Praise for The Promised One

Absolutely amazing. Great world building, storytelling is fantastic,
everything about it is perfect. My heart is so invested
and I'm so excited to read more.

~Vyktorya, Reader

Morgan gives us characters that we fall in love with,
characters that we absolutely hate (in the very best way possible)
and characters that we wish we could be.

~Katie, Reader

Epic fantasy at its finest. A unique storyline and a depth to the
characters that reminds me why this genre is so fantastic.
War, mystery, magic, immersive world-building
and a realistic love story.
Something for everyone.

~Chandler, Reader

The Promised One

The Chalam Færytales, Book I

Morgan G Farris

MINₒR 5
PUBLISHING

Minor 5 Publishing

THE PROMISED ONE: THE CHALAM FÆRYTALES, BOOK I. Copyright ©2018-2021 by Morgan G Farris. All rights reserved. Printed in the United States of America. No part of this book may be used or reproduced in any manner whatsoever without written permission except in the case of brief quotations embodied in critical articles and reviews. For information, visit http://www.minor5publishing.com.

A hardcover edition of this book was published in 2018 by Minor 5 Publishing. Second Minor 5 Publishing digital edition published 2020. Third Minor 5 Publishing edition published 2021. Designed by Morgan G Farris. ISBN 978-1-7331668-6-7

For Lance,
because we shared a chalam.

Secondary Dedication:
*For my mom, who has never read my books.
Thank God, because there's cussing in them.*

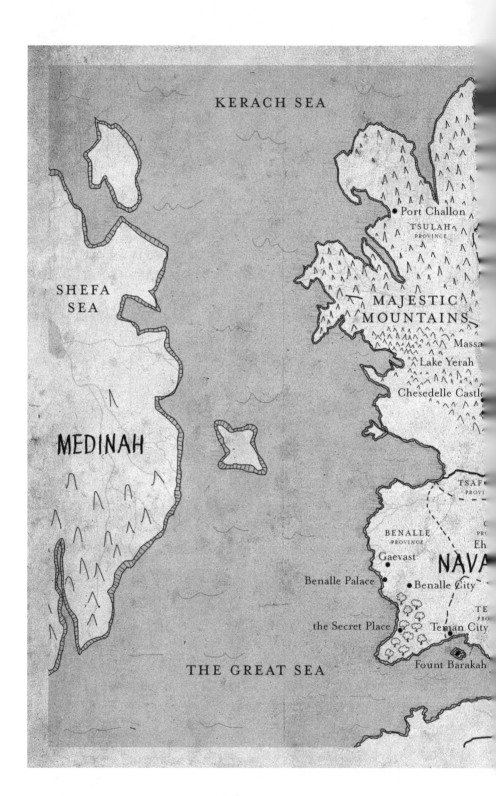

KERACH SEA

SHEFA
SEA

MEDINAH

Port Challon

TSULAH
PROVINCE

MAJESTIC
MOUNTAINS

Massa

Lake Yerah

Chesedelle Castl

TSAF
PROVI

BENALLE
PROVINCE

PRO

Eh

Gaevast

NAVA

Benalle Palace

Benalle City

the Secret Place

Teman City

TE
PRO

Fount Barakah

THE GREAT SEA

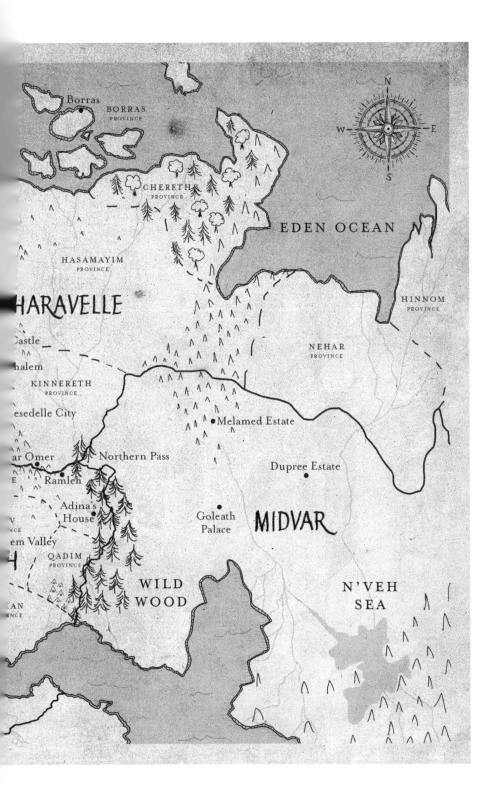

Part I

Chapter 1

I t had been love—deep, abiding, earth-shattering love—the kind about which færytales are written and wars are fought.

So she could think of no logical reason why he could not re-member it. Or her. In fact, she could only gape as she watched him ride, the morning sun casting buttery shafts of light across his back and through his unruly golden locks as he galloped away, growing smaller and smaller with each clomp of the horse's hooves.

She could think of no logical reason why the crown prince did not remember her at all.

It had been a strange morning, to be sure. Had anyone told Eliza-beth that she would wake up and tend to her duties in the stables, only to find that her dearest friend in all the world—a boy she had grown up with on the grounds at Benalle Palace, the man she had fallen in love with over the course of those years—suddenly had no earthly idea who she was, she might have scoffed and said such things only happen in stories. Færytales. Fables.

Not reality.

But here she was, staring off into the golden plains of the Navarian countryside, watching her beloved ride away like a stranger.

A strange morning, indeed.

Unsettling, really. No, not unsettling. Crushing. It was crushing dread that bloomed in the pit of her stomach.

What had happened to him?

Crown Prince Ferryl, heir of Navah, had arrived at the stables like he had every morning from the time they were children. And he had headed straight for his blood-bay stallion, Erel, just as he always did. To ride. To greet the morning with a race, with a trek to the forest, to start his morning off with his *Lizybet*. Exactly as he had every morning from the time they were children.

But unlike every other morning in her memory, this morning, Ferryl had not greeted his Lizybet with a cheerful salutation. Or a warm embrace. Or by pulling her into his arms and kissing her soundly—as had become his habit of late.

No, this morning, Ferryl had merely spoken to her as if he had never met her before.

"What's this, then?" Elizabeth had asked, her back to the prince as she fussed with a bucket of oats in the shadows of the stables, surprised that Ferryl hadn't already snaked his arms around her, planted his lips at her neck, whispered little sonnets of love and need and desire. He had always been a shameless flirt. "You make me meet you out here at the crack of dawn and don't even have the decency to greet me with a good morning?"

Yes, Elizabeth had always spoken to the crown prince with a healthy measure of nonchalance. And cheek. Such was the nature of the relationship between a prince and a servant who had known each other since they were young children.

"I beg your pardon?" Ferryl had asked.

She puffed a laugh and then, "You're in a silly mood this morning, Ferryl. Addled from lack of sleep, is it?" She grinned, biting back a smile as she kept her back to him. The heavens knew she certainly hadn't slept much last night, for yesterday had been...like a dream. So she waited...waited for the quip, the punch line. But it did not come.

"My lady, I'm afraid you must have me confused with someone else. As it is, I must get my steed saddled. I am expected in the city this morning."

"The city?" she asked, whirling to finally face him. "But I thought—" It was only then that she had begun to understand. At least as far as she *could* understand. Something...something was fundamentally different about Ferryl.

His eyes, usually so violently blue as to make a sapphire pale in comparison, were hazy, cloudy. Like a foggy autumn dawn, like the mists settling over the ocean. And in his countenance she did not find the familiarity that a decade and a half of friendship afforded. No, in his countenance she found a stranger.

She swallowed back the barrage of retorts she had thought up and heard herself instead say, "The city. Of course, Ferryl."

It was then that a grin found his sensuous mouth. And in a gesture so familiar, he pushed his hand through the messy thatch of blond hair spilling over his brow. For a blessed moment, relief tapped on her soul at the sight of that effortless smile, that familiar gesture. But that fledgling little bud of relief was short-lived, dying a sudden death when he said, "Do you always address your superiors in such a manner, then?"

She found she had no retort and instead stared with mouth agape as he continued. "Indeed, it would not bother *me*, but seeing as you are new here, ah, what did you say your name was?"

"Lizy—I mean, Elizabeth," she stammered. "My name is Elizabeth."

A smile. One that could melt chocolate, damn him. He slipped his hands into his pockets. "Well then, Mistress Elizabeth, seeing as you are new here, I feel that I should inform you that while it might not bother *me* to be called by my given name, were you to make such a mistake around my mother, I'm afraid the consequences might not be so pleasant."

"Of course, Your Highness," she managed, the title strange, foreign on her tongue. She could not ever remember a time when Ferryl had insisted she use such a formality.

With a tremble in her hands, she made her way to the wall of saddles so that she might retrieve Ferryl's. Never mind that she had never once had to saddle his horse for him because he had always insisted on doing it himself. Never mind that she couldn't have lifted said saddle with her scrawny arms if her life depended on it. She made her way to the saddle wall anyway, acting on instinct like...well, like a stable hand. But while she might have been a stable hand in name, she knew no more about the beasts than Ferryl apparently knew about her at the moment.

Ferryl, still a gentleman even when a stranger, noticed her ineptitude and quickly came to her aid.

His nearness was simultaneously unsettling and so achingly familiar that she had to close her eyes for a moment just to breathe. She had loved him for so long, so many years, that now, this unfamiliarity was... well, it was gut-wrenching, to say the least. She had half a mind to just grab him by his jerkin and kiss the sense back into—

"Are you all right, Mistress Elizabeth?" he asked. It was only then that she realized she was standing before the saddles. Eyes still closed. Just...breathing.

Awkward behavior for a stable hand, to be sure.

"Uh, yes. I'm fine. I—"

"Here," he said, making to retrieve his own saddle, his solid arms pulling taut his gauzy white shirtsleeve. She found she could not tear her eyes from him, not as his deft hands strapped the heavy leather onto the back of the sleek stallion, not even when he finally met her eyes again.

"I'll be off, then. It was a pleasure to meet you, Elizabeth."

She couldn't remember what a proper response should be. Couldn't think past the desire to yell, to cry *What in all the realms of Sheol is wrong with you?*

Oblivious to her inner turmoil, Ferryl mounted Erel and turned to ride out of the stables and into the sunrise with nothing more than a nod of his head and a lingering chuckle on his mouth.

And then he was gone, leaving a thousand screaming questions in his wake.

* * *

Chapter 2

Well, if it isn't my long lost little brother!" Prince Ferryl exclaimed, throwing his arm around his brother as soon as he reached him in the palace corridor. After having spent a day in the city meeting with some of the nobility to discuss the presence of Midvarish rebels, he had returned to Benalle Palace as soon as he had seen the horses and wagons coming up the road—Commander Titus's men, returned from their long stint on the other side of the kingdom. He had quickly finished up the last of the pointless meetings his father had scheduled and rushed back to greet his wild-tempered little brother...who was anything but little.

Derwin returned the embrace with equal enthusiasm. "Brother," he said, clapping Ferryl's shoulder whilst inadvertently crushing him under the solid girth of his arms. "It's good to see you."

"How was Qadim Province?"

"As much of a wasteland as it has ever been," said Derwin, his tanned skin even darker from the days he must have spent in the sun the past few months, his auburn hair a mess of disheveled curls atop his head.

"You smell like shit," laughed Ferryl.

"Well," said Derwin. "At least I have an excuse."

Ferryl punched his brother's arm with a chuckle. "Any updates?"

"The commander is still under the impression that he has everything under control. But from where I stand, the rebels are only growing. The border was teeming with them. Much more than we had anticipated." Derwin walked past his brother, trudging down the black-and-white marble corridor, shrugging off his dusty riding cloak and handing it to a servant girl who waited patiently, her hungry eyes practically devouring the returning prince. Derwin ignored the ogling servant, a gesture that didn't go unnoticed by his older brother. Flirtation with any female in their vicinity had been a favorite pastime of the brothers since the moment they realized they were surrounded by a gaggle of willing candidates.

Derwin marched off, and Ferryl could see the tension practically trailing him. "Well, that was new," said Ferryl, following in step behind his brother.

"What?"

"Please don't tell me three months on the road with the army and you've lost your taste for women."

Derwin didn't attempt to hide the ire in his glare. "Spare me, Ferryl. She's been eyeing both of us like that for years."

"Which seems an awfully long time not to do anything about it."

"I thought you, of all people, had tired of court games."

"Indeed, but I didn't think you had. Unyielding service to king and country has changed you, brother." He had meant it as a joke, but the humor was painfully lost on his little brother.

Derwin ignored him, rounding a corner, pushing into his private receiving room, Ferryl following. "Derwin, are you all right?"

"I'm tired. I've been on the road with a hundred stinking brutes for the better part of three months. I've seen nothing in the way of progress toward ending this ridiculous rebel threat, and I've had to bite my tongue about it because of a commander who is only interested in ignoring the problem for the sake of so-called peace. Indeed, Ferryl, I'm tired."

Derwin collapsed into a plush chair before a warm and otherwise useless fire that his servants had no doubt lit in anticipation of his return. He scrubbed his face with his calloused hands and sighed heavily. He might have been Ferryl's younger brother, but in that moment he looked a thousand years old. Weary. Worn. What had happened in Qadim?

"Dinner is in fifteen minutes," Ferryl said, hoping to lighten the mood.

"Mother and Father can wait to hail their returning warrior. I'm in no mood for Mother's prying."

A sentiment Ferryl could understand entirely.

"So what has happened here since I've been gone?" Derwin asked.

Ferryl made his way across the spacious room—large, certainly accommodating, but nowhere near as vast as his own. The second son, that's what Derwin was. Although Derwin was the second-born son to the greatest king Navah had ever known, his chambers were modest in comparison to the rest of the royal family—a fact that had puzzled Ferryl most of his life. He crossed the room and took a seat near his brother, pushing a hand through his hair. "It's the same as always. Mother is busy plotting advantageous matches with the most groveling noblewomen she can find. Father shakes his head and says nothing of it. And I get to sit and wait for the puppet strings to be pulled, like a good prince."

"How is Father?"

Ferryl looked his little brother in the eye, knowing the weight of the question, the worry that had been plaguing them both for months. "He's still having headaches. I think they're getting worse."

Derwin turned his head, resting it against the back of his chair as he rubbed his temples. "Do you think he is ill, Ferryl?"

Ill? Ferryl would have been lying if he hadn't wondered the same thing many times. But his father was still young, capable. A formidable king, only approaching his mid-forties. There could be no reason for him to be ill. "I think he's unhappy with his marriage. That's what I think. He's fine, Derwin. Mother is just—"

"Impossible."

Ferryl chuckled, albeit a bit sardonically. "Yes."

"And what of Elizabeth? Any news?"

Ferryl had to think a minute about whom he could mean. "The stable girl?" he finally asked, wondering why in the world Derwin was asking about her, of all people. The unfairly beautiful stable girl who apparently had not one iota of knowledge of horses. Or court politics.

Derwin only scoffed. "Yes, the *stable girl,* you ass."

"I suppose she's busy working in the stable," Ferryl answered, thinking he was just about done tolerating his brother's short temper for the evening.

Derwin laughed. "Well, it seems we are both biding our time, then, doesn't it?"

"Biding our time for what?" Ferryl asked.

Derwin rolled his eyes and this time, the gesture was lost on Ferryl. "I'm tired, Ferryl."

And Ferryl knew he was being brushed off. "I'll make your excuses at dinner," he offered, standing to his feet.

"Thank you."

Ferryl returned to the door, but he didn't get a chance to open it before a smiling blonde servant pushed it open. "Hello, Leala," Ferryl said warmly. "Come to greet our returning warrior?"

Leala's laugh chimed with mirth and beauty, her wavy blonde hair cascading over her shoulders and down her back. Ferryl was well aware of how his mother preferred her maids to keep their hair in perfect, polished braids or sleek buns. And he also knew that Leala had just enough of a mind of her own to ignore such asinine demands from the queen of Navah. "Hello, Ferryl," she said, but when she turned to say her hello to Derwin, Ferryl could have sworn he spotted a hint of rose coloring her cheeks.

Derwin immediately stood and ambled over to the door, his hands in his pockets. "Hello, Leala," he said casually, but Ferryl did not miss the smile in his eyes. It was...consuming. For Leala was not just one of those ogling servant girls. She was one of Derwin's closest and most trusted friends. Derwin hesitated for a moment, but soon gave Ferryl a sidelong glare before pulling their childhood friend into his arms and hugging her rather unashamedly. Leala seemed to melt right into his embrace.

"How was your trip? Successful?" she asked, her eyes sparkling.

"If by successful, you mean that we made it out of the province alive, then yes, it was successful."

Leala laughed again, and this time, Ferryl didn't miss the lingering look she gave his brother.

"I got your letters. It sounds like things are more complicated than you anticipated," she said.

"To say the least," Derwin responded, his arm still slung casually around her. "Ferryl was just leaving," he added, nodding his head in Ferryl's direction without taking his eyes off of her.

Well then.

Derwin and Leala had always been close. Much closer than Ferryl had been with her. She had grown up in the palace right alongside the princes, and no one had batted an eye when their friendship extended into adulthood, even though she was merely a servant and they the sons of the king. Never in all the years he had known her had he recalled feeling like a third wheel. But now—

"Yes. I have to get to dinner," said Ferryl, glad of an excuse to leave. "I'm glad you're home, brother. It's been painfully dull without you."

"I'm sure you were able to find *something* to do," said Derwin, a twinkle of mirth in his eye.

"Right," said Ferryl, thinking his brother seemed a bit addled from his trip. "Enjoy your night off."

"Goodnight, brother," said Derwin, and Ferryl didn't even bother to wave as he walked out of the chambers, thinking Derwin had been in a strange mood, indeed.

* * *

"Your brother isn't joining us?" asked Queen Meria, her perfectly arched brow striking a healthy amount of fear into her eldest son. Her garish russet gown filled her chair, billowing in yards and yards of fabric like a cascade of shimmering autumn leaves. Her jewels shone around her neck like a crackling fire. She had a habit of overdressing, no matter the occasion. Tonight, she looked more appropriate for a banquet with every nobleman from the province, not a quiet family dinner.

Ferryl sat down at his father's dining table and cleared his throat. "He is tired, Mother. He sends his apologies."

"Yes, I'm sure he is exhausted," said King Aiken, already digging into the first course. Asparagus soup—his favorite.

"But not too exhausted to see you," said the queen, eyeing Ferryl with her cold gaze. Her golden hair had begun to gray in recent years, just as his father's had, but she still had it fashioned into the most complex and elegant styles, which of course only added to the long list of reasons why Queen Meria of Navah was perhaps the most terrifying person on the planet. Ferryl didn't miss the growl in her voice either. It seemed that no matter what Derwin did, it was never right for their mother. No wonder he had stopped trying years ago.

The queen didn't release her cold glare from her son for quite an excruciating moment, and Ferryl found himself particularly interested in the consistency of his soup as a result. He wondered at her effect on him, considering he had done nothing wrong.

He sipped on a spoonful of soup by way of distraction, wincing at the earthy, acrid flavor of the asparagus soup his father so often requested.

A servant ambled by, offering wine, and Ferryl didn't hesitate to have his goblet filled to the brim. Despite the summer heat, the room seemed uncomfortably cold, and he welcomed the warmth the wine offered.

"Has Derwin anything to report from the east?" asked the king.

"I'm sure he can fill you in on the finer details," answered Ferryl, thankful for the conversation. "But he did tell me that the rebel situation is worse than we had assumed."

The king looked up from his soup. "What do you mean?"

"I do apologize, Father. I did not pester him for more information. He was particularly tired. I assumed we could discuss it with the council tomorrow."

"Well, there's no reason to get our feathers ruffled," said the queen. "Derwin is not exactly levelheaded when it comes to things about which he is passionate. I am sure that Commander Titus has the situation under control."

The king only gave his wife a sidelong glance before he returned to his soup, and Ferryl knew why. If there was one rule they followed religiously in the palace, it was to never argue with the queen.

Alas, the anticipated return of his warrior brother and here Ferryl was, participating in yet another uncomfortable dinner with his parents with no little brother in sight. Indeed, Ferryl was tired as well. It had been an off day, to be sure—like a misty, icy fog had settled on his mind, never mind that it was never cold in Navah, even in the dead of winter. And besides that, it was summer anyway, the sun beating down hot, the humidity making his hair particularly unruly. There should be no reason for such a winter-like weight to be coursing through his very veins. But he concluded the mental heaviness had something to do with the absence of his entertaining and smart-mouthed sibling and the quiet worry that pulled at the back of his mind any time he let himself think too long about his father's strange, untreatable headaches.

Whatever the case, he was more than ready for that blessed monotony of court life to return once more.

* * *

Chapter 3

Everything all right, dear?" her father asked as Elizabeth plopped herself down into one of the two expertly carved chairs that faced the hearth in her little cottage. Gifts from Ferryl—not that he would remember that. No fire burned in the fireplace, the coals from the night before waiting for her to relight them and begin the nightly routine all over.

Except she had absolutely no desire to prepare dinner tonight. Not since—

"Elizabeth, love?"

Elizabeth slid her gaze to her father as he emerged into the small living room; he took a seat in the matching chair beside her, his silver hair glowing in the evening light that streamed through the windows of their quiet cottage. His eyes, so kind and colored with concern, searched her thoroughly. "Has something happened, love?"

She let her gaze flick back to the empty fireplace. "Something is wrong with Ferryl."

"What do you mean?"

"He..." How could she say this? It made no sense. Absolutely no sense at all. "I don't think he knows who I am."

"Love, I'm fairly certain that could never be true," chuckled Bedell, taking her hand across the chairs. His hand, speckled with age, the veins showing clearly through his papery skin, was surprisingly warm on top of hers, his grip somehow both impossibly strong and heart-breakingly tender. "He has had eyes and a heart for none but you for as long as I can remember."

She only managed to huff a sardonic laugh.

"Tell me what's happened," he went on.

"That's just it," she said. "I don't know what's happened. Yesterday...yesterday, he..." She hadn't told him. She hadn't yet told her father what had happened. The question Ferryl had asked. The one a crown prince should never have asked a servant. But the promise he had made nonetheless. And she as well. "Yesterday, he was fine. But this morning he...well, it was as if he had no idea who I was."

"What do you mean?" Bedell asked, his voice kind but not terribly concerned. She wasn't sure whether to laugh with relief or cry with frustration.

"I thought maybe he was just playing with me. Some sort of game." Never mind that Ferryl wasn't one to play those kinds of games. Not so *thoroughly* anyway. "But then he just...left. And when he returned— which wasn't until just an hour ago, by the way—he had a page bring Erel back to the stables. He never does that, Father. He always brings him back. Always." Always an excuse to see her again. To kiss her once more. In nearly fifteen years of friendship, he could never seem to keep away from her. Which was convenient, considering she did not want to be away from him, either.

"It's as if...it's as if he's never met me before, Father." She hated it—the tear that threatened to fall. The lump in her throat. She should not be so upset. For surely—surely there was some sort of logical explanation for it all. But the tear fell despite her. And she rushed to wipe it away.

Bedell only squeezed her hand.

"Have you..." She paused to swallow back the tears. "Have you ever heard of such behavior?"

"Hmmm," he said, stroking his long, silvery white beard. He, too, stared into the cold hearth.

"Could he be ill?" she offered. "Is there some sort of illness that would cause such a thing?"

"I suppose it's possible," her father responded. "Logical, perhaps. But I've not heard of such an illness."

She knew then. She knew what he was about to say. The explanation he would offer. The impossible, improbable, useless explanation. Her father, the Chief Advisor to the king of Navah, was little more than a believer of færytales. She gritted her teeth and waited as he finally said, "I have heard rumors though."

"Rumors?" she asked, despite herself. "Rumors of what?"

"The Midvarish. They are rumored to have such abilities, though it is merely conjecture, of course."

"What abilities?" she ground out. Waiting. Waiting for the answer she did not want to hear.

"Magic, my dear. Not true magic, of course. But the dark magic of Midvar. Dark magic that can take a person's most cherished memories. Wipe them away with no trace or hope of return."

No hope? *No* hope of return? Fear pounded in her veins, even as her mind—her logical, capable mind—knew better than to believe such folly. Magic? There was no. Such. Thing. As magic. But still... "Why would someone want to take away Ferryl's most cherished memories?"

"Why would someone want to take anyone's memories, love?" Bedell asked with that annoying habit he had of answering a question with a question. Or a riddle.

"Father," she muttered, glaring.

A quiet chuckle. "Memories, love, are powerful things, are they not? Perhaps in taking Ferryl's memories, one might hold the power over Ferryl's future."

His future? "But, Father, Ferryl seemed perfectly lucid. It's as if... it's as if he has only forgotten me. What benefit could there be in taking such a memory?"

"Are you or are you not his future, love?"

"The prophecy," she said, leveling a flat look.

Bedell nodded, a twinkle in his wizened eyes.

The *prophecy.* How many times had he mentioned it? She could recite it by memory, he had reminded her of it so many times over the years.

> *A queen in the shadows*
> *Who will bring forth the light*
> *A king's song sung through the night*
> *On the wings of eagles they would fly*
> *That the way for the Promised One would be made.*

But it was nonsense. That she—a nobody, a servant, an orphan—was somehow the subject of some sort of Providential prophecy. Never mind that she didn't believe in prophecies. Never mind the prophecy made no sense whatsoever.

"Your destinies are entwined, love," her father went on. "Should it really surprise you that there might be someone out there who would thwart such a thing?"

Yes. Yes, it should surprise her because she was no one. Not just in some self-loathing *I'm not worthy* sense. But in reality. She was no one. A nobody. An orphan, abandoned, nameless child, taken in by a kind old man who fancied himself a prophet—much too old to be a father and much too kind to leave a little girl to her fate. And what a fate it would have been—abandoned for her death in the midst of the Wild Wood when she was little more than five years old. Had it not been for the old man beside her, she would surely be nothing more than dust and a forgotten memory.

But that didn't mean that she was a somebody. And it certainly did not mean that she was a somebody about whom prophecies had been written. And certainly not prophecies about the Promised One, whoever that was.

She was certainly no promise.

She was nothing but a stable girl in love with the crown prince. The crown prince who apparently no longer had any idea who she was.

A nobody, indeed.

But this nobody was bound and determined to find an explanation for what had happened to Ferryl. And it would be an explanation founded in logic and reason, not magic and færy stories, thank you very much.

"Why don't you use that calculating mind of yours and go and find an answer?" he asked, tearing her from her stricken thoughts.

"You're actually advising me to find a logical explanation?"

A pursed smile rested on his face as he brought her hand to his lips and kissed it softly. "I've no doubt that if there is anyone who can find the truth, it is you."

"And so, is this the advice of the prophet or my father?"

"You will find, love, that I am inextricably both."

* * *

"ELIZABETH, DEAR! WHAT BRINGS YOU here?" asked Mary, a pleasant smile on her rotund face. The morning had dawned bright and cheery, replete with hope and the promise of answers. So Elizabeth had bounded out of bed, swallowed a couple of quick bites of last night's bread and practically run the short distance from her cottage near the stables to the old healer's infirmary at the back of the castle.

"I was wondering if you had a moment to talk." The ocean breezes had already begun whipping loose tendrils of her hair out of her plait, but Elizabeth only absently tucked them behind her ears as she stood before the old woman—a dear friend.

"Well, of course, of course! Come in, child!"

Mary opened her door and ushered Elizabeth inside, the smell of various savory spices assaulting her nostrils as she entered the healer's infirmary. Elizabeth had always found the room to have an odd smell, what with the vast array of herbs and potions it boasted. At the attack of the pungent aroma, she wondered how Mary could stand it all the time.

"Everything all right?" Mary asked, as she pulled up a couple of chairs around a tiny table.

Elizabeth sat down across from the healer, wringing her hands in her lap. She hadn't thought about it before she arrived, but it became suddenly imperative that the subject of her concerns remain anonymous, considering that an onslaught of rumors in the prattling busybody court of Benalle Palace could be disastrous for Ferryl.

"Yes, Mary, everything is all right. But I wondered if you might have some insight for me regarding a friend of mine."

Mary's eyes twinkled, and Elizabeth knew she was probably assuming who that friend might be. Ferryl's infamous affair with the stable girl was by no means a state secret. Still. "You don't know her," she added lamely.

"I see," said Mary.

"Well, you see, it's just strange because my friend, h—*she* lost her memory recently and I cannot seem to figure out why."

"Lost her memory, you say?"

"Yes. It's the strangest thing. One day she was fine, then the next day, out of nowhere, she couldn't remember who I was."

Mary cocked her head. "Couldn't remember who you were?"

"Yes, and the strangest part is that's all h—*she* forgot. Just me! Have you ever heard of such a thing?"

Mary didn't answer for a minute, drumming her fingers on the scarred table between them as she stared into the fire. "That is strange."

"Do you suppose he's ill?" Elizabeth asked.

"He?"

"I mean *she* of course." Elizabeth could feel heat rushing to her cheeks. Well, if nothing else were gained from this meeting, it was at least painfully evident that she would make a terrible spy.

"Well, my dear," said Mary, "I'm aware of many illnesses that can cause memory loss. Fevers, especially. Has *she* had any signs of illness?"

Elizabeth did her best to ignore Mary's emphasis of the pronoun for fear that she might give herself away. Heavens, she was most certainly a terrible spy. "None that I've noticed."

"Hmm, hmm, hmm," the healer said, drumming her fingers on her chin. "That is strange, indeed."

Elizabeth's stomach was a pit of nerves, not only because she knew Mary was no fool, but also because of the fact that the old healer seemed genuinely perplexed. What if something was truly wrong with Ferryl?

"Of course," said Mary, "even if she showed signs of illness, I've never heard of any such malady that could take away only parts of memories. Or entire people. Usually, if someone suffers memory loss due to fevers or injuries, it's as if entire seasons of their lives are erased. Like time just stopped for a while. Not memories of individual people. That is a strange illness, if indeed that's what it is. I've certainly never heard of such a thing."

"Nothing?" Elizabeth asked, knowing a strange mixture of disappointment and relief. So Ferryl probably wasn't sick. But if not, then what in the world was going on?

"No, child, I don't know of any such illness that works that way. I would venture to guess that she's not sick at all."

Not sick. Not sick, but then— "Have you any idea what could be wrong?"

"It could be a great number of things, of course. But if I had to guess based only on what you've told me, I'd say it was likely the product of a spell."

"A spell?" Elizabeth asked, resignation giving her shoulders reason to slump. "You mean like magic."

"Yes, magic. A spell. A curse. Something meant to take a specific part of her life away from her."

"But magic, Mary. Surely you don't believe in such nonsense."

"What is nonsensical about magic, my dear?"

"Well, for one, it's not real. Not to mention it's a silly, antiquated notion." One that had, thanks to the much more logical and realistic minds of the powers that be, been thoroughly and completely eradicated from the more educated sectors of modern society. But not, apparently, from plump and aging healers. Or questionably old, adoptive fathers.

"My dear, just because you don't believe in something doesn't mean it's not real."

Elizabeth huffed a defeated laugh. "Now you sound like my father."

"I know that it is the plight of a teenage girl that she should never believe a word out of her father's mouth, but rest assured, my dear, magic is very real, and I daresay someday, you'll believe that for yourself."

Elizabeth resisted the urge to roll her eyes or cross her arms—a very *teenage*-like thing to do. Instead, she only toyed with the charm that hung from her neck—one half of a stone, cut so expertly that the glittering insides shimmered in even the most wan light. A trinket she had worn for as long as she could remember, though she had no idea where it had come from. Her family, perhaps? Her past? But what was her past? She had never known. Nor had Bedell. It was a mystery she supposed would never be solved.

Of course—of course the world was full of things that couldn't be explained. But just as the wind cannot be seen but for the stirring of the trees, just as thunder answers lightning without remorse, some mysteries were better left to poetry and song. To the imagination.

Some mysteries were better left unsolved. She just hoped whatever had happened to Ferryl wasn't such a mystery. Because to explain it away with something as naïve as magic…

The world—her world—had always been divided into two categories: those who believed in magic, and the realists who comprised the remaining majority. She, proudly, had always been a part of the latter. Her father, obstinately, had always been a part of the former. And apparently, so too had Mary, which was surprising, considering there was nothing particularly odd or naïve about the kind old healer. Unlike her sweet, well-meaning father.

The problem was that if Ferryl wasn't ill and had not been the victim of some sort of magic spell, then what was wrong with him?

"Of course, dear, without seeing her, I couldn't be sure. Can you bring her here?"

"Oh, umm, well…" Sweat slicked her palms as Elizabeth tried to think of an excuse on the spot for why her mystery-friend-who-was-really-the-crown-prince couldn't come for an examination.

"Of course," said Mary, "it would be strange to ask your friend to come see me when she doesn't even know there's something wrong!"

Elizabeth practically stumbled in relief. "Yes, yes, I wouldn't want her to become worried over something that is probably nothing. I'm sure it will correct itself."

"Yes, things have a way of working themselves out," said Mary.

"Thank you for your time, Mary. I'm sorry to have wasted it."

"Come now, child, you haven't wasted a thing! Have some tea with me! I haven't gotten to see you much lately."

And so Elizabeth obliged the kind healer, drinking tea and chatting for a good while, listening patiently as the old woman prattled story after story of her glory days and the creative herbs she had used to heal the royal family—a salve to heal the king's mysterious injury, a concoction she had made that once helped the queen overcome crippling melancholia. But even the long-winded reminiscing couldn't distract her from what was beginning to dawn on her: that whatever was wrong with Ferryl wasn't going to correct itself anytime soon. Nor was it going to be easy to solve.

Chapter 4

The room glittered and shimmered in the candlelight like the lights of a thousand upon a thousand stars. She laughed as she ran, her shoes click-clacking on the stone floors. But she soon threw her hand over her mouth. She couldn't be caught. Not this time. She was determined to win the game, even though she had yet to. The sound of her father's counting faded the farther she ran.

She soared across the golden floors—it was as if she was flying! She stifled another giggle before crouching in the tiny alcove. The alcove into which only she could fit—her favorite hiding spot.

She waited.

And waited.

Her patience growing thin, she was determined to wait it out. She wouldn't giggle and give herself away this time—

* * *

ELIZABETH WOKE WITH A START, her heart pounding wildly in her chest, only to be greeted by the wan light of the sunrise peeking through the old curtain on her tiny bedroom window. It had only been a dream.

A familiar dream. One she was fairly certain she had dreamt before.

But a dream, nonetheless.

Something oddly familiar washed over her at the thought of the glittering rooms. The laughter. The happiness she had felt. Had it been real? A memory? Even as the details slowly ebbed from her mind, she couldn't put a finger on why they had stirred her so deeply. Yes, it must have only been a beautiful dream. So she stretched her arms high into the air and yawned with a sound she was sure was completely unbecoming.

With a sigh, she caught sight of the necklace that dangled from her neck—the stone and its crystalline center, sparkling in flecks of every color she could name and several too impossible for words, as glittering as the halls of which she had just dreamt. Beautiful, really. A trinket she had worn as long as she could remember—a mysterious link to her unknown past. For while she remembered every moment of her life here in Navah—every horse race with Ferryl, every picnic in their Secret Place in the cliffs, every stolen moment, every tender kiss—everything before it was a fog. A blur. A smear of oil across rippled glass. Close, so close, and yet untouchable. She was no one, really. Elizabeth probably wasn't even her true name—just the name Bedell had given her when he found her. And for what felt like the thousandth time, she wondered if she'd ever know who she truly was. Spiraling down the chasm of her thoughts, she took hold of the stone and ran it along its golden chain as she stared out the window.

She thought about her father's words, his implication that magic was somehow a sufficient explanation for what had happened to Ferryl. The mystery was no closer to being solved, never mind that it had been nearly a week since he had forgotten her. Or did not remember her. Or was cursed. Whatever.

Magic.

Running the stone along the glittering gold chain, she breathed a sardonic laugh, knowing that by the end of all of this, either she or her father were sure to be proven a fool.

At the moment, she didn't really care which. All she could think about was the fact that the man she loved was due to arrive at the stables soon, as was his habit. And well, why would she miss an opportunity to see him? To even hold out the paltry hope that perhaps this had all been just a bad dream. Or that this ridiculous turn of events had somehow corrected itself.

She could not dress fast enough.

* * *

BEDELL WAS STILL ASLEEP WHEN Elizabeth tiptoed through the quaint cottage, pausing only to stoke the embers in the fireplace to warm the room before her father woke. An ancient book sitting on the mantel caught her attention, its worn edges and frayed leather telling the story of just how old it was—and how loved. She paused for a moment, admiring its beauty, ancient mysteries whispering secrets around it. The faded black leather cracked in many places, the gold leaf embossing nearly faded. Its age was anyone's guess, but the words in the book were said to have been penned many centuries before—by the forefathers of these lands. Most didn't think it anything more than a quaint collection of fables and færy stories, Elizabeth being no exception. But not Bedell. Bedell believed every word of it. Built his life by it. And as Elizabeth stared at the well-used book on the mantel, she wondered why she didn't possess the same devotion as her father.

She shook her head as she finished her work, determined to think about her dilemma another day.

Slipping out of the cottage on silent feet, Elizabeth practically skipped to the nearby stable grounds, the gray light only beginning its journey to the golden splendor of sunrise. The ocean lapped lazily against the cliffs behind her, bathing the air with the soft hiss of the relentless procession and recession, procession and recession of the fathomless depths. She breathed a deep sigh, her heart thrumming to a gallop with anticipation.

Ferryl. She would soon see Ferryl. Stranger or not, she did not care. For even just the sight of his handsome face was enough to refill her soul with hope for the answers she so desperately sought.

She wanted to get her chores done as soon as possible on the off chance that Ferryl decided to show up early. She didn't want to be in the middle of shoveling out the stalls when he arrived. Despite the fact that Ferryl vehemently disagreed, particularly once he had made known his love for her, Elizabeth had insisted that she have an actual job in the palace, claiming that she had to earn her keep just the same as any servant.

"You're not a servant, Lizybet! I won't have you shoveling dung and feeding horses," Ferryl had said.

"If you think that just because you're in love with me, I'm suddenly going to prance about like an overprivileged courtier, then you don't know me very well. I'll stick to the horses, thank you. They're much more civilized than most of the courtiers I've had the privilege of meeting."

Ferryl had only chuckled as he shook his head. "And what will you do when I make you my princess? Become my personal servant?"

"Ferryl, don't be daft. The day I become your princess is the day Eagle flies."

"Just you wait, Little Lizybet. You'll see. Father has told me that I can marry whomever I want. And unlike my father, I intend to marry for love."

"It's not your father I'm worried about."

Ferryl had wrapped his arms around her waist and drawn her close, kissing the end of her nose and tucking a strand of hair behind her ears. "I wouldn't worry about my mother, Lizybet. She's not nearly as vicious as she likes to pretend. And besides, it's not as if she can stop us from being together."

Ferryl's unfailing ability to see the best in his mother had been the subject of much scorn from his younger brother for as long as Elizabeth could remember. *Overbearing* only began to explain Queen Meria's brand of mothering. She had always seemed keen to remain at the very center of her sons' lives—and the sealer of their fates as well.

And as the morning began to stir around her—doves cooing, crickets chirping, birds greeting the sunlight with joyous songs—and with Elizabeth's mind clear and keen, she began to wonder: could his mother have something to do with Ferryl's unexplained memory loss?

* * *

ELIZABETH WAS THANKFUL THAT SHE had finished the most pungent of her chores by the time Ferryl arrived in the stables that morning. He had never minded her unkempt state before, but considering that he seemed to have no idea who she was, she was determined to put her best foot forward. She had opted to muck out the stalls first, affording her enough time to get washed up before continuing with her work, seeing as it would be to her benefit to smell, well...better than manure. Who knew? Perhaps Ferryl would fall in love with her all over again and all of this could be a distant memory.

Reaching—but she supposed it wasn't out of the realm of possibility.

She was in the middle of brushing Erel down when she heard his voice. He sounded to be in a pleasant mood—a promising start, anyway.

"Good morning! Elizabeth, was it? How are you today?"

Elizabeth smiled to herself, a flutter of delight dancing in her belly. "I'm well, F—Your Highness. And you?" She bobbed a nervous curtsey and hoped he didn't notice the blush rising to her cheeks.

Ferryl smiled that smile of his—the one that could convince any breathing being within a thousand miles to fall at his feet and kiss the very ground upon which he walked. "I'm well, actually."

It was strange having a conversation with someone she knew as well as she knew herself but who didn't know her from a stump in the forest. Still, she could tell by the smirk on his face and the spring in his step that something was definitely better than "well."

"Forgive me, Sire, but you seem particularly cheerful today. Any reason?" she asked, risking the dive into his personal affairs.

Ferryl inspected her for a moment before answering. "There is, actually. My mother, she...well, let's just say she's not exactly known for her agreeableness."

"I'm aware of her reputation," she agreed, doing her best to stifle a chuckle.

"Well, she has just been particularly agreeable the past few days. I suppose it's nice to not feel like..." He paused, toeing a rock on the ground. "A constant disappointment."

Elizabeth considered his words. A constant disappointment? She knew Ferryl and Queen Meria's relationship was strained, to say the least. But a constant disappointment? She hadn't quite realized he felt that way.

"I'm glad to hear it, Sire."

Ferryl only leaned against a stall and crossed his arms, his build solid from years of training with the army commander, his silver tunic taut across his broad chest, his unruly, sandy-blond hair set off against the tan of his skin. And his eyes. Oh, his eyes. Even with the depth-less blue somewhat less pronounced for reasons she had yet to explain, they could still pierce right to her soul. Elizabeth found herself staring a little longer than she should have. As if after fifteen years of having the privilege of staring at him, she had only just now opened her eyes.

It was only at the clearing of his throat that she was startled out of her trance. She felt the heat rush to her cheeks as the prince chuckled.

Because who wouldn't stare at the prince?

She resisted the urge to growl. Or punch him. The unfairly attractive, smug bastard.

"Well?" he asked.

"I'm sorry?"

"Are you going to saddle my horse?"

"Oh!" said Elizabeth, jumping into action, still unable to get used to the fact that Ferryl—in his memory-less state—seemed to expect his stable girl to actually know something about horses. She wondered if this time he would wait to see if she could indeed saddle his horse, which of course she could not.

Stable girl, indeed. The folly of their arrangement was only just beginning to dawn on her—how ridiculous it must look to him to be faced with the proposition of getting help with his horse from a scrawny-armed and otherwise painfully inept girl. No one had batted an eye that Ferryl had given her the job in the stables all those years ago. Ferryl had done most of her work for her, anyway. It was really nothing more than an excuse to have her near him without crossing his mother's not-so-subtle rule that Elizabeth was not to enter the palace. Ever. But to this Ferryl—the Ferryl who knew none of that—the clueless stable girl must have looked—

"Anything wrong?" she heard him ask from behind her.

"Oh, um..." She wasn't one to lie. Nor was she ever one to think on her toes. But in that moment, she was eternally thankful that she thought up a lie anyway. "It's just that I recently injured my shoulder, and, well, I can't—"

"Oh! Please allow me," he said, stepping to her side as quick as lightning so that he might lift the saddle from the rack.

"Your Highness, I sincerely apologize. I—"

"Elizabeth, please don't apologize," he said, turning to meet her eyes. "I'm truly sorry your shoulder is injured. Is there anything I can do? Should I take you to see the healer?"

"Oh. Um, I have seen her, thank you," she said quickly, hoping her stumbling wouldn't give away her lies. At least she could take comfort in the fact that she was terrible at lying. Add that to the list of spying. And horsemanship. Truth be told, she was more hung up on the fact that he had asked if there was anything he could do—and the sincere kindness in his question—than the fact that she had just lied about her reason for seeing Mary in recent days.

To her surprise, Ferryl placed his hand on her arm, his warmth and solid sureness coursing through her veins like a summer wildfire. The last few days had felt like she might never know the thrill of this man's touch again. And here she was, melting at a single, chaste gesture of chivalrous concern. She swallowed and met his eyes, willing herself not to just throw caution to the wind and kiss the man. He was grinning.

Oh Ferryl, never one to miss the infatuations of the opposite sex. She might have laughed in his face had she been anything more to him than an acquaintance of late.

"Would you perhaps like to join me for a ride today?"

Wait, what?

"Wait, what?"

"You can use one of the palace horses, if you like. Perhaps some fresh air and sunshine might do you some good. I know I'm looking forward to it."

If she wasn't mistaken, Ferryl was flirting—a favorite pastime of his that had resulted in a nuisance of a reputation that had followed him long after he had given up such habits. Which begged the question—had he returned to his old habits now that he had no idea who she was? She didn't allow herself to think about it too long. No, no, she would not go down that rabbit hole. Not now. Instead she smiled her most coquettish smile—if he could play that game, then so could she—and said, "I would love to."

She knew her answer pleased him—because she knew that look on his face. He had always liked getting his way, especially when it came to her.

"Take your pick of any of the horses. Although I wouldn't recommend that one," he said, pointing to the restless dapple stallion she knew to be the king's.

A wicked grin turned the corner of her mouth. "I have a mare of my own, actually."

"Do you?" he asked. "It can't be one of these. They're all palace horses."

"No, no. She's out there." She pointed towards the mossy hazelnut forest just over the hill that stretched beyond the stable grounds.

"Out there? What do you mean *out there?*"

"I'll show you," she said, eager to see the look on Ferryl's face when he saw her mare, Eagle. Would he remember her? What an interesting and entertaining predicament this was turning out to be.

Ferryl led Erel by the reins out of the stable, following Elizabeth. She crossed the grounds and went up the hill that divided the land from the forest. It wasn't until they crested the hill that Eagle was visible. And all Elizabeth had to do was whistle for the mare to come running, always eager to join in on the day's ride.

"*That's* your horse?" Ferryl gaped, and Elizabeth couldn't help but laugh at the incredulity in his voice.

Eagle trotted up the hill with the grace of a dancer, her white mane blowing silky in the wind, an unearthly shimmer to its tendrils. At the sight of Elizabeth, she extended a set of glorious, impossible wings, feathered and vast, spreading out from either side of her as if she would take flight. Except that she never had. Not that it had made her any less miraculous. Winged horse, indeed. There were none other of her kind in all of the kingdom of Navah.

Eagle whinnied eagerly and lowered her head, bending at the knees in a bow, waiting as she always had for Elizabeth to mount and ride. They had been companions, friends really, for as long as Elizabeth could remember.

"How...? Who...?" The crown prince of Navah seemed to be at a loss for words. Elizabeth had often felt the same in the presence of the glorious beast before them.

She laughed and nodded her head towards the open plains spread wide around them. "Shall we, Your Highness?" And before he could answer, before he could form another word, she took off atop the nimble agility of her mare, laughing as the sun kissed her cheeks and the wind whipped her hair. She heard the unmistakable thud of Erel's hooves from behind and smiled.

Maybe there was hope after all.

Chapter 5

"Y̶ou told him you had an injured shoulder?" Leala laughed.

"What else could I say? *Oh, sorry I can't saddle your horse, Your Highness. You see, you used to be in love with me and wouldn't let me saddle your horse on principle, so the truth is, I have no idea how.*"

Leala spooned a heaping serving of creamed potatoes onto her plate and giggled as she sat across from Elizabeth. A council meeting had called her father to the castle for the evening, so it was just the two of them having dinner by the fire in Elizabeth's cottage, laughing and chatting about males of their species. As was the usual topic of choice for two young women around the dinner table.

"True. Maybe you could have hinted or something, I don't know."

"How do you hint to someone that they're in love with you but they just can't remember it?" Elizabeth laughed.

"When you figure that out, maybe you can help me figure out how to get a man to admit he's in love in the first place."

Elizabeth met Leala's eyes. "He loves you. He's just…stubborn."

"Well, that is an understatement if ever I heard one," Leala grumbled.

Elizabeth chuckled, sipping her water. "He's the kind of man that makes up his mind and then dives right in. I'm telling you, once he decides it's time, he's not going to ask to court you. He's going to ask to marry you."

"I find it a bit presumptuous that a man should think so much of himself that courtship should be skipped," said Leala, stabbing a bite of roast with her fork.

"Leala, how many times have I heard you say that you'd marry him tomorrow if he asked?" Elizabeth laughed.

"That is entirely beside the point," Leala said, abusing the poor bite of beef as if it were the face of the man she loved. The man who hadn't made a single move to tell her that he loved her too, even though it was painfully obvious to anyone paying attention.

"Why are men so clueless when it comes to women?" Leala asked, finally giving up on the battle with her dinner and plopping the shredded meat into her mouth.

Elizabeth swallowed a bite of potatoes. "Maybe for the same reason they're forgetful."

Leala pouted, cocking her head to the side. "I wouldn't worry too much, Elizabeth. You know how Ferryl is. We've all been waiting for him to ask for your hand. Maybe he's just playing some sort of game with you before he finally proposes."

The bite in Elizabeth's mouth suddenly turned to ash. For what Leala didn't know—what no one yet knew—was that Ferryl had already asked for her hand in a sweet, intimate proposal at their Secret Place not a week ago. He had taken her hand in his, and she had marveled at the way he trembled, as if the crown prince of Navah should be nervous to speak to a common-born nobody. But then he had proceeded to tell her words sweeter than any she had heard. And when he had said that only spending the rest of his life with her would suffice, she had shed a tear and kissed him thoroughly.

But then, like the snuffing of a candle, it had all been taken away. Because the very next morning, he hadn't known who she was. Perhaps that was the most perplexing part of all—the timing was too coincidental. Was someone trying to keep her away from Ferryl?

Leala shook her head and took a bite of her roast. "This is delicious, by the way. If at the end of all this you are relieved of your duties as a stable girl due to severe ineptitude, you can always work in the kitchens."

Elizabeth managed to smile. She did enjoy cooking and was a fairly decent cook, a trait at which Ferryl had always marveled on their many excursions to their Secret Place. Elizabeth had cooked many a fireside meal there—usually some animal Ferryl had caught or shot—while they flirted and laughed and dreamt of their lives together. But the thought soon brought a frown to her lips.

"What's wrong? I thought we were having fun," said Leala.

"Sorry. It's just...sometimes I fear he might never remember. What if I never get him back, Leala?"

Leala furrowed her brow, appraising her friend for a moment. "You just have to have faith, Elizabeth. Faith that there's a reason for all this. Faith that there's a plan."

A plan. By Providence, she meant. Now Leala was sounding like Bedell.

Where was Providence in all this? Elizabeth failed to see how such a being—god or creator or cosmic force or whatever—could have any interest in the comings and goings of something as insignificant as human lives. Yes, Ferryl was the crown prince of Navah. Perhaps that gave him higher priority. But Elizabeth? The orphan? The stable girl? She was no one. No one Providence would notice, anyway. And certainly no one he would have time for.

Father had always said that Providence was not only interested in, but also intricately planning the comings and goings of his creation. But truth be told, Elizabeth wasn't sure if she believed such ideologies, such naïve færytales. But Leala did. Leala had always believed in Providence, in his wisdom, his "plan" as she called it. And here, with an ache in her heart, Elizabeth wondered if she could borrow some of that faith. At least until something more practical—like a solution—came along.

"You think I'm crazy, don't you?" asked Leala.

"Not crazy, just idealistic." Elizabeth shrugged. "You're too much like my father."

"And you—you're the consummate realist, aren't you? Logic!" she cried, shaking a mocking fist. "And let the dreamers be damned!"

Elizabeth chuckled despite herself.

But Leala's teasing tone turned altruistic as she added, "I'm here to tell you that not everything is logical, Liz. Faith makes a fool of what make sense. Sometimes...sometimes you just have to trust that there's a bigger plan than what you're seeing. That's all I know to tell you."

Elizabeth pushed the bits of roast and vegetables around on her plate, turning her thoughts over one by one. "Do you believe in magic, Leala?"

A shrug was her friend's response. "I don't know that I'd call it magic, but I believe in a power beyond our own."

A power beyond our own. Like something that could cause Ferryl to lose his memory selectively. For no apparent reason.

Then again, perhaps there was a reason. Perhaps it wasn't quite as hidden as she had thought.

"Ferryl mentioned that Queen Meria is in a good mood these days. Have you noticed anything?"

Leala, being a palace servant assigned to the queen's personal chambers, typically stayed abreast of the latest gossip, particularly that which pertained to Her Majesty.

She raised her brows, nodding as she considered the question. "She *is* in a good mood. Markedly so. But I hadn't surmised as to why."

"When did it start?" Elizabeth asked, her heart having apparently found a new home in her throat.

"Hmmm, I guess about a week ago," Leala said indifferently, helping herself to another bite of roast. But as if she had been frozen in place, her fork stopped on its journey to her mouth and she slowly slid her eyes back to Elizabeth. "You don't think..."

"If I'm being honest, the thought has crossed my mind. What if she's behind this ailment, for lack of a better word? It's common knowledge that the king always seems to develop headaches when he's been around the queen for any length of time. What if it's not just because she gets under his skin? What if it's something more? And what if she's done the same thing to Ferryl?"

"What? A potion? Poison? What are you implying?"

"I don't know. A curse?"

"A curse!" Leala exclaimed, nearly dropping her fork. "Since when do you believe in such things?"

"I don't. I didn't, I guess. But I can't think of any other logical explanation for what's going on. It's not a game. He's not sick, at least not in any other way, and Mary has never heard of an illness that limits memory loss so specifically."

"You spoke with Mary about Ferryl?"

"I didn't tell her it was about him. I didn't give any specifics. I just... fished." Elizabeth shuffled the food around on her plate with her fork, her appetite having suddenly disappeared. Had she really just suggested that Ferryl had been cursed? Leala was right. She, of all people, would never stoop so low as to believe such nonsense. But if not a curse, then what had happened to Ferryl? What else could explain such bizarre and isolated behavior?

"I don't know what's going on, Liz. I wish I did. Honestly, I do. But you're talking treason, you know that, right? To suggest that the queen of Navah is cursing her husband and son—the king and the crown prince—"

"I know, Leala. I know. It was just an idea. Forget I mentioned it." But even as she said it, she knew Leala wouldn't forget it.

And neither would she.

Chapter 6

"How was your meeting, Father?" Elizabeth asked from one of the small armchairs around the fireplace. The dying embers cast a haunting glow about the dark room as her father entered the cottage, his shoulders heavy, his eyes limned with a thousand thoughts.

"I thought you'd be asleep," he said, absently hanging his cloak by the door. Not even the moonlight was bright enough to penetrate the cottage tonight.

Elizabeth shrugged. "Can't seem to sleep."

No, couldn't seem to stop *thinking*, actually. Of course. Because who could sleep after admitting to her best friend that she thought the queen capable of cursing her own son?

The paltry orange light from the dying fire cast the deep lines of her father's face into shadow as he smiled kindly, taking a seat beside her.

"Your meeting was long," she mused absently.

A heavy sigh. "It is a pity that the length of a meeting is no indication of its actual use. Or success."

She patted his hand where it rested on the carved arm. "I think perhaps a sip of tea is the antidote to both of our ailments." She smiled.

He chuckled warmly. "I'll stoke the fire."

Elizabeth nodded, standing to fetch the kettle and cups while her father tended to the hearth.

"What was the meeting about that it should last so long?" she asked over her shoulder.

She heard the unmistakable huff of the bellows, and soon her father had the fire licking merrily along the logs. "It would seem that the troubles with Midvar are far from over."

"I thought the army had been able to subdue the attacks at the border," she mused, ambling back to her father's side, accouterments in tow. She set the cups down on a small side table, handing her father the kettle.

He hung it from a hook over the fire and all but collapsed back into his chair. "They had. But now there are more along the northern end of the border. It seems that Midvar enjoys keeping our soldiers busy at all times. The king is eager to devise a better strategy. But alas, what strategy is there against pandemonium and senselessness?"

"Why do you suppose they are so relentless, Father?"

"Who can say? To hear the queen tell it, our relations with Midvar have only improved. And I suppose, in some ways, they have. Sir Thomas insists that these are rebel attacks and have no association with their king. But I cannot help but wonder..."

Elizabeth tore her gaze from the dancing flames, looking at her father's profile beside her. "You're not suggesting..."

He sighed, even as he kept his attention rapt on the growing flames. "Alas, I have no answers to the games of kings, love. But I know this. The Midvarish claim to all of these lands goes back centuries. It may be a new king and a new generation, but those claims run deep into the very fiber of their being. And they have been relentless in their pursuit over the centuries. Of course, their tactics have changed, evolved. And it's true that since the reign of King Aiken and Queen Meria—or more specifically, since the birth of their first son—the Midvarish attempts have been thwarted, to say the least. But that doesn't mean they won't keep trying. They want Navah. And they want Haravelle. I think maybe they want the whole known world. And yes, I fear that the rebel attacks are not rebel attacks at all, but instead some sort of diversion. But of course, there is no proof of my claims, as they are nothing more than a hunch. And I'm sure when the king of Midvar finally pays us a visit, he will be prepared with a list of reasons a thousand strong why the rebels have nothing to do with him. And Sir Thomas takes a personal affront at such a notion, as well. And I would likely do the same if someone were accusing my country of sedition. So in the end, tonight's meeting was little more than a beating of a long-dead horse. And we are no closer to a solution than when we started."

"And this old man is tired," Elizabeth said with a sympathetic grin, standing to pour her father a mug of the steaming beverage.

"Indeed, this old man is tired," he said, patting her hand as she handed him a cup. "But the more important question is, why aren't you asleep, my dear? Have the cares of this world already burdened you so that, at the tender age of nineteen, you're unable to find rest on such a beautiful night?"

Elizabeth sighed. "I know I must sound like a lovesick girl, but I can't seem to take my mind off of Ferryl. And I am no closer to finding a solution about him than it seems Navah is at finding a solution regarding the Midvarish rebellion."

"Then we would both benefit from a diversion this evening, wouldn't we?" Bedell smiled.

Elizabeth returned his smile, knowing precisely what kind of diversion he meant. "Yes, Father. Tell me a story."

A proud smile turned her father's wrinkled mouth. "What story would you like to hear?"

Elizabeth thought for a moment, savoring the idea of hearing one of her father's stories. There were so many—about the ancients, tales of Navarian kings, of great magic—færy stories. But there was one that stood out above the rest. One that she loved to hear most of all. "Tell me my favorite story."

"Ah yes, the story of how the man you love became the miracle of the Great War. A fitting choice, is it not? For the subjects of the story are the very subjects that weigh heavily on our hearts this night."

"I'm sorry, Father. You're right. Perhaps another, then?"

"No, no," he said, patting her hand. "You're wise, my dear. For often when we cannot find the answers we seek, it is best to go back over the very information we think we understand. For it is only in the telling and the retelling of stories that we begin to unlock their secrets."

Bedell settled more deeply into his chair, preparing himself to launch into his memories. Elizabeth, too, relaxed into her chair, relishing the sound of her father's soothing voice, the way he made his stories come to life. She closed her eyes and let him transport her.

He sighed deeply, drawing long on his cup of tea, the steam curling in silvery tendrils around his long beard and wiry brow.

"For a thousand years, the people of Midvar have held to the notion that the thrones of both Haravelle to our north and our great country of Navah were rightfully theirs. For a thousand years, Midvarish kings have launched attacks against both kingdoms, battles and skirmishes, raids and rebellions. And for a thousand years, they have failed each time. And even though it was the most organized and brutal of their attempts, the Great War was no exception.

"Midvar is known the world over as a mysterious kingdom, keeping their secrets well hidden, their people quiet and unfriendly, but not without undeniable mysteries—which are more legends and whispers, really. Midvar is vast and powerful, stretching far north past the Majestic Mountains all the way to Haravelle and far east into Unknown Lands. It is by far the most mysterious of the kingdoms in the realm. It has been said that the Midvarish people are giants, descended from the 'fallen', which some call the Nephilim. They are powerful and sure of blade and bow, fearless and tenacious, and everyone, whether believers in magic or not, says their abilities are nothing short of otherworldly."

Even though she had never seen a soul from Midvar—not even their diplomat to Navah, Sir Thomas Nachash—for some reason, every time her father spoke of these giant-like people, Elizabeth thought of Ferryl's brother, Prince Derwin. He was tall—much taller than Ferryl even though he was the younger of the two. His hair was darker than anyone in his family. Not black like Elizabeth's, but nowhere near the sandy blondness of Ferryl's, or King Aiken's or Queen Meria's. She always pictured a Derwin-esque warrior, wielding blade and shield, as her father talked of the Great War.

Her father went on, the pleasant lilt of his voice quavering softly with his age. "Not twenty years ago, Midvar had been marching from the south into the mountains of Haravelle. They had planned a surprise attack, a ploy to take over the peaceful kingdom, but King Aaron of Haravelle was no fool. He had spies everywhere, and had known for some time that Midvar had been planning an ambush. By the time the Midvarish army arrived in his great country, his army was ready.

"But that didn't mean the war was easy. In fact, it was brutal and bloody. Many lives were lost on both sides. Even when it was clear that Midvar would lose, they never relented in their advance. It seemed that King Darius, the aged father of King Derrick, was intent on finishing his mission, no matter the cost. And Haravelle, growing weary from the months of battles and losing countless numbers by the day, finally decided to call on the help of Navah. King Aiken was eager to lend aid: troops, food, supplies, whatever he could offer. Queen Meria, on the other hand, was hesitant. Their son, Prince Ferryl, was only a boy then, and she didn't like the idea of his father departing for a battle that wasn't his, on the chance that she might be widowed and her son rendered fatherless. But King Aiken was torn between the duty of a father and the duty of a king, as are most kings when faced with a choice between what is right and what is easy.

"It was then that I had the vision. As clear as if I had been there myself. The vision of what would happen in the war if Navah didn't intervene. Chaos. Bloodshed. A Midvarish takeover of the peaceful people of Haravelle—and Navah would be next. Brutal. Relentless. Unyielding.

"But it would all be avoidable if only for one reason: Ferryl.

"It was clear from my visions that Ferryl was special, an integral part of the Great War. Yes, he was only a little boy. But everyone knew there was something special about him. More than just the beloved prince, Ferryl had a special power. Of course, none of the practical people of this kingdom would call that power *magic*." At this, Bedell gave Elizabeth a wink, his eyes twinkling in the firelight. "But he had an unquestionable power about him nonetheless. So without hesitation, I requested an audience with the king and told him what I knew in my heart: that Navah must join forces with Haravelle, and that if they did, the common enemy would be defeated. But only if Prince Ferryl traveled with his father to the country to the north.

"It took some convincing, but eventually Queen Meria agreed and allowed her son to travel with his father to Haravelle on the condition that she travel with them.

"And sure enough, no sooner did the boy step foot on the soil of Haravelle than the Midvarish attempts began to falter. The war ended within the month, and Haravelle was free of the threat of infiltration once and for all. And all thanks to the little hero, Prince Ferryl of Navah. The Protector of our realm."

Elizabeth sighed and smiled. Ferryl. The Protector. She had always loved to hear her father speak of him in such a way.

"But, my love, as with all things, the Great War did not come without a high price. On the very night that Midvar surrendered, little Princess Adelaide, the beloved and only daughter of King Aaron and Queen Avigail of Haravelle, was taken from them. Stolen like a crown jewel, slaughtered in her own home by Midvarish soldiers who held tightly to their fanatic ideals. She was only a toddler, little Adelaide. An innocent in the games of kings. Murdered for nothing more than her birthright."

"But why did they kill her, Father?" Elizabeth interrupted, asking the question she had never asked. "Why kill a little child?"

"Some destinies, love, are too great to be contained. Some destinies can only be thwarted in death."

A chill ran down Elizabeth's spine. This was the part of the story that had always haunted her. What kind of monster abducts and kills a child? No matter how badly you might want to prove a point, it takes a special sort of demon to do such a thing to an innocent. Too often— too often she thought of King Aaron and Queen Avigail, of their tear-streaked faces, not monarchs mourning the loss of an heir, but a father and a mother, mourning the loss of their only, beloved child. What a fate. What a terrible fate for all of them!

And little Adelaide of Haravelle—the stolen princess. She was a haunting reminder that the price of birth, the price of *fate* can be high.

Insurmountable.

And Ferryl—he would be king of Navah someday. He would rule the land with his pure heart, with his protection.

What would be the price he paid? What would be the cost of such a destiny?

She was immensely thankful that she lived in a kingdom with a prince like Ferryl. Ferryl the great protector. The boy who had turned the tides of the bloodiest war in the kingdom's history. Whatever power that was within him, she understood it. Somewhere in her soul, she understood it. The way she had always felt about him went beyond just the safety and protection of his love. She had always known that Ferryl's power went far beyond what he understood, what he even knew of himself. And while she knew her father would call it magic, she didn't care. It didn't have to be magic, but it was Ferryl. And her heart beamed with pride at the thought of this man she loved.

Bedell pulled her out of her trance with a gentle squeeze to her hand. "Love, you look like sleep might cooperate now. Perhaps you should go to bed."

"Yes, Father," she agreed. But instead of going to bed just yet, she stood and bent low over her father that she might kiss his wrinkled brow. "Thank you. I always love your stories."

He wrapped his arms warmly around her and drew her into him. She gladly curled into his lap, just as she had a thousand times before, her father's arms steady, sure. A fortress of peace and safety in a world full of mysteries.

"I suppose there will come a day when you are no longer under my care and I cannot tell you stories," he said, cradling her against him. "But until then, I shall cherish every chance I get to sit by the fire with you. It reminds me of when you were so very tiny and I would hold you in my arms, telling you stories until you fell asleep."

Elizabeth smiled. "It will always be one of my favorite memories. And when I have children of my own, Providence-willing, I will expect you to tell them stories just the same."

"*Providence*-willing?" Bedell mused.

"You know what I mean."

"Indeed. I just wonder if you do," he said, absently patting her arm.

"What does that mean?" she asked, sitting up to better see him.

A twinkle of mirth shone in his watery eyes. "Your favorite story is one of a boy prince ending a war with his very presence. Tell me, to what do you attribute such heroics?"

"Strength of character?" She smiled innocently.

Her father chuckled warmly, pressing a kiss to her brow. "My daughter, for a girl who prides herself on practicality and sensibility, you've certainly held fast to a notion that is, at best, idealistic."

Maybe it was idealistic to believe that there was something special about Ferryl. Maybe it was her love for him, or maybe it really was a kind of magic.

Or maybe love is its own kind of magic.

Either way, when Elizabeth slept that night, she dreamt not of færytales or fantastic notions, but of a blond prince and a raven-haired servant, of stolen kisses in the stables, and the abiding love between them.

* * *

Chapter 7

The sunlight had only just pierced the deepest corners of the stable, tendrils of golden sunshine shimmering hither and thither upon piles of hay, upon buckets of feed, upon flicking tails of mares and stallions—and there in the corner, upon the cascade of raven hair that fell down the back of the stable girl.

And at the sight, his heart thundered to a gallop.

He ambled his way to her slowly, sure that if he didn't mind every step, he might run and make a fool of himself.

Because Providence above, this woman...

He had never known that he could love someone so deeply. Thoroughly. Ravenously. She was all he had ever wanted. From the moment he had met her. His best friend. Turned into his greatest love. Could she possibly know it?

He made his way to her, but she kept her back to him, affording him a glorious and lingering view of her slender waist, her curvaceous hips hidden beneath her simple dress. She had unbound her hair, letting it fall free and wildly about her shoulders, and when he finally reached her, snaking his arms about her waist, pulling her to him, he had to brush her glorious tendrils away that his lips might find purchase on that irresistibly kissable neck of hers.

"Good morning to you too," she laughed, though he did not miss the quiet little sigh that escaped her at his touch.

His blood thrummed in response. "Good morning, my love."

"Did you sleep well?" she asked innocently—an attempt on her part to toy with him. It wasn't working.

He grinned against the velvety soft skin of her neck. "Oh, off and on."

"You did not sleep?" she asked, attempting to turn that she might face him. He allowed no such thing, too busy with her neck, her ear, her jaw.

"Not much," he admitted.

"Why?"

Because all he could think of was her. How much he had wanted her by his side. To touch. To hold. To not let go. Because it was time. Time, and he damn well knew it.

"No reason in particular," he finally said.

"Ferryl," she said, managing to turn in his arms, which he kept firmly around her waist.

And heavens above, at the kiss of color on those cheeks, at the sight of those gloriously supple lips...he did not hesitate to let his lips find hers.

And linger.

And linger.

Because that taste. That smell. Of honey. And lavender.

He could taste it all day and it would never be enough.

He took no small amount of pride in the fact that she was just as breathless as he when at last he relinquished her lips.

"Ferryl—"

"I love you, my Lizybet. Do you have any idea how much?"

A becoming shade of rose blossomed on her cheeks even as a smile threatened her glistening lips. "An inkling, I suppose."

"Well, that simply will not suffice," he said, letting his lips find hers again. She snaked her arms around his neck, drawing herself into him, into his embrace, deeper into his arms until there was nothing left between them, no space, no distance, no secrets, nothing but Ferryl and Lizybet. And all the dreams they shared.

There could be no sweeter thrill than this. Than her. And he knew it. To the very marrow of his bones, he knew it.

* * *

IT HAD ONLY BEEN A dream.

A dream of the raven-haired stable girl. A rather poignant, realistic dream. But still, just a dream.

Never mind he hadn't been able to get it out of his head. The taste of her. The smell of her. So real. As if...as if he had tasted it before.

But it had only been a dream.

Yet for some reason, even as he walked to another one of his mother's insufferable dinners with yet another grasping noble family from Navah, he could not shake the dream.

He had not been able to shake it all day.

And he could only wonder as to its meaning.

That he should dream something so...vivid, so...intimate...about a complete stranger. It was...what was it? Unsettling? Not really. It hadn't unsettled him. Not in an unpleasant way, anyway. No, the dream had... it had branded him. Marked him. Left him reeling. Wondering...

Wondering if he'd ever get to taste those lips of hers, that's what.

But it hadn't been a playful, flirtatious kiss she had given him. It hadn't been a dallying servant toying with a prince.

It had been...it had been love.

Deep, abiding, earth-shattering love.

The kind about which færytales are written and wars are fought.

And yet still he wondered...would she ever let him taste those lips of hers?

"It is not of this meeting that you are thinking," said King Aiken, startling Ferryl from his thoughts as he rounded the corner of the corridor near the king's private dining chambers at Benalle. The king chuckled knowingly. "You are in another world, my son."

"Good evening, Father," said Ferryl, bowing, knowing the false alacrity in his voice only confirmed his father's assessment.

"Any reason in particular?" his father asked with a knowing wink.

Ferryl couldn't understand why his father should know something he didn't. "Not that I can think of," he admitted.

"Hmm," said the king. "If I didn't know any better, I would say that my son has finally given his heart away."

Ferryl froze in his steps, dumbfounded.

King Aiken chuckled again. "Don't look so surprised, son. I'm not as ignorant of your comings and goings as you think."

"What—" But Ferryl didn't get a chance to finish his question before Prince Derwin arrived, gruff and sour as usual when forced into one of their mother's *prospect dinners,* as he called them. As if finding a wife—a partner, a mate—were as easy as selecting a choice cut of meat from a smörgåsbord.

"What's on the menu tonight? Another courtier from the Tsafone Province wearing so much fur she looks like a bejeweled grizzly bear? Or perhaps this time she'll actually be smart enough to bring appropriate attire for our climate, but with teeth large enough to rival a horse. Either way, you're a lucky fellow, Ferryl." Derwin clapped his hand on his brother's back with a smirk, never one to play the silent, approving type.

Ferryl only laughed. It was true—his mother had terrible ideas on the qualities of a fitting wife. It seemed it mattered not that their personalities had the depth of a teaspoon, nor that their looks left much to be desired, so long as they came with a handsome dowry and numerous political advantages. And for some reason, his mother had also decided that twenty-one was much too old to still be a bachelor, thus increasing these insufferable *prospect dinners* to no less than two a month.

"Don't be too smug, brother. Your time will come, you know," grumbled Ferryl.

"Thankfully, I'm a patient man," he said, to which King Aiken chuckled, as the three royal Navarian men made their way through the giant wooden doors and into the grand dining hall of the king.

The outer walls of the chamber, like all the outer walls of Benalle Palace, were lined with windows from which could be seen Benalle City to the east and the crystal-blue ocean to the west. The dining hall, like the rest of the chambers of the royal family, was located on the top floor—a perfect vantage point for the breathtaking vistas the cliffs of Benalle offered.

"It's a beautiful evening, isn't it?" asked Ferryl as he stared out the window, his hands clasped behind his back.

"Well, aren't you just the romantic?" chided Derwin. "Finally take the plunge, did you?"

"What?" asked Ferryl, taken aback by the strange question.

"Your Majesties," interrupted a scrawny page as he stood proudly at the doorway. "Her Majesty Queen Meria and honored guests, Sir Matthew Westerly of Teman, his wife the Lady Abbey, and their daughter, the Lady AnnaMaria Nanette Danae Westerly."

Lady AnnaMaria Nanette Danae Westerly of Teman. An obnoxious, ridiculous name. As if she were a queen descended from a throne of the heavens. Who in Sheol would do such a thing to their own daughter? Ferryl resisted the urge to laugh at the idea of owning up to such an atrocious name.

"So pleased to have you with us," said King Aiken in that kind way he had of speaking to even the most groveling of courtiers as if they were old friends. Ferryl wondered if he'd ever learn to mix authority with sincerity as effortlessly as his father.

"The pleasure is ours, Your Majesty," said Sir Matthew, and it was only as he fell into an exaggerated bow that Ferryl caught first sight of his wife and daughter trailing behind him. They, too, followed suit with an equally exaggerated curtsey, and Ferryl couldn't help but notice that the bodice of Lady AnnaMaria Nanette Danae Westerly's dress was cut rather low, her curtsey angled just so, her eyes never leaving the prince. And what with the generous view she was offering him of her rather voluptuous breasts, it was entirely evident that Ferryl Prince of Navah was her target tonight. And she was determined to hit her mark.

Ferryl extended his hand to take hers, planting a featherlight kiss on the silky soft skin he found there. "A pleasure, my lady," he said, sliding his eyes back to hers. She held his gaze with predator-like intent. Target, indeed.

"Sir Matthew and Lady Abbey, it is certainly a pleasure to have you with us this evening," said Queen Meria as everyone took their seats around the grand table. "Sir Matthew hails from one of the most *wealthy* noble families in Navah," the queen prattled on, touting the information as if ungodly wealth could be counted a virtue.

The servants arrived immediately, pouring wine and offering the first course. But Ferryl found himself transfixed on Lady AnnaMaria Nanette Danae Westerly as she nibbled tiny bites from her fork. Perhaps her mother had taught her that ladies should only eat enough to satiate a small bird. Or perhaps this was her idea of charm and appeal. All Ferryl could think was that she bore a striking resemblance to a squirrel. Albeit, a rather generously endowed one—but a squirrel, nonetheless.

"Thank you for inviting us, Your Majesty," said Lady Abbey. "We were most pleased to receive your invitation. AnnaMaria has spoken of nothing since."

AnnaMaria blushed, breathing a throaty giggle. "Mother."

Ferryl eyed the courtier over the top of his goblet as he took a generous drink of his wine.

"Prince Ferryl, we've been told that you have been working hard with your brother to devise a strategy for the armies along the border. I'm told you have quite the mind for preserving the interests of Navah," said Sir Matthew, his wealth apparently unable to keep his hair from becoming more and more like a haystack with age, his teeth so yellow they reminded Ferryl of freshly shucked corn.

"Yes, Prince Derwin is the mastermind, really. I've a mind to make him commander of the Royal Army when I am king."

"Really? I didn't know that about you, Prince Derwin," said Sir Matthew. "That is most impressive."

"My brother, as usual, is understating his contributions to the strategy for dealing with the Midvarish rebels," said Derwin.

"Yes, from what I understand, if it weren't for you, Prince Ferryl, Haravelle would have lost the Great War all those years ago. It would seem that you're something of a good-luck charm," raved Sir Matthew.

Ferryl laughed. "A fluke, I'm sure."

"That's not what I've heard," said Sir Matthew.

"It's true, brother. Wherever you are, our troops are impenetrable. No one can deny that there is something to—"

But Derwin's speech was cut off by an exasperated sigh from the noble and obviously bored Lady AnnaMaria Nanette Danae Westerly of Teman. "Oh Father, must we always talk of war? It's exhausting." She rolled her eyes, plopping her pointed chin down onto her waiting palm.

Well then.

"Yes, let's not talk of such masculine interests," said Queen Meria. "You wouldn't want to bore your guest within the first hour of dinner, now would you?" She laughed merrily, the wine obviously already going to her head. Ferryl looked over to see that nearly all of her goblet had been drained. Wonderful. Keeping the conversation on topics that would suit her seemed a winning prospect.

"So, Lady AnnaMaria, from what area of Teman do you hail?" he asked.

"Not far, Your Highness," she said, her narrow chin tilting ever so slightly as she spoke. "Our family's land borders Benalle Province just to the south. The journey is little more than an hour from your palace."

He nodded, taking another sip of his wine as she continued.

"Of course, we cannot claim such exquisite views as Benalle Palace offers. Our land is not nearly as close to the ocean," she said. "But close enough that I have spent many days on the black sands of the Great Sea. I suppose you have too, Your Highness."

"Indeed."

"So much in common," beamed Lady Abbey proudly.

She was practically gushing—as if he had already proposed marriage. It would seem that Lady AnnaMaria Nanette Denae Westerly of Teman was not the only person here with an agenda.

"Lady AnnaMaria, do tell us about your initiatives with the lower classes in Teman City. We are all eager to hear of your benevolence," said Queen Meria.

Lady AnnaMaria Nanette Danae Westerly blushed demurely, promptly launching into a long-winded explanation of her self-proclaimed brilliant plan to rescue the poor, miserable lower classes from themselves. And Ferryl, genuinely trying to listen, was so bored out of his mind that he soon found himself staring out the window behind her, letting the glorious pink sunset distract him as he gazed, thinking longingly about going for a long ride on Erel, a pastime to which he usually resorted when faced with less than thrilling princely responsibilities—prospect dinners being no exception. Of course, it didn't escape him that upon visiting the stable to retrieve his horse, he would likely have to run into the stable girl, the girl about which he had dreamt. Of her glossy black hair, her slender waist, her supple lips—

"Your Highness?" he heard vaguely. Someone cleared their throat.

"Ferryl!" He was instantly plunged back into reality by the threatening voice of his mother from the other end of the table.

"Yes?"

"Lady AnnaMaria has marvelous ideas for Teman City, does she not? Perhaps we could devise a plan to implement some of her inspiration here in Benalle City as well," said his mother.

"Oh. Indeed. Yes. Inspired," said Ferryl, knowing full well that he had failed at feigning interest.

His mother glared disapprovingly from her very large and ornate seat, and even with the distance between them, Ferryl understood the threat to be very, very real. He shifted in his seat and vowed to do a better job at playing the game this evening, if for no other reason than to avoid the sound tongue-lashing he would receive from his mother otherwise.

But he didn't do a very good job. And by the end of the dinner, with his mother fit to be tied, his brother cheered rather pleasantly by the wine, and his father predictably quiet, Ferryl took a bite of the assortment of fruits and cream before him, thanking Providence that if nothing else, dinner was almost over.

"The dinner has been exquisite, Your Majesty." Lady Abbey beamed at Queen Meria.

"As has been your company," she replied. "We are happy to have you as our guests. We hope that you will find the palace to your comfort."

"We certainly appreciate the invitation to get better acquainted with your beautiful palace and city," said Sir Matthew.

"Of course," said Meria.

Of course. *Of course* this would end up being a days-long parade of accolades and accomplishments, a dog and pony show for his benefit, so that dear Prince Ferryl might see that there could possibly be no other woman on the planet for him but the lovely and perfect Lady AnnaMaria Nanette Danae Westerly of Teman. Of course.

"And now, if you will excuse us, His Majesty and I shall retire for the evening. Please do make yourselves comfortable. Your servants will be waiting to escort you to your chambers when you are ready," said the queen as she stood, taking the king's arm. King Aiken only nodded, a faint smile on his lips, his eyes squinted from another one of his headaches.

Sir Matthew, Lady Abbey, and the eager Lady AnnaMaria Nanette Danae Westerly all stood, bowing and curtseying in farewell, and Ferryl knew that if he didn't come up with an excuse soon, he would be doomed to spend the evening escorting the courtier around the palace—a prospect which sounded a bit like having a tooth pulled.

"Alas, it has been a lovely evening," said Derwin eagerly, unable to hide the smirk begging to curl his mouth. "But I, too, must depart. I have a long day ahead of me tomorrow. My lord, my ladies, a splendid evening to each of you." Derwin nodded and practically ran to the door.

Wonderful.

The three Westerlys turned their eager faces to Ferryl, and for a brief moment, panic stole over him like a tidal wave. Something. He had to think of something. Anything. For Providence's sake! He grinned toothily and scratched the back of his neck like a fool, his doom impending.

"Forgive me, Your Highness," cried the eager young page boy. "His Majesty wishes to see you."

Bless him. Bless that man.

"I am truly sorry, but I must see to my father. A lovely evening to you!" Ferryl didn't miss the look of disappointment on Lady AnnaMaria's face as he practically skipped out of the room, his heart finding a regular pattern again as he tore through the halls like an antelope on the run from a hungry caracal.

He made his way down the hall and through the door to his father's private receiving room, knocking on the door of his bedchamber just beyond, knowing full well that no one but the king would answer. His mother hadn't slept in the same room for as long as he could remember, and her departure on the king's arm this evening had been nothing more than a show for their guests.

"Come in," said the king.

Ferryl hesitantly opened the door, realizing in that moment that he hadn't stopped to think about the reason for his father's call. "You wanted to see me, Father?"

"Yes, yes, I mainly wanted to give you an excuse to escape that girl." He smiled.

Always the voice of reason. Bless him, indeed.

Ferryl chuckled more with relief than mirth. "So it wasn't just me. She was terrible, wasn't she? Why does Mother insist on only bringing around the most pretentious of potential mates?"

"Alas, son, she has no concept of love in marriage. Only political gain. The Westerlys, while severely lacking in intrigue, make up for it tenfold with their name. They are one of the oldest noble families in all of Navah. And consequently, the richest. I'm sure you can see why your mother might consider that girl an advantageous match."

"I suppose it's rather apolitical and selfish of me, but I've never quite had the desire for an advantageous marriage."

The king's face shone with silent understanding, and it gave Ferryl the gumption to ask a question that he had wondered for many years.

"Father, were you ever in love with Mother?" he asked.

King Aiken sighed. "When we were young, son, when you were a new distraction for us, there was a time when I thought we might fall in love. I certainly loved her. Or at least I tried, anyway. But things changed when..." The king trailed off, his eyes distant. Ferryl wondered what he wasn't saying. "Well, things just changed, and it seems that whatever we might have been has been lost forever. I wish I had a better answer for you. You certainly deserve better."

Ferryl searched his father's eyes, seeing the secrets behind them. What had happened between them that their love could be so lost? Whatever it was, he feared that an arranged marriage would only lead to the same fate for himself. "Father, what am I to do? I don't think I can stomach many more of these dinners. Nor do I have any idea of how to convince Mother that I am capable of making my own decisions."

"Son, as I have always told you—there is nothing I want more than for you to have the freedom to make your own choices. I don't want you to settle. I know your mother means well, but she is shortsighted when it comes to your marriage prospects. In the end, I want you to choose your own life, not have it handed to you."

Ferryl had known this. He had always known it. But why did it always seem to be so complicated?

"Of course, you must remember that you will also have to face the consequences of the choices you make, good or bad. And I daresay your mother would not hesitate to offer any *consequences* she saw fit regarding choices you might make that are contrary to her plans."

Ferryl met his father's eyes, only to find relief when the king chuckled softly. "Then again, you already knew that, didn't you?"

Ferryl sat down next to his father in chairs that faced the king's ornate fireplace, carved from white Navarian stone and resembling a caracal's open mouth. The snarl, the fangs, the wickedly tufted ears of the caracal had always struck fear into his heart, ever since he was a child. But here, with his father beside him, the caracal seemed a great deal less formidable than his mother these days. Ferryl exhaled a sigh. Yes, he had always known that whatever choices he made, he would have his mother to answer to. He longed for a change in subject.

"You seemed unwell tonight, Father. Another headache?"

"Pay no mind, son. I don't want you to worry about me. I want you to focus on your duties as prince and heir. There is much on your shoulders, what with the rebel attacks. Don't let your mother burden you with the unnecessary."

"Sometimes I feel like you are the only one who understands me, Father."

"We are much alike, you and I. And I don't want you to make the same mistakes I did. But Derwin is your ally too. Never forget that. The road ahead may be riddled with twists and turns, but Derwin is blood. And he loves you. I am eternally grateful that you have him."

"Father, you speak as if...well, you speak as if you are ill. Is there something you're not telling me?"

"My son, I will not be around forever. And I may not always be in my right mind. So for now, while I am, I want to make sure you know where I stand. Do you understand what I'm saying to you, Ferryl?"

Ferryl met his father's eyes. His right mind? His father was nothing but brave. Strong. Loyal. Wise. He couldn't imagine him any other way, and certainly not in a poor state of mind. Truly, he knew he would give anything if only to have an ounce of his wisdom and experience. What a good king he was. The kind of king Ferryl could only hope to be.

"I understand, Father."

Chapter 8

A knock on his door had Ferryl facing the day much earlier than he had intended. But it was not so much the early hour that surprised him as who stood on the other side of his threshold.

"My lady," he said incredulously.

"Good morning, Your Highness," said Lady AnnaMaria with a curtsey and another generously offered view of her generous breasts on display yet again in a low-cut gown.

"What brings you here at this hour?" he asked, keeping his eyes fixed on hers.

She pursed a wolfish grin. "I have it on good authority that you are quite the horseman. I was hoping you might take me for a ride."

He could think of about ten thousand things he would rather have been doing than entertaining a potential bride on horseback. As it were, none of them were suitable excuses—at least where his mother was concerned. One hint that he had brushed off the daughter of the richest lord in Navah in order to play cards with Michael the guard or practice his archery skills with Derwin would surely incite a war with the queen to put all other wars to shame.

So he merely sighed and said, "It would be a pleasure, my lady."

* * *

THE MORNING DAWNED BRIGHT AND cheery, clouds of gnats glittering in the sunlight that danced on the grasses. He crossed the palace lawns with the Lady of Teman in tow, barely listening to her idle prattling on the temperature, on the ocean humidity, and the havoc it was wreaking on her otherwise perfect hair. Ferryl made a point to nod in all the right places.

"Ah, what lovely beasts," she said as they finally made their way inside the stables. "Even if the smell is...less than savory."

Ferryl had always found the smell of horse dung and hay to be rather a comfort—a reminder of simpler times, of a childhood filled with horses and sunshine and races across the grounds with...with whom did he race? He found suddenly that he could not think of a soul that he might have raced with. Not Derwin; he'd never liked races. But surely—*surely* he had a thousand memories of races. Every day, nearly. And he hardly ever won, either. Who could he have raced with? And who had a horse faster than Erel?

"Let me guess. Is this one yours?" the lady asked with a delighted grin, gesturing to a black mare.

"No."

She frowned, glancing around the stables again, as if trying to prove that already she knew him so well as to be able to pick out his horse just on a hunch. Ferryl resisted the urge to roll his eyes.

"This one?" she asked, gesturing to his father's dapple stallion.

Ferryl shook his head, leaning against a stall post.

Undeterred, Lady AnnaMaria Nanette Danae Westerly continued her pointless guessing game.

"Oh, I know. Of course I know," she said, making her way to yet another erroneous guess. Ferryl wasn't sure whether he would be more entertained by letting her continue to guess wrong or by seeing the look on her face when he told her that he had been standing next to Erel the entire time. But he did not get a chance to decide before a distraction emerged on the other side of the stables. He froze in place as he beheld her, only remembering to speak after the horrid realization that it had been an excruciatingly long silence.

"Good morning, Elizabeth!" he said, eagerly. Too eagerly, damn it. That dream—that damned dream—it all came flooding back to him the moment he took her in. That raven-black hair, that alabaster skin—it looked so damn soft.

"Servant," said Lady AnnaMaria curtly. "Prepare two horses. His Highness and I would like to ride this morning."

"Of course, my lady," Elizabeth said with a curtsey and promptly made her way across the space between them—straight towards Ferryl, he noted with no small amount of alarm—and anticipation. But that smile she gave him when at last she reached his side...

"Your Highness," she said, with another curtsey, though her eyes did not leave his. Then again, nor did his leave hers.

"Sleep well?" he asked. As if that were an appropriate question to ask a stranger. Damn it. Damn it all to Sheol.

"I did, Your Highness," she said, clearly flustered by the question as she moved to pull Erel from his stall. The horse did not shy from her touch—not like he usually did around strangers. No, Erel seemed to... well, he seemed to like Elizabeth, nickering rather gaily at her touch, accepting an apple from her without hesitation. And she, too, brushed those alabaster hands of hers down his mane and neck with a kindness, a familiarity that called to Ferryl somewhere deep down.

"He likes you," Ferryl said.

"I've always liked him," she said with an absent smile. But then, "I mean, as long as I've known him, of course."

"Of course," Ferryl said, unable to take his eyes off of the creature before him, the way her hair fell down her back in a single, thick plait, unruly wisps caressing her cheek and neck with the breeze that blew through. The way her brows furrowed ever so slightly as she concentrated. The way her eyes—

"Your Highness," said Lady AnnaMaria with a rather loud clearing of her throat.

Ferryl whirled, having completely forgotten that the lady was still there.

"What horse would you recommend for me?"

"Oh," he said. "Well, you are welcome to any of them, of course. But I would suggest one of the queen's geldings."

He walked to a stall that held four black horses, their coats glossy and well kept. But then it occurred to Ferryl that Elizabeth would likely need help with the saddles, considering she had been nursing a shoulder injury, and he promptly—and rather eagerly—marched back to her side that he might saddle Erel himself.

"Thank you," she said with a hint of rose to her cheeks as, without a word, Ferryl took the saddle from her and lifted on to his steed.

"There is no need, my lady," he said. "I do hope you're feeling better."

"What's this?" Lady AnnaMaria scoffed as she marched her way back to Ferryl, her hands resting on her hips. "The crown prince saddling his own horse? I won't hear of it!"

"There is no need for offense," said Ferryl by way of placating the surely well-meaning but entirely too presumptuous courtier. "Elizabeth has—"

"Servant!" Lady AnnaMaria interrupted. "What have you to say for yourself that you should make the crown prince do your work for you?"

Elizabeth darted her gaze to Ferryl and then back to AnnaMaria. "I—"

"You are quite lucky His Highness is so humble that he would not scold you for such insolence! You should be sacked for your laziness!"

"My lady," Ferryl said. "Calm yourself. The Lady Elizabeth has simply—"

"Lady?" AnnaMaria scoffed. "Oh, Your Highness, you are most certainly a humble prince," she said, a sudden oiliness to her voice as she placed a hand on his chest—which he promptly removed. "I know you are simply too kind to scold her for her behavior, but I will tolerate no such thing for my sovereign prince. And as for you—" she said, turning and pointing a rather sharp finger at Elizabeth. "His Highness is too kind to do anything about this, so I will do it for him. Rest assured, rat, I will see to it that you are reported for your brazen insolence, your downright laziness!"

"My lady," Elizabeth said with a bow of her head, but not before Ferryl caught sight of the thin layer of silver in her evergreen eyes.

A righteous indignation welled in his gut.

"You will do no such thing," he spat at AnnaMaria. "In fact, you and your family will be leaving. Today."

"Excuse me?" she hissed. Gone was that syrupy sweetness. In its place was nothing short of venom. Here—*here* was the true Lady of Teman, and by her vitriol, Ferryl knew exactly what a marriage to her would be like.

"You will not send me away like a scolded child," she growled. "Have you forgotten who I am? Why don't I remind you, Your Highness? I am the wealthiest, most coveted daughter in this entire kingdom. There can be no more profitable match for you, let me assure you. And if I didn't know any better, I would say that you are throwing all of this away just for a tumble in the hay with a filthy stable rat, is that it?" She shoved a slender, knotted finger towards Elizabeth, all the while keeping her raging eyes fixed on Ferryl.

"You are out of line," Ferryl said, his voice a low growl.

A crazed sort of laugh. "So you do not deny it."

"I am not in the practice of explaining myself to grasping courtiers."

"Oh, no? Do you want to explain to me why you've been looking at her like you might devour her all morning? Is she a new conquest, then? Or an old faithful whore you like to turn to when the well goes dry?"

He stepped across the gap between them, nearly nose to nose with the vile courtier. "You will apologize," he spoke with deadly calm.

A scoffing laugh.

"Apologize. To. Her," Ferryl ground out.

"My father will hear about this. Mark my words. You are going to regret this day, Prince Ferryl of Navah," she snarled, and before Ferryl could stop her, Lady AnnaMaria spat in Elizabeth's face before turning on her heel and marching out of the stables.

* * *

"Elizabeth, I am so sorry," Ferryl said, fumbling through his pockets for a handkerchief. Mercifully, he found one quickly.

"There is no need to apologize," she said, wiping her face with the gossamer cloth. He could plainly see that she was embarrassed.

"Are you all right?" he asked, closing the gap between them.

"I'm fine," she said quietly, unable to meet his eyes. "I'm so sorry that I—"

"Elizabeth," he said, lifting her chin. And Providence help him if her skin wasn't even softer than he had dreamt. A consuming kind of softness...familiar. He promptly dropped his hand to his side and cleared his throat. "There is no need to apologize," he went on. "I am the one who should be apologizing to you."

"Why should you apologize?" she asked, furrowing her delicate brows.

"I knew she was rather forward. I had no idea she could also be so vile. She had absolutely no right to speak to you like that."

A deeper rose kissed her cheeks at the mention of the lady's accusations and the insinuation she had made regarding the nature of his relationship with the stable girl.

"Please forgive me," he said quietly, taking hold of her hand despite himself. She was trembling softly, but she nodded her head briefly all the same.

She tried to hand him back his handkerchief, but he closed her fingers around it. "Keep it," he said softly before going on. "Tell me, Elizabeth, do you know which of the horses belong to the Westerly family?"

A question in her eyes and then, "Of course, Your Highness. They are right over there," she said, pointing to stalls down at the other end. Ferryl turned and headed towards several rather dull horses.

"Where are you going?" she asked, as he heard her following behind.

"I meant what I said, Elizabeth. I will see to it that they leave today. And never come back," he added as he marched to the first horse.

* * *

Part II

Chapter 9

King Derrick, Son of Darius, Sovereign of Midvar reclined in the plush chair, crossing his hands behind his head. "So we are in agreement, then?"

"Of course, Your Majesty," said the duke, his slender frame bending into a sniveling bow.

The king snorted. How easy his brother-in-law was to convince. Had he known it would be this simple, he might have thought to do something a long time ago. Then again, the brink of poverty and ruin has a way of providing ample motivation for any man.

"Good," said the king, rising to his feet. "And my niece? Will she be as bullheaded as my sister was, or can we count on her compliance?"

"She will be made to agree whether she likes it or not," said the duke, a hint of fear in his beady eyes as he took a seat.

The king chuckled. "I like you, Hevel. I always have. You've always known your place, unlike my impudent sister."

The duke fidgeted in his chair. "And what of their king and queen? Will they be in agreement with the plan?"

King Derrick paused for a moment, allowing his brother-in-law to squirm in the silence. "Do you doubt me, Hevel?"

"No, Majesty. Not at all. I simply—"

"Their queen and I have conversed thoroughly on the subject. All will go as planned. And that is the last time you will question me. Understood?"

The duke bowed his head low, but even so, the king could see his trembling. "Of course, Majesty. I would never question you."

Fool.

The king crossed the room to the door, his black brocade cloak trailing behind him as if on a phantom wind. "I will look for you both there soon."

"As you wish, Majesty," said Hevel, bowing again to the king as he disappeared.

* * *

DUCHESS DELANEY DUPREE SAT IN her father's oversized office, her arms folded across her chest, fuming. The overstuffed chair in which she sat felt surprisingly uncomfortable, the room stifling hot as the afternoon sun poured in like molten lava. Suffocating, that's what it was. Her whole life, however short, had been nothing but suffocating.

"I don't see how this helps anything, Father," she said, not bothering to quell the edge to her voice. Duty. Respect. Obedience. Pounded into her head since her childhood.

Well, duty, respect, obedience be damned.

"This matter is not up for discussion or your opinion," the duke said, shuffling papers on his desk.

Delaney huffed. "But father, it's so unfair! I'm only seventeen! Why must I be married now?"

"Because the time is right."

"Because the *money* is right," she huffed again.

Her father lifted his face from his work. "You know, my dear, I've never had cause to mourn the loss of your mother," he said dryly. "With your smart mouth, it's like she never died."

"What a thing to say," Delaney said through her teeth, a cold rage welling in her gut. How dare he speak of her mother that way!

"My dear, it matters not whether you like the arrangement. In one month, you will be headed for your new fate." Duke Hevel of Sheqer stood from his desk, his black eyes never bothering to so much as glance at his daughter. Such haughtiness, such disdain from a man who not twenty minutes ago was trembling like a yellow-bellied coward in the presence of her uncle, the king of Midvar. She knew, for she had watched the whole scene unfold through the keyhole on his office door. "This arrangement will seal our family's fate. Ensure our wealth and name for generations. Do you care at all for what happens to your little sisters? Or are you as selfish and childish as your mother was?"

"Father, of course I care about them!" she pleaded. "But I don't see how being shipped off to marry our enemy is going to help our family."

"Then you are as shortsighted as you are impertinent."

"And I suppose I'll be expected to produce his heirs, won't I?"

Her father donned a crooked smirk. "You will be expected to fulfill all of the necessary duties as wife and princess."

"Necessary duties," she scoffed. "You mean for me to be his whore."

"I mean for you to bear his heir, you insolent brat." When she rolled her eyes, he went on. "Oh, don't look so glum. Most girls your age would give anything to marry a prince, even if he is the enemy. You'll never want for anything—don't forget that. And with your lineage and his, you'll be the most powerful princess on the continent."

"Why, Father? Just tell me why. Of all people. Of all countries, for that matter. Why ship me off to marry *their* prince?"

Her father stood with his back to her, his hands clasped behind his back as he looked out the windows at the countryside beyond their manor, rich and thick with summer vegetation. "My dear, you will soon learn that in matters of state, there is no personal opinion. There is only duty. There is only the king's wishes and nothing more. The sooner you understand that, the better."

* * *

DELANEY LAY IN BED, HER arms wrapped around a pillow at her chest, still fuming from her father's declaration. She stared out the window of her room, watching the gnarled branches of the oak outside as they danced and swayed in the wind. All the times she had sneaked out, climbing down those branches. All those nights, just her and her friends. And Ravid. She had marveled at how long she had gotten away with having a life right under her father's nose.

But now it seemed that was at an end. For now her life was being ripped right out from under her and there was nothing she could do about it.

And a prince! Of all people to marry! She could only wince at the thought of what a spoiled, selfish pig like him must be like. If she could have sprouted wings and flown away that very moment, she would have.

She closed her eyes, the moonlight still dancing through the wind-tossed branches even through her eyelids. She exhaled a ragged sigh, and that's when she heard it—that familiar *tap tap* on her window. Her eyes shot open, and she sat up in bed, unable to stifle her growing smile.

She climbed over and unlatched the window, her heart racing a little faster at the sight of her visitor.

"If I didn't know any better, I'd say you were angry just now," said Ravid, climbing into her room from the branches just outside. "Was that a scowl on your face?" Delaney only pinched his arm, but she didn't fight him when he drew her close and kissed her soundly. "Take a deep breath, wildcat. It could be worse."

"How could it be worse?" she grumbled, pushing him away and crawling back onto her bed. "I'm to marry some Pig-Prince, or hadn't you heard?"

"Pig-Prince. I like that one," he chuckled, plopping down onto the bed beside her.

"I fail to see how this is funny."

Ravid's eyes still held a smile, but there was pity in them too. She wasn't sure she could stand his pity. "Don't," she said.

"Don't what?"

"Don't look at me like that."

Ravid draped a heavy arm around her shoulder. "Cheer up. It's not as bad as it seems."

"How can you say that?"

He kissed her nose. "Because I'm coming with you."

"What?" she asked, pushing away enough to look him in the eyes.

He grinned, that feral grin that made her heart explode. "It was decided just today, right before the king left. As your father's vassal,

I've been commissioned to join you on the journey. Your father and I will come with you and stay until the fated wedding day. And if all goes as planned, I'll earn myself a place on the Pig-Prince's court. Perhaps even a title, not that I care about that."

"Are you serious?" she asked, a flicker of hope blooming in her heart—a promise of something more than the burden of duty and expectation.

"Yes. And you can have your secret life on the side while the Pig-Prince remains blissfully unaware."

Delaney chuckled and nestled deeper into his embrace, letting his warmth wrap her like a cocoon.

When she didn't respond, Ravid asked, "Aren't you going to say something? Like *thank you*, perhaps? It took some pretty clever arranging to make this happen, you know."

"Well, it turns out you're not as useless as I had thought." Delaney tried to hide the smirk behind his shirt, but he caught her and pinned her down, tickling her side and showering her with kisses until she laughed out loud. "Don't! My father will hear us."

But Ravid only gave her an I-don't-particularly-care grin and kissed her right on the mouth. Thorough. Ravenous.

She couldn't help but return the gesture.

* * *

Chapter 10

Most days, Titus Melamed enjoyed being commander of the Navarian armies. It usually suited him just fine to hunt down rebels like prey, hiding in the brush like a caracal on the hunt, sniffing them out until he could devour them like the worthless scum they were.

And today was no exception.

The wind blew briskly through his hair, stinging his eyes with bits of dirt and dust, but he wasn't complaining. He and his men were downwind of the band of rebels they were currently tracking through the woods, which meant he could smell the rutting bastards from a mile away, while they remained blissfully unaware of the ambush that awaited them.

Gods, he loved this. The freedom of the battlefield, the power that came from the credo by which he lived: hunt or be hunted.

He would take the former, thank you very much.

He crouched down low, using a boulder as a barrier between him and the rebels that were now camping in a cramped ravine below. He turned to give his men the signal, nodding to his loyal general, whose trademark Navarian blond hair tossed about like an unruly haystack atop his head. The general smirked back. He loved this as much as Titus.

One last sweep of the camp and then—

Arrows whizzed through the air like a swarm of deadly bees. He had trained his men well. Few arrows missed their mark, and within seconds, thirty men crumpled to the ground below them.

Chaos resulted. Arrows whizzed towards them, shouting ensued, and the little band of pain-in-the-ass rebels began scattering like confused ants on a rain-sodden mound.

Idiots. Each and every one of them. If they had any idea just how much of a pawn they were, they wouldn't be playing this game. This game of kings. Of lies and empty promises.

Titus, Midvarish by blood, had faithfully served the king of Navah as commander for the last ten years. King Aiken had never questioned his loyalty to the throne. Titus had never given him reason to. And as he shot the rebels one after another—men of his own kingdom, his own heritage—he didn't even feel the slightest bit of remorse.

Perhaps he should have.

But he didn't.

After all, fools deserved a fool's death.

The battle was over quickly. Too quickly. These little attacks against the rebels had gotten too easy. It was going to be difficult to keep up this charade much longer if all Midvar could come up with were these young boys who were much better at pissing in the wind than engaging in any real warfare.

The question was, where were the real Midvarish soldiers—the ones Titus had trained with as a boy? These so-called rebels, they weren't soldiers. They were nothing more than the expendable pawns.

Still, it was fun. And oddly satisfying. And perhaps Titus's favorite—deliciously contradictory. For here stood the Midvarish-general-turned-Navarian-commander, taking down his own people with the ease of a predator cat. And he was paid to do it.

Yes, Titus enjoyed days like today very much.

* * *

THE MEN HAD SET UP camp deep in the forest that separated Qadim Province from the border of Midvar, a smattering of bedrolls and frayed blankets smeared across the forest floor. But Titus had taken to setting up a tent in recent months, affording him a place to hold private meetings and a quiet place to sleep at night. The gods knew he needed it, because for the past few months, Titus hadn't been sleeping well. At all.

He couldn't pinpoint the reason. Perhaps it was the monotony of hunting down rebels day after day—a task that should have been assigned to some captain, not the damned commander of the rutting army. Then again, at least it was some kind of engagement. For King Aiken was, if nothing else, a peaceful man. War was not in his vernacular. He preferred a more diplomatic approach to ruling the western half of the continent.

So very different from the king of Midvar.

But no, it wasn't the daily Midvarish rebellion squashing that had contributed to his lack of sleep. Perhaps it was the guilt of knowing that he served one king and betrayed another. Perhaps it was the exhaustion that he did his best to ignore, the exhaustion that had begun creeping in like fog and mist, slowly, almost undetected over the last few years. The exhaustion of serving everyone's needs but his own. Of living at the constant beck and call of a king whose primary and sole objective was his own glory.

Yes, he was fairly certain that could exhaust any man.

He sat down on his bedroll, puffing a heavy breath before drawing deep from his skein. A few parchments lay scattered beside him—orders and reports, no doubt. He shuffled through them, fairly disinterested in whatever new objective his king had for him. But he stopped in his tracks when he saw a parchment on the bottom of the stack, black, scrolling handwriting—more like art in and of itself—sprawling across the front. It only had his name, but he knew that penmanship. He had grown to love that penmanship. He wondered what it said about him when his heart skipped like a schoolboy at the sight of it. He didn't hesitate to open the letter, eager to devour its contents.

Well, I must say, Qadim sounds beautiful.

No preamble, no small talk. Just straight to the point, as if they were carrying on a conversation in person instead of by letters that took a month to reach each other. Gods, he loved that about her.

You make it sound like a luxury destination, not a battle zone. When did you become such a poet, Titus Melamed? (I'm smiling as I write this, can you tell? General Titus, a poet? Well, gods, the world has gone straight to Sheol, hasn't it?)

Penelope—his wife—had such a smart mouth. He loved—absolutely loved—that about her. She hadn't spoken to him that way in many, many years. But somehow, since they had been writing to each other, things had become...different.

I'll have you know that I'm sitting at the dining table right now, thinking about whether or not I could manage a garden on my own. That field—the one just south of the manor—I think would be perfect. What do you think? Would I make a good farmer? Better yet, would you like to be a farmer's husband? I'm talking dirt under my nails, mud on my boots, farmer.

But gods, it would be wonderful, wouldn't it? Fresh vegetables whenever we wanted them. The chance to plant a little seed and watch it grow. To bask in the fruits of hard labor. For some reason I can't quite place, I am bound and determined to have a garden someday.

What say you to that, Titus Melamed? Do you think less of me now? Do you think me a peasant girl at heart? Maybe I am.

He laughed out loud at that.

Then again, you seem full of surprises. Why shouldn't I also be?

Maybe by the time you're able to come home next, I'll have a bushel of fresh vegetables waiting for you in a basket on my arm.

The next sentence had been scratched out, but not enough that Titus couldn't make out what it said after a few tries.

Speaking of which, have you any idea when you'll have your next leave?

He stopped for a moment, just to take it in, reading the scratched-out scrawl again just to be sure. Did she miss him? After all these years, and the marriage that was little more than two acquaintances who shared a manor that he rarely visited, could she possibly be missing him? Titus had been in love only once before. When he was young, when the world seemed ripe for the picking. He had met a Navarian girl and fallen in love quickly. Their torrid romance didn't last past the fateful summer when he found out his parents had been wiped out by the sickness that spread its tentacles across the lands of Midvar as fast as lightning. But he had loved her. He was sure of it. And now, reading letters from Penelope—from his wife—the way his heart caught in his throat, the strangeness of it, the foreignness of it, he wondered if he wasn't actually missing his wife. Gods above, after all these years, was he falling in love with her?

Whenever you get to come home next, maybe I'll have a few vegetables ready for the servants to prepare something from the fruits of my labor. Then again, I would imagine I have a lot to learn before my garden is successful. There's a life lesson in there somewhere, I just know it.

Well, I'm sure I've dazzled you with my talk of dirt and seeds and mud and vegetables. Quite the intrigue, I am. Write back soon and tell me where you're headed next. And tell me all about its rolling hills and lush forests with that newfound poetic prowess of yours.

I'll be waiting with bated breath.

Until then....

Penelope

Titus read the letter again for good measure, loving the way she wrote—as if she were standing right here beside him, her slender arms akimbo, chastising him for questioning her desire to garden. She was a lady in her own right, after all. To tend to a garden should have been beneath her.

But Penelope wasn't like most women. She was different. He had known that from the very beginning. And somehow, reading letters from her month after month had begun stirring a desire in his heart to remember—no, to relearn—all those wonderfully different things about her. To hear her smart mouth in person again. To feel her auburn hair in his hands again.

And that's when Titus understood. For the first time in many, many years, Titus finally understood that the exhaustion that had begun to settle on him was solely because he had chosen the wrong life.

Maybe it was time he did something about it.

* * *

Chapter 11

Good morning, Mistress Elizabeth," said Ferryl as he sauntered into the stables. Half-hidden in the shadows, it was only as his eyes adjusted that he realized she was fussing with a rather heavy pail of oats. "Let me help you with that," he said hastily, springing to her aid as she attempted to lift the heavy pail.

"Good morning, Your Highness," she said, turning to bob a small curtsey. She caught his eye and held it for a moment before he realized that he was staring and that he was supposed to be helping her.

"You look well this morning," she added.

"As do you," he said without thought. It was true, wasn't it? No, it wasn't true. It was a paltry response for how she looked, because Providence above, she looked...she looked...

"Thank you for your help," she said, biting that supple lip of hers.

Oh, he was in such deep, deep trouble. There were so many things he should be doing this morning—a council meeting, a private meeting with some of the generals regarding the rebel threat, mountains of paperwork to sort through with his father. Yet here he was, avoiding responsibility...just for an excuse to "get Erel out," as he had put it. He wondered how he would pay for his frivolity.

At the moment, he didn't really give a damn.

He cleared his throat. "Of course. How is your shoulder?"

"Hmm?" she asked, as if she hadn't a clue as to his meaning.

"Your shoulder. Is it better? You had mentioned an injury and—" It took a moment for her eyes to show she understood him.

"Oh! My shoulder! Yes, it's...much better, Your Highness. Thank you for asking."

She turned quickly away, tending to his mother's stallion.

"I hope I haven't offended," Ferryl added, unsure as to the meaning of her reaction.

Only then did it occur to Ferryl that perhaps she had feigned an injury in an attempt to hide her ineptitude with the horses. And at her sudden and harried fussing over his horse, he knew he was likely right. He pursed his lips to stop the chuckle that was threatening to escape, stifling the urge to take hold of her hand, to kiss it, to laugh with her and tell her that she shouldn't worry—she was not the only fool here this morning.

"Not at all, Sire," she said, her back still to him.

So she was embarrassed—and Ferryl was fairly certain he knew the reason. She had been found out. Well, she didn't know she had. But she had. And from where he stood, there was only one thing to do about it.

"All the same, let's be careful, shall we? I don't want to risk further injury. Just save the heavy work for me, and I'll help you with it when I get here."

"Sire, I couldn't ask you to do that. There is much work to be done every day, not to mention you're the crown prince. It wouldn't be—"

She stopped when Ferryl placed his hand on hers, and when she met his eyes again, he smiled. "It would be a privilege, Elizabeth." Her breath grew shallow as he held her gaze, and while Ferryl knew full well that he had that effect on women, there was something distinctly different about her. Different and...sincere.

Oh, he liked sincere. He very much liked sincere.

"Elizabeth?"

"Yes?" she said, her voice only a breath.

"There's somewhere I'd like to take you today. If you have the time. And if you'd like to come with me, of course."

"Oh? Where is that?"

He grinned, leaning a fraction closer to her. "It's a secret."

It was only for the briefest of moments, but Ferryl could have sworn he saw her eyes flash as if she knew exactly where he could be taking her, never mind the fact that he had never told another soul in the world about his Secret Place in the clifftops. He brushed it off. Surely he had only misread her reaction, for she was smiling now too.

"I'd love to," she said, and with that, she turned on her heel and headed towards the forest where he knew she kept her wild, winged mare.

Ferryl chuckled at the notion that she had left the crown prince alone in the stables to tend to his own horse without a backward glance. Any other stable hand would have long since been sacked. He made a mental note to warn her about being so careless around the likes of his mother. The last thing he wanted was to see her leave over something as ridiculous as the queen's unwillingness to lift a finger for herself.

This girl. This impossibly intriguing girl. What fool in his right mind would have ever hired her to work in the stables?

* * *

THE RIDE THROUGH THE FOREST was quiet. It seemed Elizabeth was at a loss for words, which might have bothered Ferryl had he not gotten the distinct impression that she was as nervous as he was. It was strange, however, that he felt he could read her so easily. It was almost as if... well, it was almost as if he knew her somehow. But that was impossible, of course. Perhaps they simply shared a connection of sorts—two souls on the same wavelength. He couldn't completely explain what it was about the girl that drew him in so, but he would have been lying if he said he didn't enjoy it thoroughly. Which only made him want more if it. More of her.

They made it to their destination within an hour, and strangely enough, Elizabeth never asked where they were going. Even when they had to guide the horses through narrow gullies and down steep hills, she never complained, never questioned Ferryl. To add to the mystery, she even rode ahead of him at times and stopped as if on instinct when they arrived at the granite cave Ferryl had always called his Secret Place.

Truly, he might have even taken the time to ask her about her perceptiveness had he not been utterly and completely distracted by her dismount from the winged mare. Her hair tossing to one side, falling in gentle curls around her face, her slender leg momentarily exposed from under her simple blue dress as she made her way down the side of the beast, the smile she donned when she caught him looking.

"Everything all right, Your Highness?" she asked.

"Yes. Yes, of course. Sorry, I just..." But stupidly, Prince Ferryl of Navah could think of no good reason for his gawking and opted instead to dismount his own steed and distract himself by giving her a grand tour of his favorite place in the kingdom.

"It's beautiful here," she said.

"I'm glad you think so. This happens to be my favorite spot. I come here often to think. It's my escape, really."

"I can see why. It's quite peaceful."

It was true. The place was tucked away under the side of what was too small to be a mountain and much too large to be called a hill. It was surrounded on all sides by thick forest, ferns, and moss, but from the vantage point of the shallow granite cave, the ocean was visible just through the trees, where the curled, moss-covered tendrils of the hazelnut forest abruptly ended at the edge of the cliffs that towered from the depths of the Great Sea. *Breathtaking* only began to describe the place.

But Elizabeth seemed almost as if she were feigning awe.

"Have you been here before?" Ferryl asked, plucking a sprig of long grass that he might chew on it.

"What? Oh, umm, I think maybe. I can't remember."

"Truly? I didn't think you could forget a place like this."

Elizabeth studied his eyes for a moment before responding. "Yes, I've been surprised to learn what things we're capable of forgetting." When Ferryl didn't respond, she continued. "Do you come here often?"

"I haven't been in a while. But yes, I used to come all the time, just to get away. I call it my Secret Place."

"Have you ever brought anyone here with you?"

Ferryl chuckled. "Now what kind of a secret would it be if I told others about it?"

Elizabeth looked to him quickly. "But you've told me about it."

Ferryl met her eyes. Such candor with this one. So very different from the grasping palace courtiers desperate to tell him what he wanted to hear. So he decided to reciprocate. "I trust you, Elizabeth. I can't explain it, but I do. Does that sound strange?"

He let himself linger in her eyes for a moment, enjoying the flecks of gold and green shimmering like a forest of rain-speckled evergreens in the sunlight, rimmed with thick black lashes that kissed her dewy cheeks every time she blinked. Honey and lavender. That's what he had dreamt that she tasted like, smelled like. And the urge, the damned desire to find out if it was true was gnawing at him like a wolf at a kill.

He promptly shut out the traitorous thoughts.

"No, it doesn't sound strange. I think we understand each other, Your Highness."

"Exactly," he said with a roguish smile. "That's exactly what I meant."

Elizabeth played nervously with a necklace Ferryl had failed to notice before. "What is that?" he asked, gesturing to the rustic charm. A stone. A stone cut in half. Radiant with heat, energy. As if, well, as if it were—

"This? Oh, it's just a trinket. I've had it as long as I can remember."

"If I didn't know any better, I'd say that's an amulet."

"An amulet?" she questioned. "Why would you think that?"

"Can't you feel it? The power?" Yes, in his very bones, he could feel the power coming from it. Could she not?

"Power?" she asked in awe, but then she didn't say anything else, observing the charm for herself, lost in its crystalline depths.

An amulet around her neck about which she knew nothing. A winged horse that did not fly. A stable girl who did not seem to know much about horses. And a dream about her that threatened to devour him body and soul.

Who was this Elizabeth? And why couldn't he get her out of his head? His every thought?

"I just mean that it looks like it belongs to someone important, that's all."

"Well, I'm not important, rest assured. It's just something I've always had. I don't know much more other than it seems I'm the only one capable of removing it."

"What do you mean?"

"I mean I can take it off if I want. But no one else can. Not my father, or my friends. And even when I take it off, it always seems to find its way back to my neck when I'm not looking. It's as if no one is allowed to wear it but me. Strange, isn't it?"

"I've never heard of such a necklace," Ferryl admitted, curiosity getting the better of him. "Do you mind if I try?"

"Try what?"

"I want to see if I can remove it."

Elizabeth chuckled. "Go right ahead. You've never—" She cleared her throat. "I mean, yes. You can try."

Ferryl stepped around Elizabeth as she lifted her hair to reveal the clasp that rested on the nape of her neck. He might have been taken aback at how quickly the sight, the nearness of her skin consumed him, had he not been so distracted. Her neck, slender and delicate, her skin like cream, in stark contrast to the inky blackness of her silken hair. He found himself feigning a struggle with the clasp to have the excuse to linger, to let his fingers brush against her, to bring his body closer to hers. And then he realized he could smell it. The lavender in her hair. He wanted to devour her for that smell. The aching familiarity of it. The need to just...touch her. He closed his eyes. Closed them and just breathed.

But that was a terrible idea, for the scent only grew more powerful, seeping into blood and bone, bringing him alive, awake. As if he had been asleep his whole life. He abruptly opened his eyes again, taking a step back lest the shredding vestiges of reason and self-control give way to the desire—the aching need—to hold her, to taste her. This stranger before him who was unwittingly devouring him body and soul.

It was only then that he realized he had the amulet in his trembling hands.

"How did you do that?" she asked, turning to him with awe in her evergreen eyes.

"I don't know. You say no one has ever been able to remove it before?"

"No one," she insisted. "Not even y—" But she stopped herself, clearing her throat before she said, "See if you can wear it."

"What?"

"Go on. See if you can put it on."

"I don't... Why? What for?" He did not want to put it on. No, for some reason he knew that was a terrible, terrible idea.

"I want to see if it will stay on you."

Ferryl raised his brow. If he didn't know any better, it would seem she was implying there was some sort of magic to the necklace. But that would be impossible. Necklaces couldn't have magic. Magic wasn't real. Still, he found himself complying with her request, clasping it around his neck, surprised when it fit him. He was sure it was entirely too small to fit around his neck, for it had only extended to the small of hers—much too short for any man. But it fit. It fit perfectly. And when he held it in his hands as it rested against his breast, he could feel that indeed, there was a kind of power in it. Something he couldn't put his finger on. A depthless well of ancient power, thrumming and pounding and slumbering...

Chapter 12

This is an amulet, Elizabeth. I have no doubt."

But she didn't answer, instead staring at him with eyes wide and mouth partially agape.

"I won't keep it. You needn't worry." He chuckled, quick to remove the charm and return it to her, to make light of what they both knew to be a significant moment. Though for what reason, he could not be certain. But sure enough, when it rested on her breast again, it was small and delicate, falling at a length that he knew would be much too short for him. What in all the realms of heaven and Sheol?

"Where did you say you were from, Elizabeth?"

"I've lived in Navah as long as I can remember, Your Highness."

"You don't look Navarian. You're the only person I know with hair that color. And your skin..." He stopped himself before he got lost thinking about her skin. He cleared his throat and continued. "But you only recently came to work in the palace?"

"I suppose that's one way of looking at it, yes."

She was hiding something, that was certain. But what it was, he couldn't imagine. Why would a girl with a mysterious amulet and winged horse suddenly show up in his kingdom to work in his stables? Who was she, and why did she seem so familiar?

Either she was a good actor, or she, too, seemed genuinely surprised by his observation that her necklace was an amulet. Regardless, this girl intrigued him in more ways than one, and he was not opposed to the idea of spending as much time with her as possible. To get to the bottom of things, of course.

"It looks like there's a storm headed this way," she said, interrupting his thoughts.

He turned to face the direction she was pointing and saw clouds gathering in the distance, a menacing black belly peeking through the labyrinthine trees. It wouldn't arrive for a while, but it was surely headed right for them.

"I think you're right, but if we hurry, I think we can make it back to the palace before it hits."

"Do you need to return soon?" she asked.

"No. Why?"

"Because I think we should stay and watch the storm roll in. Thunderstorms are one of my favorite things."

Ferryl couldn't help but grin at such a declaration. For indeed, thunderstorms were one of his favorite things as well. "You won't be frightened?"

"What would you do if I was?" she asked, looking down, kicking a small stone.

"Why, I would protect you with my life, my lady," he said, taking her hand in his, placing it on his breast. Flirting. Shamelessly. Both of them. He knew a sweet thrill of anticipation at the thought.

She didn't remove her hand from his as she said, "I would expect nothing less."

* * *

IT TOOK MORE THAN AN hour for the storm to make its way to the Secret Place, but Ferryl and Elizabeth didn't seem to notice. In fact, the time passed quickly as they laughed and shared stories. She was easy to talk to, full of memories of growing up at Benalle. Why hadn't he noticed her on the grounds before? He was quite certain he would have, even from a distance. But he supposed it didn't matter anyway. He had noticed her now, and he had no intention of forgetting.

"Elizabeth, may I ask you a strange question?"

"Are you hoping for a strange answer?" She nudged his shoulder with her own as they sat side by side under a canopy of stone and moss, watching the black-bellied clouds tumble slowly in. Thunder rumbled menacingly in the distance.

Ferryl might have basked a little more in her response, at the casual familiarity of it, had he not been so nervous for what he was about to ask, his traitorous heart pounding in his chest. What would she think of such a question? Still, for some reason beyond his comprehension, he felt compelled to ask.

"Have you ever been in love?" he managed, his voice nearly a whisper.

"What?" Her eyes shot to his.

"I mean, do you know what it's like to be in love?" he corrected.

She looked out through the trees, past the small circle of rocks where Ferryl built fires sometimes. Thunder clapped a few times before she answered.

"Yes, I... I suppose I do."

"Anyone I know?" he asked before he could think better of it.

She only laughed and looked down at her feet. "I suppose you know him. In a way. Or at least, I wish you knew him."

"Oh," was all he could say.

"Why are you asking me this, Your Highness?"

"Elizabeth, I know this is going to sound strange but..." Ferryl fidgeted with his fingers, wishing his nerves would calm. Why *was* he asking her this? "I keep having these dreams."

"Dreams?"

Providence, he was a fool. A damned fool. But his traitorous mouth kept talking. "Of a woman. A woman I don't know. Not really. But I think...I think I might be in love with her."

"What makes you think that?" she asked, and he couldn't tell what she thought of his preposterous line of questioning.

"I don't know, Elizabeth. I don't know how to explain it. I don't even know her, you see. But she...she's all I think about. All I want. Do you think it's possible? To love someone you don't know?"

She was trembling. He could see the faint tremolo in her fidgeting fingers. Damn it, he shouldn't have said anything. A fool, that's what he sounded like. A blithering, rambling fool.

"I suppose it's possible," she finally said.

"I know it's strange. I know there's no reason for it. But I do—I think I'm in love with her."

"But you don't know who she is, this girl in your dreams?"

"Not in a manner of speaking, no." How could he tell her the truth? What would she think if he admitted to her that it was she who occupied his every waking thought? She who consumed his dreams? She who was little more than an acquaintance? Why in all the realms of Sheol did he think he was in love with her anyway? Did he even know what love was? Could he say that he had ever been in love?

"It's ridiculous, isn't it?"

Elizabeth seemed to deflate. She sighed heavily and looked again through the trees. "It's not ridiculous, Sire. Strange, perhaps. But not ridiculous. But you haven't any idea who she might be?"

"In my heart, in my mind, I know her. But in reality, no, I don't know her. Or I should say I know very little of her. Does that even make sense?"

"Not, really, I must admit. But it does explain things a little better, I suppose."

"What do you mean?" he asked.

"Nothing, just... I agree. I think you're in love."

"That's what it sounds like, right? Is that how you feel? About the man you love, I mean?" The question tasted like ash in his mouth. Jealousy. He was jealous of whoever it was she loved.

He was such an insufferable, damned fool.

She sighed again. "My situation is...complicated."

"Why?"

"He's not...he's not here."

"He's gone?" Ferryl asked in awe. Who would leave a girl like her?

"Gone, yes."

"Surely he'll return for you, Elizabeth. He'd be a fool not to."

She met his eyes and lingered again before giving him a rueful smile. "I do hope so. Every day I hope."

Ferryl and Elizabeth didn't say anything for a long while, the not-so-distant thunder rumbling as the storm approached ever closer. The lazy pitter-patter of errant rain drops began dancing on the hazelnut leaves.

"So what will you do, Your Highness? Will you look for her?"

"Elizabeth." The prince placed his hands over hers as they rested in her lap.

"Yes?" she asked.

"I'd like it very much if you called me Ferryl."

Elizabeth turned her hands under his, palm to palm, and gave them a gentle squeeze.

It was a moment before he could continue, too thrilled by her touch to concentrate on much else. "To answer your question, yes. I won't rest until I find out who she is."

She didn't say anything for another long moment. "I hope you do find her, Ferryl."

"And I hope you find him."

"He's getting closer," she said. "I can feel it."

* * *

PERHAPS IT WAS A BIT strange to tell a woman that you think you're in love with someone you've never met and then proceed to hold her hand, but that's exactly what Ferryl did. In fact, he found that as soon as their hands rested in each other's, he didn't want to let go, couldn't help but to trace lazy circles on the back of her hand with his thumb. And Elizabeth, it seemed, didn't mind either, for she offered her hand willingly, entwining her fingers with his in a way that was oddly comfortable...familiar. Like...like her hand had rested in his a thousand times before. Like it had been made to rest in his.

The thunderstorm had come, but it wasn't nearly as powerful (or frightening, frankly) as Ferryl had hoped. Still, Elizabeth shuddered a time or two when the lightning hit close and the thunder clapped violently. And Ferryl seized the opportunity to inch a little closer to her, savoring the way his whole body warmed at even so simple a touch as her shoulder against his. It was almost as if...well, almost as if there was a kind of magic between them.

"I've always loved storms," Elizabeth admitted.

"As have I. I've been coming here to watch them ever since I was a child. It's my favorite place to be when they come in."

"You have good taste," she agreed.

"I'm glad you are here with me, Elizabeth."

"I'm glad you asked me."

"I should like to ask you again, if you're so inclined," he said.

"You showed me your Secret Place, Ferryl. How could I deny an invitation?" she grinned.

He chuckled, bringing her hand to his lips that he might kiss the soft pocket of skin between her thumb and her forefinger. And Providence help him, she tasted like honey—wild and sweet and untamed. Just like in his dream. So he kissed her hand again and grinned over her fingers as he said, "You cannot, my lady. You cannot."

* * *

"As much as it pains me, I must be getting back to the palace. Everyone will be wondering where I've been," said Ferryl, but he didn't move a muscle in preparation for a departure. The thunderstorm had long since passed, the leaves of the forest dripping leftover rainwater lazily around them. But he and Elizabeth had sat under the stone for hours, enjoying the petrichor, the balmy breeze, one another—as if old friends come for a long overdue visit.

"We've been here quite a while, haven't we?" she asked.

"It's past the noon hour. The sun is in front of us now. You must be hungry. I'm sorry I've been so thoughtless."

"I hadn't noticed until you mentioned it, but yes, I am a bit hungry."

"Well then, it's settled." Ferryl jumped to his feet. "I shall have to retrieve sustenance for the lady before we depart. Should you like to come with me? There is a tree not far from here with the sweetest little fruits. I usually stop by before I leave."

"That would be lovely," said Elizabeth, and she, too, stood, taking Ferryl's hand when he offered, following him through the mossy grove to a small clearing in the forest where stood a lone fruit tree kissed by flickering shards of sunlight, its inky branches slender and curled on the ends like beckoning fingers of midnight, its shimmering leaves and plump fruits lush and golden, glowing and sparkling in the mottled light like fireflies dancing about the branches.

"These are called chalam. Have you ever had one?" he asked as he picked the two ripest from the tree.

Elizabeth grinned and toyed with her amulet, running it along its chain. "I've lived here my whole life, remember? I've had a chalam."

"Oh, it's just that—"

"They only grow around the cliffs. I know." She grinned, her fingers brushing his as she took the fruit he offered.

He gave her a skeptical grin. "Well there is an old legend about the fruit. Have you heard of it?"

She shook her head as she bit into the juicy snack.

"In the ancient tongue, chalam means dream. It is said that those who share of chalam from the same tree shall be forever knitted by the same destiny."

She raised a brow. "Do you believe that's true?"

He took a casual bite of his fruit, its sweetness bursting in riotous flavors on his tongue. "I don't know." He shrugged. "I suppose we'll have to find out."

She eyed him skeptically as she took another bite, and he found that he couldn't take his eyes off of her. And when a rogue drop of juice began to slide down her delicate chin, it was all he could do not to reach out and wipe it away. But alas, he could think of no good reason to touch that chin of hers, concluding that such an explanation as, "I couldn't help myself" or "you're simply irresistible, Elizabeth" would hardly suffice for an excuse. So instead he focused on finishing the honey-sweet fruit in his hands and calling on every reserve of self-control he knew himself to have.

She was in love with someone else, he reminded himself.

She was in love with a fool.

"That was delicious," she finally said, wiping her hands. "Thank you, Ferryl. You're quite the gentleman. Don't let anyone tell you otherwise." And at this she winked.

Winked.

Well.

Ferryl, fool that he was, swept his thumb across her chin before he thought better of it, wiping the drop of chalam juice she had missed. But the juice wiped and the moment expired, Ferryl's traitorous thumb lingered, his eyes wandering to her lips. Full, the most perfect of pinks, slightly parted.

Irresistible.

And had it not been for the nuisance thunder that startled them, those lips would have been thoroughly kissed.

As it was, the two of them only laughed and agreed to head back to the palace before the next round of storms hit. For if the clouds on the horizon were any indication, the rain hadn't finished for the day. And Ferryl knew better than to keep Elizabeth there another second. Because if the storm didn't claim her, he would. And he wasn't sure what that said about himself.

* * *

Chapter 13

Y ou seem in good spirits, my darling," said Bedell, the steam from the freshly-baked breakfast kissing his silvery beard.

Elizabeth finished cutting an apple and set it on a platter along with cheese, a peppering of golden coconut macaroons, and hot, crusty bread. She smiled as she spoke. "Maybe I am."

"Falling in love all over again, are you?" her perceptive father asked.

She pursed a smile as she bit into the macaroon, the coconut a sweet and crisp contrast to the salty stickiness of the treat. Oh, this was a good batch. She made a mental note to write down exactly what she had done this time, finally managing to perfect the recipe she had attempted and failed too many times before.

"He has always had your heart, hasn't he?"

"He always will."

"Yes, like the twining branches of the chalam tree, your destinies are of one purpose," said Bedell before he took a bite of a macaroon.

Her eyes shot to his at the mention of the tree, only to find him preoccupied with admiring the pastry in his hand. "Are you speaking in prophecies, Father, or is this your attempt at poetry?" she chuckled.

"Prophecies, like love, are usually poetic, my dear. How else could we speak of that which is yet to be but with songs and sonnets?"

Elizabeth shook her head with a laugh. "Father, you speak nonsense."

"Nonsense," he retorted. "Where would the beauty in this world be if not for love and poetry? And speaking of poetry, I believe I am inspired even now by this macaroon."

Elizabeth beamed. "Do you like it, Father?"

"*Like* is a severe understatement. You've been making them a lot lately."

"Macaroons are one of—well, I've just been trying to master them for years." And considering they were Ferryl's favorite confection, she had all the more reason to perfect them these days.

Bedell took her hand across the table and gave her a sympathetic smile. "My dearest, I am glad to hear that Ferryl has captured your heart all over again. I pray for nothing less than the most glorious of what life has to offer you."

"Do you think he will ever regain his memory, Father?"

"It's hard to know these things. But take comfort that even if he doesn't, you're creating new memories now that will last a lifetime."

New memories. Yes, she hadn't thought of it that way. But certainly since he had forgotten all about her, they had shared many new moments to enjoy for as long as they lived. So many questions left, yes. But still so many things for which to be thankful.

She looked down, catching sight of her necklace out of the corner of her eye as it shimmered in the shafts of morning light. She picked it up and looked at her father.

"What do you suppose this is?" she asked.

"Why it's your necklace, my dear," he said, happily taking another macaroon.

"Ferryl told me he thinks it's an amulet."

"Yes, well, amulets are necklaces, are they not?"

Elizabeth frowned. "Do you think it has powers?"

"Now that is an interesting question coming from you," said Bedell, his eyes sliding to Elizabeth's.

"It's just that...well, you know no one can remove it. Not even you. Ferryl was never able to remove it when we were children, either. But just the other day, he did. He removed it! He could even put it on, and it stayed! What do you suppose is the meaning of that?"

Bedell didn't say anything for a moment, leaving her mind to wander into the thousand questions that had been nagging at her for days. "I told you that your destinies are of one purpose."

Elizabeth furrowed her brows. "I'm talking about the necklace, Father."

"As am I." Bedell was silent for a moment before he said, "I would imagine the reason he couldn't remove it when you were children is because he wasn't in love with you then."

"He can remove the necklace because he's in love with me?"

"He's right, Elizabeth, dear, that amulet has powers. You have had it since I found you in the Wild Wood, and I have known all along that its powers belong to you and you alone. But if Ferryl is capable of wearing it now, that tells me that my inclinations are correct—your destinies are entwined if for no other reason than because he is your match and you are his."

"I don't understand. How can our destinies be the same? He doesn't even remember who I am!"

"There is power in commitment, love. And the commitment you have both made to one another is no doubt the reason that the power in your necklace now applies to him as well."

"But how can he be committed to me? He doesn't even remember me!"

"The heart, my love, weighs much more heavily in such matters than the mind. But commitment alone is not enough."

"Why?" she asked.

"While there is power in the commitment your hearts have made to one another, there is only fulfillment in covenant. You cannot live out your united destiny without it."

"I don't understand," she admitted.

"Like most things in life, it is not meant for you to fully understand today. It is something you will have to discover over the course of your life. But for now, I want you to understand that there is no higher calling, responsibility, or privilege than the love of a man and a woman. What you and Ferryl share is real and lasting, incapable of being thwarted by any spell or curse forever, so long as the commitment remains. Should you choose to enter into that most sacred of matrimonial covenants, I believe that you will find the destinies you have, the powers you wield, and the love you share exponentially increased and thereby blessed. These are the ways of Providence, you see."

Elizabeth thought in silence as she chewed her macaroon. Destinies inextricably linked. Her father's words had always perplexed her, always left her with more questions than answers. But in truth, she had come to understand that the questions pressing on her heart of late weren't going to be easily answered.

Perhaps her father wasn't as naïve as she thought.

* * *

Chapter 14

"You look to be in a pleasant mood, brother," said Ferryl with a sarcastic smirk as he strode alongside Derwin through the palace corridors, the black-and-white marquis marble spreading before them in endless monotony. Sunlight streamed in through the breezy halls, casting golden swaths of afternoon sun along the considerable expanse before them.

Derwin's brows furrowed even more. "I find it ridiculous that King Derrick felt the need to travel all the way from Midvar just to reiterate what he's been insisting all along—that he has nothing to do with the rebels. All this diplomacy is tedious, if you ask me. And it's severely infringing on my schedule."

Ferryl snorted. "Your schedule? What exactly are you missing, brother?"

But Derwin, ever silent on his own affairs, didn't answer.

"Well, I think we should hear him out, even if he is the so-called enemy. Just because his father waged war against our kingdom does not mean he will follow in those footsteps. And if he felt it important enough to make the month-long journey to our kingdom, perhaps King Derrick has something worthwhile to say," Ferryl offered.

"Or he's as manipulative as Mother and he's more effective in person."

"Ever the pessimist." Ferryl laughed.

"You mean you actually want to hear what this ass has to say?"

"I mean, simply, that he might very well offer a perspective different from our own."

Derwin snorted his disagreement. "Yes, I'm sure he'll be full of insight. Just as he will be most helpful as we give him a personal tour of the locations and conditions of every one of our outposts."

"What?" Ferryl demanded, stopping in his tracks.

Derwin stopped too, turning to face his brother. "You didn't hear? He's not just here for this meeting. He's going to be visiting all of our outposts with our generals in the coming weeks."

Ferryl didn't answer, surprised that he hadn't been informed about this. Then again, maybe he might have picked up on it had he not been so preoccupied as of late.

"Are we really this naïve?" Derwin asked, interrupting his thoughts.

"What do you mean?" Ferryl asked, resuming his trek through the corridors.

Derwin fell in stride. "I suppose if we take him at his word, then these rebels have nothing to do with him and any insight he offers is most welcome. But if he's lying, as I strongly suspect he is, then we're blindly handing over valuable information to the enemy. We might as well hand him a map of the kingdom, conveniently marked with every vulnerable outpost and unmanned region. I cannot believe Father is this much of a fool."

"He's not a fool, Derwin."

"He wasn't. Not when he was young. But his mind is addled in recent years. And he's being played a fool."

"What makes you believe that?" Ferryl asked as they came to the giant doors separating them from the fated meeting.

"I know it in my gut."

Ferryl eyed his brother for a moment, wondering which he should trust—his father's credentials or his brother's instincts.

He didn't have an answer as the two of them entered the royal meeting room, resplendent with the abundant afternoon sunlight pouring in through the wall of windows. Their mother and father sat at one end of the giant oak table, talking pleasantries with the guests. King Aiken seemed in lively spirits, as if his headaches had mercifully subsided for the time being. And Queen Meria, in an ostentatious black-and-crimson gown and equally obnoxious diadem, stared down the table as if she were drinking in every guest, even as she kept up an air of casual conversation with Sir Thomas Nachash, the diplomat from Midvar, who sat a little more proudly today. Several crusty old lords and dukes lined both sides of the table, along with his father's chief advisor, Bedell; the Royal Army Commander, Titus Melamed; and sitting at the end opposite King Aiken, looking as pompous and snobbish as Ferryl would have assumed, King Derrick of Midvar. His hair was a deep auburn, and his features were as severe as his expression. It didn't help that he was clad in black from head to toe. He looked to be the kind of man who never laughed, and Ferryl found himself inexplicably uncomfortable around him, wondering what kind of diplomacy could result in a meeting with such a man.

But more than the severity of the monarch, Ferryl was caught off guard by the sudden look his mother shot to the visiting king. Sitting beside her husband, her shoulders back and chin high, Queen Meria slid her eyes to King Derrick from across the long table as if he and only he held the key to a secret treasure beyond imagination. In fact, she didn't even take the time to greet her sons with some sort of underhanded compliment, as was her habit. Her gaze never faltered, even for a moment. And Ferryl couldn't help but be bothered by her fixation.

"Ah, sons, glad you could join us," said King Aiken, rising to his feet with a happy, somewhat relieved smile on his mouth. "Sit, sit, and we shall commence." He gestured to the two empty chairs to his right and the sons obliged before King Aiken continued.

"As you all know, we have called this meeting to discuss our current situation with the Midvarish rebels and determine a strategy in dealing with them. We are honored to have with us today His Majesty King Derrick of Midvar." Aiken turned his attention to the king at the opposite end of the table. "King Derrick, we are glad of your visit, as we know it will bring much-needed insight to the situation with the rebels."

King Derrick's self-satisfied smile never left his face as he nodded slowly in agreement, and Ferryl didn't miss the extra sparkle in his mother's eyes as her husband addressed the monarch. Sir Thomas, too, adjusted himself in his chair, sitting a little straighter, throwing his shoulders back. Proud to be in the presence of his king.

"Well then, let's get down to business, shall we?" said King Aiken. "As you are aware, in recent months, the attacks from Midvarish rebels have increased exponentially. As of yet, we have been unable to thwart their efforts. We have strategized at length both with our commander and our advisors and have yet to come up with an adequate solution to the problems the rebels present. So, King Derrick, we look forward to your fresh perspective regarding our situation. But first, Commander Titus, can you fill us in on what you know to date?"

Although he was only about forty, Commander Titus Melamed had an air about him that made him seem much older. Having fought in the Great War when he was young, and sworn his loyalty to Navah sometime thereafter, he had earned a place among the king's army as one of its fiercest warriors, unwavering in his dedication. Ferryl wondered what King Derrick thought of the fact that he sat at the table with a man who no longer pledged his allegiance to Midvar. Regardless, Ferryl, along with many others, knew that the commander was as good at his job as he was tired of it. And it shone not only in his silver eyes and salt-and-pepper hair, but in the lines around his eyes and the slump of his shoulders. He moved to the edge of his seat and cleared his throat.

"Thank you, Your Majesty. It is true that the rebels have posed a more significant problem than we originally projected. What started off as disorganized factions of peasants has culminated into relentless attacks along our borders for the past several months. My officers inform me that every time we get a handle on one faction of attackers, another appears in a completely different region. And having dealt with many of the rebels myself, I can attest to their relentlessness. No matter how thoroughly we eliminate them, there are always more. It seems that they are more adamant in their agenda than we had originally assumed."

"And what agenda, pray tell, would that be?" asked Sir Thomas, with an unmistakable air of offense in his voice.

"To that end, we cannot be sure," continued Commander Titus. "Your people assure us that they are random and disorganized. But our evidence would suggest otherwise. It seems they remain a step ahead of us at all times, poised to attack exactly where our soldiers are not. And aside from stationing our legions in every possible corner of the kingdom, the only other solution I suggest is to stop responding in defense and begin an offensive counterattack. We cannot keep pretending that these rebels are harmless. They have killed too many of our—"

Sir Thomas interjected with an emphatic tone. "I beg your pardon, Your Excellency, but it seems to me that you are suggesting that these rebels are not random, and I think His Majesty and I have made it clear that there is nothing organized about these bandits. We do not know why they are attacking, nor do we know any more about how to stop them than you do."

"Well then, I suppose our best plan is to sit back and watch as they destroy our kingdom, one village at a time," said Derwin.

"I'm not suggesting that at all," said Sir Thomas.

"Then what are you suggesting?" asked Derwin.

"I suggest we enter into negations and—"

"Negotiations!" scoffed Derwin. "You're a greater fool than I had already assumed."

"Derwin," scolded Queen Meria, eyeing her youngest son with a healthy measure of disdain. "You will not speak to anyone at this table in such a manner."

"I will speak to fools as the fools they are," Derwin replied, and Ferryl opted to give his brother a look that suggested he tone it down, at least for the time being. For while he appreciated his brother's candor, and found it rather entertaining, he knew it wasn't exactly going to be received with open arms at this juncture.

One of the crusty old dukes spoke up next. "The bottom line is, we have no way of proving that this is an organized faction of any kind. And until we do, we had better tread lightly, for any accusation—false or true—could trigger an all-out war."

"Better yet, let us trigger the all-out war and be done with these bastards!" said Derwin.

"You speak of war rather flippantly, Your Highness," said another of the noblemen.

"Well, I suppose what you call flippant talk I call dealing with the issue," chided Derwin.

Sir Thomas retorted, his tone placating, patronizing, "I find it dangerous to operate on the premise that these attacks are getting worse. Evidence I have would suggest otherwise. While they are still happening, they are certainly waning. These rebels cannot keep this up forever."

It was then that an argument erupted, every man around the table attempting to get his word in, save for Bedell, who sat in ponderous silence, King Derrick, who watched as if attending a circus, and Ferryl, who wondered how in the world anything was to get done with meetings such as this.

"Commander Titus," said King Aiken, his commanding voice finally interrupting the madness, "do you have a suggestion for a new strategy regarding the rebels?"

Commander Titus swallowed and sucked in a breath before answering. "You are all correct that we do not know why we are being attacked in such a way. And you are correct that we have no proof that any of these attacks are sanctioned by a particular group or movement. But from my observation, whatever their motivation, they're relentless. Unfortunately, Your Majesty, in my opinion, the only real solution..." he paused, looking around the table, "may be war."

There was a palpable silence around the table for a good minute before anyone spoke, eyes bouncing from one person to the next, brows furrowing, exhaling. Derwin was back in his chair, arms folded across his chest in apparent agreement with the commander.

It was Bedell who caught Ferryl's attention, his hand to his chin, stroking his silvery beard.

"Bedell, what have you to say of this?" Ferryl asked. Of all the opinions at this table, he valued the old man's the most.

The king's chief advisor looked Ferryl in the eye, his old voice quavering but still strong, commanding authority. "I believe that before any talk of war, it would behoove you to speak with your neighbors to the north. Perhaps they will have insight as to how to deal with these rebels. After all, it wasn't that long ago that they were in your very shoes."

"Haravelle," said Ferryl, and Bedell nodded.

"If you're implying that Midvar is poised to attack Navah in the same manner in which my father attacked Haravelle nearly two decades ago, you are sorely mistaken." This came from King Derrick, speaking for the first time, his voice a deep, resonating timbre, his tone commanding a fearsome brand of authority.

"I am implying nothing," said Bedell, visibly unbothered by the Midvarish king's warning tone. "But our kingdom would be remiss to ignore the fact that your country has incessantly attacked both ours and our neighbors to the north for the past thousand years."

"And while I would concur with your assessment," said King Derrick, "I would be equally remiss not to point out that under my reign, our kingdoms have all been in peaceable agreement. I can hardly be blamed for the sins of my forefathers."

"No more than we can be blamed for our misgivings concerning your sudden change of heart," said Bedell, and Ferryl couldn't help but feel a fierce sense of loyalty to the fearless old man. For surely he had proven his fealty to his kingdom time and again, this meeting being no exception. Chief advisor, indeed.

"I'm afraid I'm going to have to agree with His Majesty King Derrick," chimed Queen Meria. "And while your wise insight, Bedell, is no doubt valued at this table, it seems a foolish notion to begin a process of gathering allies against an enemy that is little more than a band of rebels. I fear that if we make a journey to Haravelle, it will only send the message to Midvar that we are preparing for war. A war, I might add, that we are neither prepared for nor financed to fight."

"It is true, Your Majesty," said King Derrick to Meria, and Ferryl was taken aback at the way the visiting king's eyes lingered on his mother. "I fear what my people would think if they knew of any measures to organize an army on your part."

"Well now, that's an asinine excuse if ever there was one, isn't it?" said Derwin.

"How do you mean?" asked King Derrick.

Derwin scoffed as he looked the Midvarish king in the eye. "You *are* Midvar, Your Majesty. So any ideas your people get regarding what Navah is doing would come from you, wouldn't they? And since you are obviously here at our table today, you are privy to our plans and the notions behind them. It would seem to me that any panic on the part of your people would be not only unmerited but completely fabricated, considering that any information they get would come from you."

Ferryl was surprised at the look on King Derrick's face. He had fully expected an uproar to ensue at Derwin's audacity. Instead, what he saw was a smirk and a small chuckle. It was almost as if the king was amused by Derwin's boldness.

"Well, Prince Derwin," countered King Derrick, pressing his hands in front of his lips like a prayer, "you make an excellent point." The Midvarish king paused in thought, and Ferryl noticed that, whether because of need or effect, it made its mark, for everyone in the room, save for a select few, began shifting uncomfortably. Finally, the king's deep timbre rang through the stiffness like a gong. "If Navah decides to go to war against these rebels, you will have our full support."

Derwin looked to his father quickly before looking back at King Derrick, as surprised by the visiting king's reaction as everyone around the table. What sort of game was going on that a king would sanction a war against his own people? Ferryl couldn't help but to feel as if he was missing an entirely large piece to this puzzle.

"I appreciate all of the input here," said King Aiken, "but I would strongly advise against any plans of war at this time. We still do not know why these rebels are attacking. And if we do not know our enemy, we cannot know how to defeat them. We should not be hasty in making a decision to put the lives of our men on the line for a threat we do not understand. We do not even know what these rebels want."

"Agreed, Father," said Ferryl. "But I also think it is in our best interest to figure out this enemy's purpose as quickly as possible, for delaying a decision too long could be equally as catastrophic."

"You are correct, young prince," said the commander. "But I must concur with my king. War is not something to be taken lightly. Our soldiers are already weary from defending our borders all these months. If we are to wage a formal war, we must take this into consideration."

"We must do something to show these rebels that we are a united front," said King Derrick, surprising everyone around the table. "We must beat them at their own game."

"Yes, well, that would require knowing what game they are playing to begin with, now, wouldn't it?" asked Derwin.

"Indeed, Prince Derwin," said King Derrick, nodding. The king eyed the young prince pointedly, and Ferryl could practically feel the venom rising within his brother, and he braced himself for whatever retort Derwin was preparing. But it wasn't his brother who spoke next, but the queen, interrupting the conversation with a hastiness to her voice that seemed out of place.

"Well now, I don't know about the rest of you," said Queen Meria, "but all this talk of war is making me hungry. I say we table this discussion for the time being and adjourn to the dining hall for our dinner. We will all think more clearly with full bellies, don't you agree?"

Ferryl watched King Derrick as his gaze turned to the queen from the opposite end of the long table, his eyes hungry, devouring her as if she were a delicacy. His mother returned the gaze, but while her eyes were affixed on the dark king, her face remained expressionless. And while she never broke his stare, she slipped a hand to her husband, gripping his arm where it rested on the table beside her. King Aiken didn't so much as flicker at her touch, although Ferryl didn't miss the glassy fog that settled in his father's eyes. There was some sort of knowing in Derrick's eyes as he practically ravaged Ferryl's mother from the other end of the table. Some sort of silent allegiance the two shared. And while Ferryl had no idea what it could be, he knew he didn't like it at all.

Chapter 15

After dinner, negotiations and strategizing did not recommence as promised. Instead, with ample amounts of wine and food in their bellies, the motley crew ended the evening with raucous laughter and storytelling, card games, and plenty of wine to fuel the impromptu party for hours. The only people who didn't participate were Derwin, who disappeared just after dessert; Bedell, who excused himself on account of being tired; and Ferryl, who watched the strange scene for a while from the edge of the room before disappearing to his private chambers.

It was strange—too strange—to have a visiting king—an enemy king, no less—laughing and jesting with the royal family's most trusted inner circle. Ferryl hardly knew what to make of the behavior, much less that of his mother's shared looks with King Derrick. And while the meeting was certainly insightful, it created an onslaught of new questions for the crown prince. Chief among them: what possible show could their kingdoms put on that would display a united front to rebel attackers?

Ferryl sighed and shook his head, standing abruptly from the settee in front of his fireplace, weary from the silence of his chambers and the thoughts swarming his mind like moths. He marched to his door, a man on a mission.

"Everything all right, Your Highness?" asked a guard as Ferryl passed him.

"Michael, I need to speak with Derwin," said Ferryl, not bothering to pause as he marched past.

"I don't believe he's available, Sire."

Morgan G Farris

Ferryl turned on his heel to face the guard. A friend since they were boys training under Commander Titus, Michael was someone he had trusted for as long. "Where is he?"

Michael's knowing eyes were colored with a hint of guilt. "I am sworn not to say, Your Highness. I'm sorry."

"Sworn? By whom?"

"Prince Derwin," Michael said quietly.

"So whatever it is that Derwin is up to, he's even going so far as to make sure his own brother stays out of it."

Michael didn't look the prince in the eye, and Ferryl couldn't help but chuckle at the guard's guilt. He clasped him on the shoulder. "It's all right, my friend. You and I both know Derwin is as stubborn as a mule. I won't hold it against you."

"You are absolutely correct about that, Sire," said Michael.

"About what?"

"That Prince Derwin is as stubborn as a mule."

The two men chuckled, and Ferryl turned toward the large stone staircase at the end of the corridor.

"If it's a reprieve from your thoughts you're in search of, my rotation is almost over. I believe we're due for a game or two."

Ferryl considered the offer. And while he appreciated the respite their card games often gave him, he also knew that tonight, he just needed out of the castle for a while.

"I appreciate it, my friend. But I need some fresh air. I think I'll go for a walk. Perhaps by clearing my mind, I can figure out whatever nonsense my brother is up to."

Michael bowed. "Your Highness."

"When are you going to stop calling me that?" Ferryl asked over his shoulder as he walked away.

He heard Michael's answering chuckle echo down the corridor.

Ferryl strode off, wondering what in the world he was going to do with himself. He couldn't stand the idea of stewing in his own thoughts before the fire all night, and he knew himself well enough to know that it was exactly what would happen if he stayed in his chambers. He heard laughter ring from the other end of the corridor, but he had equally little desire to rejoin the bizarre party going on this evening.

115

Still, he needed to think, to clear his head. Perhaps even to be distracted. He could think of only one distraction that would suffice. And his pace quickened in response.

* * *

"I was hoping I might find you here."

"Your Highness," said Elizabeth, turning quickly with a look of surprise on her face. It soon faded into a smile which rendered Ferryl dumbstruck. Somehow, she was even more beautiful by starlight than the golden sunrises by which he had grown accustomed to her face. She bobbed a graceful curtsey. "You're out here late. Is everything all right?"

The moonlight cast a heavenly glow on the porcelain skin of the girl before him, and Ferryl found his heart racing at her nearness, marveling at the speed at which she had so thoroughly bewitched him. "Yes, everything is all right. I didn't mean to frighten you." He finally reached her side, took hold of her hand, and kissed it tenderly. Even in the wan twilight, he could see the blush in her cheeks, and he took no small amount of satisfaction from it.

"You didn't frighten me, it's just that you don't typically come out for evening rides unless you're upset or you need to think," she said.

"I don't?" he asked, wondering how she knew that.

"Well, I mean, I...thought so."

"No, you're right." He grinned.

"So which is it?" she asked.

"Hmm?" he asked, finding himself distracted by her hair as it tousled lazily in the salty evening breeze.

"Are you upset or do you need to think?"

"Oh, um, I just needed to think."

"I see," she said. "Shall I leave you alone then?" She took a step away, but he grabbed hold of her hand before she could get too far.

"I was hoping you might want to think with me."

"You were?"

Ferryl nodded, knowing a keen sense of satisfaction in the way her eyes flashed with...with what? Anticipation?

"What about?"

"Well, you see the King of Midvar is here, visiting with my family as we discuss the situation with the Midvarish rebels. The only problem is that there seems to be no simple solution, and for every answer, there are a thousand problems. It seems we're getting nowhere in our negotiations."

"Oh," she said rather quietly.

"Everything all right?"

"Of course, Your Highness. I just...don't know how much good I'll be. I don't know much when it comes to wars and kingdoms and the like. I'm just a servant."

"I thought we had established that you were going to call me Ferryl."

"Oh, yes," she said, looking down. Prince Ferryl cupped his hand under her chin and lifted her face to meet his again. "Ferryl," she said when she met his eyes.

"Thank you." He smiled. "And that's not true."

"What's not true?"

"That you are just a servant. In fact, you are the most unservant-like servant I know."

"Yes, well, I know I'm terrible with the horses but—"

Ferryl barked a laugh. "Well, at least you're aware," he said. "But that wasn't what I meant."

"It wasn't?" she asked, and he could see a hint of laughter in her eyes too.

"No," he said, pushing a stray strand of hair behind her ear. "I meant, Elizabeth, that there's something special about you. I can't put my finger on it. But you're just...well, different."

"And is *different* a good thing or a bad thing?" she asked with a raised eyebrow.

"Good." He smiled. "Definitely good."

"I see," she said, pausing for a moment and pursing a smile. But Ferryl could see a hint of mischief in her eyes as an idea bloomed. "Would you perhaps like some tea while we discuss this conundrum?"

"That would be perfect, yes," he said.

Elizabeth turned to head towards the back of the stables. Ferryl followed in stride. "Where are we going?" he asked.

"My cottage."

"Ah." Ferryl couldn't help himself, placing his hand at the small of her back as they walked the short walk to a small cottage on the edge of the stable grounds. He couldn't miss the way her green eyes, flecked with bits of gold, shimmered like molten stars in the moonlight when she stopped to open her door, her smile equally as irresistible.

The cottage was quaint and had the unmistakable touches of femininity all around. Intricately painted flourishes on the walls, kept and tidy, fresh flowers in a vase on the small dining table in the middle of the room. A set of armchairs and matching settee that looked exactly like the ones in his receiving room in the palace.

"Did you do all this?" Ferryl asked, admiring the painting around a small window.

"When I was young, yes. I used to love to paint." Elizabeth didn't hesitate to get a kettle started, and Ferryl took it upon himself to stoke the fire as she worked in the tiny corner kitchen.

"But you don't paint anymore?"

"Oh, I suppose from time to time I get the urge. But it's no longer my creative expression of choice."

"What is?" Ferryl asked, genuinely curious.

"Cooking," she said, offering the prince a plate of tarts with a smile on her beautiful face.

"You cook?" he asked.

She only nodded as Ferryl took a bite. "By Providence, woman!" he exclaimed around a mouthful. "Where did you learn to cook like this?"

She chuckled. "My best friend always told me I had a knack for it. He encouraged me to cook from the time we were young. I'm fairly positive he did just so that he could benefit from the hobby."

"Wise man, that friend of yours," said Ferryl, enjoying the delicious little treat.

"Indeed," she laughed, setting the plate on the table and sitting down. Ferryl, too, sat down at the table, his eyes fixed on the glorious creature before him.

"So this best friend of yours, where is he now?"

"He's...gone," she said.

"Gone?" Ferryl asked. But no sooner did he ask the question that it occurred to him. "Is he the one you loved? The one who left?"

Elizabeth nodded.

"You were in love with your childhood best friend?" he asked.

"Yes," she answered quietly.

"Elizabeth, that's beautiful."

"Isn't it?"

"And are you any closer to finding him? Any sign of him?"

Her brows furrowed and she held his gaze, a steady brand as she said, "Only that which is in my heart."

Ferryl nodded, turning his jealous attention to the fire.

"And what about you, Ferryl? Have you found the woman you're in love with yet?"

Ferryl met her eyes. "Possibly, yes," he finally answered.

"Possibly?"

"Well, it's just that...I'm not sure how she would feel about the idea of my being in love with her."

"Have you asked her?"

Ferryl looked up. Asked her? Now there was a novel concept.

"Your Highness!" Their attention turned to the voice coming from a small room just down from them.

"Bedell," Ferryl said standing to his feet. "You...live here?"

The old man chuckled. "Well, yes, I believe so."

"Yes. Yes, of course," said Ferryl, realizing he had known that Bedell was Elizabeth's father. Yes. Of course he was. He wondered why he had forgotten it. "I only meant I didn't realize you would already be in bed. I hope we haven't woken you."

"No, not at all, son. I wasn't sleeping. It seems I have too much on my mind."

"It must be an epidemic," said Elizabeth. "Looks like the tea is ready. Would you like some, Father?"

"Why, yes, love. Thank you."

Ferryl gestured to his seat at the table. "Here, Bedell."

"No, no, son, I would never impede on a young man's opportunity to sit across from a lovely young woman. I'll just sit over here by the fire. Don't worry about me."

While Ferryl appreciated the old man's generosity, he wondered at the consequences of being found out by his father's most trusted advisor. Then again, Bedell was Elizabeth's father. Perhaps he would choose protecting her over revealing that the crown prince was visiting her house. After all, he knew Bedell to be the kind of man who only spoke when necessary. Perhaps he needn't worry about an onslaught of court rumors. Or an onslaught of his mother's wrath.

"If you're worrying about my revealing your presence here tonight to your mother or father, you needn't," said Bedell with a twinkle in his eyes. "I have made it a practice over the years to leave the private business of the prince private. And after all, why would I want to do anything that might inhibit what is blossoming between you?"

"Father," Elizabeth muttered warningly. Ferryl could see the embarrassment in her eyes and chuckled.

"I've always liked you, Bedell," chuckled the prince.

"As I've always liked you, Ferryl."

Elizabeth handed the men their cups before she sat down at the table with the prince, obviously mortified by the conversation. She began to fuss with the stone around her neck.

"You have much on your mind too, Prince Ferryl?" Bedell asked, sipping his tea.

"The meeting tonight was pointless, was it not?"

"Oh, I think it was rather insightful," said the old man.

"How so?" Ferryl asked, shifting forward in his seat.

"It is so very rare when a man says anything remotely as complex as what is going on in his heart. And King Derrick was no exception tonight, in my opinion."

"What do you mean, Father?" Elizabeth asked.

"He said very little with his mouth, as it were. He spoke mostly with his eyes. Which, by my observation, rarely left the queen's," said Bedell.

"I noticed that," said Ferryl, a tinge of disgust rising in his gut. "But what could it mean?"

"A great many things, I'm afraid," said Bedell.

"Did the queen return his stare?" Elizabeth asked.

"Yes. Why?" Ferryl asked.

"Then it would seem to me that whatever King Derrick is saying, Queen Meria is saying it as well," said Elizabeth.

"Exactly," said Bedell.

"But what could they be saying?" asked Ferryl. "And why is my mother on the same page with our enemy?"

"Don't forget that he swears he is no longer our enemy," said Bedell.

"I don't think I believe that," said Ferryl. "Do you?"

"Not for a moment," answered Bedell.

"Midvar has always had their eyes on Navah. And Haravelle. Everyone knows that. Why would they suddenly change their minds?" asked Elizabeth.

"That's the question, isn't it?" said Bedell.

"Well, if you ask me, they haven't changed their minds. Only their strategy," said Elizabeth, crossing her arms.

"How so?" asked Ferryl.

"I've been thinking about it, ever since Father told me that the rebel attacks are getting worse. It doesn't make sense. What is a band of rebels doing attacking our army at random? And all over the kingdom, no less? They couldn't do that if they weren't organized to some degree," she said.

"I agree," said Ferryl.

"So if they're organized, then someone is behind all of it. And if someone is behind all of it, then they have a purpose. And what purpose has Midvar ever had against Navah other than to take back what they claim to be theirs?"

"What are you saying?" asked Ferryl, sitting up in his chair.

"If the rebels are working to take back the land of Navah, then the king is behind it in some way. Midvarish kings have always been about the purpose of expanding their kingdom. Always," said Elizabeth.

"But why feign allegiance with us? Why play such games?" asked Ferryl.

"Perhaps it's to distract us from whatever it is they're really trying to do. Their real strategy," she answered, sipping from her mug of tea.

Ferryl sat back in his chair again. Of course. It made sense. He wondered why he hadn't thought of it before. "I thought you said you knew nothing of wars and kingdoms?"

"I don't," she said rather sheepishly. "I'm just a girl. But my father happens to be the Chief Advisor, and as such, I have the luxury of stewing on the goings on of this kingdom in the privacy of my little cottage without the distraction of diplomacy and politics. I'm not claiming to have any idea what I'm talking about. I beg of you not to put any more stock in it than it merits."

"I would dare say that it merits quite a lot of stock, my lady," said Ferryl.

"She's always been my logical one." Bedell beamed. "My little thinking one."

Ferryl grinned. "It would have been quite a sight to have you at the table today, Elizabeth. I dare say you would have put King Derrick himself in his place."

"Yes well, there is no one at that table that would find the opinions of the stable girl worth their while," said Elizabeth with a laugh.

"That's where you're wrong," said Ferryl, and when she met his eyes, he made a point to hold them for a moment.

"It would seem that Prince Ferryl has found himself a replacement for when I am gone," said Bedell with a smile.

"Indeed," said the prince, still holding Elizabeth's eyes. "I think it would be in my best interests to keep the lady Elizabeth as close as possible."

Elizabeth turned away, chewing on her bottom lip. "Would either of you like another tart?" she asked, a quick, decisive diversion.

"If I eat another one, I'm afraid I shall turn into one," laughed Bedell.

Ferryl, however, gladly sampled another. "Does she cook for you like this all the time, Bedell?"

"Every day," he said.

"Now I know why I never see you at my father's table." Ferryl grinned.

"Precisely," chuckled Bedell. "I am quite spoiled."

"Enough, you two," said Elizabeth. "If I didn't know any better, I'd say all this false adoration is just an attempt to get me to make more pastries."

"It is by no means false, my lady," said the prince. "But it is most certainly my attempt at getting you to make more pastries."

The three of them laughed, settling into more pleasant topics of conversation for the remainder of the evening, enjoying themselves immensely around the warm fire and tea.

"Well, I'm afraid I've kept you both long enough," Ferryl said, standing to his feet. "But I must thank you both for the pleasant evening."

"The pleasure is ours, Your Highness," said Bedell. "You should come back when Elizabeth makes her famous pot pies."

"Pot pies, you say?" said Ferryl, his eyes lighting up.

"And macaroons. Have you tasted her macaroons?"

Ferryl didn't miss the look Elizabeth gave her father before he himself looked her in the eyes. "Now *that* I shall have to return for."

"Good night, Your Highness," said Bedell, rising to his feet. "I think I shall retire as well."

"Good night, Bedell." Ferryl gave the old man a small bow.

"Sleep well, Father," said Elizabeth, kissing Bedell's cheek.

"Good night, love," he said, and with that, Bedell disappeared into his tiny bedroom.

Elizabeth bustled back to the table, busying herself with tidying up after their impromptu party.

"Your father loves you very much, Elizabeth," said Ferryl, helping her with the plates scattered about the table.

"I count myself lucky every day that he found me," she said, her gaze on her father's door as she cleared the last saucer.

Silence as thick as an autumn fog settled between them. She kept her eyes fixed on her father's door. He kept his eyes on her.

And when at last he could stand it no longer, he crossed the remaining steps between them, took the plates from her hands, and set them back down on the table. Ferryl took both of her hands in his, kissing them first on the top, then on the palms.

"Goodnight, my lady," he said, his hand rising to her cheek.

"Goodnight," she said, her voice little more than a breath.

"Thank you for thinking with me."

She chuckled, looking down to her feet. "Of course."

Ferryl lifted her chin so that he could look into her eyes again. "And I shall expect an invitation the next time you make pot pies."

"Then I shall plan to make them soon."

* * *

ELIZABETH STOOD IN THE DOORWAY watching Ferryl walk away, leaning against the jamb long after even his shadow had been swallowed by the night.

"Everything all right?" she heard her father ask.

She turned to see him standing in his bedroom door, a look of fatherly concern in his eyes.

"Pot pies and macaroons, Father?"

"The way to a man's heart, love," said Bedell.

"You know those are his favorite things, right?"

"Why do you think I suggested it?"

* * *

Chapter 16

War, commander?" asked King Derrick, stretching himself out in a chair in Commander Titus's personal chambers at Benalle Palace. The strange dinner-turned-party had ended only a little while ago, with the visiting monarch knocking on his doors soon after.

Titus glared at the pompous king sitting at his desk, shuffling through papers—many of which were quite personal—looking down his nose with a smug grin on his mouth. He stifled a snarl at the insolence. Anyone else who dared sit at his desk like that would swiftly have received—

"War terrifies Aiken, although I doubt he would ever admit it. After he saw what happened to Haravelle in the Great War, he has no desire to replicate it in his own country. I thought it would be best to scare him up front." Titus stood firmly planted in place, determined not to show his annoyance, determined to maintain the upper hand with the arrogant king before him.

"It was excellent," said King Derrick. "I believed every word of it. And by the look on Aiken's face, they won't be making decisions about the rebels anytime soon. Excellent job."

Titus nodded curtly, without so much as a word.

The king drummed his large fingers on the desk. "Something bothering you, Titus?"

Titus ignored the jab. "I wanted to speak with you about my retirement."

"From Navah, you mean."

Titus held his breath. "Yes, from Navah. I have it on good authority that the crown prince wants to name his brother as the new commander when I retire. And I thought not only would it appease the prince's impatience if I retired soon, but it would also benefit you, Your Majesty, considering that Prince Derwin is a hotheaded young boy. His arrogance will precede any good judgment when it comes to these rebels."

King Derrick's lips were thin as he nodded slowly. Thinking. Planning. Always plotting, this king of his—the king he truly served despite his title as the commander of the Navarian armies.

Derrick's fingers steepled at his mouth. "You may be right. But I'm not quite sure I'm ready to lose your influence here just yet."

"Yes, but think, Your Majesty, if I were back in Midvar, I could be much more use to you." How long had it been since he'd been home? How long since he'd had a life of his own? No threats of war. No kings breathing down his neck. Maybe he was a fool, but Titus had learned that the only thing he really wanted anymore—the only thing that really mattered—was home.

He eyed one of her letters on his desk, King Derrick's long fingers casually drumming it, even though he had showed no sign of noticing it.

The king's smirk returned. "You're not fooling anyone, you know. I told you, Titus, that woman of yours is a distraction."

Damn it. Damn this man.

Titus met his king's eyes, but he didn't dare say a word. No, he wouldn't argue this again. Not when he was so close—so close to finally going back home after all these years serving King Derrick's interests in Navah. And right under King Aiken's nose. No, he wouldn't jeopardize his chances at having a life again.

"You have served me well, Titus. I tell you what. Let's get our little duchess here, safe and sound. And then we'll talk of your *retirement*, as you call it."

Titus bowed his head. "I am but your humble servant, Majesty."

* * *

Chapter 17

Wwhat's this about?" Ferryl asked, making his way to his father's meeting room.

"Mother said it was an important meeting for our family." Derwin shrugged as the two princes ambled through the palace together, equally hesitant to find out exactly what their mother could want. The day had been a cheery one thus far, beginning with an impromptu visit to the stables that had turned into a morning riding the grounds with Elizabeth. There seemed no reason to put a damper on it now—especially not with an *important* meeting called by his mother. Ferryl could only imagine what she wanted with such an obtuse invitation.

"Shall I stop by a temple and pray first?" Ferryl joked.

"It probably wouldn't hurt. Too bad there are none in Benalle City," said Derwin, his answer catching his brother by surprise. There hadn't been a temple in the city for over five hundred years. Why in Sheol would it bother Derwin now?

The brothers rounded the corner to be greeted by two guards outside the king's meeting room.

"They are waiting for you," said one of the guards.

Ferryl nodded, and they entered the grand room. Derwin spoke up immediately. "If this is a family gathering, I'm not sure I understand why *he's* here," he said, gesturing rather inhospitably towards Sir Thomas Nachash, who was apparently joining the king and queen for the family meeting.

"Need I remind you that you did not call this meeting, so you do not get to decide the guest list? He is here on my invitation, son," said Queen Meria condescendingly as the five of them found chairs around the large and intricately carved oak table. "You would do well to re-member your place."

"What? As the all-but-useless second son?" Derwin snapped.

"You are anything but useless," chimed King Aiken coolly. "Your skill with blade and bow alone earned you a place as an officer in the Royal Army when you were only seventeen. You are an asset to this kingdom, Derwin. But I do agree with your mother that you ought hold your tongue. It tends to run away with you."

"Well then. Why have we called this meeting, Father?" asked Ferryl.

"As you both know," continued King Aiken, "my health has been failing in recent months. My headaches seem to be getting worse and unfortunately, there seems to be no cure." It was only for a second, but the king flashed a look at his son that suggested that the cause of his headaches might not be as mysterious as Ferryl would have assumed. But he continued so smoothly that Ferryl wondered if he had imagined the look. "And with the rebel threat, now is an important time to show the world that we are formidable and determined. As such, the queen and I have decided that it is time to make some decisions regarding your futures."

"This should be rich," muttered Derwin as he crossed his arms.

Ferryl tossed him a silent nod of consent.

"Derwin, it has been decided that for the time being, you are to re-main untethered, as we have yet to decide what is best regarding your marriage arrangement," said Queen Meria. "There are many promising prospects, chief among them being—"

"Arrangement? As in you're going to tell me who I have to marry and when, is that it?" Derwin practically shouted.

"Son, that's—" but King Aiken never finished his thought, slapping a hand to his head, the telltale sign of another one of his headaches. They certainly seemed to be getting worse these days.

"Are you all right, Father?" Ferryl asked.

Aiken only waved him off, but Ferryl couldn't help but wonder if there was a bit of frustration in the gesture.

"Derwin, you are a prince of Navah," the Queen spat. "You have duties to both crown and—"

Derwin cut his mother off. "A prince now, am I? Last time I checked, I was little more than a nuisance. At least that's how you've always treated me," he spat.

"Son..." said King Aiken, but Queen Meria placed her hand on her husband's arm.

"It's all right, Aiken. Let's hear what the boy has to say. Go on, Derwin. Do your best," purred the queen.

And at her inciting words, Derwin took the bait and launched into a tirade.

"I suppose I'm just another pawn, is that it? Another piece in your ever-growing puzzle of political strategies and alliances. So you'll keep me on the side until you're ready to play me, is that right? What about me? Did it ever occur to you that I might have plans of my own? I'm not a child, you know. I'm nineteen years old. I'm ready to have my own life. And it certainly doesn't involve any of these political games you call 'duty' and 'obligation!' I am not the heir! I have no duty to this country, and I will choose my own path!"

With this, Derwin sat back in his chair, catching his breath while Ferryl prepared himself for the tirade that he knew was coming from his mother.

But she didn't yell. In fact, she hardly shifted in her chair. "Derwin, you are the second in line to the throne of this kingdom and you will do as you are told. You will marry *whom* we say you will marry. And you will marry *when* we say you will marry, and that is the final word I will hear on the subject."

The queen glared at her second son for a moment, filling the room with a tense silence. Ferryl felt sorry for his brother, but not as sorry as he knew he was about to feel for himself.

"As for you, son," the queen continued, turning her icy attention to Ferryl. "You are twenty-one, and of marrying age. It is time that you take a wife."

"Yes, I've been thinking and—"

"It matters little what you've been thinking. You have proven yourself woefully immature and incapable of making sound decisions when it comes to the opposite sex," said Queen Meria.

"Perhaps if you offered something better than the grasping fools you seem so keen for him to marry, he'd make a decision," interjected Derwin.

"It's all right, Derwin. Thank you," said Ferryl. "Go ahead, Mother." Ferryl sat on the edge of his chair, bracing for the blow he knew was coming.

"In a little less than a month, Duchess Delaney Dupree will be arriving. She has been selected as your wife and future queen of Navah."

"Selected?" he asked. "I didn't realize my say in the matter had been revoked."

"It was revoked the moment you insulted Lady AnnaMaria Westerly. That was your final straw, Ferryl. Your last chance to choose for yourself," said Queen Meria.

"Why a month? I don't understand. If you're in such a hurry to marry me off—"

"Because it will take that long for her to get here." This came from Sir Thomas, who spoke for the first time.

"A month for her to arrive?" scoffed Derwin. "It sounds like you're shipping in some poor unsuspecting girl from the edge of the kingdom!"

"She is not from Navah. She is a proud daughter of Midvar, a striking young woman, the niece of King Derrick himself. Upon King Derrick's visit, it was decided that there can be no better show of our two countries' alliance than a union of marriage. Political implications aside, there can be no more advantageous arrangement for you," said Sir Thomas, his shoulders going back and his nose climbing into the air with pride. The queen gave Sir Thomas an approving look, lingering perhaps a little too long.

"Midvar?" Ferryl exclaimed. "Why in the name of Providence would you have me marry someone from Midvar? They are our sworn enemy!"

"All the more reason to seal an alliance!" exclaimed the queen. "You were there for the negotiations, Ferryl. We need a strategy to convince the rebels that their attacks are unnecessary. We are no longer enemies."

"You've got to be joking," said Derwin.

"It is true that the relations between Navah and Midvar have been strained in the past," said Sir Thomas. "But in truth, there has been much improvement on that account in recent years, and we believe that a marriage of this caliber will only strengthen the allied bonds already forming."

Derwin slammed his hands on the table. "Relations have been strained for a millennium! All due respect, Sir Thomas, but I don't see any of the so-called improvements you speak of."

"Derwin," said the king, but the queen held up her hand in protest.

"Aiken, if he wants to make an ass of himself, let him. I'm tired of stopping him," she said.

"Meria, for the love of Providence, let me speak," growled the king, surprising everyone in the room as he uncharacteristically stood his ground with his wife. All eyes turned to him.

Queen Meria turned her gaze to him as well, lovingly placing a hand on his arm, speaking in soft coos. "Of course, darling. Forgive me."

But no sooner had he found his voice, did he lose it again, for it seemed that the great King Aiken, the mighty battle-wizened leader, couldn't overcome the headache that suddenly plagued him. His hand found his temples, his eyes squinting tightly. The room, it seemed, had gone suddenly, inexplicably cold.

"Father?" asked Ferryl, tentatively.

King Aiken looked up, meeting his eldest son's eyes. "Forgive me, son. It looks as if I shall have to give the meeting over to your mother and Sir Thomas."

Meria rubbed her husband's arm softly before returning her attention to Ferryl. "As we were saying before we were so rudely interrupted, your new bride arrives within the month. She is beautiful, Ferryl, and—"

"What sort of half-witted idea is this?" interrupted Derwin. "Have we forgotten our history with these bastards? Have we forgotten the raping and pillaging they did to both our country and Haravelle after the war? They abducted and murdered the Haravellian princess, for Providence's sake! Have we forgotten how your own grandfather fought and died to keep them out of our lands, Mother? Shall I grab the history books? They are a childish, cowardly people, given to fantastical beliefs and sorcery! I, for one, will not stand by and watch as my only brother is forced to marry one of these half-blooded demons!"

"Need I remind you that *I* am from Midvar?" said Sir Thomas with warning in his voice.

"Exactly," said Derwin, at which Sir Thomas nearly fell out of his seat with shock.

"Derwin, learn to hold your tongue," growled Meria. "This marriage is the first step of many in the right direction. And it is the only strategy that will halt the rebels."

"The only one?" Derwin scoffed. "Have we lost all of our bows and swords?"

Ferryl spoke up again. "The way I see it, Midvar has no other reason to give us one of their daughters other than to get their own blood on the throne, which has been their objective with both Navah and Haravelle for centuries, has it not? King Derrick couldn't produce his own heir, so he's resorting to—"

The queen's hand slapped the table hard, stopping him mid-sentence. "I would advise you to watch your words," she warned.

King Aiken winced and rubbed his temples, his eyes glassy and vague, a small tear escaping. Another wave of icy air chilled the room.

Sir Thomas spoke next. "It is true that Midvar has a less than stellar reputation with both your country and your neighbors to the north. But that is why I have lived here for the past few years—to offer the right hand of camaraderie and diplomacy and end this long-standing—"

"To Sheol with your camaraderie and diplomacy!" Derwin barked. "Father, what have you to say of all this?"

The queen placed her hand on King Aiken's arm again and squeezed gently, a gesture that was no doubt meant to look like dutiful affection, but to the two sons sitting at the table who knew better, came across as an act of manipulative control. King Aiken squinted again, his words coming slowly, his eyes glassy. "We must all do what is best for this kingdom." A simple, if not monotone answer.

And that was the only advice he had to offer.

"So that's it. I have no choice in the matter anymore?" Ferryl finally asked.

"Oh, you still have a choice, son," said Meria with something of gloating in her voice. "You can choose whatever you would like to serve at your wedding feast. Although I would strongly recommend consulting your wife, as I understand she can be temperamental." The queen glared at her son before continuing with her lecture. "A word of advice, son. I suggest that you end any of your remaining trysts with the palace courtiers and servants, as any word of your infidelities will no doubt spark a war with a country we are not prepared to fight. Do I make myself clear?"

Trysts. Right. Because once upon a time, Ferryl the palace playboy had branded himself with a reputation as the dallying prince. And that reputation, it seemed, was doomed to follow him forever. Never mind he hadn't dabbled with the courtiers in years. Never mind that he had no interest.

No, there was only one person with whom Ferryl was interested in flirting. Only one with whom he could imagine anything more, anything lasting. But if kissing a few courtiers had branded him a flirt, then proposing marriage to a near stranger would certainly brand him a lunatic.

It seemed that when it came to the fate of his own heart, Ferryl, prince of Navah, was faced with nothing but losing prospects.

"If the two of you are done with your rants, you may adjourn," said Queen Meria, and without another word, Derwin and Ferryl stood and exited the meeting room, shuffling silently down the corridors and around to the other side of the castle where lay their own rooms.

But before Derwin could escape, Ferryl caught his arm. "Can I talk to you?"

Derwin nodded and followed Ferryl into his private receiving room before Ferryl closed the door and turned to face his brother.

"Well, *that* was enlightening," he finally said.

"Mother is ridiculous," grumbled Derwin.

"We do have a duty to crown and country. Isn't that what Father has always told us?"

"I have only a duty to protect this country, which I will do unto death. But it has absolutely nothing to do with my love life," said Derwin with finality.

"I wasn't aware you had one," said Ferryl.

Derwin only rolled his eyes.

"Well. What did you expect me to think? You go to painstaking measures to keep me out of your life, Derwin."

"Is that what you think I'm doing?"

"That's certainly what it looks like."

Derwin exhaled deeply. "I'm sorry, Ferryl. I'm sorry I've kept you in the dark. I've only been doing whatever I can to protect the only good thing I have."

"You *are* in love, aren't you." It wasn't a question, but still, Derwin didn't bother to answer.

"What are you going to do?" Ferryl asked.

"The same thing I suggest you do."

Right, because when it came to making his own choices, Ferryl was as free as a bird. Right. "How can we do that? We have an obligation to—"

"Ferryl, we have an obligation to this kingdom, you're right. But how can we serve this country well if we're incapable of following our hearts and using our own brains? Where did any of that get Father? He's a puppet, pure and simple! And his marriage is a prime example. They are miserable! And Mother is insufferable! There can be no advantage to a marriage that leads to misery. I vehemently refuse to marry out of duty and obligation. And Father would agree if he were capable of more than three words around Mother."

"Do you really believe that, Derwin?"

"Yes, I do."

"Is there someone you have in mind to marry?" Ferryl asked.

"There is, actually."

"Who?" Ferryl asked, genuinely surprised.

"I haven't asked her; do you think I'm going to tell *you?*" Derwin chuckled.

Ferryl dropped his jaw, in awe of his little brother. "So that's it, you're just going to marry her, political obligations be damned?"

"Political obligations be damned," Derwin repeated. "Politics have no place in love, and the other way around. Hear me, brother," he said, marching across the gap between them. He clasped Ferryl on the shoulders before saying, "The best way you can serve this country is by knowing your own heart and following it to the end in all matters. Political games are just that—games. And arranged marriage is no exception."

"How can I do what is best for this country when by making the choice I wish to make, I would be inciting a war with the very people we can't seem to keep at bay?"

"To Sheol with Midvar, Ferryl!" Derwin exclaimed, his grip a vice, a passionate plea. "They will attack us whether you are married to their daughter or not! It's not going to stop!"

"What do you mean?"

"Ferryl, in case you haven't caught on, Sir Thomas, King Derrick—they're asserting that the rebel attacks are weakening. That it won't be long before they run out of supplies and energy, for that matter. And now they're purporting this ridiculous notion that marrying you off to one of their whores will somehow magically end the threat of war." Derwin relinquished his grip on Ferryl's shoulders. He marched across the room, turning his back on his brother. On his prince. "But I've been corresponding with some of our generals. The attacks are not waning. Not by a mile. They're getting worse. Much worse than we are being told. And while Commander Titus is not painting a rosy picture by any means, neither is he telling Father everything. In fact, he is leaving out a lot."

Ferryl rubbed his temple. "What are we supposed to do?"

"Stop sitting around waiting for this to resolve itself. It's not going to."

"Derwin, I am not king. Not yet. I cannot simply—"

Derwin whirled to face his brother. "Maybe not, but you are the heir. You can do much more than I can. They want something, Ferryl. They won't stop until they have it."

"What do they want?" Ferryl asked.

"Everything."

Ferryl locked eyes with his brother, considering his assertion. It was nothing he didn't already know. Midvar had been trouble all of his life, and for all of Navah's known history. That they should suddenly cease to be a problem with one marriage was grasping at straws, to be sure.

Derwin's harsh tone suddenly softened. "I know you love Elizabeth. You—"

"You do?" Ferryl gaped. If Derwin could already see how he felt about her—

"Of course, Ferryl. She is your match. She is your best friend, isn't she? And you love her. Why wouldn't you want to marry her? Who cares if she's not noble born? Marry her and she'll be a princess, simple as that. Are you telling me you'd truly rather give that up and have little miss duchess of Midvar? If so, you're not the man I thought you were. You escaped an arranged marriage once. You can do it again."

Escaped wasn't quite the right word. More like avoided by happenstance. Yes, Ferryl had once been betrothed. He was only a little boy when the arrangement had been made to Princess Adelaide of Haravelle. But once she was kidnapped and murdered, that arrangement was naturally null and void. And mercifully, his parents hadn't insisted on another arrangement. Until now.

Ferryl rubbed his temples again.

"I don't know what it is you're so hung up on," said Derwin. "The way I see it, it's simple."

"I wish things were as simple for me as they are for you," said Ferryl, but he regretted as soon as he heard it escape his mouth.

"Yes. Everything in my life is simple," Derwin spat. "Yours is the only one with complications. Pardon me, *Your Highness.*"

"Derwin, I didn't mean that. I'm sorry. I shouldn't have—"

"No, you know what? You're right. Things are more complicated for you. But only because you seem to stubbornly hold on to this notion that our mother means well. She doesn't, Ferryl. Mother only looks out for Mother. She always has. And the sooner you understand that, the sooner you will understand that your life is only going to be what you make of it, king or not."

And with that, Derwin marched out of the room, leaving Ferryl to battle with his thoughts in the deafening silence of his brother's stormy wake.

* * *

Chapter 18

Y ou mustn't cry, little Dysis," said Duchess Delaney, patting her youngest sister on the back as the little girl clung to her leg and cried.

"Will we ever see you again?" asked Dinah, the next to youngest of the Dupree sisters.

"Of course you will! You can come visit me anytime," Delaney lied. Standing outside her family's manor home—the home she had grown up in, the only home she had ever known, the one where she and all of her sisters were born, and the place she watched her mother die giving birth to Dysis—Delaney wondered how empty her promises were. Would she ever get to see her sisters again? It was certainly not something she could count on her father to concern himself with. And the past weeks had flown by too quickly, packing and preparing herself to be shipped away to enemy territory. A peace treaty—that's what they had called her. As if somehow marrying a prince of Navah was going to set aside a thousand years of distrust, a thousand years of fighting. As if one marriage could solve all the world's problems. What a laughable notion. And what laughable people who would act as if such a thing would actually work.

She watched the servants load the carriage with her trunks. A ludicrous amount of trunks, really. But she figured if they were going to insist on running her life, she wasn't going to make it easy on them. Just as she had no intention of making anything easy for the Navarian royal family.

Ravid came up beside her, his hand brushing against hers like a phantom wind—the only gesture he could risk with her father's watchful eyes nearby. But it was enough to calm her, even if only for the moment.

"I will send you presents," said Delaney, steeling herself against the emotions that were welling. She wouldn't cry. No, she wouldn't give her father that satisfaction.

"Don't send anything particularly Navarian," grumbled Dabria, the second oldest, with a wrinkle in her nose at the mention of the kingdom.

Delaney chuckled. "My first objective will be to steal the queen's jewels and send them all to you."

"Delaney, dear," said her father in a falsely cool voice. "You'd best watch your mouth lest someone think you serious."

Delaney rolled her eyes and crossed her arms.

"We are ready, Your Grace," said the carriage driver, bowing slightly to the duke.

"Shall we, then?" asked her father, gesturing to the carriage and ushering Ravid alongside him. The two men entered the carriage that would be her prison cell for the next month—the grueling journey across the world to a place so foreign, so unknown, it might as well have been a distant star in the sky. Her throat bobbed and her eyes stung as she closed her eyes and heaved a deep sigh. So this was it, then. It was really happening. This was goodbye to her life. To her sisters. To Midvar. Perhaps forever.

Ravid met her eyes through the carriage window, his mouth in a small smile. She could practically hear him. *Put on a brave face, wildcat. It's not so bad.* Delaney gave the young man a small nod before turning back to her sisters.

All five girls crowded around each other, embracing in a tight hug, little Dysis still sniffling. It was the middle sister, Demelza, who spoke. "I'll never forgive Father for this."

Delaney only chuckled through the tears that were threatening to fall. "Neither will I, Demelza. Neither will I."

* * *

Chapter 19

Is everything all right, Ferryl?" Elizabeth asked. Something had been clouding his thoughts for the past few days. Oh, he had been to see her—to her delight, he had made it a point to see her nearly every morning for the past week. It was almost as if...well, it was almost as if things were back to normal.

If normal meant she was still in love with a man who had no idea who she was. Not to mention it was painfully obvious that there was something he wasn't telling her.

And whatever it was, she knew him well enough to know that it wasn't good.

"I'm sorry, Elizabeth. I'm afraid I've not been myself lately," said Ferryl as he stood by her side, tending to Erel. The stallion whinnied at his touch, sniffing and nudging against the stall, happy to see his prince, eager to accept the apple he offered in his hand.

"Anything on your mind?"

"So very many things," he admitted solemnly.

How could she convey her trustworthiness? How could she let him know that she was already his closest friend? That he needn't worry—she would protect his secrets and his heart. She decided to take him by the hand. "If there is any way I can help, I hope that you would ask."

A rueful smile played on his mouth as Ferryl slid his eyes to her. But it was no use. Elizabeth knew Ferryl much better than he realized. There was a long silence between them, her heart aching for him and the secret he felt he had to hide. She stroked her thumb tenderly across his hand.

In the silence between them, Ferryl reached with his other hand for the amulet around her neck, exploring it lightly with his fingers, staring deep into its crystalline center. Their bodies close, that familiar magic between them burned and branded, a searing reminder of what was once theirs.

"Elizabeth?" Ferryl asked, shattering the silence.

"Yes?"

"If you were faced with a choice—a choice between duty and instinct—which would you choose?"

She searched him for a moment, those sapphire eyes of his, the gentle fog that had settled in the very heart of them like mist dancing on the surface of the sea. "I don't know what choice you're facing, Ferryl, so it's hard to answer that question. But here is what I do know. You are an honest man. A good man. You are loyal, brave, and wise. I've never known a better man than you. If you're struggling with whether or not you should follow your heart, don't question it. It hasn't failed you yet."

Ferryl looked down at the ground for a moment, and it wasn't until she saw the tear that hit the dirt beneath them that she understood why. When he raised his eyes to meet hers, silver with unshed tears, he touched his hand to her cheek. "You are beautiful, my Elizabeth," he said. "Body and soul, you are beautiful."

He took a tentative step, closing the small space between them, his eyes never leaving hers, his hand never leaving her face. His thumb stroked her cheek with impossible tenderness, and she leaned into his touch, savoring, breathing, remembering for one precious moment what it used to be like—

"Your Highness!"

Ferryl turned suddenly to see a palace guard—Michael—his black-and-white uniform a streak of gray as he ran breathlessly towards the stables.

"What is it?" he asked, and while he tried to hide it, Elizabeth could hear the exasperation in his voice.

"I'm sorry to intrude, Your Highness, but you must come now. It's your father."

"My father?" Ferryl asked, shooting Elizabeth a stricken look. "What happened?"

"He has fallen, Your Highness. Please, you must come now!" said Michael.

"I'm coming. Tell them I'm coming," said Ferryl, taking Elizabeth's arms in his hands. "I'm so sorry, Elizabeth. I must go."

"Yes. Yes, of course." She nodded. But as Ferryl turned to leave, he had only taken a few steps before she called after him, "Ferryl, what can I do?"

He stopped that he might turn to face her again.

"Pray. Pray to Providence Almighty that he's all right." And with that, Ferryl turned on his heel and ran to the palace.

Helplessness, cold and uninvited, shivered down her spine.

* * *

FERRYL RUSHED THROUGH THE PALACE halls and up the winding marble steps that led to the top floor where his father's chambers were located. He was greeted by several guards, Michael at the helm, at the doors of the king's receiving room.

"He's just in there, Your Highness," said Michael, pointing to the king's bedchambers.

Ferryl walked with purpose, simultaneously anxious for and dreading to see what lay beyond those doors. He opened them carefully, peering around to find his brother and mother standing by the king's large bed, along with the healer Mary and several servants fetching water and cloths.

"Oh, my dearest son," said the queen, bustling across the room, her acid-green-and-black gown hissing like an asp with each step she took. She took Ferryl by both hands and kissed them, surprising him with such a rare show of affection. "Your poor, poor father," she continued, dabbing at her eyes with a delicate lace handkerchief.

Ferryl looked past her shoulders to his father lying in the bed and looking particularly frail for his age. "What happened?"

"He was walking down the corridor. We had just come from a meeting with Sir Thomas and the advisors regarding the arrival of the duchess when he fell. It was the most terrible accident, son." But the queen couldn't continue her story because of her whimpering.

From the corner of his eye, Ferryl could see Derwin glaring at his mother. Did he not believe this to be an accident?

Ferryl kissed his mother's hands. "I'm sure he's going to be fine, Mother. Please don't cry."

"My brave boy," she said, patting his cheek. "You've always been my strong one." Why she had always favored him over Derwin, Ferryl had never understood. Why she had always spoken to Ferryl as if he were somehow superior to Derwin. For it was not false modesty, but a keen sense of reality that reminded Ferryl daily that while he was no coward, Derwin was by far the braver and stronger of the two sons of King Aiken and Queen Meria. So, pursing his lips and biting his tongue, Ferryl resisted the urge to argue the point with his mother, releasing her hands and sidestepping her that he might take a place beside Derwin and assess his father.

The king lay still in the bed, breathing deeply, his massive form a force unto itself, his eyes closed, a cloth over them to block out the light. "What's wrong with him, Mary?" Ferryl asked the healer.

Mary smiled meekly, ever-present pleasantness in her voice. "Oh, not to worry, my prince. He just took a tumble. I reckon those headaches of his just give him fits from time to time. He's all right."

Derwin scoffed, and Ferryl heard him mutter something like, "I wouldn't be too sure of that."

"I want to speak with my father alone," declared Ferryl, looking around the room in a motion to dismiss everyone. Queen Meria seemed hesitant, but soon acquiesced to his request.

"Yes, everyone leave us in peace," she said, shooing the servants away. "The king needs his rest."

"You too, Mother," said Ferryl.

"I'm sure your father would prefer to have his wife by his side," she protested.

"Your sudden devotion is no doubt noted. Now let's go, Mother," said Derwin, taking the queen by the arm and practically dragging her out of the room.

Once everyone was gone, Ferryl turned his attention back to the king. "Father, are you all right? Can you speak?"

King Aiken surprised his son when he removed the cloth from his eyes, rubbing them as he adjusted to the light. He sat up a bit, rolling his neck. "I must look a terribly weak and ineffective king."

"Father, I have never known anything but the opposite to be true."

King Aiken patted his son's hand before taking it in his own. "You are a good man, my boy."

"Tell me what happened."

The king didn't speak for a good while, leaving Ferryl to wonder why his father was so carefully considering his words. "One moment I was in a meeting, next moment I was on the ground. These headaches, they're getting worse. I can't seem to see or focus when I have them. Like the world is gray and foggy. I suppose I just lost my balance."

"What does Mary say?"

"She says I am perfectly healthy and should expect a full recovery." Such nonchalance. Such flippancy. As if this were somehow normal.

Ferryl deflated at his father's response.

"Don't look so glum. We're all going to die someday," the king chuckled. But the humor was lost on Ferryl.

"Father, what is going on with you?"

"Son, you have enough on your plate to worry about mine. You've got a wedding to think about," said King Aiken.

"Yes, about that."

A thoughtful pause ensued, the king searching his son's face before he said, "Ferryl, you are the future king of Navah. For the rest of your life, every decision you make will come with a wealth of implications and consequences. I just want you to promise me that you won't give in. That you won't let her—"

"Sweetheart, I've had your favorite biscuits prepared for you," interrupted the queen as she burst through the doors, an unmistakable look of determination on her face. Ferryl noticed his father's grip slacken upon her arrival. "And I've brought tea with mint. Now you sit up here and let's get you something to eat. You look a fright." The queen placed the back of her hand on the king's cheek, fussing over him like a bee at the hive. Ferryl couldn't help but notice his father wince at her touch. It seemed her presence was as distressing as the headache. But dutifully, King Aiken never complained, only closed his eyes again.

Queen Meria replaced the cloth over his eyes before addressing Ferryl. "Son, your father needs his rest now. You should leave him be."

Ferryl reluctantly agreed, but as he left the room and made his way through the buzzing palace halls, he couldn't shake the look in his father's eyes, the quiet request. It was almost like...well, it was almost a plea.

* * *

"THERE'S SOMETHING I NEED TO tell you," said Leala, and by the grim look on her face, Elizabeth knew it was not going to be pleasant news.

"Come in," said Elizabeth, ushering her friend into her little cottage. "What is it?"

Leala took a moment to answer, and even in the dim light of the evening, Elizabeth could see the tears pooling in the corners of her eyes. "Is it the king? Is he all right?" Elizabeth continued.

"He is all right," said Leala.

"What happened to him?"

"He fell. Another one of his headaches. But Mary says he will recover completely."

Elizabeth could feel a wave of relief for her king. More so for his son. He would recover completely. A heavy breath, then, "Good," she said, ushering her friend to take a seat at the table.

"But that's not what I need to tell you," said Leala, sitting across from Elizabeth. "It's about Ferryl."

"What about Ferryl?" Elizabeth asked, her heart suddenly in her throat.

Leala didn't want to answer, that much was obvious. She held her friend's eyes for an uncomfortable moment, the tears pooling ever deeper. "He is betrothed," she finally said, so solemnly, so quietly, it took Elizabeth a moment to register it.

"He is *what?*"

Leala didn't say anything, but the silver in her eyes gave her away.

Breathe. Elizabeth made herself breathe. "To whom?"

"A duchess. From Midvar. They signed the contract today."

"Midvar?" Elizabeth balked. "He is betrothed to a Midvarish duchess." It wasn't a question.

"I'm so sorry, Liz."

"It's over, isn't it?" she said, her hand at her throat. Her breath—she couldn't seem to catch her breath.

"If it helps, he's been miserable, moping about the castle. He's hardly spoken to anyone."

Which would explain Ferryl's inexplicable absence the last few days. Elizabeth had worried herself sick that something had happened to his father. She'd had half a mind to march herself right up to his chambers and find out what was going on, if it weren't for the fact that, per the queen's orders, she hadn't been allowed in the palace since they were young.

"It's all so sudden," said Leala. "But maybe, maybe there's—"

"There is nothing. A betrothal is a contract. It is binding. There is no way out except by..." But she couldn't bring herself to finish the sentence, couldn't bring herself to utter the words, the finality of it.

"Death or divorce," Leala finished solemnly.

Elizabeth sat back against her chair, hardly able to take it in, hardly able to believe it. After all this time, after all these years of knowing and loving Ferryl. His memory was taken and before she could figure out what to do about it, he was obligated to marry another. A woman from Midvar, no less.

It was over. It was truly over now.

* * *

Chapter 20

Delaney spooned the sorry excuse for stew as she sat next to her father and across from Ravid in the ridiculously small inn in the no-name village in the eastern part of the gods-forsaken kingdom they called Navah. Weary after only ten days of travel, grumpy from the carriage that seemed to grow smaller every day, and her temper on a short fuse considering that she hadn't had a chance to so much as look at Ravid for more than a second without her father's knowing eyes traveling to them, Delaney was at the end of a very short rope.

"You must eat, my dear. You wouldn't want to look wan for your waiting prince," said her father without raising his eyes to her. He sipped the lumpy, gray mess from his spoon as if dining with the king himself.

Delaney rolled her eyes. "How can you eat this mess? It's disgusting. Everything about Navah is disgusting."

With maddening calm, her father only clicked his tongue. "Temper, temper, dear."

Ravid didn't dare look her way lest her father see it. And so she huffed loudly, knowing she sounded like a spoiled brat and caring even less. Only a few days in this country and already it was boring her to death. The landscape was flat and dull. No mountains. No lush forests like in her province. Nothing but vast, flat, boring wasteland as far as the eye could see. A piss-poor excuse for a kingdom, if you asked her.

"If you are done with your dinner, I suggest we retire for the evening so that we can get started early in the morning. We still have many weeks of travel ahead of us. No time to waste," said the duke.

"Wonderful," said Delaney. She pushed her chair away from the scarred wooden table, making sure to scrape it on the floor as loudly as possible, just to annoy her father. Ravid had a difficult time hiding his grin, and the sight of those wild eyes of his made her heart a little lighter. At least he was here. And though she couldn't even touch him, his presence alone was often all she needed to remind herself that indeed, everything would be all right.

The three of them trudged up the stairs off the filthy excuse for a dining room, up to the second floor where their rooms awaited—one for the duke and Ravid and one for Delaney. She didn't even bother turning to face her father as he bade goodnight to her, shuffling into her room and falling into the lumpy bed without bothering to change into a shift.

The room was small and uncomfortable, but it was bigger than that ridiculous carriage, and at the very least, she could stretch her weary legs. And so she did, not bothering to stifle a loud sigh as she stretched her arms behind her head, staring at the dusty beams on the ceiling.

She hadn't even realized she dozed off until she heard the faint knock on her door. She bolted upright, wondering who in the world would call on her now. But curiosity, of course, got the better of her, and she answered the door, peering around the small crack she had opened.

"Hurry," whispered Ravid, his eyes alight with mischief. He shuffled in the door and closed it quickly behind him, tiptoeing into her room and sitting down on her bed with a wide grin, a green bottle and two crude cups in tow.

"What are you doing?" Delaney whispered. "Do you want us to both be murdered? Don't put it past my father."

"He sleeps like the dead, and this tavern is about as loud as they come." Ravid pulled the cork from the bottle and poured generously into the two wooden cups. He drank deeply from his own, topping it off again before offering the other to Delaney.

"Then why are you whispering?" she asked before she took a timid drink from her cup. It was warm, spicy and terribly bitter—a tang that reminded her of her father's incessant disappointment. So she tipped the cup back and swallowed its contents in a few gulps just to spite him.

"For good measure." He grinned, tossing her cup aside before grabbing her by the waist and pulling her onto his lap. He didn't bother with conversation anymore, for which Delaney was thankful, kissing him with the ferocity of weeks of pent-up anger.

"You know," said Ravid, pulling away from her just enough that he could see her eyes, "it won't be that different than it has ever been. I mean, your father has always been clueless when it comes to my tree-climbing abilities. I don't see how it's going to be any different in Navah."

"What if they don't have trees?" she asked.

"Then I'll learn to scale walls."

Delaney smiled, wrapping her arms around his neck and drawing him back to kiss him again. Ravid lifted her onto the bed behind them, until he was hovering over her, his eyes asking the question he had asked so many times before.

"Ravid," she said flatly.

"What?" he asked with feigned innocence.

"We can't."

"You always say that," he said, nuzzling his nose along her neck.

"Not here. Not now."

"When then?" he asked. "I've been waiting a long time for you, you know."

She didn't have an answer. She had never had a sufficient answer to the question. She didn't know why she wasn't ready, but she wasn't. She had never been with him. She had never been with anyone. And it wasn't that she didn't want to, it was just—

"Can we talk about this later?" she asked, pushing him off and sitting up.

Ravid rubbed a hand behind his neck and heaved a sigh. "Fine. Later."

And without a word, he got up from the bed and tiptoed back out of the room, not even bothering with a goodnight. Delaney watched him leave before falling back onto the bed, wishing she had an answer as much as he did.

* * *

Chapter 21

He just needed someone to talk to. To stew with. To make some sense of all the thoughts swirling about his brain like a cauldron waiting to boil over. Ferryl hadn't slept a wink last night. Not a single minute. And he had paced a path into the carpets of his sitting room this morning.

Which was why, he supposed, he was knocking on Derwin's door. Though he knew full well there would likely be a lot more venting with Derwin and a lot less talking.

"Derwin, it's me," Ferryl said to the carved wooden door that was the entrance to his brother's chambers. But there was no answer. "Derwin," he tried again. "It's a bit late for you to still be asleep, don't you think?"

"Just a damned minute!" he finally heard his ornery brother call.

Ferryl chuckled and let himself into his brother's chambers.

And nearly fell dead at what he saw.

Leala.

Sitting at Derwin's dining table.

In nothing more than Derwin's shirt.

And when Derwin finally bothered to drag his sorry excuse for an ass into his sitting room, Ferryl let him know exactly what he thought of his brother's dalliances.

"What in Sheol is wrong with you?" he raged, crossing the chamber in all of three steps.

"Calm down," Derwin placated, even as Ferryl grabbed ahold of his brother's lapels.

"Calm down! I will not calm down! This is Leala, Derwin! What is the matter with you?"

It was Leala who was crossing the room, coming to Derwin's defense. "Ferryl, this is not what it looks like."

"The Sheol it isn't!" the blond prince bellowed. "What has gotten into you, Derwin? Leala? Of all people? She's like a sister to us! How dare you dally with her! Of all the women in this palace! She—"

"Ferryl, take your hands off of me and calm. Down."

"I will not calm down!" Ferryl spat. "How dare you? How dare you toy with her like this! She is our friend, Derwin! Since childhood! You cannot simply take her to your bed like a common whore!"

It was Derwin's turn to growl, to snarl in Ferryl's face. "Be careful what you say about my wife."

One word.

One word, and Ferryl just...blinked.

Wife.

Not dalliance. Not a plaything that he would toss away.

Wife.

Derwin had...he had...

"You married her? You *married* Leala?"

"Don't look so surprised, Ferryl," Leala chuckled, coming to Derwin's side. She looped an arm through Derwin's, her eyes shining with mirth and happiness.

Providence help him, Derwin had married!

"When?" was all Ferryl could think to ask.

"Two weeks ago," Derwin said, and Ferryl realized that for the first time in his life, Derwin looked sheepish.

"You just...married her? Like that? Without...without asking?"

Leala chuckled, pressing a kiss to Ferryl's cheek. "I'm sorry we didn't think to get your permission for our secret nuptials, Ferryl. But I am glad to know that I have a brother-in-law who would defend my honor so gallantly."

"You're...you're like a sister to us, Leala. You always have been," Ferryl said.

"To you, maybe. But I can say with complete confidence that Leala has never been like a sister to me," said Derwin.

And for a moment—for a stupid moment, Ferryl just stood there before his brother and his apparent sister-in-law and gawked. Finally, he mustered voice to say, "Well I should hope not!"

Amazed, that's what he was. Ferryl was amazed at Derwin's gumption. "But how? I mean, do they know? Do Mother and Father know?"

Derwin practically growled as he rolled his eyes. "I'm to 'remain untethered,' remember?"

"What will you do? When Mother and Father find out, what will you do?"

"Deal with it when it comes," Derwin said. "And keep it a secret for as long as possible. Listen, I'm sorry we didn't tell you. We didn't tell anyone, though I think several guards suspect. We just wanted..." Derwin looked at his wife, and Ferryl could see it—a need. One that flowed deeper than any other. A bond, bright and beautiful between them. Love and need and joy and hope. And they were both radiating with it. "We just wanted to enjoy each other for as long as possible before..."

Before the queen found out. That's what he wasn't saying. Before their mother made life a living Sheol for Derwin for daring to make a decision on his own. For daring to defy her. For choosing...choosing his own heart over everything else.

And jealousy—pure, unadulterated jealousy washed over Ferryl. Wishing his life could be so simple. Wishing he could be so brazen, so fearless.

Wishing he could just follow his heart without all of the repercussions that came with his title, his responsibilities.

"We wanted to tell you, Ferryl," said Leala. "We've come so close several times. I'm sorry."

"No, I...don't apologize. I understand, believe me. And I'm happy for you. Truly, I am. I am happy for you both. Congratulations." Ferryl kissed Leala's cheek before he turned to his brother who, for all the world, looked not like a man who regretted his choices. Not like a man who had made a mistake for which he knew he would pay.

No, Derwin stood before Ferryl resolute. Shoulders back, chin high. Proud.

Proud of the woman on his arm. Of the decision he had made.

Proud to call the woman he loved his wife.

"I didn't even know you were in love with her," Ferryl heard himself say.

"I hadn't told anyone. Not even her," Derwin admitted.

"And you just married her? Without a proper courtship?"

"She's my best friend, Ferryl. I've known for a long time that I wanted to spend the rest of my life with her."

"And you didn't find that strange, Leala? That he just...told you he wanted to marry you?" Ferryl asked Leala.

"Of course I did!" she laughed.

"That's an awfully big risk, isn't it?"

"Perhaps," Derwin admitted. "But the greater risk was not Mother's wrath or even Leala's reaction. The greater risk was not spending my life with the woman I love. So for me, it came down to how hard I was willing to fight for her. For us."

How hard he was willing to fight. For love.

"But you didn't find the whole thing...insane?" Ferryl asked Leala. For he wanted to know... He *had* to know...

"I'd be much obliged if you could tell me what about love is actually sane," Leala laughed.

"In a different world, I would have courted her properly, of course," Derwin said. "But I couldn't risk it—not where Mother is concerned. Not when I knew I loved Leala. I thought if there was a chance at all that she loved me too, then I'd be the world's biggest fool not to marry her. So I just asked. And she said yes."

"I said yes," Leala agreed, a toothy grin on her mouth as she met her husband's eyes. Derwin kissed her softly, unabashedly before Ferryl, but even the kiss couldn't wipe the silly grin from the younger prince's mouth.

And Ferryl, who had come to vent with his younger brother, to talk through the thoughts that had been plaguing him since the moment he had been informed of his own betrothal, understood that his little brother—his brazen, foolish, temperamental little brother—had perhaps told him more than he ever knew.

And shown him that some things...some things were worth risking everything.

* * *

Chapter 22

The glittering room sparkled in the candlelight as the noises grew louder. Raucous conversation. Perhaps even yelling. Dinner must have gotten out of hand.

But Father would be searching for her, no doubt. He never passed up an opportunity for hide-and-seek after dinner. Even if she only hid under the table. He always found her before the two of them collapsed into fits of giggles.

She bit her cheek and toyed with her necklace, waiting. Waiting for Father to find her once again.

Then she heard it—shouting and a loud crash. It seemed her father was making a spectacle of the game. She giggled quietly, convincing herself he couldn't have heard her. But surely he'd hear the way her heart pounded harder and harder the closer the sounds got.

It was only a matter of time before he found her.

The excitement of the anticipation was palpable, even in the darkness of the alcove.

Then she heard them—the clomping footsteps as they traveled across the floors. Louder and louder. Closer and closer. He was coming for her, and if she didn't stifle the giggling fit bubbling in her belly, he'd find her even sooner.

"Come out, come out wherever you are!" her father said. What a silly voice he was using!

She pressed her hand hard to her mouth and giggled through her nose. Oh how she loved playing games with Father!

"I know you're in here, little one," he said, his voice strange. Oily. Almost menacing.

She pressed further into the shallow decorative alcove, hoping the dimness of the evening would prolong her being found just a little longer.

But it didn't. For soon her father's hand clamped onto her arm. Firmly. Too firmly.

"Ouch!" she giggled.

But her father didn't answer. He only yanked her out of her hiding place.

And then the candlelight streamed across his face, and she froze.

For it wasn't her father at all.

* * *

ELIZABETH WOKE WITH A START and sat up in her bed, rubbing the sleep from her eyes as she strained to adjust. The sun's light had turned the sky a dull purple, leaving her room gray in the darkness. She had been dreaming again. The glittering halls. The games with her father. The dream that almost felt like a memory. But how could it be? A memory of what?

But something had cut off the dream. Had she heard something? A knock at the door, perhaps? But who would be calling at such an hour?

The knock came again, and she knew she hadn't imagined it.

She jumped out of her bed, grabbing a robe to hide her shift, and bustled into the living room as quickly as possible. Wondering—no, hoping, really—that it might be Ferryl knocking, she opted to smooth her hair a bit before opening the door.

She was glad she had when she saw who stood in the doorway.

"Elizabeth. I see you're up with the dawn and ready for a hard day's work," purred Queen Meria with a raised eyebrow.

Elizabeth's mouth fell agape, words failing her. Never in all her life would she have expected to see the queen herself at her doorstep. "Your Majesty," she managed, remembering her manners to bob a confused curtsey.

"Well, are you going to invite me in or are you going to insist your sovereign stand outside?"

"Oh! Of course! Come in," she said, flustered. The queen's gown filled the room with pomp, black and silky, swishing obnoxiously with every step she took.

Elizabeth bustled over to the fireplace and began stoking the fire, her hands trembling as she attempted to bring light into the room.

"Is it always this dark in here?" asked the queen.

"Only before sunrise," said Elizabeth, understanding from the look on the queen's face that she had better rein in her wit for this conversation.

"Where is your father, Elizabeth?" the queen asked.

"He is out for his prayers. Sometimes he likes to watch the sunrise while he prays."

The queen looked her in the eye. "He is a faithful man, is he not?"

Elizabeth nodded.

"And do you share his conviction?"

Elizabeth lit the kindling and encouraged the tiny flame before she answered timidly. "I admit that I am a skeptic at heart."

"He loves you dearly, doesn't he?" asked the queen as Elizabeth turned to face her again. Appraising—practically devouring her whole with those depthless black eyes. Why was she asking such a question?

Elizabeth lifted her chin, unwilling to let the queen unsettle her. "He does. And I love him. I am so thankful that he took me in."

"Yes, he is a selfless man, that Bedell." Pity. It was sardonic pity that creased her narrow brow. "It must break his heart—your not sharing his faith."

Elizabeth met the queen's eyes as she knelt at the fireplace. "He is also a patient man."

The queen breathed a throaty laugh. "Believes he'll eventually make a believer out of you, does he?"

"Simply that the truth always wins." Elizabeth stared the queen down for a moment before adding a log to her fledgling flame. She stood to face her more fully. "Would you like some tea, Your Majesty?"

"Oh, why not?" drawled Queen Meria, clasping her hands before her breast.

Elizabeth fetched the kettle from the nearby cupboard and hung it over the flame before taking a seat at the table with the queen of Navah.

"I'm sure you are wondering why I am here," the queen said. Purred, really, her black eyes locked with Elizabeth's.

"The thought had crossed my mind," said Elizabeth, attempting a smile. It ended up more like a quick turn of her mouth.

The queen toyed with a cube of sugar, flicking it between her slender, knotted fingers. "It seems my son cannot stay away from you, Elizabeth. I thought I ought get to know you a little better."

Something in Elizabeth's heart checked at the queen's admission, and she knew for certain this wasn't as friendly a call as the queen was letting on.

"Are you in love with him?"

A simple question. And yet she knew the weight of the world dangled between them with those six little words.

"I am," she said. "I suppose it's a natural result of the friendship we have shared since our childhood. Yes, I love him deeply."

"And do you fancy that he loves you too?"

"I believe he does. Or did, rather."

"Past tense? Well now, that *is* a dilemma. What happened, Elizabeth?" the queen purred, tilting her head to the side like a great wildcat measuring its prey.

The words...they caught in her throat. But whether because of the terrible memory of it all, or because the queen was winning whatever game they were playing, Elizabeth couldn't be sure. "I don't know, truly. It seems that lately he has...forgotten me."

"That seems unlikely, as he spends every day with you."

"Yes, he knows who I am," she said, fiddling with the frayed edge of a napkin. Wondering why in Sheol she was admitting what she knew to the queen.

The queen whom she feared to be cursing her own husband and son.

Elizabeth went on, "But he does not remember the past. It's as if all his memories were taken."

"I've seen no evidence of that," stated the queen, sitting back against her chair.

"I should clarify that only his memories of *me* seem to be missing," she said under her breath, suddenly unable to meet the queen's black eyes.

Silence. For too long. Stretching taut between them. "And what do you suppose is the reason?"

"I don't know." Elizabeth shrugged, still unable to look up from the tattered edge of the worn cloth with which she toyed.

"Come now, Elizabeth. You admitted you're a skeptic, which means you're a thinking person. Surely you have your theories."

"They are *only* theories," she admitted, finally looking to the intimidating monarch.

"Well?" the queen asked, tilting her chin. Her perfect blonde curls did not move even a fraction from where they were piled on top of her head.

"Well, I have considered illness. But there seems to be no disease that would cause such selective memory loss. At least not any that Mary has heard of."

"You've spoken with the healer about my son?" the queen asked with an arched brow.

"No, Your Majesty," Elizabeth clarified, shaking her head. "I only asked her about symptoms. I never mentioned the prince."

"And she had no answers for you?"

"She knew of no such disease, Your Majesty."

"Well, that is indeed a relief to know that my son is not ill," drawled the queen, though Elizabeth knew from her false tone that the queen of Navah had been worried about no such illness. "So what else have you considered?"

Questions. So many questions. Did the queen know what Elizabeth suspected?

"I considered that perhaps he is playing some sort of game with me, which would not be out of the realm of possibility. He's always been the playful sort."

"Yes, that's true," Queen Meria admitted, pursing a mocking smile. "He's always been quite flirtatious with the girls at court. I've never been able to rein in his *conquests*." The monarch slid her black eyes to Elizabeth, and at the insinuation, anger boiled in her belly. Yes, Ferryl had been a flirt. But that was many years ago and—

No. No, she wasn't going to do this. She wasn't going to let the queen get to her. She swallowed down her emotions and continued.

"But the time for making his point has long-since expired. I do not believe he is playing a game. At least not one he means to play."

The queen crossed her arms before her, arching a brow. "So what then?"

Elizabeth did not dare take her eyes from the queen. "I've come to no conclusion, Your Majesty."

"Yes, but you said you had theories. And so far you have only shared failed ideas. Surely you have a more apt conclusion, little thinker."

Elizabeth wondered why the queen was pressing her so, why she was so adamant that Elizabeth admit her theories. It was nothing more than stupid, damnable curiosity that had her saying, "Well, I had considered one idea. But it's not something I put a lot of stock in."

"And what is that?"

"Magic," Elizabeth said, searching—scouring the queen's face for any indication that she was indeed guilty of magical crimes.

"What?" the queen balked with a throaty laugh, as if such an idea was as preposterous as it was naïve.

Elizabeth immediately regretted sharing such a notion with the mother of the man she loved. Because while she knew the queen was as cunning as she was beautiful, she also always seemed to be a step ahead. Maybe two. Whatever Elizabeth knew—or thought she knew—this woman before her likely knew a great deal more.

"Elizabeth, Elizabeth, Elizabeth," laughed the intimidating monarch. "Surely you, of all people, wouldn't believe in such rubbish."

"I told you I don't put much stock in it."

A tilt of her head. "But you put some stock in it?"

She wasn't sure if she was winning or losing this little game. She squared her shoulders anyway. "It's the only theory that cannot be easily refuted, I admit."

"You realize magic is forbidden in this kingdom?"

"Yes," she said, mocking the queen by tilting her head to the side. "And I suppose my question is, why would it be forbidden if it's not real?" A question she hadn't ever pondered herself. Not before this moment. But the more she thought about it, the more she realized it made no sense to ban something that didn't exist.

It made no sense at all.

"Elizabeth, my dear," the queen said, demanding the stable girl's attention once more. "There are those who would use their power for evil. There are those who would seek to control those around them with what they call *magic*. Of course, it is merely trickery and sleight of hand. But they call it magic. And much harm has been done by such charlatans. It is outlawed for the reason that it is the most base and evil form of power and control. And to suggest that someone is using such a thing against the prince, for no other reason than to keep you away from him, is not only ridiculous but embarrassingly arrogant on your part. Who are you, my dear, that someone would go to such trouble?" Triumph. It was triumph in the queen's midnight eyes.

"I didn't mean—"

"It doesn't matter what you meant, dear. You have proven yourself a fool with your theories. Could it not be that my son has simply lost interest in you?"

"I suppose that is possible, Your Majesty. But it does not explain all of his behavior."

A flick of her hand. "Pray tell, what behavior is that?"

Reckless gumption had her saying, "You said yourself that he cannot stay away from me. And while it is true that he has no memory of our past, would he be so keen on my company if he did not, somewhere deep down, still love me?"

The queen's barking laugh reverberated around the tiny room. "Rest assured, little rat, that my son is not nor has he ever been in love with you. The trysts of a prince are to be expected and I have tolerated them all these years because I know that men will be men. They have their needs. But did you honestly think you were the only woman he had ever shown interest in?"

"No, I didn't think—"

"It matters not what you think," chirped the queen, standing abruptly, as if—as if she did not like where this conversation was going. "Frankly, his sudden lack of interest in you is to my benefit. For I have come here today to inform you that whatever you think is going on with my son—*the crown prince of Navah*—ends today. For in a few short hours, his *wife* is arriving. And I will not have a grasping piece of rubbish like yourself ruin what is already a delicate situation. The duchess represents a new era of partnership with Midvar. And unless you have been woefully unobservant, we have had our share of troubles with that kingdom. This marriage will alleviate the strain in our relations only if Prince Ferryl is seen as a devoted and pure husband, which means that *you* will stay away. Do I make myself clear?"

"But Your Majesty, I love him. And he loves me. Does that not matter to you?" Elizabeth pleaded, gripping the table, knowing how childish, how desperate she sounded.

"Not in the least, silly girl," the queen scoffed. "Love is of no consequence in matters of state. And whatever you thought would happen with the prince, you were wrong. For you are a servant, and a servant you shall stay. You will never be a princess." The queen of Navah turned on her heel, marching back towards the door.

Elizabeth stood a little too quickly, righteous indignation welling in her gut as the chair scraped noisily across the wood floor. "Even if I did agree to stay away from him, how could you keep him away from me? He is the one that comes to me every day, after all. *You're* the one who banned me from the palace years ago. Have I or have I not abided by that mandate?"

The queen turned slowly. Too slowly, as she faced Elizabeth once more. She raised a brow, glaring. Devouring. "Well, then. Perhaps you are not as simple-minded as you look." One step closer. Then another. The queen's heeled boots clicked on the wooden floors, the sound like a death knell.

Elizabeth swallowed hard as the queen went on, her voice nothing more than a low growl. "I did not want it to come to this, but I see that you leave me no choice. There is too much at stake to leave someone as arrogant as you with a card left to play. So hear me now, Elizabeth. And hear me clearly. If you do not stay away from my son, and if he does not stay away from you, I will see to it that your father is hung from the gallows. For you and I both know he believes in magic, does he not? And as we both know, magic is only used by those most evil. It would not be a stretch to conclude that someone who believes in magic also practices it. If such news were to get out, the king would be left with no choice but to conclude that your father was plotting to take over the throne with his sorcery. It wouldn't be too reaching now, would it?

Considering that his daughter has had her eye on the throne since she was a child."

Elizabeth could feel the hot tears pooling in her eyes, her heart close to failing at those words, at the insinuation... "Your Majesty, I have never wanted the crown or the throne. And if you ask Ferryl, you would know that. I—"

"How dare you address the crown prince so casually!" barked the queen, flinging her arms akimbo. "I knew you were arrogant. But I didn't know you were so brazen, little girl."

"Forgive me, Your Majesty," Elizabeth tried, her voice small, quavering. "It's just that I—"

"You seem to be under the impression that there is something left to discuss. You will stay away from my son, and that is my final word. Do I make myself clear?" The queen did not flinch, did not falter as she bored straight through Elizabeth with her searing glare. To her credit, Elizabeth did not release the queen's gaze, either.

"Yes, Your Majesty." Elizabeth finally breathed, dipping her head, barely able to speak over the lump in her throat.

The unmistakable click of her boots had Elizabeth looking up again to see the queen close enough to share a breath. A serpentine smile curled her thin lips. "There, now. See? Even ignorant, grasping peasants can be reasonable!" And then she turned, ambling casually away as if they had just finished a friendly little chat. "I shall bid you adieu, little rat," the queen said merrily over her shoulder. "I have a duchess to greet, after all. And thank you for the conversation. It was most pleasant, was it not?"

She strode the last steps across the room like a peacock on display, never once bothering to look back. She was halfway out of the door when she purred over her shoulder, "Elizabeth, dear, I believe your tea is ready."

Elizabeth turned to see the kettle bubbling and hissing on its hook, wondering how long it had been boiling, wondering how long the queen had noticed its spitting and steaming without mentioning it. She stared at the iron kettle, watching it shudder and hiss over the fire, the water sizzling down the sides, boiling like the blood in her own veins.

Chapter 23

Elizabeth sat at her small dining table, attempting to write a letter, her hands trembling. Bedell had not returned to the cottage that morning. In fact, it was almost noon, and she still hadn't seen him. He had no doubt been commandeered by the queen today, making sure she could utilize his services in case any complications arose around the arrival of the duchess.

Tears welled in her eyes as she peered into his room. His neatly made bed. The candle that he used to read every night. Such a good man, he was. Such a good father. She hated to think of only leaving him a letter, but she had to get out of here as soon as possible. She had to leave and dared not risk what the queen might do if she didn't. And she certainly didn't want to see Ferryl and let him have a chance to convince her otherwise.

How did you tell the man who reared you, who dropped everything to give you love and life, that you were leaving and never coming back? How to let him know what he meant to you, what he would always mean to you? Tears dropped on the parchment as she wrote, spreading the ink into watery blotches.

Father,

I wish I had a better explanation than the one I'm going to give you. But in truth, I must leave. I know not when I will return, if ever. I am sorry it has to be this way. Someday, Providence-willing, I will find a way to explain. For now, find peace knowing that you have been nothing short of the sweetest father anyone could ask for, and I will carry the love you have given with me forever.

I love you, Father. Always.

Elizabeth

She had just finished signing her name when she heard the second knock of the day on her door. Who now? She walked hesitantly to the door, hoping the queen hadn't decided to come back and exact a new brand of revenge.

"Ferryl," she said as she opened the door to see his beaming face. "What are you doing here?"

"I...hello, Elizabeth," Ferryl said, fidgeting with his fingers. Was he nervous?

But Elizabeth didn't say a word—couldn't, really—only turned her back to him, bustling across the small room to finish gathering the last of her supplies. She packed feverishly, unsure what to say to Ferryl and certainly sure that if too much was said, she would lose her resolve. And she couldn't do that—not with her father's life at stake.

"Are you all right?" he asked, letting himself in and following her across the room. When she didn't say anything, he took hold of her hand as she reached into the cupboard. "Elizabeth, beloved, what is wrong?"

"What did you call me?" she asked, stunned, turning to face him.

His eyes were smiling. The same smile he used to wear all the time. Back when he had known that she was his Lizybet, back when he had remembered their past, their story. Back before everything had fallen apart. A lifetime ago. And at the sight of those smiling eyes, the world seemed to crumble beneath her. So when he touched her cheek, she nearly shattered.

"I love you," he breathed, his voice rough. "That's what I came here to tell you."

His touch, so gentle. So familiar. So consuming. She closed her eyes and pretended for a moment that it was just the two of them. No queen in the way. No duchess on her way. Just Ferryl and Elizabeth and all the love between them.

But the beauty of the moment was gone in an instant, replaced by the blinding reality that there *was* a queen in the way. There *was* a duchess on her way. And there was so much more than just their love at stake.

So she stepped back.

She couldn't let him touch her. Not again. Or she would lose all her resolve. She turned away from his tender sweetness and continued to gather supplies from the cupboard. Bread. Apples. Some salted pork. Yes. Yes, she would need some food. Lots of food. Anything that would keep. She packed feverishly.

"Going somewhere?" he asked, but she did not answer. His hands— Providence help her, his hands found her waist, his breath warm on her neck as he closed the small gap between them, as he brought his body so close to hers. He pressed a soft kiss to her shoulder, a gesture so familiar she wondered if part of him hadn't really forgotten. If part of his soul still remembered their love story. If it was truly dark magic that had wiped his mind but had no bearing on his soul.

Still, she said nothing. *Could* say nothing. So Ferryl took hold of her shoulder and turned her to face him. "Elizabeth?" he asked, even as an arm snaked about her waist, as his other hand found her cheek. Concern. Such deep, genuine concern in his eyes. She found she could only shut her own. Shut him out.

"What are you doing here, Ferryl?"

"I...I came to see you, Elizabeth. I came to tell you that I love you and I..." He paused, sucking in a nervous breath. "I want to marry you."

She couldn't meet his eyes; she could only shake her head, tears coming again. "You can't love me, Ferryl."

He cupped his hand under her chin and lifted it that she might meet his searing gaze. "Well then, we have a problem." He wiped tears from her cheeks with his thumbs, even as he pressed his brow to hers. "Tell me what's wrong, Elizabeth. What's the matter?"

Somehow—*somehow* she managed to pull herself away from him and bustle to her room, eager to finish gathering her things and stuff them into the small bags she would take with her. It wasn't much, but it would do.

"Will you not speak to me?" he asked, following her. "Tell me what's wrong. Let me help you."

"You can't help me, Ferryl."

"Elizabeth," he said, and she could hear the fear rising in his voice. "Why won't you talk to me? Has someone hurt you?"

"It's nothing like that."

"Are you leaving?" he asked.

She nodded, her back to him as she fussed with a homespun dress, folding and refolding it with her trembling hands.

"Where are you going?"

She shrugged, unwilling to face him, determined to do what was right, even if he didn't understand it.

"When will you return?" he asked.

"I'm not."

Ferryl didn't say anything, and through tears, Elizabeth managed to finish packing her small bag and turned to head back to the sitting room without a word. She marched to the fireplace and paused to look at her father's book—the ancient texts. Something inside her cried out at the sight. Perhaps it was the prospect of saying goodbye to her father. Perhaps it was something else. But Elizabeth took the book and stuffed it into her leather satchel, hoping he wouldn't be too disappointed at her thievery.

"Why won't you talk to me?" Ferryl asked, interrupting the pain welling in her heart.

"I have to go," she said, turning towards the door, her two satchels over her shoulders.

She had almost made it across the room when he spoke again. "Elizabeth, please." He was silent for a moment. "Is it him?" he finally asked in a small voice.

She turned to face him again. "Him?"

"The man. The man who left you. The man you loved. Is he the reason you're leaving?"

She nodded in silence, knowing how her answer would break his heart and hoping that it would convince him to forget her.

"Do you love him still?"

She held his eyes for a long moment, taking in the earnest plea in his strangely cloudy sapphire eyes, willing herself to remember every little detail about him—from his unruly blond locks to the determined set of his shoulders, the single dimple on his right cheek, the way he tended to lean on one hip. "I will love him all my days. And I will never love another."

With that, she turned on her heel and walked through the door, closing it behind her.

She went several paces before she stopped to catch her breath, unable to shake the image of Ferryl's stricken face from her mind.

But this was for the best. The only way she could protect him. Protect her father. And so this was goodbye.

Forever.

* * *

Part III

Chapter 24

Duchess Delaney swallowed painfully, dust somehow managing to find its way to her throat, despite the windows of the carriage having been closed for the duration of the day. Or perhaps it was nerves that made her throat so dry. Either way, as the carriage that had been her prison cell for the past month approached the Navarian palace, she could barely swallow.

This was it.

Home.

Or at least her father's sham-marriage-to-save-the-world idea of a home.

She fought against the stinging in her eyes, determined not to let her father see that he had gotten to her. And even more determined to not let the Pig-Prince see any sign of weakness upon her arrival.

The palace grew ever closer with every clomp of horse hooves, its spires white and towering, its vegetation lush and green, the sky impossibly blue. The tropical sea air made for quite a balmy day.

She took a tiny portion of consolation that, if nothing else, this province wasn't as hideous as the rest of the kingdom had been.

The carriage rounded a bend, turning toward the palace, and facing her window away from it. Now all she could see were hills—hills and impossible trees, gnarled and spindly, yet thick and black. Like intertwined vines covered in moss.

"What kind of trees are those, Father?" she asked, breaking the deafening silence.

"I believe they are hazelnut," was his indifferent response.

She never took her eyes off of them, haunted by their beauty. Perhaps she would ride out one day and wander through them. And if luck was on her side, perhaps she'd even get lost in them. Or better yet, eaten by some terrible creature.

She dared a quick glance at Ravid, who sat by her father. She had felt his eyes on her like daggers all morning, but she hadn't looked at him until now. And now she wished she hadn't, for she couldn't stand the pity in them. But was it pity for her? Or for himself?

The carriage stopped all too soon, and before she knew it, Delaney was climbing out, taking a moment to adjust the obnoxious gown her father had insisted she wear before looking up to the greeting party.

She spotted the king first. His smile seemed kind, but somehow strained. His eyes were like two chips of glass—vague and void. A bore, no doubt.

Next, the queen. Her hair was blonde, knotted in impossible swirls around her head, her skin fair despite the abundance of sunshine. But it was her black eyes that caught and held Delaney. Dark. Foreboding. She was dressed in a royal-blue gown that trailed behind her like a river. She looked fit to attend a royal wedding, not greet a visitor. Delaney swallowed hard. The queen *would* be attending a royal wedding—in the very near future.

Next she spotted two young men, both of them unfairly handsome. One had hair like the wheat fields behind her father's manor. And his eyes—terribly blue—bluer than the queen's ridiculous gown. He smiled, but there was a sadness to his eyes that couldn't be missed. The other man was at least a head taller. His hair was a shock of auburn amongst the blonde royal family. But it wasn't his hair that caught her off guard. It was the scowl that shone on his chiseled face, his imposing jaw—like the honed edge of a deadly blade. Clearly, he didn't approve of her arrival. She hoped against hope *he* wasn't her intended. But with her luck, he probably was.

Her uncle, King Derrick, stood with the group as well, his smugness oozing off of him like honey. She hated him. Hated him for making this arrangement. For the fact that he looked so much like her dead mother. Hated the stupid crown that sat atop his stupid head. King Aiken wasn't wearing his crown. Why in Sheol did her uncle feel the need?

A tall man walked to the front, his nose proudly in the air. His skin and hair were distinctly Midvarish, and she recognized him immediately as the diplomat who had visited her family home to discuss the arrangement.

"Your Majesties, may I proudly present to you, His Grace, Duke Hevel of Sheqer and his daughter, Duchess Delaney Dupree," said Sir Thomas, practically bursting at the seams with pride. It was settled, then. She hated him too.

"What a pleasure," said the queen, her hair constructed in such a way that Delaney wondered if it weren't meant to hide unwanted gray growing at her temples. "We are so thrilled to have you."

"The pleasure is ours," said her father, and Delaney used every last ounce of self-control to keep from rolling her eyes. Pleasure, indeed. For him, anyway. And likely the Pig-Prince, whichever one he was.

"May I present to you, my son, Prince Derwin," the queen continued, gesturing to the scowling man on the end who gave little more than a curt nod. "And the happy bridegroom, Crown Prince Ferryl."

Happy. Right. The sad-eyed prince gave a small bow as he lifted Delaney's hand to his mouth, barely brushing his lips against it.

So here was her intended. Thankfully he was as tall as she, but only just. She had endured many a nightmare that, among the other misfortunes of this marriage, she would tower over him. Instead, when he rose from his bow, he met her eyes with his blue ones, and she couldn't miss that there seemed to be some kindness in them.

Well.

That was something, anyway.

"Shall we stand out here like peasants or shall we adjourn to the drawing room?" asked the queen, and with one snap of her fingers, the servants were scampering to usher the party indoors.

The prince with the blue eyes waited for Delaney to come to his side before entering the palace, ushering her in before him.

So he was chivalrous too. That didn't mean he wasn't a pig.

Delaney took a deep breath and plunged into the palace through the towering doors that stood open for her, feeling the prince behind her like an ominous cloud.

Yes, this was only the beginning of the storm that awaited her.

* * *

DELANEY LOOKED AROUND THE VAST chambers that she was to call her rooms. Colorful tapestries hung on the walls. Plush carpets spread across every surface of the black-and-white marble floors. The palace hadn't been a disappointment—the ocean alone was incredible enough to mesmerize her every chance she looked upon it. She considered it a small mercy that her chambers overlooked the sea. And here, in the stillness of the night, she stared out the windows to the sparkling, endless mass of water stretching out before her.

Incredible, really, if she were being honest with herself.

But she didn't feel like being honest with herself.

Not with the emptiness that plagued her now. Not with Ravid staring her down like prey yet still giving her the cold shoulder whenever they were alone, not with her father so enraptured with the king and queen that she might as well be invisible And certainly not with the crown prince looking at her like a disease.

Yes, Delaney was alone in this vast palace. Alone in this task to become the princess that would save the kingdom.

What a lonely task it was turning out to be.

She shuffled from her receiving room into her bedroom and bathing room beyond, the theme of black-and-white stone continuing throughout the whole palace. Her bed—four posters and much too large for one person—loomed before her like the wasteland that separated her home from this new one. She climbed in and sprawled across it, wondering if she would ever feel like she belonged here. If she would ever see her little sisters again.

A tear fell down her cheek, the first one she had allowed herself to cry since finding out she was to become the bride of her kingdom's greatest enemy.

* * *

Chapter 25

Ferryl dismounted Erel, his heart heavy, his eyes stinging from the wind that had dried them after a long day of riding. He rubbed the neck of his trusted friend, leaning into him in exhaustion. Erel whinnied, stomping his foot.

"We'll find her, my friend." Ferryl sighed, reassuring his horse as much as himself. "I promise. We'll find her."

"Any luck?" came his brother's unmistakable voice, and Ferryl turned to see him coming into the stables.

"No," he said quietly.

Derwin didn't speak for a moment, his mouth pursed in quiet contemplation, his eyes narrowed with concern. "We'll find her, Ferryl."

"Where is she? Where could she have gone? How hard can it be to find a woman riding a white winged horse? I don't understand this at all."

Ferryl had spent the past two weeks riding out every day in search of Elizabeth, regretting the moment he had let her disappear. She hadn't said where she was going. She hadn't left any clues, only that she was leaving and never coming back. And at first, Ferryl had been too dumbstruck by her departure to argue, letting her leave, letting her disappear like a fool. But one look at Duchess Delaney Dupree, one look into the future his mother had carved for him, and Ferryl had decided he wasn't going to settle for it, betrothal or no betrothal. Duchess or no duchess. He wouldn't rest until he found Elizabeth. Until he made her see what she had become to him.

Yes, he knew that she was in love with someone else. But he had left her, hadn't he? He had disappeared, leaving her to question everything. Ferryl hadn't. Ferryl was here, ready to give her his heart. Wasn't that enough? Why would she leave so suddenly when things had been going so well between them?

Ferryl kicked a stone in frustration, watching it tumble across the ground before him.

Derwin spoke with apology in his voice. "You'd better come inside. Mother will be waiting for you. And so will the duchess. Dinner is in an hour."

* * *

"WHERE HAVE YOU BEEN?" QUEEN Meria growled to Ferryl the moment she entered his receiving room.

"Riding," he said, ignoring her frustration. Let her be frustrated.

"All day?"

"Yes, all day."

"Where?" she asked, marching through the room to take a place where she would be unavoidable.

"Anywhere. Everywhere. Nowhere." He turned his back to her and stared out the windows, looking into the forest beyond, hoping by some miracle to see the unmistakable contrast of Eagle's white wings. But there were only trees, glowing golden in the evening sun, rustling lazily in the sea breeze. Beautiful. Mocking.

"Son, you've been disappearing every day for weeks. What, pray tell, are you trying to find?"

"Answers," he said quietly.

"The answer you're looking for is waiting for you in the king's dining hall."

He turned to face his mother. "I don't love her, Mother."

"You don't have to love her. You just have to marry her."

Ferryl stared into her black eyes for a good while before crossing the room without another word, marching through the halls to the other side of the castle where his duty and obligation awaited like a festering plague.

* * *

THE ROYAL FAMILY OF NAVAH, Sir Thomas, Duchess Delaney, several of her newly-appointed Navarian ladies, her father Hevel, Duke of Sheqer, and his vassal sat silently around the dinner table, the servants eagerly serving the first course. King Derrick had stayed for the first few days after the duchess's arrival, but soon departed to continue his visits to some of the army outposts with the generals in an apparent attempt to better understand precisely what was going on with the rebels. It hadn't mattered that Derwin had vehemently protested their departure without him. The queen had insisted that he was needed here, although what for, neither Ferryl nor Derwin could say. As if reading Ferryl's thoughts, the queen stared incredulously at her youngest son from across the room.

"Not eating again tonight, son?" she asked.

"Not hungry," said Derwin.

"That's not what I hear," she said casually. Too casually.

Derwin looked up at his mother, who continued to pepper her soup without raising her eyes. The contrived merriment in her voice was nothing short of alarming to those who knew her best. "What do you mean?" he asked.

"The servants tell me you take dinner in your private dining room every night. Enough for two. You must watch out, son, or your insatiable appetite will turn you fat," she said, emphasizing *fat* with a pointed stare. Ferryl wondered if anyone else around the table understood the conversation. Regardless, one thing was clear: the queen knew Derwin was hiding something. And if she didn't already, it would only be a matter of time before she understood why Derwin was taking dinner for two privately every night. And Providence only knew what storm awaited Derwin when she found out about his secret wife.

The thought caused Ferryl's heart to sink. For, not so very long ago, he had made plans for a secret wife of his own. Yet here he was, sitting across from a stranger who eyed him silently. A stranger who was due to be his wife in a month. A young girl of only seventeen. It hadn't mattered when Ferryl protested her arrival. He had been told by his mother, under no uncertain terms, that the kingdom would be expecting heirs soon after their wedding and that a young, fertile bride only increased their chances at conception.

Wonderful.

It hadn't mattered that she was Midvarish—the sworn enemy of Navah. The sworn enemy of their allied country, Haravelle.

It certainly hadn't mattered that he wasn't in love with her.

All that had mattered was that his mother had made up her mind. And she was unflinching.

Ferryl gazed blankly as he stirred the warm soup, his appetite gone. This stranger across the table from him seemed to be boring holes into him with her eyes. Did she know she was only a pawn? That his mother was using her for political gain?

Even if she did, what did it matter now?

Dinner continued painfully with the queen, Sir Thomas, and Duke Hevel plotting and scheming the grandest wedding Navah had ever seen, the duchess nodding silently in agreement from time to time, the king silent and unreadable. Ferryl, however, did not miss that the young vassal of the duke, Sir Ravid, couldn't seem to keep his pointed stare from the duchess. Had it been Elizabeth who was the object of the boy's shameless ogling, Ferryl might have felt the need to throttle him. As it were, he truly hoped that the two might wind up in a torrid love affair that would free him from his matrimonial obligations.

But whether because she didn't notice or didn't care, the duchess paid no attention to the young vassal's obvious affections, and Ferryl wondered if there was more to the two of them than met the eye. At some point, he was going to have to get to know the girl across from him. But his heart held fast to the hope that he would find Elizabeth— bring her home where she belonged. And so he looked away when the duchess caught his eye, angry with his mother for forcing her on him, and angry with Delaney for complying.

* * *

"You needed to see me, Father?" Ferryl asked, peering into his father's vast, private office.

The king sat at his marble desk, boasting views of the lush clifftop gardens that separated the back of Benalle Palace from the ocean beyond. Strong. Powerful. A king in name, and a king in stature. Ferryl wondered if he would ever live up to such a man. "Yes, there is something I want to discuss with you privately."

Ferryl entered the room tentatively, wondering what the cryptic tone of his father's voice could mean. "Yes?"

"Son, I received word this morning that the rebels have advanced in the north and the south. They are attacking in the Qadim and Tsafone provinces. They are burning houses, even attacking women and children."

Ferryl's eyes grew wide as he took a seat across from his father's deep desk. "I thought the commander had been able to keep them at bay."

"He had, for a while," said the king. "It seems that the rebels are intent on causing as much damage as possible."

"What does Sir Thomas have to say about all of this?" Ferryl asked, crossing his arms.

The king's eyes were weary, burdened. He picked up a pen and jotted a few notes on a parchment before him. "Little. He is all but useless, and the *diplomacy* he offers is laughable. We cannot afford to play these games anymore. It's time to plan a new strategy."

"And Commander Titus?"

The king continued his note-taking, his eyes on the papers before him. "He assures me that everything is in order. But I have a feeling that he is not telling me everything."

"We need to involve Derwin, Father. He is a tactical genius. He will probably already have a plan in mind."

The king lifted his gaze, appraising his firstborn. "He is hotheaded, son."

"Yes. But when it comes to matters of outwitting the enemy, he is unmatched. I've seen him, Father. When we were sent to the outer provinces last year, it was his advice that the commander followed."

Contemplative silence. Then, "Do you still have a mind to name him your commander when you are king?"

A nod. "I do."

The king of Navah sat back in his chair, crossing his solid arms across his broad chest. "Well then, why wait?"

"What?" Ferryl asked.

"If you think he will make a good commander, then let's not wait until I am dead to see what he can do." The king pushed back his heavy chair, standing so that he might pace behind his desk. "Let's name him now. Commander Titus has made it clear that he wishes to retire soon. And you're right. Derwin is cunning, and he is smart. We need more than his bow and blade. We need his expertise. These rebels aren't relenting."

Ferryl kept his eyes on King Aiken. "Why aren't they? Mother was convinced that the announcement of my marriage would solve all our problems."

"Because, as in most things, your mother is shortsighted." The king paused his pacing, turning to face Ferryl fully. "You don't want to marry her."

It wasn't a question. Ferryl met his father's eyes. "No, sir. I am sorry." He looked down, fiddling with his fingers as he sat before the formidable man he called father and king. "I know my reputation. I know what people think of me. But I don't love her. But I suppose it doesn't matter now, anyway."

"Why is that?" the king asked, tilting his head to one side.

"Because Elizabeth is gone."

His father made his way around his desk, leaning to sit against it across from Ferryl as he asked, "Where did she go?"

"I wish I knew." Ferryl shrugged. "I've found no sign of her."

"Did she tell you she was leaving?"

Ferryl looked up at his father. It was concern in his storm-tossed eyes. But not just the fatherly kind. No, it was genuine concern—from one man to another.

And for that simple gesture, Ferryl had never loved or respected the man more.

"Yes. But nothing more. I don't know why she left or where she was going. She was in a state, Father. I shouldn't have let her leave."

The king let out a rumbling chuckle as he crossed his arms. "And what would you have done? Thrown her into the dungeons until she saw reason?"

Ferryl laughed cynically, shaking his head. "I did nothing. I just stood there and let her walk away. And now I don't know where she is or if she is all right. It's torture, wondering if she is even alive."

"What do you suppose drove her away in such haste?"

Ferryl considered his words. To admit to his father what he was thinking would mean he would have to admit what he had been up to the night before she left. And while he knew he could trust his father, he wasn't sure if he could trust his mother—and to that end, he didn't know how much his father still confided in her. Or how much she was able to coax out of him.

"What is it that you're not telling me, son?"

Ferryl met his father's eyes. Maybe it would be better if he did know. "Father, if I tell you..."

"If you are worried about me telling your mother, you needn't." There was humor in his eyes. But there was more. Something like... deep understanding.

Ferryl sighed, knowing he was right. "The truth is, I don't know why she left so quickly, but I have a feeling it has something to do with Sir Thomas."

"Sir Thomas? Why?" the king asked, furrowing his blond brow.

"The night before she left, I... Well, I went to the village of Gaevast. There is a temple there. And a priest that is a friend of...one of the servants. I was told that he would be able to help me with a secret."

"And what secret, pray tell, would you need a priest to keep?"

"A wedding," said Ferryl quietly.

The king's brow raised, but it wasn't with incredulity. It was with a smile. The king was smiling at his son. Ferryl swallowed his fear with his newfound gumption. "I was planning to marry Elizabeth." At the king's chuckle, Ferryl asked, "What is it, Father?"

"You're a brave man, Ferryl."

"Why do you say that?"

"Marrying a servant behind your mother's back? I'd sooner take on the armies of Midvar alone than her reaction to such a move." He laughed, and Ferryl laughed with him.

"I'm an impetuous fool, aren't I?" Ferryl said, shaking his head.

The king leaned forward, clasping his son's shoulder. "Perhaps you are a fool, son, but if I had ever had the privilege of the kind of love you seem to have for that girl, I might have been made a fool myself."

Silence yawned between them. An ache for his father—for what he did not have, for what he had never had with his own wife. "I do love her, Father."

"I know, my son. I've known for a long time."

"And you don't think me mad?"

"Why ever should I?"

"For loving a servant. A servant I barely know."

The king leaned back, his brows furrowed incredulously. "I don't know how you can say you barely know her, son. You two have been practically inseparable."

"Yes, I suppose that's true. But I did worry that she might think me mad when I asked for her hand."

The king barked a scoffing laugh. "Ferryl, son, I'm surprised you hadn't asked her before now."

He shrugged. "I was planning to. The morning she left. I woke with the dawn and went straight to her. But she was packing, Father. She was leaving, and it was clear that she did not want to be stopped. I couldn't help but wonder if the reason she left so abruptly had something to do with Sir Thomas. I don't have any proof of anything, really. But the night I was in Gaevast, Sir Thomas was there too. Meeting with the very priest I met with. For hours. I never saw him again, but I did see his horse in the same livery where I left mine for the night. But when the morning came, the stable boy told me that Sir Thomas had left before the sunrise. And that he was in a hurry."

Ferryl lifted his eyes, meeting his father's contemplative gaze. "I don't know why he was there. It may have been sheer coincidence. But when I finally got to Elizabeth, she was in a state, and I did nothing to stop her from leaving. I should have. I should have stopped her at all costs. For now, I fear I've lost her forever. And worse, I am running out of time, for my own wedding is rapidly approaching."

"Then don't rest until you find her."

"But I thought—"

"I know what you thought, son. You have always been my obedient one, never breaking the rules. But you have to do what you think is right. As king, that will be your first duty. Not to your mother. She will not stop until she has her way, Ferryl."

"What do you mean?"

The king only shook his head. "Nothing, son. I mean nothing by it. But I know how you feel about Elizabeth. I have watched you fall in love with her over the years. She is a good girl, Ferryl. She—"

"What do you mean *over the years?*"

The king chuckled, standing. He walked back to the other side of his desk. "Son, it took you much longer to admit you were in love with her than it took us to figure it out."

"Yes, but *years?*"

The king smiled, a warm and fatherly expression as he took a seat again. "You still have time, son. Your wedding is not until next month. Go find Elizabeth. Bring her back. Make her your wife." He picked up his pen and set about his note-taking again.

"But what about the duchess? And Midvar?"

"I'm still the king. Let me deal with them."

"And Mother?"

His pen froze, and the king met his son's eyes. "I'll deal with her too," he said. "And do hurry. I would like grandchildren while I still have my health."

Ferryl laughed, relaxing back into his chair. "You do seem better lately, Father."

King Aiken set down his pen. "I am. I haven't had a headache in two weeks, which is a drastic improvement. When I'm not plagued by those dastardly things, I feel like my young self again. Ready to take on the world." The king smiled a smile Ferryl hadn't seen since he was quite young. And for that moment, it felt like all their worries were behind them and it was just the two of them, father and son, back in the days when the world was simple and nothing much mattered except their kindred spirits and the love between them.

* * *

FERRYL SAT BOLT UPRIGHT, THE night pouring thick and undaunted into his vast bedchamber. The emptiness of his bed stretched out beside him like a wasteland. A chasm. A void where Elizabeth should have been beside him, his arms warm around her, the cadence of her breath a steady rhythm against his chest.

Instead, he was alone and Elizabeth nowhere to be found.

He was thankful for the conversation he'd had with his father, thankful for his approval. But what good would it do if he couldn't find Elizabeth? Where could he look that he hadn't already? Where could she have gone so quickly?

That's when he noticed it—in his peripheral vision. Something small. Black. Fluttering. A moth? It lingered just outside his line of sight, but he knew it was there, nonetheless. He flicked his hand, hoping to brush the nuisance away.

"Dastardly thing. Be gone!" he cried. But it didn't leave. It stayed, its wings flickering like a black flame.

He closed his eyes and thought again of what he'd shared with his father—of his theories about Sir Thomas. Why had he so mysteriously shown up that night in Gaevast and disappeared the next morning? Had he said something to Elizabeth? Had he known what Ferryl was planning? But how? And if he did, was he helping the queen in some way? There could be no doubt that the two of them were always up to something together. But what proof of that did Ferryl have other than speculation, loosely formed theories?

Had his mother been the one to scare Elizabeth away? Yes, his mother spent most of her time threatening him and Derwin to do as she bade. And she certainly didn't like when things didn't go her way, but would she have threatened Elizabeth too? What could she have possibly said to make the girl leave and never come back?

No, Elizabeth had left because of another man. The man Ferryl had known about all along. She hadn't hidden him. She had told him the day he took her to the Secret Place. She was in love with another man who had left her inexplicably. And she had left in search of him. Why hadn't Ferryl seen it coming? Was he so arrogant to think that she would give up the man she loved for a man she barely knew? Did he think himself superior? That *he* deserved her over another?

He shuddered to think he could be so haughty. What kind of man—a future king—could be so arrogant? He looked again at the emptiness in his bed, then settled down and closed his eyes.

Answers, it seemed, were as overwhelming as the questions.

* * *

Chapter 26

Delaney lay draped across her bed, listening to her stomach growl from the dinner she had refused to eat. It wasn't enough that her father felt compelled to plan every aspect of her life. It wasn't enough that Ravid refused to say a single word to her. But the prince. How he stared! She could practically feel him devouring her with his searing sapphire gaze anytime she looked down. Why didn't he say anything to her? They were to be married, weren't they? Was their marriage destined to be as cold and lonely as her new life at Benalle Palace?

The fear of such a prospect settled over her like a fog. Never in her life had she felt so alone. So afraid. So desperate for escape.

She was startled by a small knock on a door she hadn't noticed until now. Another door that led directly into her bedchamber. Perhaps a servant was coming to check on her. Who else could it be, after all?

She peered around the door and was stunned to see the pleading eyes of Ravid staring back at her.

He didn't say anything for a moment. Neither did she.

"It's all your fault you know," he finally managed, his lips almost a pout.

"What?" she breathed.

He stuffed his hands in his pockets. "The way I act sometimes. It's only because I love you so much that I act that way."

She found herself at a loss for anything to say.

Ravid shrugged. "I know I've been unreasonable. I've been beating myself up about it."

"Yes, you have been unreasonable," she said, crossing her arms. But he looked so contrite, so pathetic, she felt her heart break a little more. She had never meant to hurt him, but she realized that in her selfishness, she had likely hurt him as badly as he had hurt her. So she stepped back, opened the door a little wider, and let him in.

He shuffled in like a wounded puppy, looking around and delivering a low whistle. "Fancy."

"I was going to say obnoxious," she said, closing the door quietly.

He turned to face her and smiled. She laughed at the absurdity of their rift and then threw herself into his arms. "I'm sorry," she said quietly.

"Let's not talk about it anymore, all right?" he said, pulling her close, burying his face in her neck.

"Agreed."

Ravid pulled away, taking her by the hand and guiding her over to the bed. He sat down, patting a place beside him. She smiled and hopped up onto the high mattress to join him.

"So the prince," he said, wrapping an arm about her waist. "He's an ass, huh?"

"What?" she asked, leaning away to better look at him.

"I saw the way he was looking at you tonight. I was ready to tear his eyes out. Pompous buzzard. Who does he think he is?"

Delaney laughed through her nose, resting her head on his shoulder. And just like that, her friend was back. Her Ravid. The boy who had been her closest companion ever since her mother's death. Who had been her greatest source of comfort. The secret she had somehow managed to keep from her father for years. She kissed his shoulder, warming to her core when his hands stroked luxuriously up and down her side.

He took her chin, holding her gaze for a moment before he kissed her, and the warmth, the familiarity she had missed so greatly came rushing back like the tide of the ocean behind her.

She didn't know whether it was loneliness mingled with the relief of having him back or the homesickness plaguing her heart, but when she kissed him, she did not hold back.

Neither did she ask him to leave her chambers that night.

* * *

Chapter 27

The next morning, Ferryl did not set out in search of Elizabeth, nor the morning after, instead taking his meals alone in his private dining room. Even with the encouragement of his father's blessing, reality had hit him hard and fast once more, dancing around his mind, mocking him like the little black-winged moth that fluttered about his face. Even if he did find Elizabeth, what could he say to her that would convince her to choose him? She had made her choice, hadn't she?

The nuisance moth seemed to follow him too—like an unwanted pet. No matter how he swatted, it didn't leave his presence. Day or night. What a strange sight he must have made—a moping prince with a relentless black moth fluttering about him. He shook his head in hopes of simply ignoring the thing away. But for reasons beyond his comprehension, the tiny winged creature seemed attached, for better or for worse.

* * *

BEFORE HE KNEW IT, SEVERAL weeks had gone by and he hadn't gone looking for Elizabeth once. He had even humored his mother and attended a few meetings planning the wedding festivities. It seemed that everyone was in a good mood except him. Derwin with his new wife. The queen with her wedding planning. Sir Thomas watching a Navarian prince plan his nuptials to a Midvarish duchess. Even King Derrick, who was still touring their kingdom—much to Derwin's chagrin—still seemed in a pleasant mood anytime he was in the palace. The duchess herself didn't have much to say, keeping quiet mostly. She wasn't quite the brat his mother had made her out to be. In fact, she was surprisingly complicit in the whole matter of wedding planning, with few opinions of her own. It seemed she was eager to please the queen—which Ferryl knew to be a wise choice on her part, unless she had a particular affinity for misery.

Still, his heart ached with longing for Elizabeth and the fear that his yearnings were futile. Would that ache ever subside?

In the stillness of the afternoon, Ferryl was reading a report from the northern legions, absentmindedly swatting at the little black moth, when there came a knock on the door to his office. He looked up from his desk to see Michael peeking his head in.

"Your Highness," said the guard, "Her Majesty the queen is here to see you."

Ferryl nodded as he stood. The queen of Navah emerged into his private chambers, clad head to toe in the purest white, a striking contrast to the depthless black of her eyes.

"Hello, Mother," he said, bowing when she reached him, taking her hands in his and kissing them dutifully.

The queen didn't say anything, didn't move, only looked at Ferryl in a way he hadn't remembered since...well, since he was a boy.

"What is it?" he asked, furrowing his brow, still holding her hands in his. She held his gaze, and that's when Ferryl saw them—tears. Pooling in her eyes. "Mother? Is everything all right?"

"I could ask you the same thing," she said, her voice soft. Stricken.

"What? What do you mean?"

The queen gestured for her son to take a seat. As if this were her room. As if these were her chairs. Ferryl obeyed anyway, and only when she sat down across from him did she continue. "Son, I came to check on you. To see how you are doing."

"You did? Why?"

She sighed, looking down and wringing her narrow fingers, clad in several heavy rings. "Ferryl, I know I haven't been the easiest to get along with. And I know I've been hard on you. But I want you to know...I want you to know that I love you more than anything in the world. There is nothing I wouldn't do for you. Nothing."

"I know that, Mother," said Ferryl, failing to understand why she seemed so stricken to confess such a thing.

"I want you to be happy," she went on, her eyes limned with concern. "And I want you to know how proud I am of you."

"You are?"

Her brows narrowed in...what? Regret? "I know you loved her, Ferryl." Her voice so quiet, she had barely breathed the words.

Ferryl said nothing as he watched his mother. And he wondered why she would say such a thing. She who had made it impossible for him to choose any life but the one she wanted for him.

"I know you loved Elizabeth. And I know you were heartbroken when she left."

Heartbroken. Yes. But why did she care? Nothing—nothing but an advantageous marriage would satisfy his mother. And certainly not a marriage to a stable girl he had just met.

And yet still...still there was something behind what she was saying. More than just her signature drama.

His mother seemed...genuinely sorry.

"I thought you didn't approve of Elizabeth," he finally said.

The queen sighed—a deep, heavy breath that dragged her shoulders ever lower. "I admit I've been hard on you, Ferryl. I cannot help it, you know. I've only ever wanted the best for you." She fussed with the toggles of his jacket as she went on. "In truth, I only want to see you happy. I want to see your reign secured, your legacy sealed." She met his eyes then. Met them and held them with her own—a firmament of midnight. "But I see your grief, and I am stricken with my own." She drew him into her arms, resting his head on her shoulder, patting it softly. The most motherly gesture she had shown him since boyhood. He found himself transfixed by it.

But he pulled away from her embrace, meeting her eyes again, unable to say anything. So she kissed his cheek softly, a gesture so familiar, so aching, it reminded him of bygone days—of a simpler time when all that separated him from manhood was a world of dreams and desires.

Then again, had any of that really changed?

"I know you probably don't believe me," she went on, "but I know you will find happiness with the duchess. And I know that with her by your side, you will make a fine king someday."

"Do you really believe that, Mother?"

"Of course I do, son," she said, cupping his cheek. "Of course. You are a good man. And you have a good heart. I know it's not easy to give up what you want. I know because I had to do the same thing when I was your age. But I promise you, it is worth it. For there is nothing more important than your duty to the crown. The people are looking to you, Ferryl. You must show them your wisdom. You must show them you are fit as heir. And marrying the duchess is the first step. You have made your kingdom proud, son. And your marriage will set a legacy of peace between two countries who have struggled for centuries."

Ferryl didn't say anything, the crown suddenly a heavier burden than ever he had known. Could it really be that simple? Could peace with Midvar be as simple as a wedding ceremony?

"Mother, I appreciate what you're saying. I do. But why haven't the rebels subsided? We announced the betrothal officially two weeks ago and still they attack."

"Son, it takes time for news to travel across the kingdom. And it takes even longer for small-minded people to see reason. But you're right—the attacks should be waning at the very least."

"So why haven't they?"

A small, hopeful smile. "Because you are not married yet, of course. You'll see, son. When you are married to the duchess, this whole ordeal with the rebels will be nothing more than a distant memory."

It sounded simple enough, which was precisely why he wondered how it could be so. He, of all people, knew that nothing was ever as simple as it seemed.

Ferryl met his mother's eyes again. Her eyes that conveyed a sympathy he wasn't entirely sure he understood.

"What did you give up, Mother?" Ferryl suddenly asked, thinking how little he knew of the woman who stood before him.

"What?" She met his eyes, and for the first time in his life, Ferryl did not see a queen before him.

He saw a woman. A woman with an ocean of secrets in her eyes.

"You said you understand what I'm going through because you gave up something you wanted when you were my age. What was it?"

The queen tore her gaze from him, silence yawning long and uncomfortable as she stared absently out the wall of windows beside them. When at last she spoke, her voice was stricken, hoarse. Still, she did not look at him as she said quietly, "What I wanted, son. I gave up what I wanted."

What she wanted? What could that mean? And what was it that his mother had wanted that should still resonate so deeply? Still ache within her very soul even now?

Maybe in his mind, his mother had always been a bear. A snarling mother bear, aching to devour any threat to her or her cubs.

But in this moment, Queen Meria of Navah was no bear. No, in this moment, she was a fawn. A newborn fawn, trembling as she sought footing on unfamiliar ground.

Ferryl found himself even less settled than before she arrived, for where was the justice in giving up the heart's deepest desire? And what good could come of it? And what good was having a heart's desire when it was only one-sided?

"I love you, Ferryl. Please don't ever forget that," the queen said at last, her countenance melting back into her practiced resolve.

"I know you do, Mother. I love you too."

She didn't say another word, pressing a kiss to her son's cheek before leaving the room, her cloudy white dress trailing behind her. That's when Ferryl noticed it. Another moth fluttered to join his unwanted companion. He swatted at the cursed little beasts, but they lingered. Nothing, it seemed, would keep them away.

* * *

Chapter 28

The morning light peeked through gossamer curtains tousling lazily in the ocean breezes, a salty brine that permeated her chambers. Delaney breathed deeply, knowing she was a fool for allowing Ravid to stay this late when the servants were due in her rooms any minute. But a small part of her—that part of her that had not quite relinquished its hold on her childhood—relished the idea of a scandal, and she smirked as she rolled over, surprised to see Ravid was awake too.

"What's that grin for?" he asked.

"You."

He kissed her tenderly, trailing a finger down her bare shoulder. "You know, if anyone catches me in here, it will be my neck."

"And what a pity, for you have such a lovely neck," she said, running a finger along it. He grabbed her by the wrist and held her gaze for a moment before pouring kisses down her arm.

"You really had better get out of here before my servants arrive."

"What a little tyrant you're turning out to be."

"Yes. A tyrant who would rather not find the man she loves hanging from the gallows, thank you very much."

"Loves? That's an awfully important distinction for a plaything."

"You are no plaything, Ravid, and you know it."

He kissed her fingers. "Don't you have a prince to tend to, my lady?"

She slapped his hands away. "Don't talk like that."

"Well, it's true, isn't it? You're going to marry him, and I'm going to be tossed aside like a child's toy."

"Stop it, Ravid. You know I wouldn't do that." She sighed heavily. "And don't talk about this stupid marriage. It's bad enough that I have to watch the queen and my father practically drool over planning the wedding. I can't even think about it."

Ravid's lips found their way to her neck, where they lingered for quite some time. "I'm sorry, wildcat. You know I am."

"How can they make me do this? I don't even know him. What if he's some sort of sycophant? Or a murderer? What if he's a murderer, Ravid?"

"Well then, you should probably get to know this sycophantic murdering prince before you marry him."

Delaney slapped his arm. "Get out of here. The servants will be here any minute, and you're no help anyway."

"So sorry, my lady," he said with a smirk, kissing her quickly before shuffling out of the bed. She blushed, unable to watch him dress, turning her back to him.

He chuckled at her prudishness. "I'll see you later, wildcat."

"Go on, Ravid."

He laughed again, and before she could turn to face him, he had slipped out the door.

Mercifully, the servants didn't come knocking for several more minutes, allowing her ample time to hide any signs that there might have been anyone else in the room with her.

But for the rest of the day, she couldn't get his words out of her head. Even though they had been said in jest, she knew he was probably right—she needed to get to know this man that she was supposed to be marrying.

* * *

"My sources inform me that you have announced your retirement to our dear King Aiken," said King Derrick, leaning on the door of the commander's office. No greeting. No preamble. Just cut to the chase. Typical.

"Yes, Your Majesty," said Commander Titus, closing his ledger and standing to bow to the unannounced king.

"It was quite a surprise when I heard it. I had expected you to discuss it with me."

"Well, with you being gone—"

"Gone? I've been in Navah, traveling the countryside with your Navarian generals, Commander, trying to assess the rebel situation. They seem to be under the impression that Aiken wants a war to wipe the rebels out once and for all. Now who would give them that idea?"

Titus crossed the small room, pressing the door shut before going on. "All due respect, Majesty, but these are your rebels and this is your cockamamie idea to keep the Navarian army busy quelling uprisings while you carry out a real plan right under their noses. Meanwhile, I'm supposed to play the part of loyal commander to a kingdom that is my enemy, keep your plans secret, and keep two kings placated. Frankly, I'm tired. And it's well past time I retire. I'm sure you'll agree."

The king didn't say anything as he stared at the commander, that ever-present smirk of his never wavering. He crossed his arms and leaned against the wall. "It was a clever plan, Titus, I'll give you that. To play the part of a foggy old man, incapable of sound judgment in his age. Perhaps you thought it would be just enough to convince both kings that your retirement is imminent. But we both know better, don't we? For you are neither old nor foggy. You're just as ruthless as you were in the war." The king sauntered over to the fireplace, leaning against the mantle as the fire burned beside him, casting a reddish glow about him. A devil incarnate, if such things as devils and gods existed. "So I suppose for now, you have won. For it has already been decided that Prince Derwin will replace you. And you will go home to Midvar and that useless woman of yours. But rest assured, General, that your tenure is not up. And when I need you again, you had better be ready to answer my call—lest you find yourself at the mercy of the eager new Navarian commander. It would be a pity if he were to find out what a traitorous liar you have been."

In the same manner by which he had entered, King Derrick left the office of the commander—no farewell, no words at all. And Titus only stared into the fire as his king's words echoed in his head. Yes, he had been a traitorous liar to a king and kingdom that had been nothing but good to him over the years, serving King Derrick and the interests of Midvar the entire time.

But it was over now, no matter what King Derrick said. Titus was done. Done with being the Midvarish general turned Navarian commander. Done with wars. And games of kings. And lying. It was time— time to go home, time to rest.

And he'd be damned if he let that bastard of a king run his life anymore.

* * *

Chapter 29

Trying to best me, brother?" asked Ferryl, the scarred wooden sword flashing in the torchlight.

"I do not try. I only do," said Derwin, and Ferryl didn't miss his smirk in the golden light bathing the barn where the two of them had practiced sword fighting since they were boys.

"You know I am better than you," continued Derwin as he advanced on his brother.

"You are faster, I will give you that. But you are not better."

"Pray, remind me, O Sovereign Prince, when was the last time you won a fight against me?" Derwin laughed as their swords hit together in the darkness.

"Now what kind of big brother would I be if I never let my little brother win?"

"Bah!" Derwin scoffed, advancing on Ferryl. "I am the superior swordsman and you know it!"

Ferryl chuckled to himself, for he did know it was true, although he would never admit it. "It's true your skills are superior to most," said Ferryl. "Which is why I'm making you my commander."

"Yes, well, we'll have to wait a thousand years for that now, won't we?" Derwin spun on his heel, thrusting his sword at his brother, who deflected the blow only just. Yes, Derwin was quick and capable. Markedly so.

"Actually, it's already done."

"And what's that supposed to mean?" Derwin scoffed, brandishing his sword with expert skill.

"It means you are now the commander of the Royal Army."

Derwin stopped in his tracks, his sword dropping slowly as he stared at his brother. "Don't fool with me, Ferryl. I'm in no mood."

"Neither am I," said Ferryl matter-of-factly.

"Are you serious?"

"I am. It's done. I spoke with Father already. It will be announced tomorrow."

"And what of Commander Titus?" Derwin asked.

"He's been ready to retire for years. I suppose that's why he's been so lax about the rebels. He wants to go home, live out his days drinking wine and bedding his wife. A sentiment I can relate to, entirely," Ferryl laughed bitterly, twirling the tip of his sword in the dirt.

"Brother, do you really mean it?" Derwin asked, failing to laugh for the sheer awe in his eyes.

"I do."

And to his surprise, Derwin dropped his sword and lunged into his arms, embracing him with every measure of brotherly affection the two shared.

"I can never thank you enough, Ferryl."

"I do hope you'll remember that." Ferryl smiled, happy to share in his brother's excitement.

After the news finally sank in, the brothers resumed their sword practice, speaking little, for Derwin, it seemed, was determined to prove his worth as newly crowned commander. And Ferryl didn't mind the more aggressive sparring. But after a long while, it was Derwin who surprised Ferryl when he broke the silence.

"May I ask you a question?"

"Of course," Ferryl said.

"Why have you stopped looking for Elizabeth?"

Ferryl froze in place, taken aback by the question and equally unsure how to answer. "I don't know," he finally managed. "I don't know what to do."

"So that's it, then? You're simply not going to look for her anymore?" Derwin asked as he advanced with his wooden blade.

Ferryl parried the attack easily, his sword like an extension of his, arm thanks to all the years he'd spent as a boy training with Commander Titus. "What choice do I have? She's gone. She left. What can I do? Search every corner of the country? It's time that I step up to my responsibilities, Derwin." Ferryl spun around, thrusting the practice blade quickly. But Derwin was faster, and he deflected the blow effortlessly.

"I don't understand how you can give up so easily. You're in love with her, Ferryl. You have been since you were a boy. You—"

Ferryl retreated suddenly, his sword staying at the ready. "A boy? Why does everyone keep saying that? I only just met the girl a few months ago, Derwin. I cannot keep pretending that it was going to amount to anything. She is in love with someone else. And I have a duty to—"

"A few *months* ago?" Derwin cried, advancing on his brother, raising his sword to attack. "What in Sheol are you talking about?"

"What are *you* talking about?" Ferryl replied, hardly able to concentrate on the sparring.

Derwin scoffed. "Brother, you've lost your mind."

"Don't be such an ass." Ferryl feinted left and swung right, but Derwin wasn't fooled. It was a move he had taught Ferryl himself.

"How about *you* stop being an ass and go and find the woman you've loved your whole life?"

Ferryl could see frustration burning in his brother's eyes and wondered if their sparring match might turn into a real fight. "How can I have loved her my whole life, Derwin? How is that possible?" He lifted his sword over his head and charged his brother.

But Derwin countered easily. "Is there something wrong with you, Ferryl? Something you're not telling me?"

"I'm a vision of health." Ferryl laughed, bowing proudly before poising to attack again, but at the look in his brother's eyes, his sword came down.

"Are you? Because you act as if you've forgotten all about Elizabeth. As if nothing ever happened between you two. I thought for sure you had asked for her hand while I was in Qadim. But ever since then, you haven't said a word about it until just before she left. I thought it was strange, but—"

"Proposed to her while you were in Qadim? Derwin, that was months ago! Why would I have done that?"

"Because it's all you've talked about for almost a year!"

Ferryl just...stopped. Froze. Standing before his hotheaded little brother, exasperated at the conversation, he finally said, "Derwin, stop talking nonsense. You've lost your mind!"

Derwin swung his sword in the air, jabbing and parrying with his invisible foe. "I've not lost my mind, but it seems to me that you've lost your memory," he said casually.

Ferryl scoffed. What was his brother talking about? Loving Elizabeth his whole life? His father had said similar things too. Had his family known something he didn't? Or rather couldn't?

Derwin at last ended his invisible match, turning to his brother. "Ferryl, you've loved Elizabeth your whole life. We all grew up together. I mean, it took you a while to admit it to yourself, seeing as you're a stubborn ass. But everyone knew you loved her. And everyone knew you'd ask for her hand someday. How could you have forgotten that?"

Grew up together? Since childhood?

How could that be possible?

But even as strange an assertion as his brother was making, somewhere—somewhere deep down Ferryl knew it to be true. He knew it in the very marrow of his bones. It had to be. How else could he explain the powerful feelings Elizabeth had stirred in him if she were only a stranger?

Maybe she wasn't a stranger. Maybe he knew her.

But if he knew her in his heart, he certainly didn't in his mind. How could such a thing be possible?

Ferryl shook his head suddenly, lost in a sea of confusion. Of memories that seemed right on the edge of his mind, now that he thought about it.

"You really don't remember, do you?" Derwin asked.

Ferryl only shook his head.

"How could you have forgotten her, Ferryl? What is wrong with you?"

"There is nothing wrong with me as far as I know. My only problem is that everyone seems to remember a great love affair that I am not privy to."

"If I didn't know any better, I'd say you've been cursed," said Derwin flippantly.

Ferryl looked at his brother in shock. "Cursed?"

"It was a joke, Ferryl."

But when it was obvious that Ferryl wasn't joking, Derwin took a good while before he spoke again. "You can't be serious."

"I have no memory of knowing her my whole life, Derwin."

"How is that possible?"

"I don't know. I thought I was being impetuous, wanting to marry her. I thought it was too soon, that we had just met. But to be honest, it makes sense. It makes sense that I have known her my whole life. Because I love her like I *have* loved her my whole life."

"That's because you have," said Derwin.

"Don't you see it, Derwin? I forgot her. But I never forgot my love for her. How could that be so?"

"I don't know. Do you remember anything? You grew up together, Ferryl. We all did. Elizabeth, Leala, Michael, you, me. A thousand memories. Are you telling me you remember none of it?"

"I remember growing up with you and Leala and Michael. But only the four of us."

"How could you forget Elizabeth and nothing else?"

"I don't know."

Both brothers stood silently for a while, their sword practice on hold as they pondered the mystery unfolding before them.

"The thing I don't understand is why she left so suddenly," said Derwin.

Ferryl felt his heart sink. "She's in love with someone else. She left to—" But even as he said it, the truth began to dawn on Ferryl, steady and blinding. Bright. Like a summer sunrise.

"She left to what?" Derwin asked.

"To find him," Ferryl said, his voice far away. He stumbled to the barn wall, leaning against it to brace himself. "Of course. Of course, it makes sense. She left to find the man that had left her. It was me, Derwin," he said, locking eyes with his little brother. "She left to find answers about me. Because I left her. Gone, she said. The man she loved was gone. She must have left to try and figure out why. And all this time I thought she was looking for someone else. But it was me.

She left to help me!" Ferryl sank to the ground with a thud, sitting hard in the dirt. "Oh Providence, what have I done? I'm a fool!"

Derwin walked to his brother, squatting before him. He placed his hands on Ferryl's shoulders. But it wasn't mockery in his eyes. It was empathy. "Yes, you are a fool. A fool to let love like that slip through your fingers. It doesn't come along every day, you know."

Ferryl pushed a weary hand through his hair. "I know. Oh Providence, how I know."

Ferryl met his brother's eyes, saw the same weariness that was in his own, and thought of another childhood friend. How difficult it must have been for him to have to keep the woman he loved hidden away like a dirty secret. "Where is Leala, Derwin?"

"She is fulfilling her duties as my mother's maid."

"But she is a princess now," protested Ferryl.

"Yes, well, you, she, and I are the only three people in the world who know that, aren't we?" Derwin stood, extending his hand to help Ferryl up. "And you only know it because you figured it out. I don't like it. But what choice do I have? I shudder to think of what Mother would do to her if she found out. I fear she may already know and the worry follows me like a moth to a flame."

"Moths?" Ferryl asked, his eyes shooting up to meet his brother's. He saw them, the little moths in his peripheral, and wondered if his brother could see them too. No one else seemed to have been able to see the pests.

"It's just an expression, Ferryl."

An expression. Of course. Derwin had meant nothing by it. And Ferryl certainly couldn't see any moths around his brother. Was he going crazy? *Was* this truly some sort of aftereffect of a curse? Magic. In Navah. He shook his head. What a strange turn of events.

"What are you going to do?" Ferryl asked.

Derwin only shook his head. "I don't know yet. But I will figure out something. Father seems to be doing better these days. Perhaps he can help me. My only prayer is that I can figure something out before Mother uncovers the truth."

A sentiment Ferryl could understand, indeed.

* * *

Chapter 30

"May I help you with anything, Your Grace?"

Delaney paused her walking long enough to turn and face the voice that had come from behind. She spotted a tall guard with chestnut hair as unruly as the prince's, standing in the corridor just outside her chambers. The fit of his black-and-white uniform made him look authoritative, strong. But there was a kindness in his eyes that struck her. She realized she hadn't answered when he continued, "You seem to be looking for someone. Can I help you?"

"Oh," she said. "Yes, actually." She took a step closer to the guard. "Do you know where I can find the crown prince?"

The guard smiled, and she saw flecks of icy blue dance in his silver-gray eyes. Like steel and moonlight. "I believe he is in the armory, sparring with Prince Derwin."

"The armory. All right," she said, feeling strangely fidgety. "Thank you." She turned on her heel and walked hastily away, unsure why she was so unsettled by the stranger. But she heard him call after her again.

"Would you like for me to escort you there, Your Grace?" There was a hint of a laugh in his voice.

She paused again, but this time she didn't turn to face him, embarrassed that she was most likely going in the wrong direction.

She felt him beside her before she saw him. And to her surprise, his smile was genuine. "I would be glad to show you the way, if you would like."

She turned her eyes away from him and nodded, wishing she wasn't such a fool. The guard led her through the opposite corridor and down a large flight of stairs at the back of the castle. She memorized the way so that she wouldn't have to call on his help again. While she knew why she wasn't saying a word, she suddenly wondered why *he* wasn't. And the thought only made her more antsy.

Once they made it outside, he turned to the right and toward an open garden that she had seen from her balcony and had wondered how she could get to it.

The garden was surrounded by the towering white castle on three sides, but the fourth side was open to the ocean—the cliff's edge. The moon wasn't quite full, but it was bright enough that the silver light danced on every flower, every leaf, every branch of the lush vegetation around them, the ocean breezes kissing her face. She breathed deeply.

"It's a beautiful night," the guard finally said.

"I've yet to see one in Navah that isn't," she heard herself reply.

The guard smiled again and stopped walking, turning to face her. His eyes were even more spectacular in the moonlight. They glimmered with strength. And grace. She forced herself not to stare into them. "We're here," he said.

"Oh." She hadn't noticed the building before them. It was small, and while it, too, was built out of the same white stone as the castle, it was little more than a barn. She was surprised. While the castle itself was beautiful and grand, there was nothing ostentatious about it. In fact, there was nothing ostentatious about anything she had seen so far in this kingdom. It seemed they were much more interested in the natural beauty surrounding them than in displaying their wealth and splendor—another thing she hadn't expected about this place.

"Thank you for escorting me," she finally said.

"My name is Michael, if you need anything else, Your Grace." He gave her a small bow before turning to walk back towards the palace. She watched him walk—the power, the grace in his movements were almost a work of art. And for a wicked moment, she wondered how many excuses she could come up with to call on his services again. The thought turned the corner of her mouth into a grin as she peered into the torchlight of the barn before her.

* * *

FERRYL AND DERWIN HAD RECOMMENCED their sparring, although it lacked the ferocity that it had earlier in the evening. Both brothers distracted with their thoughts, the clashes of sword against sword became a sort of release, a rhythm, a search. For answers. For solutions. For something other than the brick wall they both seemed up against.

Even distracted, Derwin was capable of besting his older brother, though Ferryl was only vaguely aware of it.

"Getting tired yet?" Derwin smirked.

"Not a chance," said Ferryl. But it was Derwin who suddenly retreated, throwing Ferryl off balance.

"What's gotten into you?" Ferryl asked. It was only at his nod that Ferryl followed his gaze into a dark corner of the barn to find Duchess Delaney, quiet as a mouse, hidden mostly by shadows, her expression unreadable.

"Duchess?" Ferryl asked in disbelief.

"What are you doing here?" Derwin added, pointedly.

"I am sorry," the duchess said in a small voice. "I did not realize I wouldn't be welcome. It is not every day one has the privilege of seeing such skill in action."

Derwin scoffed. "If this is your attempt at flattery, you can spare us."

"Derwin," said Ferryl in a placating tone, more curious as to why she was here than irritated. "It's all right. Yes, Your Grace, you're allowed to watch. But in the future, you should make your presence known."

"Of course," she said, bowing her head slightly.

"Do you make a practice of lurking in dark corners?" Derwin sneered.

Delaney only shook her head, looking down. A picture of submission.

"Been here long?" Derwin asked.

"No. I only arrived a moment ago," she said quietly.

Derwin's scoff let Ferryl know that he didn't believe her, but Ferryl sensed something strange in her voice. Small and fleeting. Was it apology?

"Interested in swordplay?" Ferryl offered, deciding to seize the strange opportunity and attempt to get to know the mystery before him.

"It has always fascinated me, yes," she said, taking a moment to meet his eyes.

"Can you wield a sword?" Ferryl asked.

"Hardly. My father would have flogged me indeed had he ever seen me with one of those things in my hands. A duchess cannot risk such terrible atrocities as callouses or scrapes." At this, Delaney let out a small laugh, and Ferryl found himself smiling with her.

Derwin, whether disinterested in the conversation or attempting to run Delaney off with his manner, Ferryl couldn't be sure, retreated to the back and picked up a bow to practice with the targets.

"Do you two practice often?" she asked, gesturing toward Derwin.

"We used to. When we were younger. But we haven't in a while. It seems we've both been...preoccupied," said Ferryl.

Delaney nodded, an inscrutable expression on her young face. "You both seem quite the swordsmen."

"Derwin is the better one by far."

"You looked quite capable of handling yourself to me," she said.

Ferryl wondered why this girl who had yet to say two words to him was suddenly so keen on complimenting his swordsmanship. "I'm not terrible, I suppose. But Derwin has the upper hand in both speed and agility. Not to mention he's freakishly tall."

"I heard that," Derwin called from the back.

And Ferryl realized in that moment that Delaney, too, was quite tall. Especially for a girl of only seventeen. She was almost as tall as he, in fact. Why hadn't he noticed before? She shuffled past Ferryl, her hand grazing the weapons along the wall, her steps slow, her manner thoughtful. "Are you enjoying planning our wedding, Your Highness?" she asked, her back to him.

There was a tone about her question. As if she knew the answer already. "I suppose I'm enjoying it about as much as any man would. Why?"

She shrugged. "Curious, is all."

There was an awkward silence, and Ferryl felt the need to propel the conversation. "And how are you enjoying Navah?"

"I admit that it is a beautiful country. The ocean is spectacular. I have enjoyed getting to know Navah these past weeks."

Yes, he supposed the ocean was beautiful. Growing up beside it had numbed his awe over the years. "I'm glad it is to your liking," said Ferryl, wondering where the conversation was going.

"You must love the countryside."

"What do you mean?"

"You rode out to see it every day when I first arrived." At this, she turned on her heel, her brown eyes meeting his and holding him frozen. "Why did you stop?"

"I suppose I...needed a break."

She took a moment to reply, searching him with her piercing eyes. "And will you resume riding again?"

At Ferryl's silent nod, Delaney's expression returned to an inscrutable mystery. But she lingered. And after a moment, Ferryl could have sworn he saw a hint of surprise somewhere in her brown eyes.

Just then, hurried steps sounded across the garden and a stricken-faced Leala appeared before them, her eyes wide, her body tense with fear.

"What is it?" Derwin asked, appearing from the shadows of the barn, his eyes full of concern.

"She knows," Leala replied, tears threatening to fall down her flushed cheeks.

"What?" the prince asked, closing the gap between them.

"She knows, Derwin. The servants, they figured it out and...you know how they gossip. Perhaps she overheard. Or perhaps she coaxed it out of them. I cannot be sure. But she knows. She knows, and she's furious."

"What happened?" Derwin asked, taking hold of her hands.

Leala shot a look of distrust at the duchess, and without hesitation, Delaney bowed her head. "I had better get back to the palace. My father will want to see me before he retires. Good night." Delaney hurried away from the practice barn and Ferryl found his gaze transfixed on her every move. Leala waited until she was out of their sight before continuing in a trembling, hushed voice.

"I came to her chambers to dress her for bed as I always do, but one of the other girls was already there. When the queen saw me, she..." Leala drew in a ragged breath. "She wouldn't even look at me. But she asked the other maid why there was a harlot in her room. A *harlot*, Derwin. Then she asked the girl if she knew what happened to servants who were found fornicating in the palace. The poor girl, she knew the queen was talking about me. All she could do was shake her head. But the queen, she laughed. She laughed, Derwin. And she said they hang fornicators from the gallows. What's going to happen to us?" Tears fell thick and heavy down Leala's face, and Derwin wrapped himself around her, taking his wife into his arms in quiet comfort.

Surely his mother wouldn't do such a thing. Surely she was making idle threats. Hang Leala? How could she inflict such a harsh punishment? And fornication? It was not fornication by any means—they were married, for Providence's sake! Surely she was simply trying to scare Leala. It was no secret that the queen didn't like it when she didn't get her way. But Ferryl had never known her to be a calloused tyrant. Surely—surely—this was a misunderstanding.

"I'm sure it will be all right, Leala. My mother is—"

"She is cruel and unreasonable," interrupted Derwin. "But I won't let her hurt you, my love. We shall go and speak with Father. He will side with us. I know he will. I don't know why I haven't gone to him sooner." Derwin kissed his wife's temple as he stroked her hair. Leala only trembled in her husband's arms, fat tears falling down her flushed cheeks.

"Derwin, Mother means well. She does. She just doesn't like being outsmarted. She will see reason," protested Ferryl.

"When are you going to open your eyes, Ferryl? She doesn't mean well. Mother only does what is in Mother's best interests. In her whole life, there's only one thing she's ever gotten that she didn't want."

"And what was that?" Ferryl asked.

"Me," Derwin responded flatly.

"Derwin, you mustn't say such things," said Ferryl.

Leala looked down, still clinging to her husband's side, but obviously privy to his feelings on the subject.

"She hates me. She always has. What other explanation is there? I think she still loved Father when she had you. But she certainly didn't by the time I came along. And I only remind her of that. My whole life, all I've ever reminded her of is her hatred for our father. And she's treated me like a stepchild because of it. Like dung on her boot. She won't show us mercy. She won't see reason. It's the reason I had to marry the woman I love in secret, like it was a sin. And it's the reason I'll leave if I have to. I won't choose this life over Leala. Not even being commander. I won't. I will always choose Leala. Always."

Leala buried her face in his shoulder. He held her close and kissed her hair as she wept.

And Ferryl found that he understood his brother's conviction. He understood it because he felt the same fealty to Elizabeth.

Elizabeth, the girl he had forgotten. Elizabeth, the love he could never forget. But now that he understood why his heart had so fiercely belonged to her, he knew he could not rest until he found her and brought her back home.

"We must speak with Father," said Derwin. "He is the only one who can help us now."

* * *

Chapter 31

D elaney pulled the plush blankets up over her, staring out her bedroom window to the ocean beyond. The moonlight spilled over the waters, illuminating a silver pathway that looked as if it might lead straight into the heavens.

The ocean was beautiful. She had never seen anything like it. She hadn't lied to the prince—she truly loved the beauty of the palace and its cliffside views. It had provided a surprising dose of peace in an otherwise impossible situation.

And tonight, as she had watched the prince spar with his brother—observed their friendship, their camaraderie—something stirred in her, something she couldn't quite explain. She had a pretty good idea as to why he had been avoiding her all this time. Picking up little tidbits here and there around the court. Prince Ferryl was in love with someone else too. And apparently she was missing.

But he had looked for her. Relentlessly. Every day when she first arrived he had ridden out. For hours. Usually most of the day. She had originally assumed it was because he was avoiding Delaney like a child. She had assumed he wasn't man enough to face his responsibilities.

Then again, she wasn't woman enough to face hers, so who was she to judge?

But that wasn't why he was riding out every day. It was for a woman—a woman he must have loved deeply. Strangely, he had stopped his search recently, and she wasn't sure she quite understood why. But tonight he had said he was going out for his rides again—to resume his search, no doubt.

And somewhere, deep in a dark corner of her heart—a corner untouched, a corner forgotten—Delaney felt something for the prince.

Something she couldn't quite define. He wasn't the monster she had assumed. He wasn't the heartless, selfish pig she had expected to find.

He was a man. A man in love.

And somehow, she knew it changed everything.

* * *

FERRYL FUSSED WITH THE PARCHMENT on his writing desk the next morning, reading and rereading the speech he had been preparing for his brother's appointment as commander. The ceremony was to be held later that afternoon, and Ferryl wanted to deliver a speech that would make his father proud and do his brother justice. It was the first speech of its kind he had ever given, and he was nervous, to say the least.

He mumbled the words to himself as he scanned the pages, wondering if his word choices were genius or if he would look the fool he feared. This was his first official appointment as heir, and he knew he had to deliver a speech that would show the people that he was fit to be their king. He chewed on his pen as he read and reread, but his concentration was shattered by the sharp knock on his door.

"Yes?" he called.

Michael opened the door and entered. "Your Highness," he said with a bow.

"Michael, for the thousandth time, why won't you call me Ferryl? I should think we are good enough friends that we can be on a first-name basis," he chuckled.

Michael moved to shut the door behind him, pressing it gingerly to the jamb. He kept his back to Ferryl for a moment before at last turning to meet the prince's eyes. "Yes, I consider you my friend. Which is why I hope you won't find my visit out of line."

"Out of line? Why ever would I think that?" Ferryl asked, the smile fading from his eyes. Michael looked down, and Ferryl knew something serious was on his mind. "What is it?" he asked, gesturing for him to join him in the chairs by the fireplace.

"Your Highness," Michael started, sitting rather uncomfortably before meeting Ferryl's eyes again. "Ferryl. There's something I think you should know."

"Pray tell."

"I was guarding the king's chambers this morning when I over-heard some shouting. I want you to know that I wasn't spying. I—"

"Michael. Relax. I know you wouldn't spy. You are my most trusted guard. It is your job to stand outside our doors. And I, for one, know that if my mother was shouting, half the castle could likely hear."

Michael relaxed...a little.

"What were they shouting about?" Ferryl continued.

"I heard something about Derwin. And Leala."

Ferryl sat up straighter. "What about them?"

"She knows, Ferryl. She knows about them. Everyone does."

"And now my father knows."

Michael nodded. "But that's not why I came to you."

"Yes?"

"It was something the queen said that caught my ear. I couldn't help but think—"

"Think what?"

"That it was about Elizabeth."

Ferryl froze, his heart in his throat. "What about Elizabeth?" he asked, thinking he wasn't entirely sure he wanted to know what his mother might be shouting about Elizabeth. "What did she say?"

"She said that she had half a mind to get rid of Leala. That she had done it before, and she would do it again if necessary."

"What?" Ferryl asked in horror. She had gotten rid of someone be-fore? Had she been the reason Elizabeth seemed so stricken when she left? Had his mother threatened her? But how could she? The queen knew how much Ferryl loved Elizabeth. She had said so herself.

The implications of such an underhanded game made his head swim.

"I don't know what it means. But I know you've been stricken with grief over Elizabeth's disappearance. And I don't know why she left, because I know how much she loves you. She has always loved you, Ferryl. Since we were all children. I didn't understand why she would leave so suddenly. It made no sense. But when I heard the queen say that she had gotten rid of someone before, a part of me couldn't help but wonder if she meant Elizabeth. And I know it's treasonous what I'm saying to you. I'm sorry. If I'm wrong, then I should be hung from the gallows for such accusations. But you are my friend. And I—"

"Michael, I am glad you told me," said Ferryl, standing to his feet, a righteous indignation building within. Michael stood as well. "I would have been disappointed if I found out you knew and didn't say anything. And I'm glad you feel that you can trust me with such information because you *are* my friend. You can rest assured that I will not betray you, no matter the outcome. But if you will excuse me, I believe I need to speak with my mother."

With that, Ferryl marched past the guard and out of the room, through the corridors of Benalle Palace until he reached the king's receiving chambers, intent on finding his mother and settling the truth once and for all.

Ferryl burst through the doors without introduction, to find his mother and father in conversation, his father obviously frustrated, his mother with her signature determination.

"Ferryl, darling! I am glad to see you. Your father and I were just discussing you. Have you prepared your speech for the ceremony?"

"I am prepared," said Ferryl flatly, standing his ground and taking just a moment to gather himself. "Tell me, Mother. Will you stop at nothing to have your way?"

"I'm sorry. What do you mean?" asked the queen, a look of innocence on her face.

"Tell me. What method were you planning to use to get rid of my brother's wife? Anything you've used before?"

"I'm afraid I don't know what you're talking about," the queen said, and it was only then that Ferryl could see it, for the first time. As clear as the blue Navarian skies. He had been played a fool. She had been crafting a game, and he had been too naïve, too trusting to see it.

But not anymore.

"I think you do. But how convenient for you to have such selective memory. I should know. For my memory, too, has been *selective* as of late."

"And what exactly are you accusing me of, son?" the queen asked softly. Too softly. Hoarfrost iced her voice.

"Oh nothing at all, Mother. I wouldn't dare. I'll see you at the ceremony," he said with a forced smile. And without so much as another glance, Ferryl turned on his heel and marched back out of the room, his heart thundering wildly in his chest.

* * *

THE ROOM SEEMED TO BE growing smaller as Ferryl stood waiting, wringing his hands in anticipation.

"If you're going to vomit, I suggest you do it now," said Derwin with a chuckle.

"Thank you for the vote of confidence, brother," chimed Ferryl, wiping the sweat from his brow and wishing his brother wasn't so damned perceptive. And mouthy.

"It's just a speech, Ferryl," Derwin said. "Relax."

"I've never known you to be the nervous type," said Leala as she stood with her hand on her husband's arm.

"I suppose the prospect of asserting my authority as heir is a little more daunting than I anticipated."

"Yes but it's not like you're doing anything controversial," chuckled Derwin. "You're simply appointing a new commander in light of Titus's retirement. Hardly groundbreaking."

Ferryl didn't say a word, nor did he meet his brother's eye. Instead, he stared at the door, knowing at any moment Michael would emerge and beckon him to join his parents in the throne room that held the waiting guests.

"Ferryl?" Derwin asked, knowing in his voice. "Is there something you'd like to tell me?"

Ferryl cleared his throat and straightened his jerkin as he squared his shoulders, mustering every ounce of confidence he could find. He was certainly going to need it. He didn't answer his brother. Nor did he opt to look him in the eye.

"Your Highness," said Michael as he peered around the jamb. "They are ready for you."

"Ferryl, what are you up to?" Derwin tried again.

"I'll see you in there," said Leala as she kissed her husband's cheek and turned to leave the room, for she would view the speech from the back of the throne room with a smattering of knights and gentry. The lesser nobility always stood in the back. Quiet. Inconspicuous. Just as the queen had ordered.

The two princes followed the guard through the door into the throne room, crossing the short distance to the side of the dais. Ferryl, nodding to his parents, ascended the few steps to the platform where sat the ornate thrones. The symbols of their authority—white Navari-an stone garnished with onyx and gold. He cleared his throat and lifted his chin, turning to fully face the court at Benalle, a surge of adrenaline rushing like a tidal wave as he spoke.

"My distinguished and honored guests," said Ferryl. "I am pleased to address you today. As most of you know, our dear friend and commander of the Royal Army, Sir Titus Melamed, has concluded that his retirement is imminent, as he is eager to get home to his beautiful wife and enjoy her pleasant company." The audience chuckled, and Ferryl scanned the crowd as his nerves slowly began to settle. Leala stood in the back, almost hidden behind the guards. A small crowd of noblemen filled the hall, along with their wives and a few squires. King Derrick of Midvar stood to the side, not far from the dais, next to Sir Thomas Nachash and Commander Titus. Ferryl didn't miss the smirk on the king's face. Bedell stood resolute with a smattering of other council members, and Duchess Delaney stood near as well, her father on the left, the eager vassal Ravid on her right. But her eyes never left the prince's.

Ferryl cleared his throat and continued. "We have been honored by Titus's service these last twenty years. He has proven his valor, his courage, and his determination to protect the interests of our great kingdom, and we will be forever indebted to his faithful loyalty." Ferryl nodded to Sir Titus, who nodded in return as the audience applauded.

"In light of his retirement, it is my duty as heir to name a new commander. The man I have chosen is one I know to be both strong and confident, brave and courageous, honest and noble, loyal to a fault. He is wise, and he is clever, and he will no doubt serve the interests of our kingdom with unwavering conviction. Good people of Navah, I present to you your new commander, my brother, Prince Derwin."

The anticipating audience applauded and cheered in approval as Derwin climbed the dais next to his brother, the brothers shaking hands with smiles on their faces. Derwin poised himself to deliver a speech, but took a small step back, his mouth agape when Ferryl cut him off to continue his own.

"I am glad to hear of your approval, as I have even more happy news to share with you." Ferryl looked to his brother and gave him a small nod before returning his gaze to the audience. "It is my distinct pleasure to announce that my brother, your new commander, will be taking up his post with his new wife by his side." Murmurs and whispers ensued from the crowd, and from behind, Ferryl heard his mother suck in a tiny breath. He donned a smirk and continued, "Ladies and gentlemen, it is my pleasure to present to you a woman I have called friend for my whole life and whom I now have the privilege of calling sister. Loyal subjects, may I introduce to you, Princess Leala of Benalle!"

Ferryl gestured for Leala to join them on the dais, and reluctantly, she pushed through the crowd, her eyes wide with fear. But Ferryl only smiled, knowing he had gifted Derwin with the freedom to afford his wife all the luxuries of a princess while simultaneously usurping his mother's ridiculous plan to otherwise deny him that privilege.

Once Leala reached them, Derwin took her hand in comfort, but his eyes were almost as wide as hers. Ferryl chuckled. "Ladies and gentlemen, Prince Derwin, Commander of the Royal Army, and his wife, Princess Leala!"

The crowd applauded and cheered in approval, blissfully unaware of the subversion that had taken place. Ferryl turned to his father to see a smile curling the corner of his mouth as he chuckled, which Ferryl returned with exuberance. His mother, on the other hand, only sat with her shoulders squared and her lips pursed, applauding perfunctorily without a sound.

Ferryl turned back to the crowd. "Tonight, we shall feast in celebration of this happy day!"

Chapter 32

Leala, if it's possible, you look even more lovely than usual," said Ferryl, kissing her hand.

The crowd around them created a buzz of chatter and laughter, music and merriment as the festivities ensued in the golden ballroom at Benalle.

"Thank you, Ferryl," she said, a blush to her cheeks. "I'm just glad I could find something to wear that wasn't covered in stains or distinctly servant-like."

"I suppose I didn't give you much warning. I do apologize," said Ferryl. "Where did you find the gown on such short notice?"

"The duchess lent it to me," she said.

Ferryl's eyes grew wide, and when he saw that there was no jest in her admission, he scanned the crowd for his betrothed, only to find her across the ballroom, deep in conversation with her father, the queen, and Sir Thomas. He couldn't help but notice that she looked lovely in a forest-green gown and a bib of diamonds around her neck. Like a princess. His heart broke a little at the thought.

"I don't know how I can ever thank you, brother," Derwin said, clapping a hand to Ferryl's shoulder. "I must admit, you're braver than I thought."

Ferryl chuckled, happily accepting a goblet offered by one of the passing servants. He sipped his wine and perused the crowd of finely dressed guests as they danced and mingled around the room. A celebration of his making. He might have been thrilled at the idea of asserting his authority in such a manner if he didn't know his mother well enough to know that this glory would be short-lived. And likely regretted.

"I don't think I'll ever forget the look on Mother's face," Derwin continued.

"Or Father's," Ferryl added. "They were both surprised."

"Well, it was kind of you, Ferryl," said Leala.

"You are the princess, Leala. It's about time this kingdom knew it, whether my mother likes it or not."

A tear glistened in Leala's eye as she stood on the tips of her toes to kiss Ferryl's cheek.

"All right, all right," said Derwin, taking hold of Leala's hand. "Enough kissing my brother or I'm bound to get jealous. Come dance with your husband."

The three of them chuckled, and Derwin whisked Leala off to join the dancers in the center of the room. Ferryl stood alone for a moment, basking in the odd combination of confidence and loneliness that plagued him like the moths that danced around his head. After a while, he noticed Delaney again, and found himself admiring her from across the room. He had never noticed her poise before. The ease with which she spoke with the queen, her father, the ambassador. She was beautiful, there was no doubt. Was it a crime to think so?

He was surprised when he realized he was inching his way towards her. He had rounded the first corner of the ballroom when he ran into his father.

"Well if it isn't the man of the hour," said the king as he clasped his hand on his son's shoulder.

"If you're looking for Derwin, I think you'll find him dancing with his wife," chuckled Ferryl.

"I'm talking about my son and heir. The one who proved his authority to the world *and his mother* in one fell swoop." The king beamed, a gleam of pride in his eyes.

"You must think me mad."

"Your mother is not easy to stand up to. I should know. I don't think you're mad, son. But I do hope you understand that she will retaliate. Maybe not today. Maybe not tomorrow. But she will find a way to retaliate."

"She retaliated when she sent Elizabeth away," said Ferryl.

"Do you have proof of that, son?"

Ferryl met his father's eyes, unsure how to answer the question.

The king nodded silently, lowering his voice. "Tread lightly, son. Your mother is not a woman to cross."

Ferryl nodded, his lips pursed, his mind deep in thought.

"Take heart, Ferryl. For if nothing else, you've shown her that you're not one to be crossed either."

"I'm not sure I understand why my own mother would feel the need to cross me in the first place."

"Now, now," said the king, sipping from his goblet. "This conversation has turned much too serious for such a pleasant evening. Go and enjoy the spoils of your crown."

"Thank you, Father."

"To my sons!" the king said merrily, lifting his goblet.

Ferryl returned the gesture, lifting his goblet and wishing he could ignore the sinking feeling in his stomach.

* * *

"STOP FIDGETING," SAID THE DUKE as he stood by his daughter.

"I'm not fidgeting, Father," said Delaney.

"You are. You look ridiculous. You are betrothed to the crown prince of Navah—a princess. Start acting like one."

"Father, go and find someone else to torment. If you're going to insist I give up my life for all of this, I'd like to at least enjoy the party."

"I certainly hope the prince likes a feisty tongue. Otherwise he's in for quite a disappointment."

"Does it really matter what he likes?" she asked, sipping her wine.

"Would you know? Have you even taken a moment to get to know him, or have you been too busy wallowing in your own despair?"

Delaney's head twisted to see her father. "You're insufferable."

"And you're a callow child. I'm going to get more wine." And with that, the duke shuffled away, smiling pleasantly at the guests he passed. Delaney could feel the bile in her throat at the sight of him. Pig.

"You look good enough to eat, wildcat."

Delaney jumped at the warmth of Ravid's whisper as it tickled her ear.

"Did I scare you?" he asked, coming to her side, but not too close. Just a casual conversation with an admiring passerby.

"If you make me spill wine on this gown, I may murder you."

"Perhaps, but you'd get blood all over it. And what's the point, then?"

Delaney couldn't help but chuckle. "You're ridiculous."

"And you are madly in love with me," he quipped. "So who is the ridiculous one, really?"

"Shhh," she scolded. "Someone will hear you."

"In here? The room is chock-full of drunken revelers intent on kissing both the royal asses as well as yours. I don't think I have anything to worry about."

She shook her head, ignoring the grin threatening to escape, sipping her wine again.

"Looks like the Pig-Prince is ogling his catch. He looks like he's ready to eat you up."

"What?" she asked, searching the crowd for evidence of Ravid's claim. Sure enough, Ferryl was staring right at her, a look she couldn't place in his eyes. Why in the world was her heart suddenly racing? She quickly took another sip of wine. Clearly, she was much too uptight for the evening.

"I had better make myself scarce. I'll see you later," he said, emphasizing later with a wink and a pinch to her waist. She slapped him away and squared her shoulders, determined not to let her nerves get the better of her.

* * *

AFTER THE KING LEFT HIM to mingle with some of the dukes and lords, Ferryl recommenced his edging around the crowd toward the duchess. It didn't take long to reach her, standing alone and lovely on the edge of the room, sipping wine and watching the merriment with a small smile on her young face.

"Your Highness," she said, bobbing a small curtsey upon his arrival.

"You look lovely this evening, Your Grace," he said kindly.

She blushed softly. "And you look handsome, Sire."

Ferryl met her eyes and found himself lifting her hand to his mouth.

The duchess blushed at the gesture. "I've always admired a man in uniform," she said in a small voice, and Ferryl didn't miss the nerves that saturated it.

Ferryl chuckled as he looked down to his dress uniform. "It has certainly been a while since I've worn these. I'm surprised they weren't too short."

"They're perfect," she said.

Ferryl gave her a warm smile, fidgeting with the goblet in his hand. "I believe I owe you my gratitude."

"Why?" she asked.

"Leala told me you gave her a dress for tonight. I am indebted to you. I'm afraid I didn't think about her lack of appropriate attire when I announced a feast in her honor only a few hours ago."

Delaney laughed. "It was my pleasure. A princess needs a formal gown for her first appearance."

"Indeed," he said, trying to read the expression on her face. Why had she extended such a kindness? And out of nowhere.

The duchess turned her attention back to the dancers, and a pregnant silence commenced between them.

But Ferryl couldn't help himself, and after a while, he managed to ask, "Why did you do it?"

Delaney took a moment to answer. "Your Highness, if you'll pardon my bluntness, I didn't think it was right that the queen wouldn't recognize her. Derwin loves her. It shouldn't matter that she's not nobility."

"Did you know?" he asked.

"Know what?"

"That they were married?"

Delaney chuckled. "It was rather obvious. I don't think a soul in the castle didn't know. They've been the talk of the court for weeks."

"The best-laid plans, right?"

Delaney smiled and sipped her wine again.

Ferryl met her eyes, but it took him a moment to think of what else to say. "Well, thank you, Your Grace. You don't know what it means to me."

"Delaney," she said.

"What?"

"You can call me Delaney."

Ferryl paused, surprised at the gesture. "And you can call me Ferryl," he finally answered.

Delaney smiled softly. And Ferryl couldn't help but notice it was a beautiful smile.

"What a lovely couple you two make," said a woman as she passed by, smiling toothily and lifting her glass. "We are all looking forward to the wedding!" Ferryl nodded silently before turning back to Delaney.

She gave him an apologetic look, but he shrugged it off. He didn't want to think about that tonight. In fact, he was tired of thinking about everything so much.

"Would you like to dance?" he surprised himself when he asked.

Delaney met his eyes, searching them for a moment. Perhaps she thought it was a trap. Or a joke of some kind. But to his surprise, she handed her goblet to a passing servant as she finally answered, "I would love to."

Ferryl extended his hand and tentatively, the young duchess took hold, letting the prince lead her to the dance floor.

The royal couple danced gracefully together, the eager guests nodding and smiling in approval as they wound around the dance floor. Ferryl was surprised at how easily they fell in step together, how easily Delaney fit in his arms. Even the queen's scowl fell slightly at the sight of them.

Ferryl didn't mind dancing with his betrothed and found himself asking for the next dance and the next—every time one song ended, he asked for the next. The dancing, the room spinning around them, the music—it was all a welcome reprieve from the thoughts and fears that had been plaguing him—and Ferryl didn't mind losing himself in the night.

And so he danced on, thoroughly enjoying the distraction of the duchess in his arms. She moved expertly—a practiced courtier, born and bred for this life. The dress whirled about her as she spun and dipped, as she held his eyes with her own. His hand rested perfectly in the small dip of her slender waistline, her body brushing against his now and then with the moves of the dance.

And in that moment, she was everything and nothing. She was the duchess brought to be his bride and she was the great love of his life. She was his beautiful friend and his passionate lover. She was Delaney.

She was Elizabeth.

Her long black hair flying behind her as she twirled, her waist small in his hand, the intoxicating scent of the lavender in her hair. He was drunk on that scent, on the primal need it aroused in him. He found he could do little more than take her in, body and soul. Devour her. For she was his, and he knew it.

Elizabeth had always been his.

And he needed her. Providence help him, he needed her in his arms. To touch her, taste her, know her. To remember. To learn all over again.

Ferryl stopped the dance, suddenly dropping his arms and stepping away. Away from Delaney. Away from the woman whose arms had wrapped so easily around him. Away from the woman who had fit so neatly in his own. Away from this counterfeit, this woman who was not his beloved. The rest of the dancers twirled mindlessly around them.

"Ferryl? Are you all right?" Delaney asked.

Ferryl met her eyes, his breath falling short. "I am sorry, Delaney. I am afraid I'm feeling ill."

"Can I do something?"

"No, no there is nothing you can do. Thank you for a lovely evening, but I regret that I must retire." He bowed—a quick dip of his head before turning on his heel, escaping the crowded room and practically running up the stairs to his chambers. Away from the crowd and the frivolity of the evening.

And that night as he lay in his bed, for the very first time in his life, Ferryl prayed for answers.

* * *

Chapter 33

Delaney's head was spinning. Partly from the perhaps excessive amounts of wine she had ingested this evening, but also from of the shock of Ferryl's sudden departure. What had happened? Had she done something wrong? She thought they were enjoying themselves. For a brief moment, she even entertained the idea that perhaps marrying the prince wasn't going to be the bane of her existence after all.

He was kind. He was warm. He was even a little funny. And he was certainly handsome. Perhaps she could manage to be his wife after all. Perhaps this kingdom wasn't the Sheol-hole she had assumed it would be.

But then he just left. Out of nowhere. Dance after dance, smile after smile. And then nothing. Dropped like a stone.

She had stood alone on the dance floor for a moment, too dumb-struck to move. But then her father had fetched her and shuffled her to the side of the bustling room, scolding her for sampling too much wine, which, he eagerly reminded, was not behavior becoming of a princess. And after her fill of his lecturing, she marched herself to her rooms, fully intent on drowning herself in a too-hot bath.

But a nice, scalding soak would not be hers either, for much to her chagrin, she returned to her rooms to find Ravid sprawled out on her bed, his auburn locks helplessly mussed, his tunic askew. His lopsided grin was nearly obscured by a rather unbecoming hiccup.

Drunk. Wonderful. She sighed loudly, shuffling across the carpets.

"You're pathetic, Ravid."

He curled a hand behind his head, propping himself up that he might watch her de-jewel herself. "You have to admit, the stuff they serve here is much better than anything we had back in Midvar. I must've drunk several vats of it tonight." He stretched, his lithe form much like an alley cat sprawling in the sunlight.

Delaney rolled her eyes, turning her attention to the looking glass as she peeled away layers of jewels and baubles, carefully arranging them on her dressing table.

"Aren't your servants supposed to do that?" he asked.

"Well I can't exactly solicit the help of my servants when you're in here sprawled out on my bed like a stray cat, now can I?"

"I don't think they care." He laughed, crossing his ankles.

It was true, though she was hesitant to admit. Conspicuously, not one servant had stumbled upon Ravid in her chambers. Not in the many times he had visited. Not once.

Which seemed a rather lucky turn of fate. Or something far, far worse...

She shook her head free of the thought. "You're quite brazen, Ravid. It would be a pity if you were to get caught."

He sat up, propping himself on his elbows. "Well, if I get caught, you'll get caught too, *Your Highness.*"

She turned to face him. "Precisely. So quit prancing around like a git and use your head."

"You're feisty tonight," he drawled, collapsing back onto the pillows.

"I'm serious, Ravid," she said, walking to the edge of the bed so she could sit beside him. "You're too obvious. You shouldn't have even spoken to me tonight. You saw how the prince watched."

"Yes, and he seemed *utterly* offended," he said, rolling to his side, pulling at the delicate buttons that ran down the back of her gown.

She angled away from his reach.

"Ravid, this is important."

He inched closer over to her, his stupid lips finding her neck, her exposed décolletage where all those diamonds had just been. "Mmm hmm," was all he said.

Heart pounding in her throat, she somehow managed to push him away. "Stop."

His feral grin curled the corners of his lips as he ignored her protests, managing to loosen her bodice with a few flicks of his practiced fingers. "I don't think he'll mind sharing, darling. It's not like he's in love with you."

Maybe it had been a flippant remark, a passive observation. But for reasons she couldn't explain, the words stung, a bitter tang in her throat. She shoved his fingers, his hands from her bodice and stood abruptly. "Get out."

"What?" He sounded teasing, an indifferent smirk on his narrow mouth as if she couldn't possibly have meant what she said.

"I don't want you here tonight, Ravid. Please leave."

He searched her for a moment, that Cheshire Cat grin slowly hardening to ice, then to stone. He stood, straightening his tunic before sweeping into an exaggerated bow. "Goodnight, *Your Magnanimous Holiness.*"

She did not take her eyes from him as he took step by casual step out of her chambers, the snick of the door behind him shuddering to her very bones.

* * *

Chapter 34

"May I speak with you, Ferryl?" asked Delaney from across the dining table, a glorious midmorning breakfast spread before them after a late night of dancing and merriment.

Ferryl gingerly set down his fork, surprised that Delaney was speaking with him like...like they were friends. Like he hadn't danced with her all night and then run like a coward without explanation.

He glanced around his father's dining room, but either his family didn't seem intrigued by this turn of events or they were damn good at looking preoccupied.

Ferryl let his eyes wander back to Delaney for a moment, searching. Wondering if she weren't plotting her revenge for his stupidity even now.

But he found no plot; he found no ire.

No, in her eyes, Ferryl found sincerity.

"Of course," he said, swallowing back his surprise, his sudden, insatiable curiosity. He looked around the room, knowing that, despite her current state of nonchalance, his mother's eager ears would be prying from any vantage point. "Would you like to speak privately?"

Delaney nodded, so Ferryl stood, taking her by the elbow when she made her way around the table to him and guiding her out of the king's dining room to his own private chambers.

"We can speak in here," he said, opening the door to his receiving room, gesturing for her to go before him.

"Thank you," she said as she passed, her liquid brown eyes innocent and surprisingly enchanting, her hair thick with auburn curls. Elegant, poised, demure—a duchess in more than title. And she was... damn it, she was beautiful.

"I wanted to apologize, Ferryl," she said quietly, her back to him as she faced the wealth of windows before her.

"Apologize? Whatever for?" he asked, closing the door quietly behind him.

"I know you don't want this," she said, keeping her back to him.

He took a breath. Then another. "Do you?" he asked, tentatively crossing the space between them.

She turned to face him fully, a myriad of secrets, stories, hurts in her eyes. "I was sent here on a mission. I want you to know that."

"What mission?" he asked with furrowed brows.

Delaney turned again to the windows, her dark gown whirling around her. She kept quiet vigil as she at last explained her meaning. "I come from a noble Midvarish family, as I am sure you are aware. We can trace our lineage at least seventeen generations. But my father... well, my father is not wise. He squandered our family's fortunes in the Great War." She looked over her shoulder, not quite meeting his eyes as she admitted, "We have nothing, Ferryl. Nothing but our name. My marriage to you is a chance to bring our family back from ruin. I want you to know this because I think you're a good person. And I don't want you to find out later and think that I've been trying to deceive you." She paused, drawing a heavy breath before turning to face him fully. "I will marry you because it is my duty and because I know that it is important for my family's legacy."

Ferryl stared, understanding that brand of obligation better than most. They weren't really very different, were they? Ferryl and Delaney. Two children of duty, bound to family expectation and trapped between heart and mind.

How strange to feel sorry for the woman you were supposed to hate. How strange to understand her. To even like her.

But he did, he realized. He liked her very much.

So he walked with purpose as he crossed the room and placed his hands on her shoulders.

Trembling. She was trembling softly.

"Thank you for telling me, Delaney."

"There is something else." She looked down, folding and unfolding her hands before her stomacher. "I know why you rode out every day when I first arrived."

"You do?" he asked, cocking his head to the side.

She didn't answer for a moment, and Ferryl couldn't help but wonder if a lecture was coming on, if that demure sweetness was about to be violently replaced with the signature temper tantrums about which he had been warned. Repeatedly.

"I know you are in love with someone else, Ferryl," she said quietly. "And I want you to know that I do not hold it against you. I, too, had a life of my own in Midvar. But it was a life I had to leave behind."

"And you had no choice in the matter?"

"Did you?" she asked, lifting her eyes to his.

A quiet pause, then he said, "I thought I did."

"Does one ever have a choice in the games of kings?"

"I don't want to be that kind of king," he admitted, dropping his hands from her warm shoulders. But he did not step away from her. Nor did she step away from him.

"I have no doubt," she said, a ghost of a smile on her rosy lips. "But you, too, will be faced with many choices. And so will I. Choices that will determine our fates, for better or worse."

Ferryl lingered in her chocolate eyes. "How did a girl of only seventeen grow so wise?"

The duchess huffed a becoming laugh, shrugging her narrow shoulders. "I am the eldest of five girls, Ferryl. I was ten when my mother died giving birth to my youngest sister. As the oldest, it was my responsibility to look after them. I did not have the luxury of a childhood." She turned away at last, facing the fireplace, her eyes distant and glassy. "You are a good man, Ferryl of Navah. I can see it in you, even only having known you these last weeks. And I believe you will make a good king. But you must learn to trust your heart."

Those words. So similar to what he had been told not so long ago. By the girl who held his heart. A flood of longing tore anew at his soul. "I don't know how to do that anymore."

She turned to face him again, taking his hands in hers. Soft. So luxuriously soft as she stroked her thumbs across his palms. He looked down at their clasped hands. Friends. Somehow, he had become friends with the Midvarish duchess.

"Go and look for her, Ferryl. Don't give up until you find her."

"It doesn't matter now. Our wedding is only a few days away, Delaney. Even if I did find her, I—"

"Then we'll delay it."

"What?" he said, meeting her eyes. Such sincerity shone there. Such eager, beautiful hope.

"We'll delay the wedding. Until you find her. I cannot simply call it off. My family would disown me—I do hope you understand that. But I can delay it as long as necessary. We can figure something out once she is found."

"But how? How could you delay it?"

Delaney's mouth turned into a wry smile. "I told you I am the eldest of five girls, Ferryl. I am well-versed in the art of tantrum-throwing and its inevitable effects on the heart of even the bravest of men. And women. And your mother has only reared boys. She has long since forgotten what a teenage girl is capable of."

Ferryl stood at a loss before the girl in front of him.

"I'll tell them I hate my gown. I'll tell them the guest list is all wrong. I'll complain of the castle being too humid or the flowers being wilted. Leave it to me, Ferryl. I can delay our wedding until such a time as we can make other arrangements."

"You would do this for me?"

Delaney nodded, looking down.

"Why?" he asked, taking a tentative step towards her.

"All my life, Ferryl, I was taught about the people of Navah. About how selfish they are—lying, deceiving, grasping, backstabbing. When I found out I was to be shipped off to the country of my enemies to marry their crown prince, I was angry. I felt betrayed. And when I arrived, I fully expected to find a spoiled, selfish pig of a prince. Instead I found a good man. I'd like to think I found a friend. I'll do this because I believe our fathers have been wrong, and our fathers before them. The world is not divided into good kingdoms and bad kingdoms. People are not good because of their nationality, just as they are not bad because of it. And I'm learning that enemies are only those who would fight without conviction of cause.

"You are not that man, Ferryl. I have watched you tirelessly search for the woman you love. I have watched you stand up for your brother when those around him either couldn't or wouldn't. You fight for those you love. So now I will help you fight for the woman you love."

Ferryl hardly knew what to say, could hardly think to form the right words. This girl, this surprising girl, was turning out to be a friend. Not an enemy. A true friend. How many of those did he have?

He cupped her cheek. "How could I ever thank you for this?"

Delaney smiled softly, a kiss of rose finding her cheeks.

So he pulled her to him, and he wrapped his arms around her, and he held her tightly—this unexpected ally of his. Her arms held him just as tightly.

"You will always have a friend in me," he said into her hair. And he meant it. Every single word.

"And you in me."

* * *

WITH NEWFOUND EXPECTANCY AND FLEDGLING, precious hope, Ferryl mounted Erel that very afternoon and set out in search of the woman he loved. Determined to look in the places he hadn't before, in the places he already had, with little knowledge of whether Elizabeth was running or hiding, Ferryl's unexpected friendship with the duchess fueled his heart with a hope he had not known before.

He would find her this time. Nothing could stop him now. He believed it to the very marrow of his bones.

* * *

Part IV

Chapter 35

He should not be hearing this.

Standing guard outside the duchess's chambers, hearing the words—the growling shouts, the vitriol, the poison being spewed like arrows raining down on the enemy—guilt washed over Michael.

He should not be hearing this.

But thanks to paper-thin walls and his damned curiosity, Michael was hearing it all nonetheless.

Not words. Weapons. A shouting match between the duchess and her father. How well he understood such things. He had known the same with his own father too many times.

It was obvious that the girl wasn't keen on the idea of being married off to the prince. But her father was equally as obvious in his intent to keep her in line, no matter the cost.

But this.

This argument was more than just an order from a father to his headstrong daughter. This was—this was warfare.

"I don't know what you want me to say, Father!" the duchess shouted.

Michael wondered if she had any idea just how thin the walls were in this palace.

"I don't want to hear another word out of your mouth unless it is *yes, Father* or *as you wish, Father!* You've been nothing but a thorn in my side since the moment you were born, Delaney! And this behavior of yours lately is absolutely unacceptable! I will not have it, do you hear me? *I will not have it!*"

Michael shuddered at the lupine ire with which the duke growled at his daughter. That kind of hatred hit too close to home. He couldn't help but wonder what the young girl on the other side of the wall must have felt. But he could probably guess. Because he'd been there himself—on the receiving end of a father's fury. And those kinds of wounds didn't heal easily. Or quickly.

Something like white-hot rage boiled inside him. How could a father say such things to his own daughter? And no matter the circumstances, what right did he have to speak so coldly?

"I hate you, Father!" the girl shouted.

"Well, then we can finally agree on something," the duke snarled, and the iciness in his voice gave Michael a start. He took a step back, staring at the door that separated them, unable to take it anymore.

"You *will* marry the prince, and you *will* cease with this ridiculous tantrum throwing at once. Or I will see to it that you are *shipped off* with the slaves. Do you hear me?"

The duke didn't bother to wait for an answer before he stormed out her door, surprising Michael with the speed at which he walked. The door slammed so loudly behind him that Michael started. But after a moment, the wake of the duke's rage finally ebbing, Michael could hear it.

It was small at first; a quiet little sound. Like a child. A whimpering breath, a sniffle. Tears. Tears for the pain from the kind of wound that never truly heals.

His fist was at the door, poised to knock. He wanted to go in, wanted to say something. But what? Would he tell her everything would be all right? How could he say such a thing? What did he know, and what could he do? He was only a guard. A nobody. And he certainly had nothing to do with her, nor with the royal family, their lives, their choices. It was only his job to protect them, to guard them.

But knowing he couldn't guard the girl inside the room from her father's hatred—from his ire—tore at him in ways he could never have expected.

* * *

Chapter 36

The days and nights became a blur of countryside, inns, and cottages, of mindless searching. Soon a week had gone by and another, and still no sign of Elizabeth. Not a soul in the kingdom had seen so much as a glimpse of a white-winged horse or the black-haired girl that rode it.

"Oh, I'd remember that, I would," one man had said. "Who'd forget a winged horse, Your Highness?"

Me, apparently, he thought sardonically. *She'd still be here if I hadn't forgotten.*

It became clear that Ferryl would need to venture farther out than what a day's ride could afford him, and he made plans to spend the night in outlying villages to afford him time to cover more ground before having to make the return trip to the castle. But north, east, and south, no one had seen her or her fabled horse. Not a soul in the kingdom, it seemed.

Where could she have possibly gone?

After several nights away from Benalle—and Derwin purporting the notion that Ferryl's absence was a result of being sickened with grief over the delaying of his wedding—Ferryl decided he needed a change of tactics, for the business of blindly searching the vast countryside was proving frustratingly unfruitful.

So Ferryl came home and decided to visit the one person who might be able to give him answers.

It was only as he knocked on the door of the small cottage that it occurred to Ferryl that he probably smelled as terrible as he looked, for he had been riding for four days, sleeping in dingy inns and cottages—even one night under a tree—without so much as a river bath. But before he could change his mind and return to the palace to make himself more presentable, Bedell answered the door, a look of surprise on his face.

"Your Highness!"

"Bedell. Do you have a moment?"

"Of course," said the old man, opening the door and gesturing the prince inside. "Is everything all right?"

"I do apologize for my appearance. I didn't think when I knocked, but I should have at least changed my clothes before I called."

Bedell laughed. "Perhaps you had other things on your mind."

"Indeed," Ferryl said with a nod, pathetically attempting to brush the dust from his boots before entering the little house.

"Would you like some tea, Your Highness?"

"I would actually love a glass of water."

"Of course," said Bedell warmly, fetching the prince a cup right away. "I was wondering when you would call. I had expected you sooner."

"You had?" Ferryl asked, surprised. He made his way inside, settling down into one of the two chairs facing the hearth. Chairs just like his own. Because he had been too blind before to notice. Too blind to see that he had forgotten about the love of his life.

"You've been looking for Elizabeth."

"For weeks."

"And have you found any sign of her?" Bedell asked, handing the prince a cup of water.

"Nothing. Nothing at all. It is the strangest thing. It's as if she vanished into thin air." Ferryl drank heartily from the wooden cup.

"Well," Bedell chuckled, settling into the opposite chair with his own cup. "While there are many strange possibilities, I am afraid vanishing is not one of them. At least not in the strictest sense of the word."

"Do you have any idea what happened to her?"

"I don't think anything *happened* to her. I think she *happened* to decide to leave."

"Did she tell you she was leaving?" Ferryl asked, straightening.

"Why haven't you asked me this sooner, Ferryl?"

Ferryl hesitated to answer, but upon hearing the old man call him by his given name, he knew the answer wasn't as strange as it sounded. The man knew him better than most, considering he was the father of the woman he had grown up with. He settled back into the seat. "Because I wasn't sure that she even wanted to be found."

"But you've changed your mind?"

He shrugged. "I suppose I've had my eyes opened."

"What does that mean?" Bedell asked.

Ferryl fussed with a loose thread in the tapestry of his seat. "It means that if it weren't for my persistent brother, I would likely still think that Elizabeth is a new acquaintance and not a girl I have known my whole life."

"And why is it that you had forgotten that, Ferryl?"

He looked up, meeting the watery, sincere eyes of the old prophet. The man his father had trusted for advice for as long as he could remember. "I don't know. Have you any ideas?"

"No, I haven't any ideas," said Bedell, a twinkle in his eye. At his answer, Ferryl deflated. But then, "I do, however, have answers."

Ferryl sat up. "You do?"

"Well, I should clarify that I at least know where you can find them."

"Where?" Ferryl asked eagerly.

"In Haravelle."

"In *Haravelle?* Did Elizabeth go to Haravelle?"

Bedell took an excruciatingly long sip of water before he finally said, "I don't know where Elizabeth went, and I didn't say you would find her there. I said you would find your *answers* there."

"Answers to what?"

"The questions you're asking."

Frustration mounted, welling within him. He swallowed it down. "And what questions am I asking aside from where I might find Elizabeth?"

"Now that is a good question," said the old man, raising a finger as he stared into the empty hearth.

Ferryl took a deep breath so as to allay his temper for the sake of the old man. "Bedell, I don't need riddles. I know of your thoughts on

Haravelle. You've mentioned them before at council meetings. But I'm not interested in gaining allies for a coming war. I want to find Elizabeth. I *need* to find her."

"And so you shall. For your destinies are of one purpose."

"When? When will I find her?" he asked, gripping the arms of his chair.

"Your paths will converge again when the time is right." Such nonchalance. Such simplicity in his answer. As if it were really an answer. Ferryl ground his teeth.

"If you know where she is, and you're not telling me, so help me, I—"

At last, Bedell looked him in the eye. "Ferryl, you must calm yourself. Now is not the time to lose heart. There is too much at stake."

"Is she all right?"

"Now that is a question that I cannot answer."

"Who can?"

"The one who knows the answer, of course."

Ferryl threw his head back and sighed. "Bedell, please help me. I have searched high and low with no sign of her. I don't even know she is alive. No one in this kingdom has seen her. It's as if she's invisible."

"Another interesting, yet erroneous theory, for invisibility is, at least in this point in our history, impossible."

His hands were at his temples now, doing his best to keep himself from tearing the frustrating old man apart. "Bedell, please. Help me."

"The answers you seek lie in Haravelle." To the point. No hesitation. No vehemence. Just a simple answer. As if the question weren't everything.

"Are you telling me to end my search for the woman I love in order to take a road trip to Haravelle?"

"If that is how Providence prompts you, yes."

How Providence prompts him? Did Providence do such things? "And what exactly am I supposed to find there, if not Elizabeth?"

"Answers," Bedell said.

"Answers. Yes. Well, I don't want answers, I want Elizabeth."

"Yes, I know. But you also want answers. Why else would you have come here tonight?"

"To lose my mind, apparently."

Bedell chuckled. "Son, while it is true that sometimes Providence may tell us the ends before the beginnings, he almost never tells us the roads we will take to get there, nor the snares we will encounter along the way. He tells us only what we need to know precisely when we need to know it."

Ferryl crossed his arms. "You speak on behalf of Providence?"

"I speak only what is given for me to say."

"And I suppose Providence doesn't want me to know where Elizabeth is?"

"If you don't know, it is because you are not supposed to know. And when you know, it will be because you are supposed to."

Ferryl wanted so very much to take him by the shoulders and shake some sense into him. But he knew full well from watching his mother deal with the old man that Bedell only said precisely what he wanted to say and not a word more. Perhaps he didn't know where Elizabeth was after all. Perhaps he was telling Ferryl all he needed to know. "Do you think she is all right? Can you at least tell me that?"

"Have you asked him?"

"Who? Providence?"

Bedell nodded, again staring absently into the empty hearth. Ferryl followed the old man's gaze.

"No," he admitted quietly.

"You have not because you ask not."

"I asked him for guidance on what to do." The other night. When he had prayed. He had spent the better part of an hour begging Providence for answers. For wisdom. For anything, really.

"And did he give it to you?"

"I think so," he admitted. Delaney's kindness, her offer to help him by delaying the wedding...that had felt more like Providential guidance than anything. But... "But it has only led to dead ends."

"How do you know that?"

"Because I cannot find her anywhere!"

"And what makes that a dead end? That it is not the end you wanted?" Ferryl met Bedell's eyes again before the old man continued,

"Perhaps you are not finding her now because Providence has plans for her too. Plans that, for the time being, don't involve you."

"So I just need to wait?"

"I'm not saying not to look for her. I'm saying to trust that you will find her when you are supposed to."

Ferryl exhaled through his mouth and returned to his pointless vigil of the open hearth.

"I know that's not what you want to hear, Ferryl," Bedell continued. "But Providence does not make it a practice to tell us what we want to hear. He makes it a practice to carry out his will. It merely comes down to a matter of whether or not we trust it."

"I confess I don't know much about the will of Providence," said Ferryl.

"You know not because you ask not."

Ferryl sighed deeply, giving himself a moment to take in the frustrating conversation. But somewhere in the space of a breath, he understood that Bedell was on his side. He loved his daughter as much as Ferryl did. Surely he missed her too. "I don't know why I'm thanking you right now, but I feel as if I should."

Bedell chuckled again, patting Ferryl's hand on the arm of the chair. "Oh, Ferryl, you have a good heart. And I am glad that you have given it to my daughter. But you should consider entrusting it to the hands of Providence as well. You might be surprised."

Ferryl stood, a sudden need to be alone, to think, engulfing him. "Thank you for speaking with me, Bedell."

"I am glad that you came," the old man said, standing as well.

"I am too. And now I bid you good night."

"Good night, Your Highness," said Bedell warmly, nodding his head in a bow.

And without another word, Ferryl crossed the small room and emerged out into the dusk, an odd sense of peace washing over him. For once, on the brink of war, his father had entrusted Bedell with their very lives. And as strange as it was, Ferryl knew deep down that he could trust him too.

* * *

Ferryl walked thoughtfully down the corridor that led to his chambers, wishing for little more than a hearty glass of wine and a healthy dose of silence, the hypnotic pattern of black and white along the floors before him lulling him into a trance.

The spell was broken by his name, spoken with a soft coo.

"Duchess Delaney," he said as he whirled around.

"You've been gone many days," she said, concern in her eyes as she walked thoughtfully toward him. "Have you still not found her?"

Ferryl shook his head. "Not yet."

Delaney only nodded, stopping a step away from him. Yes, it was concern in her eyes. But there was something more. Something...troubling.

"Are you all right?" he asked. "Is my mother giving you a hard time about the wedding?"

Delaney looked down, her soft features alarmingly blank. "It's nothing I cannot handle," she said softly.

So he took a step closer. "Would you tell me if it becomes too much for you?"

She looked up, lingering in his gaze before answering. "Yes."

"Good," Ferryl said, taking her hand and pressing a chivalrous kiss to her soft skin. "Now if you'll excuse me, I'm sure you've smelled all of me you can stand."

Delaney chuckled, a melodic little laugh that shattered the unspoken worry. "It's not as bad as you think."

"And now you are being unnecessarily generous," he laughed, turning to walk to his chambers.

"Shall I have some food brought to you? You must be hungry."

Ferryl turned to face her again, surprised at her kindness, her thoughtful concern. "You are sweet, Delaney. But you needn't worry about me. The only things I need at this very moment is a bath and a good night's rest."

She nodded, her eyes still distant, unreadable. "Very well. Goodnight, Ferryl."

"Goodnight, my lady," he said with a small bow.

And Ferryl did get his bath, and a hearty glass of wine. But as for a good night's rest, it would not be his. For his dreams were plagued with screams and cries, moths and darkness, and the terrible sense of losing something he would never find again.

* * *

Chapter 37

Her breath came in heavy gasps, her heart pounding inside her chest like the beating of a tribal drum, and from the hollow log where she hid, she could hear the thudding of heavy footsteps all around her, angry voices shouting with a lilt she couldn't place. She slapped a hand over her mouth and willed her lungs to catch up with the rest of her body as the voices drew near.

"Did you lose her?" came a low, rumbling voice from just behind.

"She can't have gotten far," came another voice, this one with a higher timbre and saturated with nerves.

"Find her," came the gravelly voice again.

"Yes, milord," the nervous voice replied.

Light footfalls scurried off and away, but Elizabeth stayed crouched in the log, stock-still and scared for her life. She had been running all night from the hodgepodge band of ruffians, and somehow she had managed to stay one step ahead of them, despite their speed and determination.

Whether they were Midvarish rebels or not, she couldn't be sure, for she hadn't a clue where she was or even if she was still in Navah. After nearly two months of wandering the countryside without any idea as to where to go or what to do, she had run into a gaggle of riotous men, keen on having her horse—and most likely her as well—for themselves. They were fast but she was somehow faster. Maybe it wasn't speed that was her ally, maybe it was little more than her will to live. For as eager as they were to capture her, she was even more eager *not* to be captured and fall prey to whatever they had in mind.

Eagle had been wise enough to flee when the rebels had attacked them on the outskirts of the small village. Thrown from her horse dodging the biggest sword she had ever seen, Elizabeth had fled to a nearby grove of trees. And Eagle had wisely disappeared in the opposite direction. Elizabeth didn't know where her beloved horse had gone or if she would ever see her again. She couldn't blame her if she didn't, for the life of a vagabond was no life for a creature as majestic as Eagle. Still, she missed the winged mare terribly already, almost as much as she missed her prince.

Ferryl. She wondered what he was thinking, how he was faring. That look on his face the day she had left. The devastation in his eyes. It had shredded her already torn heart. But she had done it for him— she had left for him, to spare him from his mother's ire, and to spare her father from the queen's vengeance. But she had also left for the answers that had been nipping at her heart for years—who she really was, where she came from, why her past was shrouded in such mystery. She had left to find out the truth as much as she had left to protect those who mattered most. To protect Ferryl from what she had always known—even when she had been reckless enough to pretend, just for a moment, that he could be hers. She had always known the truth deep down, that she could never have Ferryl. She could never marry a prince.

Her eyes stung, and she swallowed back the lump in her throat. She would not think about that now. She would not think about Ferryl's tender words, his sure arms, always there to hold her, to keep her safe. No, she needed to stay focused. For if these rebels caught her, there was no telling what they would do to her. The heavy footfalls of the man with the deep voice still crunched around her, and she held her breath as long as she could in hopes of evading his notice.

And thank Providence, it must have worked, for from a knothole inside the log, she spied him mount his horse and gallop away. Relieved, she let out a ragged breath and began scooting her way out of the end of the gnarled log, her knees scraping against the rough wood and brambles.

But no sooner did she emerge than she plummeted to the ground again, her belongings scattering around her as the heavy weight of a man pinned her down, his filthy hand over her mouth, his sour breath in her face.

"Thought you got away, didn't you?" he asked with a toothless grin. His skin was ruddy and pock-marked, even beneath the thick layer of dirt and grime and Providence knew what else on his face. "Tell me, what's a pretty thing like you doing all the way out here in the middle of nowhere?"

Elizabeth struggled against the beastly man who was not nearly as small as he had seemed, writhing and kicking even as she bit back a gag at his stench, but it was no use. The harder she struggled, the harder he pinned her to the ground. And there would be no use in screaming either, for his grimy hand stayed mercilessly on her mouth like a muzzle, while his other hand...

She sucked in a breath. So this was it. After months of wandering with little to nothing in the way of answers, much less adventure, this was how she would die—at the hands of a filthy man who would have his way with her before slitting her throat or strangling her, no doubt. For she had heard plenty of stories of what the rebels did to women when they got their hands on them. Hot, muddy tears fell down her cheeks as she kicked and writhed like a fish on the shore. The man only laughed.

"Feisty one, aren't you? I like a woman with a little fight in her." Elizabeth would have liked very much to have spat in his nasty face, had it not been for his nuisance hand over her mouth. But she was distracted from the notion when his beady eyes slid to the stone resting between her breasts. "Now, what's this?" he asked, his spare hand drifting slowly—too slowly—to the amulet.

Panic stole over her at the thought of this man taking her only link to her past. Never mind no one had ever been able to remove it except Ferryl. What if this filthy ruffian knew how? What if he knew some secret of this kind of magic that she had never bothered to learn? She had blatantly ignored magic for so long, even against her father's insistence. And now, with this brute of a man above her, while she didn't know what her amulet was or if it had any real significance, she certainly didn't want this monster having it either.

That's when she felt the tugging at the back of her neck. It wasn't hard at first, but in an instant it became frenzied, forceful. The man was struggling with every ounce of his strength to pull the chain away, as if brute strength were a match for it. It wasn't budging, of course.

Because strength of man was no match to the power of whatever had rested at her breast for her whole life.

And of course now—when a filthy man sat astride her, pulling, yanking at her necklace—*now* would be the time when she would realize that her father hadn't been nearly as naïve as she would have liked to think. *Now* she would see the truth that had been staring in her face.

Nothing like a heaping dose of panic to help reality settle in.

He yanked harder still, the chain a brand, searing into her neck with a white-hot burn. Reality settled in for him too, because the necklace wasn't budging. His ire only burned brighter.

"Think you're smart, don't you?" he growled, grabbing her neck, his thick hand a vice, constricting, suffocating...

She wasn't sure what came over her—bravery or insanity—but in that moment, she bit the nasty hand over her mouth, and in the second it bought her as he slackened his grip, she rolled away and grabbed a fallen branch nearby.

But she didn't get a chance to knock him out before he was on his feet and shoving her to the ground again. Her mouth was free this time, and she screamed as loudly as her lungs could carry before he had her pinned down again.

He ripped her dress at the bodice, pinning her arms down as he buried his face in her neck, working his knee between her legs. "You're a strong one, I'll give you that. But unfortunately for you, I'm stronger."

She braced herself for the worst, his strength overwhelming her as her head dug into the dirt underneath. But as quickly as he had overcome her, he went slack on top of her, his head bouncing off of her like a child's toy.

It took her a moment to register what had happened, and when she looked around, she found a boy, young and dirty, with the branch-weapon in his hand, panting and wiping the sweat from his brow.

"Did he hurt you, miss?" he asked, his voice croaking with prepubescence.

Elizabeth struggled to shove the beast of a man off of her, and with the boy's help, she sat up, the man rolling off to the side like a sack of potatoes.

"Is he dead?" she asked.

"Nah. Just out cold. We better get y'out of here 'fore he wakes. Damned rebels. They won't leave us alone," said the boy, offering to help her up.

Elizabeth took his hand—no larger than her own—and stood, her knees wobbling beneath her, her entire body shaking from the terrifying ordeal. She looked around the forest floor frantically for her things. But all that was left was her leather satchel, torn to shreds and missing most of its bounty, save for a few items. She grabbed it and hugged it to her chest.

"You okay, miss?"

"Let's just get out of here," she said, hoping her instincts weren't wrong. She had no choice but to trust him. The boy extended his calloused hand again—apparently eager to hold hers once more—and she gripped it tightly as he took off at a run, surprising her with his speed, considering his size.

"Me family's farm s'not far from here. Think y'can make it?"

"I have to," she panted, ignoring the searing pain in her back as she clumsily ran through the maze of trees. "Is this the Wild Wood?" she asked suddenly.

"What?" asked the boy in shock. "Mercy, no! This is just a grove of trees, miss. S'it look cursed to you?"

"Cursed? The Wild Wood is cursed?" she asked breathlessly, for the boy's speed seemed to be increasing.

"What? You din know that? Ev'rybody knows the Wild Wood's cursed!"

Elizabeth knew her eyes must have been as large as saucers, but it was nothing compared to the shock she felt in her heart. No, not everyone knew the Wild Wood was cursed. Particularly not her. Especially considering that's where she was found as a child.

"Who were those men?"

The boy slowed his pace enough to turn and look her in the eye. "Yer not from around here, are you?"

Elizabeth shook her head.

"Them's the Midvar Rebels. Nasty folk. They been terrorizing our village for months. Nobody can seem to stop 'em, neither. Not even the king's army!"

The boy turned past a long stone fence and headed down a dusty road. Elizabeth could see a small cottage just down the way.

"Is that your home?" she asked, thankful that his run had slowed enough that she could catch her breath.

"Me momma will be glad to fix you up, lady."

"Oh no, I couldn't ask her to do that. If I could just rest in your barn for a while, perhaps."

The boy's eyes colored with a look Elizabeth couldn't quite place—as if... as if the barn were the last place in the world he would ever let her set foot. Or maybe the last place *he* would ever set foot. "If me momma knew I'd found a pretty girl like you attacked by them rebels and left you t'sleep with the pigs, she'd have me neck!" said the boy, his words carefully, casually hiding whatever secret fear she had inadvertently revealed.

What in the heavens did that mean?

"All the same, I can't—"

"Why don' we jus' let me momma decide, how's that?"

Elizabeth nodded, following silently behind the boy who was determined to be her hero.

"Where are we?" she asked.

"The edge of the world, miss," the boy said, pulling her on as they approached the tiny, dilapidated cottage he called home. "Me momma's in here. Lemme get her. Just wait here."

Elizabeth nodded, feeling nervous as she stood, filthy and trembling, at the doorstep. She looked down to realize her dress had been ripped a little more than she realized, and she quickly grabbed the rags and pulled them together, doing her best to fasten them back in place with the remaining laces of the bodice. She succeeded in at least covering herself to decency again, wrapping her cloak tightly around her for good measure, and hoped that if nothing else, the boy's mother might see fit to help her mend the dress back to one piece.

Just then the door opened and a plump woman with a pleasant smile greeted Elizabeth.

"Child! What a fright you look! C'min, c'min," she said, ushering Elizabeth inside and sitting her down in the nearest chair around their small table.

"I am sorry. I don't mean to intrude. I was attacked and your son—"

"No need t'explain, child. Them damned rebels can't seem to get enough. I'm just glad little Jo here was there to help you. Providence only knows what they'da done if they'd had a chance. My cousin's daughter weren't so lucky."

The kind lady handed Elizabeth a mug. "Drink up. It'll cure what ails ya."

Elizabeth didn't hesitate and took several large gulps of the beverage before she realized that it burned like fire in her throat. She coughed as she caught her breath and the woman laughed. "Didn't say it wouldn't burn a bit."

"Thank you for your help. I will pay you, whatever you ask. I'm afraid I owe your son my life," said Elizabeth.

"Now, now, child. Jus' rest yourself. If we don' look out for each other, who will? Certainly not the king's army. Providence knows those poor fools are as tired as we are!"

"What king? Where am I?"

"King Aiken, child. You're in Navah. But only by a short walk. Midvar is just past the bend."

Midvar? She had wandered nearly to Midvar?

"How long have the rebels been attacking?" Elizabeth asked.

"Months, child. I'd say almos' a year," said the woman.

"A year?" Ferryl had known about the attacks and had been trying to do something about it. But a year? Elizabeth was fairly certain he hadn't known about them for a year.

"The army helped when they came, mind. But these rebels, they're soulless. Relentless. The army is tired. We all are. I'm jus' glad they didn't hurt you, child. Yer one of the lucky ones. What did you say your name was?"

"My name is Elizabeth."

"Well my name's Adina."

"Thank you, Adina. For all your kindness."

"O'course, child. Now you jus' rest up. The pigs'll be needing me. If you need anything, jus' ask little Jo. He'll be keen on helpin' you."

Elizabeth smiled at Jo as he threw his mother a pointed frown, obviously unhappy with something.

Adina shuffled out the front door, whistling merrily, and Jo stood from the table, squaring his shoulders and bringing himself up to every measure of his young, adolescent stature. Something glinted on his mouth and chin in the afternoon sun as it poured through the window and it took Elizabeth a moment to realize that it was the few sprigs of baby-fine hair that had sprouted on his chin. "You hungry, miss?"

"I am, actually."

Jo eagerly bustled over to the tiny kitchen and fetched a plate full of bread and cheese. "Momma'll be makin' somethin' warm tonight. This should hold you over till then."

"Thank you, Jo."

"It's Joseph," he said.

"What?"

"I don't like it when momma calls me Jo. It's a boy's name. My name's Joseph."

Elizabeth smiled. "Well thank you, Joseph. You're a kind young man."

"I'm not that young," he protested. "I'm nearly fifteen. I'll be old enough for a wife of me own soon. I've got m'self a farm and everything."

"That's wonderful," Elizabeth said, enjoying her little feast immensely.

"You wouldn't be interested in the job, would ya?"

"What job?" she asked, meeting his eyes.

"My wife. All the boys in the village'd be green with envy if they saw the likes of you on me arm. You're the prettiest girl I ever seen."

"Well, you're certainly charming, Joseph," she laughed, now understanding his desire to hold her hand. A hero—that's what he wanted to be. Her hero. "But I'm afraid I'm a little old for you."

"You can't be that much older."

"I'm nineteen. Nearly twenty. I've lived several lifetimes, Joseph, even since you were born."

Joseph shrugged and plopped himself into the chair across from Elizabeth. "If you change yer mind..."

"You'll be the first to know," she assured him kindly. She took another bite of her bread and drank from the bitter mug again. "What is this stuff?" she asked, lifting the drink.

Joseph's feral grin did little to assuage any concerns she had as to the contents of the beverage. "Me daddy use to call it his *special tonic*. But ever since I started makin' it, me momma calls it Fire Potion. I make it a lot stronger than Daddy did."

"And do I dare inquire as to its ingredients?"

"I always find it's easier if ya jus' don' ask questions."

Elizabeth half wondered if she had stepped into a witch's lair and swallowed a potion that would turn her into a toad. But it wasn't long before she felt the effects of the beverage, its contents warming and relaxing her, and she soon found that she cared little as to whether she would sprout warts and a forked tongue. Fire Potion, indeed.

She took a deep breath and relaxed into her chair, feeling more at ease than she had in months.

"Where is your father?" she asked.

Joseph didn't meet her eyes. He only looked at the table and fiddled with a mug in front of him. "Gone," was all he said, and Elizabeth knew not to ask further questions on the subject. She felt a pang of guilt for asking the question at all.

"I owe you my life, Joseph. Thank you for saving me today."

He only shrugged.

She smiled softly, intent on earning his trust. "Why did you do it?"

"Those rebels can go to Sheol. Them's hateful bastards. I'da saved anyone I saw them attacking. But when I saw it was you, well, I reckoned you'd surely need my help. They jus' kill the men. But the women..."

Elizabeth swallowed hard against a catch in her throat. Yes, she was quite aware of what would have happened to her had Joseph not arrived when he did. "How can I ever repay you?"

"Don' need to. Savin' your life was enough payment for me." Joseph stood from the table again and left the room without another word, and Elizabeth stared blankly out the small window for a long while.

She wasn't sure why she had been so fortunate today. But she was thankful nonetheless.

* * *

Chapter 38

What are you doing here?" the duchess asked the prince as he rounded the corner of the corridor near the Royal Banquet Hall.

Ferryl only smiled as he approached. "I thought I would help you out today."

"Help me out?" she asked, her chocolate eyes sparkling.

Ferryl took Delaney's hand in his and kissed it before answering. "You've been helping me so much, I thought I would return the favor. I hear Mother has been in quite a mood ever since you tore the gown." He couldn't help but chuckle at the thought of the young duchess giving his mother a run for her money.

"What about the search?" Delaney asked.

"I need to rest. I've searched everywhere I can think of with no results. I need to regroup before I continue."

Delaney's smile was surprisingly enchanting, and Ferryl returned it, offering her his arm as he opened the door to the banquet hall where their wedding feast was to take place.

"So what is it we're supposed to be deciding today?" he asked.

"Flowers. But I have a feeling I'm going to hate every one of them." A wolfish grin flashed across her rosebud mouth.

The pair stepped down a small flight of stairs into the great room, to be greeted by the greatest assortment of flowers Ferryl had ever seen. Row after row of impossible color and beauty took over the room, as if Spring herself had decided to set up headquarters in the banquet hall at Benalle Palace. It seemed the queen was intent on calling the persnickety duchess's bluff.

"Yes, it would seem that there are no decent floral arrangements to be found in all of Navah." Ferryl laughed, shaking his head at the absurdity of his mother's ambition. "This one may be hard to finagle."

Delaney laughed too. "I make it a practice to remain a step ahead, Ferryl."

The prince raised his eyebrow, and Delaney winked in response.

"Ah, Ferryl!" cried the queen, kissing her son's cheek upon his arrival. "So good of you to come! We could certainly use your help!"

"At your service." He bowed. "I take it we're selecting flowers today."

"Indeed," said the queen. "Hopefully, we can find something that will suit your bride's impeccable taste."

The queen gave the duchess a small kiss on the cheek, and when she couldn't see it, Delaney rolled her eyes behind her back for Ferryl's amusement.

"Hello, Father," Delaney said, greeting the duke as he approached.

"Hello, darling," Hevel gushed. "You are looking well. In a better mood today?"

"I am always in a pleasant mood when these meetings *start,* Father," Delaney retorted, and Ferryl couldn't help but feel a bit of awe for the sheer dread that struck both his mother's and the duke's face, even if only for a second. Delaney had been playing her part well, to be sure.

"Ah! Your Highness!" said the duke with a bow. "It will be good to have your influence this morning."

"Oh, no, no," said Ferryl. "I am merely a spectator. The lady has exclusive taste. Whatever my betrothed wants is what she shall have." Ferryl returned a small bow to allow himself a moment to wipe away the smirk that was attempting to escape.

"I see that Your Majesty has spared no expense in bringing nearly every botanical option in the known world to the palace today," said Delaney. "Seems a bit wasteful, doesn't it?"

The queen extended her hand in a grand gesture of the room. "It is essential that we find a way to please you, dear. I wouldn't want you to be disappointed."

Delaney gave a skeptical sweep of the room, and began strolling down the first aisle of flowers, her hands clasped behind her back. The rest of the party followed suit.

"Have you seen these?" the queen asked. "It's Queen Anne's Lace. I had them at my wedding. In my opinion, there is no more delicate flower. Perfect for such a special day."

Delaney scoffed. "It looks more like a weed to me. And besides, why would I want a flower that you had? It's already been done! I need something exquisite. Something unique. Something rare. Like me."

Ferryl bit the inside of his cheek to keep from laughing out loud.

"What about these?" the queen gestured to a small white flower with five petals. "It's called the Star of Beth—"

"Too plain," Delaney interrupted.

"Perhaps something in a color, darling?" suggested the duke.

"Color? What am I, a harlot?"

"Of course not, darling," said Hevel. "But I didn't realize you could be so particular. It's only a flow—"

Delaney rounded a corner, pivoting like a soldier, glaring into the eyes of her father. "Only a flower? Is that what you think? *Only a flower?* Father, it is my *wedding* flower! It is the most important flower I will ever hold!" Tears began streaming down her young face.

Tears. Damn, she was good at this.

"How can you say it is only a flower?"

"I'm sure what he *meant* to say," said the queen, giving the duke a withering look, "was that there are so many wonderful choices here. We are sure to find exactly what you are looking for among them."

"Of course that's what I meant, darling."

The queen embraced the sobbing bride, and Ferryl put a hand over his mouth to hide his growing grin. Perhaps Delaney had agreed to delay the wedding to help Ferryl. But it was entirely evident that she wasn't exactly begrudging the task of annoying her father. Or the queen.

"If only..." said Delaney.

"If only what, dear?" asked the queen.

"If only I could have the Crown Flower in my bouquet." She sniffed delicately and wiped her eyes.

"The Crown Flower?" the queen asked.

"Yes. I saw it once. At a wedding for a friend of mine. It is so beautiful. Perfect for a princess bride. I would give anything to have Crown Flowers at my wedding!"

"I think I saw some over here!" said the queen triumphantly, bounding away in earnest, the duke following after her like a puppy.

Ferryl stepped by Delaney's side. "The Crown Flower?" he whispered.

"It's real, don't worry. The only problem is its extremely rare. It only grows at high elevations in the Majestic Mountains."

"And what are you going to do if they find some here?"

"They won't. I've already looked."

The pair of conspirators leaned into one another, snickering like mischievous school children as they watched the frantic queen and the apologetic duke search the endless rows of perfectly acceptable flowers for the elusive request.

"I've never seen my mother like this. She's positively desperate."

"I told you I had a trick or two up my sleeve."

Ferryl chuckled, nudging her with his shoulder. "Thank you for this, Delaney. Truly. You have a gift." He winked.

"Would you think me a terrible person if I told you I'm rather enjoying myself?"

"If you're terrible, then so am I."

* * *

Chapter 39

Dinner was incredible, Adina. Thank you," said Elizabeth as she helped the plump woman gather the dishes from the table. It had been so easy to fall into a routine with this little family on the edge of the kingdom. As if her life in Benalle had never existed.

Maybe in some ways, it hadn't.

"Summer's almost over. It'll be autumn soon. The nights are gettin' cooler. I always like to make a pot of venison stew this time of year. Usher in the cooler breezes as quick as possible," Adina chuckled.

"Where I'm from, there's not much in the way of seasons," said Elizabeth. "It's always warm and humid."

"Where'd you say yer from, child?" asked the portly woman as she dumped a bucket of water over the dishes in the sink.

"The coast," Elizabeth answered, having no desire to explain her upbringing in Benalle Palace.

"Benalle Province?" Joseph asked. It wasn't a particularly astute guess, she surmised, as only the provinces of Benalle and Teman bordered the ocean, with Benalle gobbling up the bulk of the coastline.

"Yes." Elizabeth hesitated.

"Ever seen the palace?" he asked eagerly, his eyes lighting up the same way Ferryl's often did. He brought the remaining bowls and platter to his mother.

"Once or twice," she said.

"S'it as beautiful as they say?" Adina asked over her shoulder.

"More so." Elizabeth smiled fondly.

"Does it really sit right on the edge of the cliffs?" Joseph asked in awe.

"The ballroom has a balcony that overlooks the ocean. It feels as if you're standing on a cloud!" she said without thought, lost in her memories of the place she grew up.

"How do you know that?" Joseph asked, dumping scraps into a bowl, no doubt for the pigs.

Elizabeth caught herself and thought up an excuse quickly. "A tour. My father took me to see the palace when I was a child."

"Did you see the king and queen?" Adina asked absently, scrubbing away at the mountain of dishes before her, the steam from the freshly-boiled water billowing about her.

"And the princes." Elizabeth smiled again as she found a towel to begin drying the clean dishes.

"Is the queen as beautiful as they say?"

The queen. Heavens above, it wasn't easy to admit to her beauty, not when she resembled a viper more than a beatific monarch. But then again, there was no denying she was stunning. Ferryl certainly hadn't gotten his flawless skin, his golden locks and sensuous mouth from nowhere. "She is beautiful, there is no doubt."

"I've heard the princes are no disappointment either." Adina winked, handing Elizabeth a bowl.

Elizabeth chuckled. "Yes, I would say that I remember the crown prince to be particularly charming."

Adina sighed dreamily. "I'd like to see it someday. Seems like all your troubles'd be gone in a place like that."

"No, I don't think that's true," said Elizabeth, gingerly stacking the worn bowl she had been drying atop a few other clean dishes. "It's certainly a different kind of trouble. But kings and queens are no stranger to disappointment."

"You speak like y'know firsthand," said Joseph with an air of skepticism as he started to wipe down the small dining table. Elizabeth caught herself, realizing she was saying much too much for her own good. "I'm merely a peasant. A servant. But I don't suppose there's any person in the world immune to its troubles."

"She speaks truths," said Adina merrily, handing Elizabeth the last clean dish to dry. "Come now, let's have ourselves some of this cake, shall we?" She gestured to a small raisin cake she had taken the time to make that afternoon, and Elizabeth knew from their ramshackle surroundings that she had used the last of her flour and oil to make it. Her heart warmed at the kindness of the strangers she had found. And the ease with which she had settled in to their simple life.

Adina cut Elizabeth a healthy slice and placed it in front of her at the table before she served her son and herself. The woman sat down heavily, the small wooden chair groaning under her weight. "So tell me, child, what's a pretty girl from the coast doing all the way out here in the borderlands? You running from something?"

"Something like that," Elizabeth said, savoring the sweet bite that practically melted in her mouth. She should ask for the recipe; Ferryl would enjoy this cake.

Then she remembered that she would never cook for him again.

Her countenance must have fallen with her heart at the thought, for Adina gave her an appraising look.

"Broken heart?"

Elizabeth looked up, nodding when she met the kind woman's eyes.

"Men are fools, sweetheart. Don' let it keep y'down forever. Pretty thing like you'll find someone else quick as lightning."

She shuffled a few crumbs around her plate with the bent fork. "That's the trouble, I suppose. I don't want anyone else." From the corner of her eye, she saw Joseph listening intently.

"You will though. Someone'll come along and steal that sweet little heart of yours again," Adina said, devouring a particularly large bite of the sumptuous cake.

Elizabeth managed a smile and busied herself with her dessert, hoping for a change in subject.

"I'd take care of you, 'Lizabeth. You wouldn't haff to worry 'bout a thing," said Joseph suddenly.

A snort came from the portly mother beside her. "Little Jo, eat your cake, boy. I know you fancy yourself the man of the house now. But that doesn't make you a man. And you've no business proposing marriage to a girl you just met on account that she's beautiful. You need mind your manners and shut your mouth."

Joseph slammed his fork on the table and stood abruptly, the loud scoot of the chair on the hard floor startling Elizabeth. "Will I always be a boy to you?" he yelled.

"Well, you'll always be *my* boy, won't you?" retorted Adina, hardly flustered by his outburst.

Joseph stormed from the room, his young face red with rage. In some ways, Elizabeth felt sorry for him. He had saved her life, after all. "It's all right. I don't mind. He's not offending me. Honestly, I think it's sweet," she offered.

"Well, o' course it's sweet," said Adina, raising a knowing brow. "But he's a boy and you're practically a woman. I won't have 'im running off getting his heart broke over some silly little boy's fantasy."

"I would never—"

"Child, you wouldn't have to do anything more than walk in the room and every man and boy in sight would start gettin' ideas. Yer too beautiful for yer own good, you know that?"

"I didn't mean—"

Adina patted her hand and chuckled. "Child, don't get in a tizzy. Yer not to blame. All men are the same, whether they're fifteen or ninety-three. They all get foolish notions in their head when it comes to the opposite sex. But it's my job to make sure my son keeps his feet firmly planted on the ground until he's ready for such things as women and marriage and children and the like. And Providence knows, he ain't ready yet. So until then, I'll be glad to burst his innocent little bubbles."

"I don't want to hurt him," Elizabeth softly, staring at the door through which he had just barged.

"Elizabeth, the boy rescued you from a terrible fate. He brought you home to take care of you. Did you really think he wouldn't get any ideas of yer undying affection?"

"I didn't mean to give him any ideas."

"Well, you don't know much about the opposite sex now, do you?"

Only one, she thought, but she shrugged. Had that been Ferryl as well? A foolish boy with foolish notions of love? A naïve dreamer intent on ideas that could never be?

"Pay no mind, child. He'll be over it soon enough. And give his heart away to the first lass that so much as bats an eye at him. And you'll find yerself a man, not a foolish boy."

Elizabeth chuckled with Adina, and the two women finished their cake with pleasant conversation and delightfully hot tea before retiring for the evening, Adina insisting once again that Elizabeth take her bed.

"Child, you looked like you hadn't had a decent night's sleep in a month of Sundays when you arrived here. So quit yer arguin' and get yer little behind to bed. And I won't take no for an answer."

"Please, I'd feel much better if you'd just let me sleep in here on the floor," Elizabeth said, gesturing to the cozy but worn living room. "Or in the barn, perhaps. I can't take your bed again."

"With the stinkin' pigs?" Adina scoffed, slinging her hands to her hips. "My mother would roll over in her grave if she knew I'd been so rude. You'll sleep in my bed and I won't hear 'nother word, child. Go on now!"

Elizabeth couldn't help herself, too overcome with her kindness. She launched herself into the plump woman's arms and hugged her tightly, grateful tears pooling in her eyes.

"Hush now, child. No need to get emotional. We all know what the rebels are like. Jus' rest here as long as you need. You can figure out everything else later."

"Thank you, Adina. Truly."

"O'course. O'course," she said, patting Elizabeth's back. "Now off t'bed with you."

And Elizabeth did go to bed, nestling down into the warm, worn straw mattress. She let her mind wander, her thoughts restless with the questions before her. Where she would live. What she would do with her life now that she was away from everyone she loved, everything she had ever known.

A nameless orphan with nothing and no one.

The weight of it all hit her hard as she listened to the sounds of the night—crickets and hooting owls, nightingales and the howls of the nocturnal beasts that roamed these hills. None of the familiar sounds of home. No ocean lapping the cliffs. No whinnies of the many horses that lived in the stables near her cottage. No crackling fire and a father reading silently by its light well into the night.

And perhaps worst of all, no Ferryl.

The aching hole of his absence seemed to only grow with every passing day.

And here, amongst the kindness of strangers, Ferryl's absence pierced more keenly, a dagger slowly cutting down and down, cleaving her weary heart in two.

She thought about what Adina had said—that she'd find someone else soon. She thought about what it would be like to be held by someone else. To be loved. To be kissed...

A tear escaped her, falling warm and slow down her temple before pooling on the pillow behind her head.

Moving on, finding a new life for herself, had turned out to be a much more difficult task than she had anticipated.

* * *

Chapter 40

Delaney picked through the berries and cream, pastries, fried pork, and eggs that loomed before her. For some reason this morning, not a single bit of it seemed appetizing.

Perhaps it was the continued absence of Ferryl, although she didn't know why it should bother her that he was relentlessly looking for the woman he loved, considering she had sanctioned the idea to begin with. Or perhaps it was the fact that Ravid hadn't spoken a single word to her since the night of the feast in celebration of Princess Leala and Prince Derwin. In fact, as she watched Ravid ogle one of her ladies that had joined them for breakfast, she couldn't help but wonder if he had found solace elsewhere.

A wave of nausea swept over her, and she nearly retched right on the table.

"My darling, you look ill," said her father in the oily, phony fatherly affection he lavished on her for the queen's benefit.

"I'm fine," Delaney replied curtly, in no mood to indulge her father's behavior.

Ravid didn't so much as look up from the no doubt *stimulating* conversation with the courtier at his side. Delaney fumed, pushing the berries around her plate as another wave of nausea hit.

"Are you going to be sick, dear?" This came from the queen. "If so, I must ask that you kindly leave the table."

Such kindness from these people. Such courtesy. Fine. She could oblige.

"If you'll excuse me," she said, rising quickly from her chair, scraping it loudly across the floor. She practically ran to the door of the banquet hall, realizing that her haste was not only a good excuse to anger her father, but a necessary one, considering that she truly felt as if she would vomit.

What was wrong with her?

She tore through the corridors, feeling as if her chambers were a thousand miles away, her stomach tying in tighter knots the farther she went.

It was the guard with the eyes like steel—Michael, she seemed to recall—who was on duty outside her door.

"Your Grace," he said, rushing to her side. "Are you all right?" He didn't hesitate as he took hold of her elbow and guided her the rest of the way to her chambers.

"Can you just help me inside?" she asked, the pathetic weakness of her voice only contributing to the nausea.

Michael opened her chamber doors and guided her into her receiving room. He tried to help her into a chair when she interjected, "I think I need the privy."

"Of course," he said, guiding her with a firm gentleness that she didn't miss, even in her weakened state.

She might have taken a moment to feel embarrassed for retching into the lavatory in front of him if she hadn't felt like death as she heaved over and over again. But Michael didn't seem fazed. In fact, he rushed to the basin, wetting a towel with warm water for her.

She looked up from where she knelt, certain she looked worse than she felt, unsure why this stranger was helping her with such an intimate issue. "Thank you," she said weakly, taking the warm, damp towel he offered.

She patted her face and neck down, savoring the feel of the warmth on her clammy skin. The nausea was subsiding just enough that she could relax a bit.

"You don't have to stay here," she finally said.

"I don't mind. Unless you would prefer if I left."

She met his eyes. There was no calculation in them. No perfunctory response. Just...well, kindness. And for some inexplicable reason, her heart quickened at the sight.

She turned back to the lavatory, breathing deeply, doing her best to decide if she thought she might vomit again. But it seemed as if she was finished. And as she braced herself against the porcelain to try and stand, Michael was at her side again, lifting her with ease and walking her back to her receiving room.

"I think I'd like to lie down, actually," she said.

"Of course." So he led her to her bedchamber, holding her steady with one hand while he pulled back the blankets on her bed with the other. After he helped her settle in, he retreated back to her receiving room. Delaney wondered if she hadn't throughly embarrassed the man. Perhaps when she was feeling better, she would realize she was embarrassed too. She would probably never see the poor fool again.

But he came back. And he brought a glass of water and another warm towel with him.

"Are you all right now, Your Grace?"

"Delaney," she said.

"Pardon me?"

"You can call me Delaney."

"My name is Michael," he replied.

"I remember." She accepted the towel he offered, wiping her brow with the welcome warmth. "Thank you, Michael."

"Of course," he said.

He didn't linger much longer, making sure the curtains were drawn to her liking and she was sufficiently comfortable before he left.

But in his wake, she couldn't help but feel as if she might have just been helped by an angel.

* * *

Chapter 41

Still nothing," Delaney said solemnly as Ferryl answered the door to his private quarters. He merely shook his head as he stepped back, allowing her into his sitting room.

"It's as if she disappeared," he said, following the duchess to a grouping of chairs around the windows. Delaney took a seat without waiting for Ferryl to offer it. Comfortable. Casual. An easiness had grown between them in the last few days. Even as Ferryl still rode every morning in search of Elizabeth, every evening was dedicated to family dinners with his betrothed.

Dinners he had come to enjoy, if he were being honest.

Ferryl ambled to a small table and poured himself and the duchess each a glass of wine, offering it to her before he took a seat next to her.

"What I don't understand," she said after sipping from her goblet, "is why she left in the first place. If I had the privilege of being loved by a man the way you love her, I would not so easily walk away."

Ferryl looked up from his goblet, surprised at the duchess's candor, the way she had so nonchalantly admitted her thoughts. "I think she left to try to help me in some way. To find answers."

"Answers to what?" Delaney asked, clearly finding such a reason paltry at best.

"Why I forgot her," he said, his voice small. This part—this I-might-have-been-cursed-by-my-mother theory—he hadn't yet explained any of it to Delaney.

"What do you mean you *forgot* her?"

Ferryl sighed, swirling the dark contents of his goblet before telling her. Everything. Every turn of events, every wild theory.

"And you think your mother did this? You think she cursed your memories of the woman you love?" Delaney asked, but it wasn't to scoff, to cast aside his ideas. No, Delaney seemed...concerned.

He shrugged. "I don't know what else to think," Ferryl admitted. "I cannot explain why I do not remember her. And yet I also cannot explain why I have fallen so deeply in love with someone I feel like I hardly know!"

Her eyes—liquid with intent—searched him thoroughly, and he realized...he realized it was jealousy he found there. Jealousy for what he shared with Elizabeth.

And for reasons he could never explain, Ferryl felt sorry in that moment. Sorry that everything was such a mess. Sorry that she—this beautiful creature before him—had been caught in the middle of such a sordid tale. Sorry that she did not know the kind of love of which he spoke.

"I know why," she finally said, her words her guttural as emotion washed over her. "I know why you have forgotten her, but are still in love with her. Because magic—dark magic—it is only of the mind, not the heart. You've been cursed to forget her, yes. But there is no such magic that can destroy love. Not real love, anyway."

She spoke so casually of it, like she was...*familiar* with it.

"You've...seen it. You've seen magic," Ferryl reeled, setting aside his goblet, leaning forward in his chair.

She stared out the windows, her eyes distant, thoughtful. "I have seen my father curse a man to forget the tremendous debts he was owed. I have seen my uncle kill a man before his court with nothing more than his thoughts. Yes, I have seen magic. And it is the most wicked, the most base of all things." She faced him, boring into him with her chocolate eyes. "Anyone who practices it, Ferryl—anyone who would use magic on another person is corrupt to their very soul."

Bile. It was bile that burned in his throat. Bile at the sight of the resolution in her eyes. Because if it was true...if his own mother had cursed him... If his own mother was cursing his father too...

"Do you know who did this to you?" she at last asked.

Damn it.

Damn it all to Sheol.

Ferryl stood, pacing behind them, pushing a clammy hand through his sandy hair. "I don't understand any of this."

Delaney did not move from her chair as she watched the prince before her.

"I don't understand why she would do this at all," he confessed.

"It's your mother, isn't it? You think your mother did this to you." Not fear, not worry, but quiet concern and tempered resolve in her words.

"But it doesn't make sense," he said, still pacing, counting patterns in the carpet as he marched. "Why would my own mother stoop to something so drastic just to control whom I marry?"

"She is a controlling person, Ferryl. And I think you know that."

"Yes, she is. But she is not wicked. She is not. I know she has her faults, I know she is many things. But my mother is not wicked. *She is not!*" he pleaded, unsure if he was trying to convince Delaney or himself.

At last he stopped his pacing, and turning to fully face Delaney, he walked the few steps between them, clasping the back of her chair as he spoke. "There is more to this, Delaney. This is more than a mother trying to control her son's choices. This is more than a queen trying to control who sits on the throne after her. She's not telling me something, Delaney. She has secrets of her own."

"Doesn't everyone?" Delaney asked, tilting her head to one side.

Perhaps. Perhaps she was right. But he thought of that day. He thought of the apology his mother had given him, of the deep sorrow limning her eyes, of the ocean of secrets between them. "Yes, everyone has secrets. But my mother's—my mother's secrets are such that she has found a need to—"

A knock on the door tore their attention away from the conversation, and Ferryl absently walked across the room to answer.

It was Michael who stood on the other side. With a heavy burden in his eyes, in the slump of his shoulders.

"Ferryl," he said, bowing his head to his prince.

"Michael, what is it?" Ferryl asked the guard, worry nearly choking his words.

Impossible silver eyes met his again for a moment before Michael finally said, "I need you to come with me."

"Has something happened to Father?" Ferryl asked, nearly panicking when he realized Derwin was behind Michael, quiet worry pulling at him too.

Shit.

"No, the king is all right," Michael said. "Just come with me."

Ferryl turned to see the duchess standing by her chair across the room, her brow furrowed in concern and question. He merely bowed his head to her before following his brother and Michael down the corridor.

* * *

"MICHAEL, WHAT ARE WE DOING out here?" Ferryl asked. Mounted on Erel, he had followed Michael and Derwin on horseback deep into the mossy, overgrown hazelnut forest. Nearly to the Secret Place—not that they knew where it was. Or the fond memories it held.

Memories, he suddenly realized, that probably belonged to Elizabeth too. Memories that had been stolen—ripped from him.

By dark magic.

By his own mother.

He gripped the reins tighter, pushing back the shattering thoughts, the consuming anger that threatened to eat him alive.

But then Michael's horse slowed, Derwin's as well. So Ferryl stopped, following in stride and dismounting from his steed. It was only when he stepped over a particularly thick and knotted root that he saw what had captured their attention.

For there, across the way, amidst a sea of moss and fern, a labyrinth of branches and brambles, was a shock of white and crimson.

A snow-white carcass.

With wings.

Ferryl stopped dead in his tracks, unable to step any closer.

"When?" he managed. "When did you find this?"

"Some of my men found it this morning," said Michael solemnly. Ferryl dared not step any closer.

"But what...what does this mean?"

"I know you don't remember this, Ferryl," said Derwin, "But Eagle never left Elizabeth's side. Ever. From the time we were children and Elizabeth found her wild and wandering these woods, one touch of Elizabeth's hand and that was it. The beast has never left her side. They were inseparable."

No. No, he hadn't remembered that. Because he remembered nothing.

A knot formed in his throat. Elizabeth would be devastated to learn of the death of such a glorious creature. Of her friend.

"There is more, Ferryl," said Michael, clasping Ferryl's shoulder and turning him to face his brother.

In his hands, Derwin held a cloak. A green woolen riding cloak, tattered and torn.

Soaked in blood.

The world.

Just.

Stopped.

"We think this belonged to her," said Derwin, unable to meet Ferryl's eyes. He didn't have to explain. Ferryl knew who he meant. He realized Michael's hand was still on his shoulder, trembling even as he tried to comfort his friend.

"But how do you know? It could be anyone's!" Ferryl protested. "Show me the body!"

"Ferryl," Michael said.

"Show me! I want to see the body!"

Panic welled deeper and deeper and deeper...

"Ferryl," said Derwin, clasping his other shoulder. "There is no—"

"Don't try to protect me. Just show me!" Ferryl barked.

"There is no body," Derwin finally said. "There is nothing left but bones and a few feathers. They were attacked, Ferryl. Attacked and eaten."

Ferryl pressed his hands to his face just to see if he was really here. If this wasn't some sort of nightmare. But it wasn't. It was real. He was here. Alive.

And Elizabeth was dead.

* * *

FERRYL COLLAPSED INTO THE SETTEE that faced the fireplace, feeling numb, speechless, lost. He said nothing, only stared blankly, as if the world had stopped turning.

"Ferryl, you need to drink something." This came from Leala, whom he hadn't even realized had followed them into his chambers. She disappeared, reappearing soon with a cup of water in tow.

Ferryl stared at the flames, realizing he had never appreciated their beauty, their mesmerizing ability to distract an otherwise broken heart.

Leala placed a warm hand on his cheek as she knelt before him. "Oh, Ferryl," she breathed, tears lining her own eyes.

Tears for Elizabeth. For her friend.

Ferryl didn't answer. He could hardly see her before him. He could barely understand anything about his room, his life.

"Drink this," Leala said, placing the goblet at his lips.

He drank clumsily, but the water felt good on his throat, and he was thankful for the attendance. Leala pressed a kiss to his brow, wrapping her arms around him for a good moment. He pressed into her embrace, the silence ringing in his ears. When at last she let go, Derwin went to her side, snaking his arm around her waist.

"What are we going to do, Derwin?" she whispered, but Ferryl caught them. Like everything else, they seemed far away.

"Pray, love. That's all I know," Derwin said.

Leala knelt before Ferryl again, placing her hands on either side of his face. Maybe she wanted to say something. Or maybe she didn't know what to say. It didn't really matter. Ferryl had nothing to say. Nothing worth saying. Nothing that mattered.

Thick tears lined his sister-in-law's eyes, her lip quivering with emotion. But he could find no strength to comfort her. To say anything at all.

As the silence yawned between them, he watched her place a hand over her mouth, her own emotion growing.

Drowning.

"Oh, Derwin, this is terrible," he heard her say softly. "How did this happen?"

"I'd bet the entire treasury that my mother is behind this," his brother grumbled.

But Ferryl didn't care who was behind it. Or why. Not anymore. He didn't care about anything except Elizabeth. Sweet Elizabeth. The woman he loved. The woman who was gone forever.

An inescapable permanence. A finality. An absolution of darkness.

And by it, Ferryl would be swallowed whole.

* * *

Chapter 42

Delaney shuffled down the front steps of the palace, determined to get some fresh air, to think, to clear her mind. The last few days had been a blur of nausea and exhaustion, not to mention a palpable silence from Ferryl. Something was wrong with him—something had happened when Michael had visited his chambers the other day, there was no doubt. But in her exhaustion, and his obscurity of late, she hadn't had a chance to ask him about it. And even if she did, what would she say? Despite their unexpected friendship, she wasn't sure she had any right to pry into his personal life.

Still, it had been unsettling enough that she needed a chance to breathe the fresh air. The sun was setting over the ocean behind the palace as she walked down the long pathway that led to the gates. The gravel crunched beneath her boots, and the ocean breeze was as welcome as it was cleansing.

But soon she noticed another shadow coming up from behind to merge with hers. She turned and saw him, walking with that confident gait of his, his shoulders back, his sword gleaming in the golden sun, his smile a work of art.

"Your Grace," Michael said warmly as his thatch of chestnut hair rustled in the breeze. "It's good to see you out and about. I take it you're feeling better."

"I am this evening, thank you," she said, wondering if he felt as awkward as she did. For the last time he had seen her...

"You've been ill the last few days. I've been worried about you."

"It's getting better, I think." And thank the gods for that, for if she retched in front of him again...

Michael nodded. "Have you been to see the healer?"

"No."

"I would be glad to take you to her, if you'd like."

"That's all right. Thank you. I'm sure I'll be fine."

Michael clasped his hands behind his back as he strode beside her, but he walked just close enough that his shoulder brushed hers every now and then. She found she didn't mind.

"I hope so," he said, and at that, she met his eyes. He didn't hesitate to meet hers, either. And his smile...gods, there was such genuine kindness in his smile. She quickly looked ahead again.

"I never thanked you for your help the other day," she finally managed.

"There is no need to thank me, Your Grace."

"Will you not call me by my name?"

Michael's steel eyes met hers, and he chuckled. "I do apologize. I have a hard time with informalities. The prince gets on to me for the same thing."

Delaney chuckled too, put at ease by his casual gait, his simple kindness. "You've seen me retch like a drunkard. I'm fairly certain we're well past propriety. You should call me Delaney or else I'm going to be even more embarrassed than I already am."

He took hold of her elbow, but dropped it immediately when she stopped walking. "You have no reason to be embarrassed."

"Yes, but of all people in this palace, it had to be you that helped me."

"Is that a problem?" he asked, a twinkle of mirth in his eyes.

"I just meant that it's beneath you to do something like that. It should have been one of my servants, although they seem to be scarce most of the time, for reasons I've yet to define."

"I would help you again, if given the chance," he said, taking her completely off guard. This one. He was too kind, especially considering he didn't even know her. Come to think of it, why *was* he so kind? Was he some sort of spy for her father? Or the queen? Delaney met his eyes again, searching for any sign of betrayal. But there was only that genuine kindness, that sparkle of wit, that glimmer in the depthless silver that reminded her of moonlight spilling across the sea. This man was a mystery.

She needed a change in subject. She began her lazy stride again, and Michael fell in step beside her.

"Do you know what is wrong with the prince?" she asked.

Michael was silent for an uncomfortable minute, and Delaney feared she had asked the wrong question. But to her relief, he answered anyway. "You haven't heard?"

"No one really talks to me," she admitted, although she wasn't sure why.

"It's Elizabeth. She is..."

Delaney stopped walking to turn to face him again. "What happened, Michael?"

She could have sworn she saw a flash of delight at her use of his name before he said, "It has been discovered that Elizabeth is dead." His voice was small, mournful.

"Dead?" Delaney breathed, more to the air than to him. She could feel her breath growing shallow, her heart picking up its pace. What would this mean? For Ferryl? For their marriage? Was she going to marry the prince after all? Or would he send her away in his grief, too stricken to even consider marriage? And why did it bother her so?

"Are you all right?" Michael asked, placing his hand on her arm. His touch was tentative yet...yet it was firm. Strong. Solid. Like a fortress, a shield. Like he would give his life to protect her. Then again, he was a guard. That was his job, she supposed.

She met his eyes again, nearly falling into his arms at the concern she saw. But she reminded herself that he was nothing more than a concerned guard. A kind one, to be sure. But he was merely doing his job. And she certainly couldn't be seen in his arms. Not now. Not now that—

"I just can't believe it," she said. "After all his searching. I had no idea, Michael. He must be devastated."

"I've never seen him like this. He loved her very much. He has loved her since they were children."

"He has?"

"They grew up together here at Benalle."

"I didn't know that," she said, her heart aching for the man she called her intended. How his heart must be grieving.

"You are kind to show such concern. I know he would appreciate to know that you care. Ferryl is a good man. I don't think I've ever known a better one."

"I had better get back to the palace," she said. "Thank you for telling me, Michael."

"Of course," he said with a small bow.

* * *

Chapter 48

Too many days had passed since Ferryl had discovered that the love of his life had been taken from him. Too many days of numbness. Too many days of nothing but blank emptiness, like a night that would never turn to day again. Black. Empty. Starless.

Ferryl, the abyss of endless black that should have held the stars—and Elizabeth, the sun that had been snuffed out, leaving behind a world of midnight. Of silence. Of emptiness so keen it tore him into shreds, minute by excruciating minute.

For any chance of hope, of love, of life, was gone forever.

Never to be had again.

Ferryl stared at the food on his plate, wondering if he'd ever find an appetite again. Wondering if he'd ever care about things like eating or dancing or living at all again.

"Are you going to eat anything?" Delaney asked quietly from across the table.

Ferryl hadn't even the energy to shrug his shoulders.

She reached out her hand across the table, taking his in hers and squeezing it gently, her face a concerned smile. Ferryl thought her hand might be warm in his and wished he could find a way to enjoy it, to appreciate it. But he could feel nothing but cold.

Empty.

Alone.

* * *

Chapter 44

"Momma! Momma! You gotta come see this!" cried Joseph as he tore into the house.

"Little Jo, quit yer yelling! What's gotten into you?" Adina said.

"Ye'll never believe what's outside!" he said, unable to mask his youthful exuberance.

Elizabeth rubbed the sleep from her eyes, the commotion outside waking her from a deep sleep. She wasn't sure she was ready to get out of bed yet, considering she had spent half the night reading and the other half dreaming vivid dreams. Her father's ancient book—one of the few possessions she had managed to salvage from her attack—had ended up being a source of great comfort as she slept in the cottage with the kind strangers. Its words were as strange as they were intimidating, speaking of the creator like he was a knowable man, a friend in times of trouble, a comforter in times of need. It had captivated her in a way she hadn't expected, keeping her up into the wee hours of the morning, reading by candlelight. And then, when sleep finally found her, she had been lost in a glittering golden world of games and laughter, of hiding and seeking. But just as always, the dream had ended just before she could see who had found her. His face was a blur, despite his voice being clear and unknown. But one thing was certain, every time she dreamt of the glittering halls, she thought she was playing childhood games with her father. And every time, just before the dream ended, she realized she was not.

She heard Joseph implore his mother again and decided she ought go and see what was the ruckus. She yawned as she bustled into the tiny living space. "What's going on?" she asked groggily.

"Little Jo's yelling wake you up, child? I told him to quit it!" said Adina.

"Momma, you gotta see this!" Joseph yelled again.

"Child, what's got you in such a state?" Adina asked.

"Come outside and see! It's a winged horse!"

Adina scoffed. "Bah, son. We see 'em all the time 'round here! Now, Elizabeth, since you're up, why don't we do something about that tattered rag you call a dress? I think I might have something to fix you right up."

All the time? They had seen a winged horse before?

Adina tried to usher Elizabeth over to her cupboard, but Elizabeth resisted, intent on seeing the winged horse for herself.

"No, Momma. Not like this. This one's diff'rent. It's tame," said Joseph.

At this, Elizabeth couldn't help herself. She pushed her way through the small cottage and outside to see what all the fuss was about. She wondered if she dared to hope. But there before her eyes, in all her glorious splendor, stood Eagle, grazing casually in the green grass, her white hair glistening in the sunrise like a diamond.

She stood dumbfounded for a moment, hardly able to believe the miracle before her eyes. But when it became apparent that Eagle was no apparition, Elizabeth tore across the ground, straight to her beloved mare, throwing her arms around her neck and weeping madly.

"Oh, Eagle! I thought you were lost forever!" she cried. She stroked the silky horse, weeping into her strong muscles and sinews, feeling immensely grateful to see her friend, her tie to home, her past.

"Miss?" she heard quietly from behind.

She turned to see the awe in Joseph's eyes.

"Is this...yours?" he asked in a small voice.

Elizabeth smiled. "Her name is Eagle. She is my friend."

"Your friend? But how...?"

"What's all the fuss about?" Adina called, shuffling her way across the field to the scene.

"Momma, she's got a tame one!" Joseph said.

"Heavens, child. Where'd you find the likes of her?" Adina cried.

"She just showed up one day. When I was young." Elizabeth shrugged—as if it were normal that a rare beast should show up and befriend a child.

"And she didn't run wild? And buck and whinny like a madwoman?" asked Joseph.

"She did," said Elizabeth, wondering what in the world they would think of her when they knew the truth.

"But how did you...?" Joseph stumbled.

Elizabeth shrugged quickly. "I don't really know. I just...asked her to calm down."

"You *what?*" Adina asked, huffing as she approached.

"You asked her?" Joseph gawked. "And she just obeyed?"

"I wouldn't say she obeyed. I would say she just...relaxed." Elizabeth shuffled her feet and tried to look at anything but the boy or his mother, unsure what in the world they could be thinking of her. For she wasn't lying—that's exactly what had happened. One morning when Ferryl and she were out playing, two children exploring the forest, they had stumbled upon the miraculous mare—her wings extended, her eyes wild and violet as she tore through the forest. But at the sight of Elizabeth and Ferryl, for whatever reason, Eagle had stilled. Long enough for Elizabeth to approach her. To touch her. And in that touch, everything had changed.

Adina and Joseph stared with gaping mouths at Elizabeth. Perhaps they would decide she was a witch and must be burned. Or mad. No matter their conclusion, she wasn't prepared for their reaction.

"That's some might powerful magic you got there," said Adina, and the awe in her voice wasn't lost on Elizabeth.

"Magic?" Elizabeth balked. "No, no, I don't have magic. I don't even believe in magic." But didn't she? Wasn't that why she was running in the first place? Didn't she want more than anything to find an answer to what had happened to Ferryl?

"Yes, I've heard that about you folk from Benalle Province. It's like you've got a blindness to it," said Adina matter-of-factly, as if magic were as mundane and regular as the air.

"Jus' because you don' believe in it don' mean it ain't real," said Joseph.

"Magic? It's...real?" Elizabeth knew she must have looked like a gawking child, but she hardly cared.

"What do you think happened to all th'other horses?" Joseph asked, inching his way closer to Eagle, obviously eager to touch her, as if she were a rare jewel.

"What do you mean? What other horses?" Elizabeth asked, gesturing for Joseph to feel free to touch the mare.

"The other winged horses. They're not feral, child, if that's what you thought. They're wild. Cursed. Haunted," said Adina.

"There are more?" Elizabeth asked, awed at the prospect.

"Lots, lots more."

"And they're haunted?"

"By the darkness. The magic of Midvar," said Joseph with an edge to his voice, as if he were proud to know something she didn't. He stroked the horse's neck, gently pulling her soft mane through his fingers.

"The magic of Midvar?" Elizabeth repeated. Hadn't her father spoken of it? Hadn't he told her it was likely the culprit for whatever had happened to Ferryl? And now she was being told it was that same magic that had once haunted Eagle. Before she was tamed...at Elizabeth's touch...

Adina nodded as Joseph stepped around the majestic beast, marveling at her beauty, her grace, her otherworldliness.

"You must have some kind of power to be able to reverse the curse, child. I've never heard of anyone doing it, and believe me, I've seen many hurt trying, including my harebrained husband, Providence rest his soul." Adina placed a hand over her heart at the mention of her late husband. Elizabeth shot a glance to Joseph, who only looked down, suddenly fascinated with a pebble under his worn boot. But Adina didn't back down.

"I don' know a soul around here who wouldn't give their eyeteeth to tame one of these things," she said, petting the glorious mare down her silky mane. "And you say y'did it just by asking?"

Elizabeth met Adina's eyes for only a moment before feeling too exposed. She looked away, unsure how she felt knowing that she had magic of her own. "I guess," she backtracked, hating the lie as it passed her lips. Why did the idea of having magic bother her so?

She remembered the moment like it was yesterday. And the horse, so majestic yet so dangerous, seemed instantly at peace with one word from her mouth. Even Ferryl had admitted it was a miracle. Perhaps it was that they were only children when it happened, or perhaps time had robbed her of the significance of the moment, but here, as she stood next to her winged friend, seeing the awe in the mother and son's eyes, she knew it was no fleeting moment. She had used magic. Even without knowing she had it. Which led her to wonder—did anyone else she knew have magic they were unaware of? Did Ferryl? She thought of her father's stories, of how he knew Ferryl had a special power about him. That's why he had been sent to Haravelle during the Great War. Hadn't Bedell always called him the Protector of their realm? Did Ferryl have magic too?

"You mean y'really didn't know what you were doing?" Joseph asked in disbelief.

"I was a child," said Elizabeth in a small voice.

"A child?" Adina cried, her eyes alight with shock...and wonder. "Your magic was powerful enough as a *child* to do this?"

"Is that...not normal?" Elizabeth asked, looking at her beloved mare, wishing her long-time companion could offer some sort of comfort at the moment. *No, Elizabeth. You're not crazy. You just have magic. Does it really come as that much of a shock?*

Yes, Eagle. Yes, it does, she mused.

"Child, there's magic everywhere, but there's very few who ever find it. And even fewer who know what to do with it when they do. That you could tame such a feral beast on your own with nothing more than your words when you were a child is something, believe me. I've seen grown men get nearly trampled by the things. They're monsters!" Adina said, nodding her head toward the forest beyond her land.

Monsters? It was difficult to think of Eagle as anything but a rare creature of grace and majesty. And certainly not a monster.

"You say there are more around here?" Elizabeth asked.

"There's a whole herd of them. They run like banshees through the Wild Wood. By the thousands," said Joseph.

"By the thousands?" Elizabeth gawked again.

Adina nodded.

"And you said they were cursed?"

Adina nodded again.

"But why?"

"Magic, child. Magic is power. I told you—there are few who know what to do with it when they discover it in themselves. But I didn't say they don't try. Especially the Midvarish. They are known for their... experiments."

"Experiments?"

It was Joseph who spoke next, a little too eagerly. "Them's mad men, the Midvarish. They won't stop until they know everything there is to know about magic. And their favorite creatures to experiment with are the ancient winged horses. N'body knows if there're any left they haven't turned wild with their 'speriments and games. They're ruthless, the Midvarish are."

"D'your parents know the kind of magic you got, child?" Adina asked.

"I don't really know who my parents are," she answered without thinking.

"You don't?" asked Adina.

"I was taken in by an old prophet in Benalle when I was a child. I have no parents."

"Does he know?"

Elizabeth thought about the question. Did Bedell know of her magic? Logic would tell her that he had to, for he believed in magic deeply. And if he believed in it, then surely he recognized it. And if he knew it, then what did it mean about her prophecy? The prophecy that called her the *Promised One*. Did that have something to do with her powers?

"I suppose he must," she finally admitted. "I never asked."

"Don't know how he could miss magic like that," said Joseph, and Elizabeth noticed the newfound respect in his eyes, which she was fairly certain was doing nothing to waylay any ideas he had about convincing her to marry him.

"Can you take me to them?" Elizabeth suddenly asked.

"To what?" he asked.

"The horses. Can you take me to see them?"

"To the Wild Wood?" Adina balked, and Elizabeth didn't miss the motherly protest rising in her voice.

"Yes, I can," said Joseph without hesitation, his adolescent chest sticking out proudly.

"Now just a minute," said Adina.

"Momma, yer always saying I need t'grow up. Well, how can I grow up if y'won't let me?"

Elizabeth wanted to jump in, to plead on his and her own behalf, but she couldn't imagine anything to say that wouldn't sound desperate. After all, what mother in her right mind would allow her still young son to escort a female to whom he was obviously attracted into a dangerous and unknown place like the Wild Wood, just for the sake of seeking out some feral horses? Yes, it was a crazy request, but one she was making anyway.

"Besides, you said it yerself—she's got mighty powerful magic. What's gonna happen to us?" he added.

Never mind that she had absolutely no earthly idea how to wield said magic, but if it convinced his mother, then she figured it was a decent enough argument. She tried to her best to don a convincing face as she watched Adina's eyes jump back and forth between her and the boy. But after an excruciatingly pregnant pause, Adina didn't back down.

"Yer too much like yer poppa, Little Jo. Too damned curious for yer own good. Got himself killed dabbling in things he shouldn't'a dabbled in. The answer is no, and that's my final word. Now come on and let's have some breakfast." The plump woman turned on her heel and marched back across the field to her little cottage without waiting for protest.

And all Elizabeth could do was look at Joseph and shrug before following in the stubborn mother's wake.

Chapter 45

Elizabeth sat up in her bed that night, her belly full of leftover stew and cakes, straining to read by the wan combination of candlelight and moonbeams. She couldn't help herself. It was as if the moment she opened the pages of the ancient texts, they drew her in and held her like a vice. She had decided to stop fighting it.

> *Providence—He is near to the broken-hearted*
> *The weary find rest in Him*
> *For in Him is Truth*
> *And in Truth is found freedom*
>
> *His magic howls within like the wolf*
> *Like the mighty wolf high in the mountains*
> *It awaits the call—the call of hunger*
> *The hunger for more*
>
> *Deep calls to deep*
> *Magic calls to magic*
> *Like a well*
> *Like a vast ocean*
> *And only in Him will it arise*

She closed her eyes for a moment, unable to read another stanza. Why was her heart pounding like a war drum?

She was startled at the sound of Joseph's voice at the threshold of her door.

"Why is it you want to see 'em so bad, 'Lizabeth?" he asked as he sneaked into her room.

"What will your mother say if she sees you in here?" she asked, sitting up in the bed and closing the tome, half horrified, half amused that the boy had dared come into her room. Never mind that she had never had a boy alone in her room at night or that it was an eager, prepubescent boy with large gaps in his not-yet-grown-into teeth, the humor was not lost on her. If only Ferryl could see her now. Ferryl with his beautiful, perfect teeth and smile that she was convinced could give sight to the blind. She would have been lying to herself if she were to say that she hadn't imagined this very scenario with him a dozen times. Sneaking into her room, stealing kisses, whispering his heart into her ear. Not that Ferryl would have, though, for in all the years they had known each other, and in all the time that he had loved her as his own, he had never taken her to his bed. Exactly why, she couldn't say, except that she had always assumed that his choice had much more to do with chivalry than a lack of desire. On either of their parts.

The thoughts pulled at her heart. Would she ever stop missing him this much?

"What's gotten inta you?" Joseph asked, pulling her out of her trance.

"Hmm?" she asked, realizing she had been staring out the small window, gazing at the stars beyond. "Oh, sorry. I was just thinking of someone."

"Him," he said.

"Who?"

"The man you love. The man who broke your heart."

"He didn't break my heart, Joseph. I broke his."

"Why?"

"Because when you love someone, you do whatever you have to do to protect them. Which is why I left him. But it's also why I need to see those horses." She couldn't explain it further than that. She wasn't sure she could ever make a young boy understand why she needed to see the magic in person. She hardly understood it herself. But she thought of her father's words—how he had told her that she needed to go back to the beginning to find the answers she sought. Was this what he meant? Where he found her? Her earliest memories? Perhaps she had lost her mind. Or perhaps, without her father or the man she loved anymore, she figured she had nothing to lose. Either way, she had to see those horses. Somehow, she knew it in her soul.

"That don't make sense."

"I'm beginning to realize that very little that has to do with love makes sense."

Joseph inspected her in the wan moonlight for a moment before answering. "I'll take you," he said resolutely, standing from the bed.

"What? When?" she asked, confused, seizing the moment his back was turned to grab a robe and cover her borrowed and much too large shift.

"Now. Tonight."

"But your mother, she—"

"She's wrong. I'm not a boy anymore. I'm a man, and I can handle meself in the Wild Wood."

"You've been before?"

"Well, no," he said quietly. "But I helped you jus' fine th' other day, didn't I?"

That much was true, and Elizabeth nodded, a little reluctant at her brilliant plan to have this boy escort her into a dark and terrifying place.

"Now even you don' believe me. Perfect," he said, squaring his shoulders. "Fine. Even if y'don go, I'm goin'."

"What? Why?" she asked, jumping to her feet and fumbling around for her newly-repaired dress.

"Cause I'm tired of Momma callin' me a boy. It's time she knew that I'm grown. I know I'm all she's got left, but I'm not a baby. And it's time she knew it." He turned on his heel and marched out of the room. "I'll wait five minutes outside and then I'm leavin'." He didn't wait for an answer before disappearing into the black room beyond.

Elizabeth stood for a moment, dumbfounded at the boy who in one fell swoop seemed more like a man. She dressed quickly and scurried out the room and after him, only to find him staring with unadulterated appreciation at Eagle, still grazing in the field beyond.

"You don't even have t'saddle her, do ya?" he asked.

"She wouldn't have it, even if I tried."

"An' I bet she won't stay in a stable, neither."

Elizabeth only smiled, taking a moment to marvel with the boy at the wonder that was Eagle.

"I'll get me gelding. Be right back." He practically skipped off to the small, nearby stable, and Elizabeth wondered if he would be so keen once they arrived in the Wild Wood. Still, she ambled over to her beloved friend with high hopes for the night, whatever it entailed.

"Hello, girl. Did I ever tell you thank you for coming back?"

Eagle whinnied and nudged her strong head against Elizabeth before assuming her bow to allow Elizabeth to mount. But before she did, Elizabeth took a moment to kiss the mare on the mane. "You're all I have left, you know."

She had barely mounted the horse when Joseph returned on a small, decidedly less majestic brown horse who hardly looked up to the task of braving whatever awaited them tonight, much like his rider.

The unlikely pair set off at a canter without much spoken between them besides the occasional warning from Joseph about roots and steep drop-offs they were approaching. Elizabeth took comfort that, if nothing else, he knew the area well.

But knowing the area well and making polite conversation apparently didn't go hand-in-hand, because Joseph was hardly loquacious. Too quiet, actually. Which did nothing to calm her nerves—the nerves that were threatening to convince her to turn around and never come back if she didn't find a distraction. And soon.

"So what's in your barn?" she asked, the idea hitting her suddenly. She hadn't shaken the way he had reacted when she had mentioned it that first day. And curiosity, of course, had always gotten the better of her.

As it was apparently doing now.

By Providence, if she wanted a distraction, she certainly had one— for Joseph seemed even less eager to discuss his barn than he seemed to discuss whatever horrors awaited them in the Wild Wood.

Wonderful.

The hoot of a nearby owl nearly scared her off the back of Eagle when Joseph finally said, "I don' go in the barn if I can avoid it."

"Why?" she asked, knowing it was rude to pry.

More silence and then, "That's where we found me dad. And that's where he..."

She didn't have to hear it to know the answer. That's where his father had died.

To her surprise, Joseph added, "Me momma don' know. She don' know what really happened to Poppa. But he didn' die of no 'speriments. He was...he was..."

Murdered. That's the word he couldn't say. The word hanging between them like a black-bellied cloud. Joseph's father had been murdered. And he had carried that secret—that burden—without ever telling his mother.

Joseph didn't say anything, and she could see the tears he was wrestling to keep from falling.

Providence, she hadn't meant to bring up such a sensitive subject. But still, as she watched the young boy who rode beside her, the way his shoulders had slumped at the mention of his father, the way his eyes had darkened to a haunting that her kept, easy existence had rendered her too innocent to understand, she couldn't help but wonder what horrors of the story he was leaving out. Adina had mentioned something about her husband being too curious for his own good.

But what sort of curiosity would lead to a murder?

"We're getting close now," he finally said. "Can you feel it?"

End of discussion. Noted.

And then Elizabeth realized she *could* feel it. She had wondered all along how they were supposed to tell the difference between the regular woods and the Wild Wood, but as soon as he mentioned the difference, she felt it all the way to the pit of her soul. It was heavier. The night somehow seemed thicker. The air somehow thinner, as if oxygen itself was in short supply here.

But it wasn't until they crossed over a small stream that Elizabeth knew—straight to the marrow of her bones—that they had at last emerged into the famed, dreaded Wild Wood. If the surroundings weren't telltale enough, the feeling certainly was.

Electric. Buzzing. Magical. That's what it was—*magical.* She could practically taste the magic in the air. Acrid. Piercing. Like vinegar and lightning. If she had ever questioned the existence of magic before, one step across the threshold of this place and there was no denying that it was real. It was powerful. And it was deadly.

"Know what that is?" Joseph asked.

"What?"

"That feeling."

Elizabeth only shook her head, afraid to ask.

"It's old magic. That's why the Wild Wood is cursed. It's reeking of all th' old spells Midvar used over the centuries. Magic tried and magic failed. Greedy bastards. They'd stop at nothing, those damned half breeds. Nothing until they figured out the secrets."

"What secrets?" Elizabeth asked.

"How to wield it. How to use it. How to use magic like a weapon instead of it using you. But they can't, see. That's why they're such greedy bastards. For a thousand years, they've tried to take control of the magic. And for a thousand years, they've failed. But that hasn't stopped 'em, no. They just keep taking and killing and cursing. I reckon they won't stop till the whole world is spent on their 'speriments."

"Why can't magic be controlled?" she asked.

"Cause it ain't ours to control," said Joseph.

Elizabeth hardly understood what he meant, but before she could press the subject, he interjected. "So tell me, what's the Wild Wood got to do with the man you love?"

Elizabeth met his eyes for a moment as their horses sauntered through the rugged, dank woods, as leery of their surroundings as their riders. "I think he might have been cursed, Joseph. And magic, well, it's not something I've always believed in. I had to... I had to see it for myself. I had to know if that's what really happened to him."

"Why'd ya think he's cursed?"

"He lost his memory."

"So? People lose their memories, 'Lizabeth. S'not so strange."

"Of only me," she amended.

Joseph met her eyes this time. "Well now, that is strange."

"Have you ever heard of such a curse?"

"Yeh. The Midvar rebels use it all the time. It's right convenient, wouldn't you say? Bein' able to wipe memories and all. It's what happened to my dad. It's why he left. They wiped his memory, and he left us. 'Twas killed by them not two days after he left. Knew too much, he did."

"It's a Midvarish curse? To wipe memories?" Well. If that was true, it changed everything. Because either Ferryl was cursed by someone from Midvar...or the queen of Navah was dabbling in the dark magic of Midvar.

"Yeh. They do it all the time."

"Can it be reversed?" she asked.

"If it could, d'ya think my dad would still be gone?"

At his answer, her heart sank. Irreversible. So Ferryl's memory couldn't be recovered. Gone. Forever. But at least she could warn him, right? Warn him that whatever this was—this curse that happened to him—it went much farther than his mother. It wasn't just her selfish desire to control his life. It had something to do with Midvar. Her heart shuddered at the thought.

"So the man you love forgot who you are and you left, huh?" said Joseph casually.

"Something like that," she answered, trembling when Eagle—deft, fearless, agile Eagle—paused and looked around, as if she wasn't sure she wanted to proceed. Joseph pulled his own horse to a stop and turned around.

"Everythin' all right?" he asked.

"This place. It's so..."

"Evil. It's pure evil, I tell ya. Whatever ya do, don' touch the trees."

"What?" she asked, wondering why he hadn't thought to relay such important information sooner. "Why?"

"Cause they don' let go."

* * *

EAGLE SOON FOUND HER COURAGE again, and the two resumed their careful trot through the engulfing darkness—a darkness that slithered along the spine, that lurked in every crevice. The forest was eerily quiet. No sounds of nocturnal animals prowling. No winds rustling the leaves. Nothing but stillness. Blankness. Blackness.

Elizabeth used every ounce of her gumption to push it out of her mind and press on.

"If you'll pardon me, miss, I don't see how any man could forget a woman like you."

Elizabeth managed a chuckle. "Thank you, Joseph."

"I'm serious. Yer as pretty as a princess."

"If this is your attempt at flattery, I do hope you will remember that my answer has not changed, Joseph. I cannot marry you."

"I'm not attemptin' to flatter ya, miss, though I don't see why a girl like you would wait around for a numbskull who'd forget you. I'm just sayin' that in all my days, I ain't seen a girl like you before. Where'd ya say you was from again, 'Lizabeth?"

"Benalle Province," she answered, wondering why the sudden change in topic.

"No, that's where you lived. Where you from?"

From? As in where she was born? Well, that was anyone's guess. But why did he care? "I don't know, actually."

"How can y'not know?" he asked, crouching painstakingly low under a low-lying branch as he guided his horse beside hers through a narrow gulley between the trees. She took pains to do the same, unwilling to find out why in the world they shouldn't touch the trees.

"I'm an orphan. I don't know my parents. I was taken in by an old man when I was a girl. He found me. Probably not far from this very spot, actually."

Joseph looked positively shocked. "In the Wild Wood?" he asked. "He found you in the Wild Wood?"

"Yes, when I was just a child. He took me in. I had no one else. My parents abandoned me, I guess."

"Abandoned you? In the Wild Wood? Who in Sheol would ever do that to a soul?"

She didn't know. Providence help her, she had so often wondered the same.

"An orphan," he went on.

"Something like that. Yes," she said, unsure why the conversation was bothering her.

"Hair as black as the night. Don't know where ye come from. If I didn't know no better, I'd say you was Haravellian."

"What?" Elizabeth asked, and as if she knew the shock in her rider's heart, Eagle suddenly came to a screeching halt.

"Hair that color only comes from one place I know of."

Elizabeth snorted in protest. "Joseph, I'm sure that there are plenty of people in the world not born in Haravelle who bear black hair. Your hair is black. Did that ever cross your mind? It's as black as mine."

"Yeh, that's cause I'm half Haravellian. That's where me dad was from. All Haravellians got black hair. It's in their blood. And ain't nobody else got hair that color. So black it's almost blue. Like th'wings of a raven, that's what me momma used to say about me dad's hair." He trotted onward, utterly oblivious to the shock that welled deeper and deeper in Elizabeth's heart.

Haravelle? Could she be from Haravelle?

"As pretty as y'are, 'Lizabeth, y'could be a princess."

Elizabeth could hardly breathe, hardly think. Here in the Wild Wood, where she knew she would be an utter fool to lose her wits, she was losing them, for the asinine reason of idle musings by a prepubescent boy. The irony was not lost on her.

"In case you've forgotten, the Haravellian princess was murdered when she was a child," said Elizabeth.

"I din say you *was* the princess, I said you *looked like* a princess," he said, urging his skinny gelding on. Eagle followed suit as he went on, "And that stone around your neck," he added, "It's Haravellian. I'd bet me life on it. Y'said y'din' know where y'were from. Maybe you're from Haravelle."

Elizabeth took hold of the little amulet and ran it along its golden chain, her heart a steady thrum in her throat. Who was this child so say such things? What did he know? She was on the brink of panic stealing over her when he spoke again.

"Look! Just there. See them?"

The boy was pointing to a nearby clearing in the otherwise impossibly dense forest. There in the moonlight, as graceful and impossible
as Eagle, grazed a herd of winged horses. Elizabeth's heart thundered
in her chest. They were real. Winged horses. Hundreds of them. Eagle
wasn't an anomaly, she was one of many—so many. Beautiful. Majestic.
Regal. Free, just like her.

Their manes and tails blew as silken in the breeze as Eagle's, their
bodies the picture of equestrian perfection. Eagle seemed eager, as if
she knew them. Elizabeth could tell she wanted to run and join them.
But something—some inexplicable bond between them—kept her
companion at bay, more faithful to her rider than her herd.

"They say their eyes are purple, but I noticed Eagle's ain't," said
Joseph.

"They were," said Elizabeth. "When I found her. But they changed
when—"

"When you reversed her curse," said Joseph.

Elizabeth shuddered. Is that what she had done? Reversed Eagle's
curse? And if so, could she do it for Ferryl? How many times had she
held Ferryl, touched his hand, his face? Why hadn't it worked before?

"They don't seem wild to me," she said. "They seem quite docile."

"Believe me, they ain't."

"Can they fly?" she asked.

"'Course not!" said the boy. "Why'dya think they been cursed in
the first place?"

"I don't know," she admitted. "Why?"

"Cause the Midvarish was tryin' to make 'em fly with their magic!"

Elizabeth marveled at their beauty, the effortless ease with which
they grazed and sauntered. They were cut of the very same cloth as
Eagle. More than a horse. Powerful. Impossible.

Magical.

Yes, magic was real. It wasn't a myth, wasn't a fable as she had believed all her life. It was real. And it was *power*. She could sense it here
in this dark wilderness as easily as she could see or hear or taste. It was
another part of her. She could feel it now. It had been awakened—she

could no more deny it now than she could deny the stars that twinkled and shimmered above.

"Joseph," she said suddenly, and it was only at Eagle's reaction that she realized she'd spoken too loudly. Eagle's neck stiffened, her animal instincts heightened, and at the thundering of her heart Elizabeth knew she had caught the attention of the herd below.

In one fluid motion, all of the winged beasts lifted their majestic heads and looked up the gulley into the thickness of the forest. Elizabeth could see the rage of madness in their eyes even from such a distance. And they saw her. They saw Eagle, too. She could only imagine what that meant.

"Oh Sheol," said Joseph slowly, quiet at first. But his voice rose. "Oh Sheol! Run, damn it!"

He turned his horse, and Elizabeth didn't hesitate as Eagle's agile limbs turned too, running back the way they came, back through the forest. Running for their lives. For the stampede behind them was swift, sure, and unrelenting.

Joseph tore through the forest on his small horse, Eagle only a breath behind—not because she was slower. No, Eagle stayed a breath behind...to protect him. The pounding of the hooves beneath them was only masked by the thunder of the chorus of hooves gaining on them. Slowly. Surely. Menacingly.

"Joseph, look out!" Elizabeth cried, but it was too late. For the boy had run into a low-hanging branch of one of the gnarled trees of the wicked forest surrounding them. And if it hadn't been for his earlier warning, she might not have believed what happened next.

Instantly—as quick as lightning—Joseph was taken up by the tree, its branch like an arm, grabbing him, wrapping around him, choking him. As if some punishment for daring to come near.

"Joseph! No!" Elizabeth cried. But he didn't answer. Nor did the tree relent, curling and choking the boy like a toy, his garbled, sickening sounds causing her stomach to turn.

He was being murdered before her very eyes. By a tree.

Chapter 46

By Providence, if she hadn't believed in magic before, she believed it now.

But Elizabeth didn't have time to consider the implications, much less panic. She didn't even have time to figure out a plan, for the massive herd of maddened beasts drew ever nearer, the thunderous hooves a knell of her own impending death by trampling. Eagle faltered and whinnied, throwing Elizabeth to the hard forest floor. She grabbed her shoulder in pain, falling against a tree.

It was a moment before she realized what was happening.

The tree wasn't attacking her. In fact, it was still. It wasn't tousled by the winds stirred by the neighboring tree, busy strangling its prey. In fact, she realized the whole forest had awakened, groaning and swaying in the madness, apparently intent on encouraging the captor tree to enjoy its bounty.

But not Elizabeth's tree. Elizabeth's tree stood still—patient, peaceful.

Uncursed.

Without thinking, Elizabeth sprang to her feet and ran to the tree that held her companion, ignoring the deafening rumble of hooves that came ever closer.

"Joseph!" she cried, throwing her arms around the trunk like a hug, thinking she must look a fool. Then again, who was here to witness her madness?

But it wasn't madness. And just as her tree had calmed, so Joseph's attacking tree relaxed immediately at her touch, dropping him to the ground like a stone. Still. Motionless. No anger in its branches.

She only had a moment to take in what had happened before she scampered over to the boy, her hand on his forehead, her ear at his mouth. Was he breathing? Was he still alive? Had she been too late?

"Joseph!" she cried again, but she understood that there was no time to relax. For the stampede was upon them, thunderous and unrelenting.

She threw herself on top of the boy and rolled his body to the side, managing to get them out of the way just before being trampled to death. But in the corner of her eye, she saw Eagle, lost in the chaos as the beasts pounded through the forest like torrential rain.

"Eagle!" she cried. "EAGLE!"

But it was no use, for Eagle couldn't have heard her for all the screaming in the world. And there would be no way of knowing if she had survived the stampede until it was over. So she turned her attention back to the motionless boy beside her. "Joseph," she said, her hand on his cold cheek. "Are you okay?"

"You...you saved my life," he squeaked, coughing as he curled on his side, grabbing his stomach.

She nearly sobbed in relief. "We're even now."

"No. No, we're not," he said, attempting to sit up. "No one survives the Wild Wood. Not when the trees get 'em. The trees, they're cursed, same as the horses, 'Lizabeth. I should be dead!"

"Well, you're not," she said with a smile, hoping to placate the frenzy she could see building in his eyes.

"How...how'd you do that?" he asked, inching away from her.

"Do what?" she asked, knowing full well what he meant.

"The tree. How'd you stop it from killin' me?"

"I didn't. It stopped on its own."

"No, it didn't," he said. "They don' do that!"

"I don't know, Joseph. It just stopped. It—"

"It didn't just stop, 'Lizabeth. You stopped it. You stopped it with yer magic."

Elizabeth's breath caught, and she stared into the wide eyes of the young boy beside her. But her attention was drawn away when she realized the stampede had passed and without hesitation, she jumped to her feet.

"Eagle!" she called again, searching through the dense forest for a sign of her beloved mare.

It was only a few seconds before she heard a familiar whinny, and after a little longer, she saw her companion coming through the trees beyond, looking harassed and tousled by the frenzy that had just crossed between them. It was all she could do not to burst into tears in relief. Eagle made her way to Elizabeth and nudged her gently. Elizabeth breathed deeply, thankful beyond measure to have survived such a fool's errand.

"Let's get you home, Joseph," she said, helping the boy to his feet.

"Where is my horse?" he asked, looking around desperately, but Elizabeth knew the answer to the question without having to search the dark forest.

"I'm so sorry, Joseph. He..."

"I shouldn'ta brought 'im in here," he said. "I shoulda known he couldn't handle this place."

Elizabeth threw caution to the wind and wrapped her arms around the boy, bringing him close and hugging him tightly. "I'm so glad you're okay, Joseph."

The boy took a moment to return the embrace, but when he did, he wrapped his arms just as tightly around her and she could feel his body relax with relief.

"Let's get you home," she said, taking his shoulders in her hands.

Joseph shrugged, no doubt feeling a little helpless at the notion of having to be rescued by the very girl he had rescued himself. But when Eagle bowed her head at the boy, his eyes grew in wide wonder, which was replaced with joy when he mounted and rode her home. Elizabeth smiled as she walked alongside the beast and the boy, utterly thankful that they survived the ordeal.

For now she knew three things to unequivocally be true.

Magic was real.

Ferryl had certainly been cursed.

And she just might have the power somewhere within to reverse it after all.

* * *

ELIZABETH JUMPED OUT OF BED, the morning light kissing her face. And despite the paltry amount of sleep she had managed after their journey into the dangers of the Wild Wood, she dressed at a fever pitch and nearly stumbled her way into the small kitchen of the cottage on the edge of the world.

"In a hurry, dear?" Adina asked, stirring some sort of batter in a clay bowl.

"Do you have any idea how long it takes to get back to Benalle Province from here?"

"Leaving?" the woman asked.

"I need to get back home as quickly as possible." Elizabeth bustled around the cottage, gathering the few remaining items she had: her cloak, one satchel that had ripped in the scuttle with the rebels and which Adina had kindly patched, and her father's copy of the ancient texts.

"You should eat first," Adina said.

"No, it's all right. I need to get going."

"You've got at least a few weeks' journey ahead of you, and you think it's a good idea to leave without a bite in your belly?"

"A few weeks?" she gawked. *A few weeks?* She knew she had wandered far away, and perhaps she knew the border was a long journey from the coast. But weeks? How could she have missed just how far away she was? And what of Ferryl? Was he married yet? Surely by now he was. But it didn't matter. Married or not, Elizabeth still needed to get home to him as soon as possible. He needed to know the truth. He needed her help.

"That's just to the border of the province, child. If yer wanting to get back to the palace, it'll take at least another week from there."

Elizabeth's eyes shot to Adina, who wasn't doing very well to hide a smirk. "I'm no fool, child. They don' give tours of th' palace. So who are you really? With your fancy white horse and hair like the night sky? You're not from Navah, that much is clear."

Elizabeth could feel the heat in her cheeks at the embarrassment of getting caught in a lie by the woman who had helped her so much. "I don't know who I am," she answered honestly. "But I think if I get home, I might be able to find out." At least find out why she had magic. For that, she would need to see her father.

An appraising look, the portly woman resting a fist on her hip before she said at last, "Well then you better get. But not before breakfast." Adina plopped a large plate of cakes, bacon, and some cheese and fruit on the table and motioned for Elizabeth to sit down. It smelled as good as it looked, and Elizabeth realized the woman was right—she needed to eat. This would probably be the last decent meal she'd have for nearly a month. The thought made her wary for the journey ahead.

"I'll pack y'some vittles for the road too."

"Leaving?" Joseph asked, emerging from his room looking like he had slept all night with the pigs. Hopefully, he would use that as an excuse as opposed to admitting to his mother that he and Elizabeth had, well, disobeyed her direct orders. He rubbed his eyes and yawned rather loudly, stretching his arms high above his head.

"She's going home, and you ain't stopping her," said Adina. "And Little Jo, if yer so keen on snagging a woman, I'd suggest at least combing yer hair."

Joseph rolled his eyes and rumpled his hair before he looked at Elizabeth. And even though he tried to hide it, she could see the disappointment in his eyes.

"I have to get home, Joseph," she said. "There's someone I have to help."

"Him," he said gruffly, collapsing into the chair across from her at the small table and downing an entire mug of tea in one gulp. Elizabeth momentarily marveled that he didn't so much as wince at the hot liquid as it must have burned down his throat like fire.

"Up all night, son?" his mother asked, a knowing in her eyes that made both of them uncomfortable.

Joseph shot a stricken look to Elizabeth, who only shook her head ever so slightly, her eyes wide with fear of being found out. She had never had a mother. Or at least, she did not remember her mother. But if she had been anything like Adina, Elizabeth was momentarily thankful that she did not remember such motherly smothering.

"I...uh...forgot some of me chores," he said, and Elizabeth wondered if the woman would buy the pathetic lie.

But apparently she did. "Yer always forgetting yer chores," she grumbled.

Joseph's shoulders sagged in relief, and he began helping himself to the pile of bacon before them. Elizabeth relaxed as well, although she couldn't help but wonder if Adina wasn't simply sparing the boy from a good chewing out until after she left.

"Do you have anything left, child?" Adina asked.

"What?" Elizabeth turned to face the woman.

"Yer satchel. It was ripped to shreds. Not much could have survived. Did y'lose anything?"

Only every last bekah she owned. Come to think of it, she had no idea how she would survive such a long journey again. All her money was gone, lost in the scuffle with the rebels. She understood that many nights sleeping under trees were ahead. She only shrugged, opting to sip her tea in lieu of explaining that.

"Here's all I got," said Adina, bustling over to the girl and placing a small pouch in her hands. It clinked with coins when it hit her hands.

"What? Oh, no, Adina. I couldn't do that."

"You can and you will."

The kind woman held her eyes with intent, even as Elizabeth felt tears threaten, stinging as she tried to find words. "Why would you do this?"

Adina looked to her son before she brought her gaze back to Elizabeth. "B'cause I know what it's like to lose someone you love. And if y'got a chance to get 'im back, y'gotta take it. But you won' have a fightin' chance of makin' it all the way back to Benalle without a roof over yer head and a decent meal in yer belly now an then. It's not much. You'll have t'use it sparingly. But you'd be surprised how far it can go if yer careful."

"Adina, I..."

Adina patted Elizabeth's trembling hand. "Go home, child. Go find the man you love."

* * *

ELIZABETH STOOD OUTSIDE THE RAMSHACKLE cottage on the edge of her kingdom, the cool autumn breeze whipping her hair around her face. Joseph's sunken shoulders, his simmering pout gave her a chuckle. "You better be careful, or you'll step on that lip."

He only grimaced and rolled his eyes.

Elizabeth risked the scolding from his mother and wrapped her arms around him. "Thank you for everything, Joseph." She kissed his cheek and smiled as he flushed with embarrassment.

She turned next to Adina. "I don't know how I'll ever thank you for all your help. You both saved my life."

"S'the least we could do. If we can't help our own, what's the point?" Adina's eyes glistened with unshed tears, and Elizabeth fell into the woman's arms, feeling a welcome sense of peace as the woman returned the embrace. She wondered if perhaps her mother had been something like this woman, after all. Warm, kind, generous, with an affinity for cooking just like her. She smiled at the thought and pulled away, quick to wipe the tears that had fallen down her cheeks.

"I s'pose this is goodbye," said Joseph.

"I hope our paths cross again," said Elizabeth.

"Providence-willing." Adina nodded, a twinkle of hope in her eyes.

And with that, Elizabeth turned on her heel to find her winged friend.

She didn't have to look far. Eagle was never far. And as she suspected, she found her grazing in the nearby field. "Are you ready to go?" she asked as she approached the mare.

Eagle snorted and bowed her head, and Elizabeth smiled, petting her friend before mounting her for the long journey ahead.

"Then let's go home," said Elizabeth.

And as if she understood the anticipation in her rider's heart, the need to get home and help the man she loved, Eagle soared across the countryside as if she were flying.

* * *

Chapter 47

Commander Titus Melamed mounted his trusted steed and set off from Benalle Palace without a backward glance. The sun cast shadows long and wicked before him, but he didn't care. He didn't care that he had little more than an hour of light before he would need to bed down for the night—he could not depart fast enough.

He had said his goodbyes to the king and his two sons. He had said goodbye to the few of his soldiers who remained in the province, most of them being deployed throughout the kingdom on rebel duty. He had even given King Derrick a curt nod, eager to get out. To feel the Midvarish sun warming his face again. To reach the dense forests and rolling hills of Midvar and the woman who waited patiently for him.

He had sent word to her a week ago that he was coming home. And as his horse set off at a gallop towards the east, the sun setting gloriously golden behind him, he couldn't get there fast enough.

* * *

Chapter 48

Ferryl stood in the stables, brushing down his trustworthy companion, watching the sun set behind the cliffs at the edge of the palace. He swatted at the nuisance moths that now swarmed his head like bees. There were at least ten of them now, a relentless reminder that he had failed, that he had lost everything that mattered. He wondered if the emptiness would ever go away, if he would ever breathe without pain like a dagger in his heart.

Elizabeth. The girl he had forgotten. The love he could never forget. She was gone. And in her absence, a hollow emptiness. Black as a starless night.

He wondered if he would cry. He hadn't—not since he found out she was gone. He had barely remembered his own voice. And even in the short time since her disappearance, he was already forgetting small things. Her smell. He couldn't remember it anymore. Her eyes. What color were they? Why hadn't he taken the time to memorize every minute detail? Why hadn't he committed every part of her to his heart? How could he have been such a fool to have someone like her within his grasp and do nothing about it?

"I did try," he said to Erel. "I was simply too late."

Yes. He had been much too late, and Elizabeth had left before he'd had a chance to explain to her what she meant to him. He had scarcely understood it himself. It wasn't until she left that he knew he couldn't live without her. And now, in her death, he knew he had been right.

He wouldn't survive this heartache.

Erel nudged the prince with his nose, and Ferryl offered him the last carrot in his hand, stroking his mane with his free hand. A small breeze rustled the trees beyond and Ferryl turned at the sound of quiet footsteps behind him.

"You miss her, don't you?" the duchess asked quietly, her eyes burning with a sort of pity the prince wasn't sure he could stand.

He turned away from her without a word. What was there to say to the woman who was the reason he couldn't have Elizabeth in the first place? If the duchess hadn't been forced on him, none of this would have happened.

But in truth, the duchess had been his friend. She had helped him in his search for Elizabeth. And as much as he wanted someone to blame, even in his grief, he knew it couldn't be her. It shouldn't be. She was as much a pawn in his mother's games as he was.

Delaney was beside him now, standing close enough that their shoulders touched. She didn't say anything, didn't look at him. Only stood beside him. And in her silent act, Ferryl found gratitude for her. For her nearness. For her understanding. She, of all the people in his life, understood the game they were forced to play better than any.

"It wasn't supposed to be this way," he finally said. She only looked at him, and he returned her gaze. "I was supposed to marry her."

"And you were supposed to be my enemy," she said.

Ferryl's smile was small, but he hoped it would convey his appreciation, however incapable he was of giving her anything more at the moment.

It must have, for she took hold of his hand, letting her thumb caress it tenderly. He looked down, understanding that he had never taken the time to appreciate her beauty. Her small, delicate hands. Her tanned skin, even darker than his. The way her auburn curls spilled over her shoulders. She was as unexpectedly kind as she was beautiful. Had he ever told her?

"I think you're lovely," he said in a small voice.

She breathed a small sigh. "Ferryl?" she asked, a faint tremolo to her voice.

"Hmm," he breathed.

"I know I'm not her. And I will never try to be. But I will love you. And I will take care of you. I want you to know that."

His throat tightened, and he held her hand ever tighter. He closed his eyes hard, feeling the ache deep in the pit of his stomach. He managed a small nod. "I know," he said, his voice rough with emotion.

Had his eyes been open, he might not have been so surprised when he felt her warm breath and soft lips on his cheek. But as it was, he startled a little when she came near, his eyes shooting open, his heart hammering feverishly. Could she ever know how much he needed her now? Would he ever have the courage to tell her?

Delaney let go of his hand and walked away without another word, and Ferryl turned to watch her disappear into the twilight beyond. She would be his wife in little more than a day. After all this time, after all the searching, all the delays, all the hope and all the heartache, the time had finally come. No more games. No more attempts to stop the wedding. For what point would there be in stopping it now? In only a few hours, Ferryl would marry the beautiful stranger walking away from him.

* * *

"ARE YOU READY FOR THIS?" Derwin asked, leaning against the bureau in the corner of the large chamber.

Ferryl let a servant fasten the last of the gold buttons on his black-and-white uniform jacket, touches of intricate gold on the neck and shoulders—the royal colors of Navah. He squared his shoulders before the looking glass. The crown prince. That's what he looked like. Like a royal about to celebrate his marriage.

But nothing about tonight felt celebratory.

"I'm as ready as I'm going to be, I suppose."

"It's only First Feast. Just look pretty and drink wine while the nobles fawn over you," chuckled Derwin.

Ferryl huffed a laugh. "Yes, tomorrow is when my life really ends, right?" The young servant finished fussing over Ferryl and skittered out of the room as the princes conversed.

"Marriage is not so bad, you know. There are many benefits, after all. Benefits that don't necessarily require you to be madly in love, my doe-eyed, idealistic brother. And rumor has it, there has never been a king who sat on the Navarian throne that has not indulged in said benefits on the night of First Feast. You're as good as married by this point, I suppose. Why not?" Derwin chuckled again.

Benefits. Yes, he would have been lying if he hadn't entertained the idea of indulging in the marital benefits with Delaney. But the thought of giving Delaney the one thing that belonged unquestionably to Elizabeth made him sick with disappointment.

Derwin raised his brow, as if reading his thoughts. His little brother was certainly perceptive. "Providence, Ferryl. Do me a favor and never ever let Mother find out what you're thinking right now."

"What do you mean?"

"The moment you two say I do, she will be breathing down your neck for an heir. Honestly, I'm surprised she hasn't before now, if I know her. If she gets even so much as an inkling that you haven't taken that girl to your bed, we'll never hear the end of it. And if she cannot get to you, believe me, she will harp on me to set your mind right. And the last thing I want is to be commissioned with the task of convincing my brother to consummate his marriage."

Ferryl chuckled, rubbing his temples. "It's not that I have no intention. It's not even that I'm not attracted to her. Providence knows she's beautiful. But I still love Elizabeth, Derwin. I don't think it would be fair to Delaney if I led her to believe otherwise."

"So what do you plan to do, then?"

"Take it one day at a time."

Derwin clasped his brother's shoulder, branding him with a pitying gaze. "I'm sorry, Ferryl. I'm sorry for how all of this happened. I'm sorry you lost the woman you love. I don't know what I would do without Leala. She is like the air I breathe."

"I do care for Delaney. I do. But I'm not in love with her. I think I can be, someday. I have faith it will happen. I just... I need time."

"Who are you trying to convince?" Derwin asked.

Ferryl only shook his head and ambled to his sitting room. He took a deep breath. "So this is it, then."

"This is it, brother. The start of a new chapter."

A new chapter. He stopped himself from saying it, knowing he'd sound like an ungrateful ass if he did, but in truth, he wished very much that he were reading a different book.

Chapter 49

I'll meet you down there," Derwin said, parting from Ferryl at the bottom of the steps on the second floor. "I must fetch my wife. It's no good to show up at a party without a beautiful woman on your arm."

Ferryl attempted a smile. Yes, if nothing else, at least he would have that tonight.

He ambled down the corridor towards Delaney's chambers, taking his time, savoring this last moment before his whole world would change. Who was he kidding? His whole world had already changed—collapsed, really—the moment Elizabeth had died.

Now he was just...going through the motions.

So he might as well pull up his bootstraps and get on with it, then.

A quiet knock had her lady's maid answering the door. "Sire," the old woman said with a curtsey. "She's almost ready. Please come in." The maid ushered Ferryl into Delaney's foyer, where he waited quietly for the duchess to emerge from her bedchamber. He fumbled with his fingers, willing away the nerves that were threatening to make a fool of him.

She was his friend, he reminded himself. That was as good of a start to marriage as any, and he should be thankful.

He looked up the moment he heard her door open. The person who emerged could only be described as spellbinding. Gone was the young, scared girl that had arrived in Navah months ago. The woman who stood before him was majestic. Demure. And he would be lying if he didn't admit that she was downright breathtaking. Yards of palest pink silk trailed around her like a summer cloud, and the diamonds that spilled down her décolletage only accentuated the sparkle in her eyes and the glow to her cheeks.

Perhaps...perhaps his self-imposed marital abstinence was a fool's hope.

He took her hand. "My lady," he said, his lips lingering over her soft, tan skin. "What a privilege it is to have you on my arm." He kissed her hand softly, taking his time about it. When he met her eyes again, he couldn't help but to return the smile he found there.

* * *

DELANEY TOOK A DEEP BREATH. This prince—the crown prince of Navah—he was kind, he was thoughtful. She wasn't above admitting that she might very well fall in love with him. They were to be married, after all, even if it was painfully obvious that he wasn't exactly fawning over the idea. But he wasn't being unkind either. He was trying, she could see that. So she smiled.

"You look quite handsome, Ferryl. Don't let anyone tell you otherwise."

He laughed and tucked her arm in the crook of his. "Well then, Your Grace. Shall we to our feast?"

"Lead the way."

Ferryl escorted her out of her chambers and down the corridors to the grand staircase that led to the first floor and the Grand Hall that awaited them.

"I don't know how much you have been taught about our traditions," he said.

"Not much, I admit."

"Well, tonight is the precursor to tomorrow's festivities. A chance for the nobility to prattle and fawn over us, offering their *heartfelt* congratulations and well-wishes."

She looked at him at his emphasis of the word and chuckled at the wink he gave her.

"Then we feast until our bellies cry out for relief, so that we can wake up tomorrow and feast some more before the wedding ceremony tomorrow night. It's all indulgent, really. But Navarian royal weddings don't happen very often, so we like to make a spectacle of it, I suppose. Any excuse to have a days-long party, right?"

"Right," she said.

He led her down a set of deep and wide steps that led from the main atrium into the Grand Hall, the sounds of mingling and merriment kissing her ears. The minstrels played merry tunes on their fiddles and lutes. The white pillars reached so high she had to crane her neck to see their heights. Ivory fabric draped the ceiling in billowy clouds, making the lights of the chandeliers glow like molten starlight. And flowers. White flowers as far as the eye could see, spiraling up every pillar, kissing every chair, spilling from every vase and bowl. The room looked like a dream.

She hadn't realized she was gripping Ferryl's arm so hard until she felt his other hand pat hers softly.

"I'm nervous too, Delaney." She met his eyes and almost looked away at the kindness she saw. "But we're in this together." He kissed her brow, and to her surprise, the crowd erupted in applause and coos of approval.

The King of Navah stood to his feet on the dais across the room, his wife dutifully by his side, her hand on his arm. "Ah! If it isn't our honored guests arrived at last!" There was an icy strangeness to his voice. Barren, cold hoarfrost coated his every word. The few times she had ever even heard the man speak, his voice had been distant, strange. But tonight... "My son, Crown Prince Ferryl, and Her Grace, Duchess Delaney!"

The crowed erupted into even more exuberant applause, and Delaney took the respite to scan the room. Her father sat at the head table with the royal family, the queen on his right, her uncle, King Derrick, to his left. King Aiken stood to the right of his wife, and high nobility flanked the royals on either side, save for the two empty seats at the very head of the table, reserved for her and the prince, no doubt. Prince Derwin and Princess Leala sat just to the right of the empty seats.

But standing just behind the king, she spotted another black-and-white uniform. Different from the one Ferryl was wearing, but equally as distinguished. The man's broad shoulders were back, his hand on the pommel of the sword at his side. Even from a distance, his silver eyes gleamed like steel and moonlight.

Michael, the guard she now knew to be one of Ferryl's closest friends. The guard who was turning out to be one of her closest friends too.

His face was masked in careful expressionlessness, but in his eyes... in his eyes she could have sworn she saw...disappointment.

She searched him for a moment from across the room, wondering what could be bothering him.

"Tonight, we feast in your honor!" said King Aiken, tearing her gaze from Michael's eyes as the King of Navah lifted his goblet in her honor. In Ferryl's honor. "Let the matrimonial festivities officially commence!"

* * *

DINNER. AND PRATTLING. AND FAWNING. This Navarian tradition of First Feast was bizarre, to say the least. Not the wedding—more like a pre-wedding excuse to drink wine and kiss ass.

Delaney found she hated it. No dance to offer respite from the monotony of well-wishes and patronizing. Nothing but course after course of rich food, richer wine, and endless, endless prattling. She had never realized just how insufferable the Navarian court could be until tonight.

But all the strange customs were truly the least of her concerns, for sitting at her left, fidgeting like a maniac, Ferryl seemed as if he might come out of his skin. Was he, too, wishing he were anywhere but here? Or perhaps dreading tomorrow like one might dread the plague?

Earlier he had seemed kind. Resigned, to be sure. But kind.

And now...now he seemed tortured. As if he were struggling with a wild beast threatening to swallow him whole.

Delaney had no idea what to make of it. Nor did she have any idea what to make of it when, as soon as dessert had been removed from the long banquet table, he kissed her cheek and bid her goodnight without a word of explanation.

Happy marriage, indeed.

Delaney swallowed one more healthy gulp of wine, smiled and nod-ded her way across the banquet hall, and made her way to her room, ready to fall asleep and pretend as if none of this were happening.

* * *

Chapter 50

Ferryl trudged through the empty palace corridors, a strange mixture of loneliness and confusion working like a tonic in his broken heart. He had almost apologized to Delaney for his lack of explanation but...but what could he say? He just had to get away. Away from all the well-wishing, all the postulating as to how soon the kingdom would have another heir, all the smiling and flirting and ass-kissing and...Providence-above, he just had to get away from it. Even if it so obviously bothered Delaney that he had left with no explanation.

When was he going to stop letting everyone else determine his life? When was he finally going to be his own man, a king in his own right? He was tired—so very tired—of the games. Of being a pawn. He wanted nothing more than to take the reins, to step up—to be like his little brother and just take control. No consequences. No fear. Just... confidence. Knowing that he had a heart and mind of his own, and that it was about time he did something about it.

What had he become? Certainly not the king his father was. He was heir to a throne beholden to an entire *kingdom* and he was barely ready. And now he was to be husband to a wife he barely wanted.

But didn't he?

Hadn't she been so unexpectedly warm? So understanding? Hadn't she given him more than he ever hoped for? If he couldn't have Elizabeth, why shouldn't he want Delaney? Why shouldn't he find love again? Where was the justice in denying the heart the ability to love?

No. He *would* find a way. He would learn to love this girl who was his friend, this duchess who would be his wife. She would be a good wife. Kind. Warm. Beautiful. A fitting princess. She had been so demure tonight, so lovely as she patiently received well-wish after well-wish. A poised duchess, bred for this life of court games and politics.

No, she wasn't anything at all like Elizabeth. But even she understood that.

So why couldn't he?

He could. Even in the hurt. Even in the pain, the desperate longing for the woman he loved—he could understand that. Delaney wasn't Elizabeth. Delaney was Delaney. Delicate, beautiful Delaney. His betrothed.

Broken heart be damned.

* * *

FERRYL BARELY RECOGNIZED WHERE HIS feet were taking him as he marched through the palace halls and up the stairs to the second floor. Delaney's floor. She would be there, in her chambers. He knew it. He had dawdled in the quiet corridors of the palace long enough to know that the festivities were long over. His heart pounded madly the closer he got to her chambers. He needed her. He needed her love, her understanding. Now more than ever, he just needed Delaney.

He knocked on the door perhaps a little more loudly than he meant to, the redheaded guard—Amos—at her door perceptive enough not to say a word to the stricken prince. He could feel his breathing grow heavier with each passing second as he waited for her response. Perhaps she wasn't there after all. Perhaps neither should he be.

But she was there.

"Ferryl," she said, her eyes lighting with a mixture of confusion and something else. Elation, was it?

He didn't say a word. He only looked at her. Took her in. She was already in her robe and shift, retired for the evening. And here he was, asking her for more than he was capable of giving her at the moment. But even in that knowledge, Ferryl pushed on the door and let himself into her room, falling into her arms, his lips finding hers with a feral need he hardly knew existed within.

He managed to shut her door behind him with his foot as he poured himself over her like hot wax. Every place he touched—her hair, her back, her hips—was like fire beneath his fingers. But she must not have minded, for her arms wound around his neck and she pulled herself closer to him.

The kiss deepened, and Ferryl knew he was losing himself with every movement of her soft, silken mouth on his. With every hungry touch of her fingers.

His wife. She was to be his wife.

He gripped her hair and pulled her head away to look her in the eyes just for a moment. Perhaps to make sure she wasn't positively mortified at his sudden need for her affection.

But to his surprise, she stepped backward, unwinding her arms from around his neck and untying her robe, her hungry eyes never leaving his. It fell to the floor in one fluid motion, a wave of silk and velvet, revealing her gossamer and much-too-thin shift beneath.

And Ferryl was finished. Done for. Claimed.

Providence above, at the very least, he would have a gorgeous wife.

He lifted her small frame to himself, her legs locking around his waist as he carried her over to the four-poster bed beside them, pressing her against it as his hands feverishly explored and his lips found hers again.

Her lips—oh her lips. Supple. Plump. Familiar somehow.

Yes, they were familiar. But how? The taste of them. Like honey. Almost floral. Divinely sweet like—

Like chalam. The rare golden fruit that grew on the cliffs of Navah.

Like the chalam they had been served for dessert tonight.

Like the chalam he had shared with Elizabeth near the Secret Place not so very long ago.

Ferryl suddenly pushed away from Delaney, pulling his hand through his mussed hair and breathing, breathing, *breathing*. He nearly stumbled as he backed away. Space. He needed a wide berth between them. His heart hammered like a war drum, and she, too, was breathing heavily, her eyes stricken in confusion, her shift hiked to expose her slender legs, her tanned thighs...

He raked his eyes back to her face, wanting her. Wanting desperately to finish what he had started. To lose himself in her, to feel something again. Anything.

But he couldn't. Not when Elizabeth still felt so near.

So near and yet so very, very far.

Delaney's eyes burned with desire too, but Ferryl only stepped farther away. He couldn't explain. He couldn't say a word. For all the feral need that had swallowed him whole only a moment ago, he was every bit as regretful now. Disgust and shame burned like bile in his throat as he backed out of the room, a criminal on the run from the sensibility he had just stolen. For a panicked moment, he was unable to find the knob on the door for the darkness of the room and the trembling of his hands.

But he found it. And he bolted like a thief in the night.

* * *

FERRYL SANK INTO THE SCALDING bath, scrubbing his face with his hands, wondering how it had come to this. How had he come to need Delaney so badly? And how had he lost nearly all of his self-control so easily?

Shame. Fear. Desire. Loneliness. Need. All swirling about him like a hurricane. He wasn't sure what bothered him more—that he could forget Elizabeth so easily in the arms of Delaney...

Or that he wanted to.

For the first time since Elizabeth died, the crown prince wept, lost in the storm raging around him. He sank ever deeper into the water, submerging even his head, wondering if he should dare emerge again.

The moths sank with him.

* * *

Chapter 51

"Y ou all right?" Michael asked when Ferryl answered the door. A fog, that's what surrounded Ferryl. A fog of guilt and need and aching, incessant loss. And the way he had kissed Delaney—

"Ferryl?" Michael tried again.

Ferryl slid his attention back to the guard before him, the darkness of the night a weight on his shoulders. "Sorry. I'm fine."

It was a look of apology his friend gave him. Wedding day. This night-not-yet-turned-morning was his wedding day. He wanted to retch right onto the floor for it. He had tried and failed to fall asleep for hours. The knock on his door was a welcome reprieve.

"Ferryl, Mary has asked to see you."

"Why?" What in the world would the healer want with him? In the middle of the night? Hours before his wedding?

"She didn't say." Michael shrugged. "But she was insistent that you come. Alone."

Alone? What in Sheol for? Ferryl didn't like the feeling welling in his gut. The foreboding. He didn't like it one bit.

"Tell her I'll be there."

"She's at the prophet's cottage."

"Bedell's house?" Elizabeth's house. Bile burned in his throat. "Michael, what is going on?"

"Providence only knows."

* * *

THE PORTLY OLD WOMAN ANSWERED the scarred door with a marked sorrow in her eyes.

"Mary?" Ferryl asked, torn between the desire to ambush her with a barrage of questions and comfort her for whatever worry was currently plaguing her.

"He's in here," she said without preamble, ushering Ferryl inside the dark, quaint cottage, a fire blazing bright in the hearth. His heart fractured as he caught sight of the little paintings scattered about the room. On the sills of every window, on the legs of every table, on the door of every cupboard. Flowers, sunshine, stars that seemed to glow on their own. Elizabeth's paintings. A fresh ache tore at his heart.

Mary led him through the cozy sitting room to the small bedchamber attached, where Ferryl found the old prophet sleeping quietly in his bed, nestled under a wealth of heavy blankets.

"Mary?"

"He's taken ill," she said. "And he cannot seem to shake it."

"What's wrong?" Ferryl asked even as he took a seat by the bed, taking hold of Bedell's cold, frail hand.

"It was just a cold. But it hasn't gotten better. In fact, it's only gotten worse. And I'm afraid..."

She couldn't say it. Come to think of it, neither could Ferryl. He couldn't stand the thought that the man before him, his father's most trusted advisor, the father of the love of his life, might be dying.

Not here. Not this day. It was too much.

"What can be done?"

"I've done everything I can for him, son. He's in the hands of Providence now."

Ferryl turned his attention back to the old man, to the labored breathing, the wheeze in his chest, the sallow color of his papery skin. Candles were lit all around the room—a vigil to the passing of a mighty man.

"I'm glad you're here, son," Bedell said to the shock of everyone else in the room, his voice gravelly and rough.

"Just rest, Bedell. I won't leave," said Ferryl, brushing an errant strand of the old man's cottony hair from his brow.

"There's something you must know, Ferryl." The old man's voice was too strained. Ferryl didn't like the idea of him using the last vestiges of his strength for a conversation he was too weak to have.

"Bedell—"

"Just listen, Ferryl. You must do this for me. You must promise."

"Anything. Of course."

A taxing cough, then, "Take her to Haravelle."

"Take who?" Ferryl asked, furrowing his brow.

"Elizabeth."

He shook his head, pursing his lips. "Bedell, Elizabeth, she…" But what was the point in reminding him? He was obviously too addled to understand that his daughter was dead. That there would be no taking her anywhere.

"She's coming, Ferryl. She will return soon for you. You must promise me that you will take her to Haravelle."

"Bedell, I—"

"Promise me," Bedell barked, and a coughing fit overcame his entire body.

Ferryl didn't like it. Promising a lie to the old man on his death bed. But he felt the need to promise all the same. "I will."

"The answers, Ferryl. The answers you seek lie in Haravelle. She must return there. And you must go with her."

Return? When had she ever gone to Haravelle? It was clear that Bedell's time was running short, his mind playing tricks on him, confusing people, stories of his past. He was quite old, Ferryl knew it. In this moment, he seemed to be centuries old.

But something gnawed at Ferryl, all the same. *The answers you seek lie in Haravelle.* Hadn't he mentioned it once before? When his mind was not addled with illness and death?

Was Bedell spouting nonsense in his last moments?

Or something of terrible importance?

The old man chuckled, a rough, strained sort of sound that resulted in another coughing fit. But he recovered soon enough and said, "Your destinies are entwined, Ferryl. Or did you think so little of Providence that his will could be thwarted by we who are lesser beings?"

"Haravelle," was all Ferryl could manage, too dumbstruck to form sentences.

"The answers you seek lie in Haravelle."

And then he recited it, a passage from the ancient texts.

"His evergreens never wither,
Growing tall and lush in even the darkest of winters
That come the spring, the promise might shine
Golden and glorious through her boughs."

Bedell's voice was reverent, even though it was strained as he spoke. And Ferryl recognized the verse immediately. He had read it once before at the temple in Gaevast. The night he had arranged for the priest to marry him and Elizabeth.

"Take heart, Ferryl," Bedell went on. "Your love approaches."

Ferryl fussed with the blankets as the old man drew a taxing breath, then another. It wasn't long before a quiet, steady rhythm returned to his breathing. Asleep.

Ferryl sat in stone silence in the quiet room, Mary having disappeared at some point that Ferryl did not recall. Motes floated in the candlelight. Dust motes, dancing and flickering with a casual elegance, taking their time about the journey to their final destination, wherever that would be. He found himself transfixed on their star-like movement, taking it in. Every word Bedell had uttered. Wondering as to the meaning.

"Sleep, my friend. And rest well," Ferryl finally muttered, stooping that he might kiss the old hand he still clasped. A warm tear fell down his cheek as he slid his gaze again to the dying prophet.

And that's when he heard it. The sweetest sound he could ever hear, coming not from his dreams, but from somewhere behind. A voice soft and delicate, rife with concern and understanding that could only come from having known and loved the same person for a lifetime.

"Ferryl?" she asked.

And when he finally turned, when he finally dared to see if the voice had been real or just his imagination, he found a pair of evergreen

eyes staring back at him and knew then that, indeed, his love had returned.

Chapter 52

What happened?" she asked as she slid her gaze to her father's bed.

"You're alive," he breathed as he stood slowly from his chair. One step at a time, closing the gap between him and the woman he loved.

Worry traced her depthless eyes. Worry for her father before her. Ferryl took hold of her arms as he stood before her, finally lifting her chin that she might meet his gaze.

"He was right," he whispered. "Oh Providence, he was right." He swallowed back the lump in his throat as he took her in. Her alabaster skin flushed and glowing, her inky black hair falling wildly about her shoulders as if she'd ridden hard and fast to make it here, her eyes. Oh, her eyes. Depthless evergreen. Glistening emeralds.

Lost. He was utterly and completely lost in her.

"My Elizabeth," he heard himself breathe.

He closed the small gap remaining between them, pulling her to him, kissing her brow as he wrapped his arms about her waist. Trembling. He was trembling with tears, with disbelief. With sheer and utter joy.

To his delight, she wrapped her arms around him too, burying her face in his chest.

"Oh Ferryl," she breathed. "Oh my Ferryl."

He kissed the top of her hair again and again, so afraid that if he stopped, if he paused even for a fraction of a second, she might vanish and he might realize this was just a figment of his weary, sleep-deprived, brokenhearted imagination.

But then she pulled back and he looked into those evergreen eyes of hers again.

His evergreens never wither.

Providence above, she was alive. Real. In his arms.

And smiling, tears limning those eyes of hers.

He brushed the back of his fingers down her cheek, and as she closed her eyes at his touch, one of those tears slipped down her face. He brushed it away with his thumb.

"Ferryl," she breathed again, as if she couldn't believe it was real, either. He pressed his brow to hers.

He didn't know when she had opened her eyes to peer over his shoulder, didn't know when she had understood the scene, but he heard her ask, "Is he all right?" and turned to face Bedell's bed again, keeping an arm about her waist, unwilling to let her go. He just needed to touch her. Needed to feel her in his arms. Forever.

"I did not know anything was wrong until this morning when Mary sent for me. He apparently became ill a few weeks ago."

Slowly, so slowly she crossed the room to her father's side. Kneeling beside the bed, she took hold of his hand and kissed it tenderly, burying her face against his arm. Ferryl could think of nothing to say, nothing that would suffice. So he only knelt beside her, wrapping an arm around her, giving her the comfort of his warmth.

He realized he shouldn't have been shocked, not since the familiarity between them was likely nothing new to her, but he was shocked—and delighted—nonetheless when she leaned into his embrace.

* * *

"WE SHOULD LET HIM REST," she said quietly.

"Yes," Ferryl agreed, following her out of the small bedchamber, snicking the door shut quietly behind him as they emerged into the sitting room beyond.

He froze by the door, taking her in, the way the firelight blazed and glowed about her like an angel, a goddess. Breathing. Just breathing. Mostly in disbelief. But also in awe, in—

"What's wrong?" she asked, at last turning to face him.

"I'm trying to decide if you're a phantom. Or if you're real."

"I'm real, Ferryl," she smiled softly. "I'm sorry I left without explanation. But I had to. I had to find out what happened."

"What did you find out?" he asked, though he was fairly certain he already knew the answer.

"Ferryl," she said, remorse in her eyes. "I don't know how to tell you this. But you need to know so I suppose I shall just say it."

"You're going to tell me that I have been cursed. That someone has taken all of my memories of you, to keep me from you. You're going to tell me that magic is real, right?"

Her eyes grew as wide as two full moons. "You know? You...remember?"

"No," he admitted. "And yes." He took a few steps toward her. "I remember nothing of you before a few months ago." Another step. "But that's just it: my mind does not remember, but my heart has not forgotten." Another few steps. "And I've been going out of my mind trying to understand why I should fall in love so quickly, so completely...with a stranger." A few more steps, the gap almost closed between them. He could see her breaths coming in short now. "It was Derwin who figured it out. And in truth, his was the only explanation that made sense. Because I understood then." Another step; he reached her now, extending a hand that he might cup her cheek. She was trembling. Then again, so was he. "I understood that the only explanation that could suffice, the only one that made sense was that I had not fallen in love with a stranger. I had fallen in love with my best friend. For the second time, as it were."

She huffed a small laugh even as a tear fell down her cheek. He wiped it with his thumb, wrapping his other arm about her waist.

It was strange to be confessing his love to a woman who likely already knew, a woman who had likely heard all of this before. But Ferryl hadn't. No, in this moment, Ferryl was as nervous as a schoolboy. For in this moment, it felt as if he were spilling his heart for the very first time.

"The way I feel about you, Elizabeth, the love I bear for you, it is not something that could happen overnight. It is only something that could grow steadily, surely. Over the course of a lifetime."

Another tear, this one he dared to kiss away. To his utter delight, she did not shy from his touch. No, she was as familiar to him as the smell of the lavender in her hair, the honeyed sweetness of her skin. He breathed her in and let it fill his soul.

"But your marriage, Ferryl. Your betrothal."

"I am not married. As it turns out, you have impeccable timing."

"You're not?" she asked, looking up at him through tear-soaked lashes.

He shook his head as he pressed his brow to hers. "I am not married yet. But I hope to be soon. If you'll have me."

She fussed with a toggle on his jerkin as she breathed a small laugh. "And so this is the second time you've proposed marriage, Ferryl."

"Is it?" he asked, pulling his brow from hers, hating that he did not remember, that there were so many memories between them—memories that he would not even know to ask about. "And what was your answer the first time?"

A smile. The most beautiful smile he had ever seen. "The same as it is now."

He tucked his hand into her hair at the nape of her neck, pulling her closer to him with his other until no space was left between them, until his body rested against hers.

"I want to remember everything, Elizabeth. I want to remember every story. I want to know when you fell in love with me and when it was that I fell in love with you. I want to know what I said when I first asked for your hand. I want to know every story, every memory of our childhood. Everything. Will you help me, Elizabeth? Will you help me remember?"

"Ferryl, that will take a lifetime."

"Exactly." He smiled. She returned the gesture in kind.

"There is only one question left for me, then. I must know, Elizabeth. Do you love me? Do you love me the way that I love you?"

She stopped fussing with his jerkin, snaking her arms around his neck and looking eagerly into his eyes. "I could no more explain how I feel about you than I could explain the stars in the firmament." She glanced at his lips for the briefest of moments before she continued, "There is only one way I could answer such a question."

And then she kissed him.

So soft. So soft were her lips as they moved expertly over his. Not the kiss of a stranger, of a woman who had never kissed him before.

The kiss of the woman who knew him, body and soul. The only woman for him. He found that her kiss was perhaps the sweetest thrill he had ever known. It was warm and intoxicating, a consuming heat like...like fire.

Blazing, burning flame. From her lips to every place her fingers touched, to the length of her body against his, there was nothing but heat and need and desire and fire. She gave and gave with that kiss of hers. And he gave and gave in return, fire scorching—scorching but not burning—in her arms, devouring, consuming as...

* * *

"Ferryl," she cried, dropping to her knees by his side, panic tearing through her. "Ferryl, what happened?"

She shook his shoulders as he lay still on the ground beside her, passed out. A kiss to rival any kiss ever kissed and then he had just... collapsed.

What happened to him?

"Ferryl, can you hear me?" she tried again, shaking his shoulders once more. He did not move, did not rouse.

The panic welled deeper.

"Ferryl, my love, talk to me. Can you hear me?"

She knelt down that she might put her ear to his heart, relieved to hear the steady thrumming in his chest. So he was alive, but—

A groan had her sitting bolt upright again, her hands on either of his cheeks as he slowly, surely came to.

"Ferryl," she tried again. "My love. Can you hear me?"

And then he laughed. Laughed.

Sitting upright on the floor in front of the hearth, he pulled her into his lap as the prince of Navah laughed. As if passing out whilst kissing was somehow a laughing matter.

"What happened to you?" she spat.

It was his eyes she noticed first. The inexplicable fog gone, the returned shock of sapphire a fathomless ocean in which she could so easily get lost.

His lips soon found her neck even as she spotted a roguish grin on his mouth. "You know, if you would have just kissed me a long time ago, none of this would have happened, Lizybet."

And then she froze, even as his lips danced down her neck, her shoulder. "What did you call me?"

"Fifteen years with the same nickname and you choose now to protest it?"

"Ferryl," she said incredulously, trying to push out of his solid embrace that she might meet his eyes. His arms did not slacken around her. "Do you...do you...remember?"

"It would seem that your kiss has a sort of magic of its own, wouldn't it? Considering that it has cured me of my ailments in one fell swoop." He did not waver in his relentless exploration of her neck, her chin, her shoulder.

She found she did not mind.

"What happened?" she managed to ask, her fervor for answers waning with every heady brush of his lips against her skin.

"I told you, my love. Your kiss is magic."

"Kisses are no such thing."

To her chagrin, his kisses ceased as he pulled away that he might meet her eyes. "Oh, aren't they? Are you telling me it was not magic that just passed between us? Did you not feel it, too?"

Heat and fire and scorching flame. Yes, she had felt the inferno blazing between them. But...magic? Was it truly magic?

"Yes, my love. It was magic," he said, as if reading her thoughts.

"But, Ferryl, what does it mean?"

His kisses resumed, lazy and intent upon her skin. "It means simply that we kiss entirely too little in this relationship. For if you had just kissed me a long time ago, we might have avoided a substantial amount of inconvenience."

She chuckled as she said, "So you mean to tell me that had a stranger walked up to you in the stables and just planted her lips right on yours, you wouldn't have had a few questions?"

"My love," he purred, "if it were you, I would have kissed first and asked questions later, rest assured."

And then his lips found hers again. Solid. Hungry. So beautifully familiar. Gone was the timid prince kissing his beloved for the first time. No, here was her Ferryl. Her friend. Her love. Her very heart. A stranger no more.

Providence above, he remembered. Maybe...maybe the kiss had been magic. Or a conduit for magic or...

Did she really care? As he kissed her and held her in his sure arms, as she let it all sink in—that he was not married. Not yet. But he remembered. He remembered everything.

Maybe...maybe the world would be righted once more. Maybe the prince would marry the stable girl, after all. Maybe...maybe færytales sometimes come true. That is, if the queen didn't stand in their way again.

"What are we going to do, Ferryl?" she managed to ask after a bit. "We must find why this happened. This is not...this is not just about us. About our love. This has something to do with our greatest enemy. This is the work of Midvarish magic and..."

The rising panic suddenly waned at the touch of his warm hands on her face, his eyes intent and boring into hers. "We will find out, my love. We will figure it out together."

Together. Yes. Together—as they should be. They would figure everything out. One day at a time. Together.

"Magic," she said disbelievingly. "Magic is real, Ferryl."

"I should have known," he said, tucking an errant strand of hair behind her ear. "Of course I should have seen it. For our love, Lizybet—the kind of love we share—it's the sweetest kind of magic there is."

End of Book One

The Purloined Prophecy
The Chalam Færytales, Book II

Sneak Peek Chapters

Lavender and The Unknown

I t was by a feather-light touch that he had awoken. Like a flutter of wings against his cheek, the intoxicating scent of lavender whirling about him as he opened his eyes and understood it hadn't been a dream.

She was alive. Elizabeth was alive. And she had kissed him good morning from the place where she had slept beside him. His back barked in protest as he shifted from his seated position on the floor of her cottage, feeling as if he had been thoroughly beaten from where the settee had apparently dug in all night. Prince Ferryl hadn't even re-membered falling asleep. He had only remembered that kiss of hers—the one that had shifted the entirety of the firmament, had changed his whole world—and the ensuing conversation. Of dreams forgotten and remembered once more, of a purloined past that had been mer-cifully restored. He couldn't recall when that conversation had drifted into dreamless sleep as they sat arm in arm against the settee on the floor of her small sitting room. The fire that had burned brightly in the hearth only a few hours ago had died to nothing more than embers.

But he didn't really care when they had fallen asleep, exactly. For she was beside him, waking as she stretched her lithe limbs, the feel of her curves in his arms a welcome, beautiful distraction. He buried his face in her neck in response.

"Good morning to you, too," she said as she tilted her head back, giving him better access. He obliged her by peppering kisses along her honeyed skin.

Providence, this woman, this love of his life.

She was alive. And she was back.

He would never let her go again.

His lips found their way to her mouth, and he claimed her with a savagery that could only come from loving and missing one person for so long. She ran her hands through his hair and he took no small amount of satisfaction from the little groan that escaped her as he pulled her onto his lap.

"I wonder if you have any idea how much I love you, my Lizybet," he said onto her skin, his lips migrating down her cheek and neck to that inviting place where it met her shoulder.

"An inkling," she said, with a smile in her voice.

Lavender encircled him once more, threatening to intoxicate him into oblivion. Heavens above, that scent. He had loved it for years. He knew it, because he remembered it, thanks to the magic that found him with her kiss last night. But while he knew the scent, he had never thought to ask why she seemed to wear it so often.

"Why is it that you always smell of lavender, my love?" he asked as he dared to pull aside the shoulder of her dress to kiss the alabaster skin he found there.

She didn't immediately answer. And while he might have remained distracted by the velvet softness of her shoulder, he found himself slightly curious as to her silence.

"My love?" he asked, lifting his head to meet her eyes. It was heat that kissed her cheeks. A grin threatened his mouth.

She fussed with a toggle on his jerkin, not daring to meet his eyes. "It's embarrassing, Ferryl."

"Embarrassing?" he asked, lifting her chin.

She bit her lip, likely knowing the effect such a thing had on him. But he was as stubborn as she was. Perhaps more. So he merely draped his arms around her waist and waited.

She sighed in resignation, pursing a smile. "For my sixteenth birthday, Mary gave me a vial of lavender water, but I thought it was too fine a gift for a servant, so I wouldn't wear it. I put it away, thinking such things should only belong to someone important."

Her cheeks heated once more, and he didn't resist the urge to kiss them as she continued. "But then one day I decided...I wanted to know, you see, what it might be like..." She finally dared to meet his eyes as she said, "I knew I was falling in love with you, Ferryl. And I wanted to pretend—just for one moment—I wanted to know what it might be like...to be your princess."

Rose colored not only her cheeks but her neck and her décolletage, but Ferryl did not laugh at her, did not poke fun.

"So I washed my hair with the lavender water and put on my best dress that day. And you..."

Oh, he remembered. He remembered that day, indeed. She had walked to the stables, her hair falling in soft, humid curls about her shoulders, her dress so simple and yet so invitingly fitted to her slender waist...

"If I recall, I think I told you that you smelled like an angel," he said, laughing at his adolescent attempt at flirtation. He had wanted to tell her that she was the most beautiful creature he had ever beheld, too. But even knowing the closeness they shared—had always shared—the thought of revealing his feelings for her had terrified him then. So he had opted to flirt instead.

Apparently it had worked.

Elizabeth bit her lip again, and so he tilted her chin and claimed her lips once more.

"That was the first time I knew that I wanted you. Not just that I loved being with you—I had known that for years," he said. "But that was the first time I knew that I wanted to taste those lips of yours."

"You didn't, though."

No, he hadn't kissed her that day. It had taken him nearly a year to get the courage to kiss her. But by the time he had, he understood that he had been falling for her—slowly, surely, steadily, roots to a mighty oak—for all of that time. And all the years they had known each other.

"I kissed you, my love, when I knew for certain that I would never kiss another."

For a blinding moment, guilt flashed down his spine. For he *had* kissed another: Delaney—the Midvarish duchess to whom he was currently, inconveniently betrothed. He had kissed her only last night.

But not because he had loved her—not the way he loved Elizabeth. He had kissed Delaney because he had needed her. Needed her to help him feel something again instead of the numbness that had plagued him from the moment he had thought Elizabeth to be dead.

But she wasn't dead. Elizabeth was alive. Alive and in his arms, looking at him for all the world as if she too had known she would never—could never—love another.

Providence above, should he tell her that he had kissed another?

"Ferryl?" she asked, her hand on his cheek, looking at him with that way she had of knowing him down to very marrow of his bones. Guilt nipped at his soul once more as he opted to press his brow to hers.

"You've always been my princess, Lizybet," he said, stroking a hand down her hair. "And soon, the world shall know it."

"Today is your wedding day, Ferryl," she said with a hint of reprimand.

"Yes, and that is as good a reminder as any that I should get back to the castle and inform my parents of my change in bride."

She chuckled a bit sardonically. "If only it were that simple."

"It will be," he said, making to stand, offering her his hand that he might help her stand as well. "I will settle for nothing less." Easy words. Such easy words when he knew that when it came to his mother, nothing was ever simple.

There was skepticism in her eyes, which he knew he would find. His Lizybet was nothing if not practical. But behind that skepticism, a whisper of longing. It was the sight of that longing that had him pulling her to him once more.

"Trust me, Lizybet. Nothing will stand in our way this time."

A coughing fit momentarily stole her attention from him, and when she looked back, that longing had melted into worry and dread.

Because her father was ill. Irrevocably ill. And she had arrived last night only to discover a damning truth—Bedell was dying.

Another cough, this one deeper, more strained, and Elizabeth didn't hesitate to tear across the small space to the adjoining bedchamber where her father had been sleeping.

Ferryl followed her, thinking he could delay the dreaded conversation with his parents—a conversation that would likely change much more than just the person he would marry. Yes, he could delay that conversation just a little while, if only to comfort the woman he loved at her dying father's bedside.

* * *

A Guard's Duty

Duchess Delaney Dupree stood before the edge of the gardens at Benalle Palace—before the edge of the world, it seemed—letting the ocean winds whip her hair around her face, letting the endless waters, the pounding waves soothe as the dawn approached. The cliff-side garden nestled in the heart of the bow-shaped castle had become a favorite retreat. To escape. To think. No one really visited it much either, which she didn't understand, considering the breathtaking views and lush flora. But while she would never understand the ignorance of such beauty by the court at Benalle, nor did she complain as she stood alone on the cliff's edge, watching the sky brighten from gray to purple, from purple to the palest pink. She closed her eyes, willing herself to breathe deeply, the briny tang of the air like a tonic to her churning stomach.

But whatever relief it offered from the insufferable nausea she had had for weeks, it did nothing to ease the twist in her gut from the conversation she had just had with her father.

"Get yourself together," he had snapped, barging into her chambers this morning without so much as a preamble. "You're acting aloof and disinterested. Your little performance last night was abominable. Leaving early from your wedding feast? You had better thank the gods that the prince left early too or else you would be hanging from the gallows this morning."

"Father, I don't feel well," she tried to protest. For it was true. She had been sick to her stomach for almost two weeks. "I do apologize. I—"

"I don't want to hear excuses. You're marrying the crown prince of Navah. It's about time you stop acting like a selfish, spoiled cow."

Her father had turned on his heel and marched off without so much as a good day, and Delaney stood alone in the foyer of her chambers, wishing she had a different life. Wishing she had a different father, anyway. She hadn't asked for this. It wasn't in her plans to be shipped to this gods-forsaken kingdom to be married off like chattel.

But she had been shipped off anyway, forced to leave behind her life in Midvar and her beloved little sisters—the only piece of her mother she had left—without a second thought. It didn't matter what she had wanted. It didn't matter what she had thought. All that mattered was that she was of marrying age, eligible, and a prosperous match for both her kingdom and Navah.

Prosperous, indeed.

Never mind their kingdoms had been sworn enemies for a millennium. Never mind there was no chance in Sheol that this marriage would be anything more than a sham, if they even married at all.

For indeed, today was her wedding day. And while Ferryl had surprised her—no, shocked her, really—when he visited her chambers last night, when he poured himself onto her, touching, kissing, holding her with a need that had set her blood to boiling, the shock had been nothing compared to the moment he suddenly pulled away, a look in his eyes of devastation, of complete loss. For one moment she had thought he wanted her as much as she was beginning to think she wanted him.

And then he had just left.

No explanation, no apologies. The crown prince of Navah had just kissed her and disappeared. And she wasn't sure if she could face him today.

Their wedding day.

She wrapped her arms around her waist and squeezed tightly, breathing deeply again, willing away the tears that were threatening to fall.

What about her life? What about what she wanted?

Apparently, it didn't matter. Not only did it not matter to her father, or her uncle—His Insufferable Majesty King Derrick of Midvar—it apparently didn't matter to Ferryl, either. Or Ravid.

Ravid, who had followed her here to Navah, who had schemed with her, made promises to her. Ravid who had loved her. Yes, for a little while, she would have sworn he loved her. But he had apparently forgotten all of that.

Like a phantom, Ravid came and went through her life as he pleased these days, visiting her chambers little, speaking with her even less. For every bit of fun and laughter they shared in their years in Midvar, they shared equal silence and avoidance now.

Maybe there was a time when she would have said she loved him. But now—now, she wasn't so sure. While Ravid had always showered her with affection, he hadn't exactly been a friend. But Ferryl had. Ferryl had been her friend, had been unexpectedly kind and warm. And the way he kissed her...

But she had been wrong. Terribly, terribly wrong. Wrong about Ferryl. Wrong about Ravid. Wrong about too many things.

Despite herself, a tear slipped down her cheek. She quickly wiped it away, staring across the quiet waters, the endless void before her.

The sound of footsteps crunching in the gravel tore her from her thoughts, and she peered over her shoulder, the winds whipping her hair wildly about her face, to see Michael—the palace guard—strolling towards her with a careful grace, which could only mean one thing.

Of course.

She wondered what bad news the guard was harboring.

"Your Grace," said Michael with a smile. And not an apologetic one, either. Despite the caution with which he had approached her, it was...it was *delight* in his eyes. "What are you doing up so early?"

The rising sun glinted on the pommel of his sword, his black and white uniform crisp and perfectly-tailored to what was surely a beautifully-sculpted form, if the broadness of his shoulders, the strong column of his neck, and girth of his arms were any indication. She tore her eyes from his body only to be transfixed by the shock of silver in his eyes, illuminated all the more by the piercing rays of the early morning sun...and the kindness she found there.

"Are you all right?" he smiled, and she realized with no small amount of horror that she had forgotten to answer his previous question. Whatever it had been.

"I'm fine," she said, lying for the sake of sparing him the gory details of the stomach issues that wouldn't end. Another wave of nausea swept over her, and she turned back towards those glorious ocean breezes.

Michael stepped closer—close enough that their shoulders almost brushed. Almost. She cut her eyes to him as he stood beside her, staring at the ocean before them. His glossy chestnut brown hair—like sunshine and earth and honey—tossed wildly in the winds. He looked much like the crown prince in many ways—that signature Navarian tan, those high cheekbones. But Michael had a ruggedness about him that no prince or nobleman she had ever known possessed. Forged. Like a blade. Like the steel silver of his piercing eyes.

Nausea ebbed at her again, waves lapping at her feet. She bit back a grimace.

"Are you sure?" he asked, and she wondered about his keen observation of her health and wellbeing. Then again, he was a palace guard. Paying attention to every detail was his job, not a kindness. She merely nodded.

Michael stood wordlessly by her side, his hands clasped behind his back as he, too took in the sunrise as it spilled over the ocean, staining the waters with violent shades of gold and pink, silver and red.

Why was he here?

"Are you on duty?" she asked, shattering the blessed silence.

"Hmm?" he asked, as if robbed from a daze. "Oh, no. I'm off rotation until tonight's festivities."

Until the wedding, he meant. She stifled the urge to make some baiting comment about the likelihood of said festivities—not after the way Ferryl had fled from her last night. "Do you ever *not* wear your uniform, then?"

He faced her, a grin threatening his mouth. "Do I offend, my lady?"

"*My lady. Your Grace.* Such formalities. I thought I asked you to call me by my name." Gods, she was snappy this morning. And she didn't mean to be, but—

He chuckled. "I'm sorry, Delaney. Old habits, and all of that."

She wasn't sure whether to laugh or roll her eyes. She opted to look back at the ocean instead. "You haven't answered my question."

"What question?" She could hear the mirth in his voice. Was something funny? She resisted the urge to bare her teeth at him for being so stupidly chipper at such an ungodly hour.

"I never see you in anything but that old thing," she said, gesturing to his uniform. "You said you're off duty. Don't you have regular clothes?"

She felt more than saw his grin. "I do. I suppose I prefer to stay in uniform. Just in case."

"In case of what?"

"In case I am needed." Needed for his sword, he meant. Because if nothing else, Michael was loyal to his kingdom, even to a fault. She had observed his friendship with the crown prince in her time here—their quiet conversations in the corridors, their card-playing and wine-drinking into the wee hours of the morning. But she had also observed that Michael, perhaps above all other guards in the palace, was loyal. Dedicated. A servant to Crown and country. And he thrived on such loyalty.

Which begged the question... "What are you doing here?"

She immediately regretted the question, the way it sounded. She hadn't meant to be so abrupt, but if the prince had sent the guard here to spy...

"I can leave if you want. I didn't realize my presence would bother you."

She might have told him good riddance, might have let him walk away if it weren't for the hint of hurt she could have sworn she heard in his voice. As if...as if he had chosen to be here, to come stand by her. It was that thought alone that had her recklessly grabbing him by the elbow as he moved to walk away.

"It doesn't bother me," she said when he turned to face her. "I'm... I'm glad you're here." And she realized she was. In some strange way, Michael, of all people, had become something of a friend. Perhaps it was the fact that he had held her hair back as she had vomited her guts up a few weeks ago. Perhaps it was the fact that he always spoke to her with such kindness. Perhaps it was that wherever she was, he always seemed to be there, too.

Maybe...maybe the crown prince was having Michael keep an eye on her.

Or maybe Michael just wanted a friend, too.

He returned to her side, and she didn't fail to notice that it was a little closer this time, their shoulders brushing. And her skin—gods, it was as if her skin came alive at that whisper of a touch. So she leaned slightly away, just because she was a stupid fool. Everything that had happened thus far only proved it. No need to drag another man into the idiocy that was her life. And certainly not Michael, even if it seemed like his offer of friendship might actually be genuine. No, she would not stand close enough to let her shoulder brush his, to let her stupid, foolish mind wander down paths it had no business going.

"Any word about tonight?" he asked. The question suddenly reminded her of last night. Of emerging into the ballroom for First Feast, observing the waiting crowd...and being taken aback by the look on Michael's face as she stood on Ferryl's arm.

Had it been disappointment?

And why?

Despite herself, she turned to see his face, to see if it held any of the same disappointment. But it was cool disinterest she found instead. She quickly faced the ocean when she sensed him turning to meet her stare. But then she registered the question he had asked. And the strangeness of it.

"What do you mean *any word?*"

"The prince. Has he said anything?"

Gods. Oh gods. Had Ferryl told Michael about their kiss? Or his disgust with it? Heat flooded her cheeks. And nausea. Oh gods, the nausea.

"Delaney," Michael said, his hand suddenly at the small of her back. Warm. Steady. Calming. "Let me take you to Mary."

"No. It's fine, it's..."

"I beg your pardon, but you're not fine. You've been ill for a while. You should see the healer. Let her help you."

She shook her head as she covered her mouth with her hand. "No, no. It's fine. What did you mean about tonight? Has Ferryl told you something? Does he not wish to marry me?"

"He hasn't spoken to you? I thought maybe that's why you were out here so early," Michael said, his hand still at her back. She resisted the urge to lean into his steady touch, instead shaking her head as she met his eyes once more. There it was again. Disappointment.

"Delaney, I—" His other hand found the back of his neck, and he looked to the ground as he fussed with his hair. She got the distinct sense that he wanted to tell her something. Something he had no right to tell her.

To her eternal shock, he told her anyway.

"It's Elizabeth, Delaney. She..."

"Elizabeth? What about her?" she asked, her heart pounding in her throat.

He met her eyes again, and oh gods, that kindness. It was mixed with regret. And worry. She would have had half a mind to console him if she hadn't suspected that he was about to deliver news that would require her own consolation.

"She's back, Delaney. She returned in the middle of the night."

Elizabeth. The woman Ferryl loved. The woman he had searched for, that he only stopped searching for once he thought she was dead. She apparently wasn't dead. She was apparently very much alive. And back.

Which meant that the wedding—

"Are you all right, Delaney?"

"I'm fine," she managed, holding her hands to her stomach as if somehow she could coax the nausea, the stupid, childish panic to subside. Breathe. It was becoming hard to breathe.

"Please, let me help you to Mary," he said, turning her, resting his arm at her waist as he took her other elbow that he might guide her back through the gardens.

She attempted a lighthearted laugh, firmly planting herself in place. "I'm fine, Michael, truly."

"Forgive me, but it is obvious you are not. You have been ill for some weeks now, haven't you?"

She nodded despite herself, a cold sweat beading on her brow.

"Delaney," he said, and she met his eyes at the way her name sounded coming from his mouth, taken aback by the concern in his voice. "I shouldn't have told you. I—I'm so sorry. I didn't mean to upset you.

Please…please just go and see her. I should like to take you to her now, if you will."

"I'm fine, Michael. It's just a bit of a stomach malady. Nothing to worry about." Delaney tried to turn and walk away, for if she didn't leave soon, she wasn't sure if she could contain herself. Vomit. She was going to vomit. Was she nauseous because she was ill? Or because she was broken-hearted? And why should she be broken-hearted about a man who never loved her anyway? Another wave of nausea rose, this one burning her throat with bile. Michael caught her by the elbow, his grip firm but gentle as he stepped in front of her. He caught her by the chin and tilted her face to meet his.

"You're going, Delaney. I won't take no for an answer."

Maybe it was the look on his face—the sweet concern, the kindness. Maybe it was the air of authority with which he spoke, the firm but gentle reprimand for daring to ignore his wishes. Or maybe it was just those silver eyes she couldn't avoid. Whatever it was, she found herself nodding her head and letting him walk her to the infirmary, reminding herself that there was nothing wrong with leaning into his embrace. He was simply doing his duty, after all.

* * *

Acknowledgments

I WILL PREFACE THESE ACKNOWLEDGMENTS by saying that these are a bit of an update, but not a complete departure from the previous ones I wrote for the first edition released in 2018. That's because while some things have changed, some have not. I am incredibly blessed to say that four years later, the people I mention here are still an integral part of my life, my career, my dreams, and my cheerleading squad (proverbially speaking, of course, because dear GOD if I had a squad of cheerleaders following me around I would likely be in prison for mass murder. But I digress...) Thank you all from the bottom of my heart for supporting me so shamelessly. I wouldn't be where I am without the rockstar feeling you all inspire in me on a daily basis.

And now for the actual acknowledgments... (That was my *Monty Python*-esque segue. Impressed?)

Where do I even begin? This book was birthed from an idea a long time ago—an idea that required a lot of thought, a lot of time, and a lot of dedication to bring it to life. If it weren't for my husband, it never would have happened. Lance, what would I do without you? You've put up with my hyper-focused, neurotic self, with my late nights and long days pouring over this manuscript. You've put up with this crazy idea I had to write a book and actually publish it. And not only that, but you inspired and encouraged me the entire time.

You are my best friend, Lance. And you are the reason I can do any of this. You are my muse, my *joy,* my *Monty Python*-loving, *The Office*-watching buddy, my Prince Ferryl, my mate.

I love you forever.

To Arielle, sister-friend I adore you. Your quick wit. Your take-no-prisoners personality. Your insatiable thirst to know more. Your uncompromising perfection. My goodness I am so thankful we found each other. Not just because of our incredible professional relationship, but because you have become a true friend. I adore you. Now move to Texas already.

To my parents, who always encouraged me to create—thank you. You taught me faith and you gave me passion to pursue the unconventional. You put up with a kid banging away on the piano all hours of the night. And you put up with an adult clicking away at the computer all hours of the night. You'll never know what it means to me.

To my babies, Virgil and Addie—it is no coincidence that I wrote about a passionate prince and a determined young girl. These characters were modeled after you both—your spirits, your hearts, the wonder in your young eyes. I hope someday you can read these stories and see just how much of you is in them. I love being your mom.

To Loisa, Elena, & Haley—you girls are my tribe. You've rooted for me, encouraged me, read my books, and listened to me ramble on and on in my over-thinking. Each of you has helped me see the potential in this little world I made. I love you all for it. (And Loisa, I'll never forget that bitmoji you sent me after reading the cliffhanger in the first draft. *chuckles* You'll never know what it meant to me to see someone invest in my story.)

To my loyal fans (which is such an incredible thing to say, but honestly there is no better word to describe you ravenous bunch of lunatics)—I know that a book is a bit of a departure from the music you've come to know from me. But I thank you from the bottom of my heart for believing in me and giving Ferryl and Elizabeth a chance. Their story has only just begun and I'm so excited to go on this journey with you.

And most of all, to Providence—you gave me a story. I'll give it back to you. That was the promise, wasn't it?

About Epic Færytales

Love fantasy books and movies? I've teamed up with authors, editors, and fantasy-loving fans from around the world to create a group just for people like us. Discuss new releases, old favorites, movies, and music all of the fantasy genre. Meet your favorite authors, win free gear, and most of all, share your love for all things fantasy!

This is your official invitation to join our group.

The Magazine » EpicFærytales.com

The Group » Search Fantasy Books & Movies on Facebook

About the Author

So LET'S JUST BE REAL here... My name is Morgan and I'm a chronic overachiever and avid binger of *The Office*. When I watch *Lord of the Rings,* I watch the extended versions, and they're still not long enough. I won arguments in elementary school by out-quoting everyone with my vast knowledge of *The Princess Bride.* So yeah, I'm kind of a big deal.* I used to have a mohawk‡. And once I had purple bangs‡. But I try not to let that dictate my current fashion choices, which are just as confused, I confess. Bless.

In my spare time, I write. A lot. Songs, stories, articles, novels... It's just this thing in me that I have to get out. The book you're reading, part of *The Chalam Færytales,* is sort of a magnum opus of all the things that have been stirring in me from the time I was a kid—musing about the existence of humanity, pondering the wonder of God and the ongoing work of redemption...you know, kid stuff. I'm real proud of it. (That's my Texan coming out. Fight me.) I'd be honored if you left a review of it somewhere on the interwebs. (Consequently, I'm convinced that novel writing is just an acceptable form of psychosis, but it's definitely a beast within me that roars to be freed. So I pet it and feed it and let it dictate my fingers on the keyboard without regrets.)

But even if you don't ever read another one of my novels or listen to one of my songs, I can't thank you enough for reading this one. I hope I can bring a little magic to your world in some way.

The art in me manifests in various forms—from my books, to my music, to my digital art and even the occasional article. I get confused about what I should call myself: author or musician or songwriter or graphic designer or armchair theologian. I think it's probably safe to say I'm just an artist at heart exploring the magic around us. Thanks for exploring with me!

*This is sarcasm.

‡This is not sarcasm.

And if you made it this far and you were wondering, "If she's a graphic designer, too, does that mean she designed the covers for these books?"

In which case, I will answer with a yes. I drew them. I laid them out. I set them up for print. All that jazz. Because I'm controlling like that. And because I like doing it. And because I think they're pretty freakin' special.

At least that's what my momma told me.

Also by Morgan G Farris

The Chalam Færytales series continues…

The Purloined Prophecy (Book II)

The Parallax (Book III)

The Perdurables (Book IV)

The War and the Petrichor (Book V)

Book VI (Volume 2) — Coming Fall 2021

Sign Up for the Newsletter

I don't send out newsletters a lot. Honestly, it's a pain. But I do use them from time to time to update you when things are releasing, or when something new is happening, or when I set out on another out-of-the-blue artistic endeavor. So that being said, I don't do the whole spammy, weekly, buy my stuff email thing. It's obnoxious.

You're probably wondering why I'd bother asking you to sign up to begin with. Well, it's because all the experts tell me I need a newsletter. And I suppose it's also a sort of doomsday when-all-the-social-media-fails-us mindset on my part.

So yeah, sign up for my newsletter in the event of Armageddon, or if you're so inclined to support a lowly author like myself.

When you visit my site, this annoying pop-up shows up asking you to sign up. Just add your email there.

Man, I should go into sales.

Visit MorganGFarris.com

WRITER. MUSICIAN. ARTIST.